"The blizzard will keep anybody from searching for us."

When she turned toward him, he didn't back away.

"I wanted you to know. I'm one of the good guys, and I'm not going to hurt you."

She'd heard that promise before. The smart thing would be to step away, to put some distance between them. But they were awfully close. And he was awfully good-looking.

In spite of her resolution to steer clear of dangerous men, gently she reached up and rested her hand on his cheek. His stubble bristled under her fingers. Electricity crackled between them.

His hand clasped her waist as he lowered his head. His lips were firm. He used exactly the right amount of pressure for a perfect kiss.

She pulled away from him and opened her eyes. His smile was warm, his eyes inviting. *Perfect! Of course!* Guys like Cole—men who lived on the edge—made the best lovers.

"That was good," she said.

"I can do better."

HIGH-STAKES MOUNTAIN RESCUE

USA TODAY Bestselling Author

CASSIE MILES

&

LEONA KARR

Previously published as *Mountain Midwife*
and *Shadow Mountain*

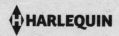

HARLEQUIN

HARLEQUIN

ISBN-13: 978-1-335-42480-8

High-Stakes Mountain Rescue

Copyright © 2021 by Harlequin Books S.A.

Recycling programs
for this product may
not exist in your area.

Mountain Midwife
First published in 2011. This edition published in 2021.
Copyright © 2011 by Kay Bergstrom

Shadow Mountain
First published in 2007. This edition published in 2021.
Copyright © 2007 by Leona Karr

This edition published by arrangement with Harlequin Books S.A.

For questions and comments about the quality of this book,
please contact us at CustomerService@Harlequin.com.

Harlequin Enterprises ULC
22 Adelaide St. West, 40th Floor
Toronto, Ontario M5H 4E3, Canada
www.Harlequin.com

Printed in U.S.A.

CONTENTS

Cassie Miles, a *USA TODAY* bestselling author, lives in Colorado. After raising two daughters and cooking tons of macaroni and cheese for her family, Cassie is trying to be more adventurous in her culinary efforts. She's discovered that almost anything tastes better with wine. When she's not plotting Harlequin Intrigue books, Cassie likes to hang out at the Denver Botanic Gardens near her high-rise home.

Books by Cassie Miles

Harlequin Intrigue

Mountain Retreat
Colorado Wildfire
Mountain Bodyguard
Mountain Shelter
Mountain Blizzard
Frozen Memories
The Girl Who Wouldn't Stay Dead
The Girl Who Couldn't Forget
The Final Secret
Witness on the Run
Cold Case Colorado

Visit the Author Profile page
at Harlequin.com for more titles.

MOUNTAIN MIDWIFE

Cassie Miles

Here's to my buddy Cheryl.

And, as always, to Rick.

Chapter 1

Some babies are yanked into the world, kicking and screaming. Others gasp. Others fling open their little arms and grab. Every infant is unique. Every birth, a miracle.

Rachel Devon loved being a midwife.

She smiled down at the newborn swaddled in her arms. The baby girl—only two hours old—stared at the winter sunlight outside the cabin window. What would she be when she grew up? Where would she travel? Would she find love? *Good luck with that, sweet girl. I'm still looking.*

Returning to the brass bed where the mom lay in a state of euphoric exhaustion, Rachel announced, "She's seven pounds, six ounces."

"Totally healthy? Nothing to worry about?"

"A nine-point-five on the Apgar scale. You did good, Sarah."

"We did. You and me and Jim and…" Sarah frowned. "We still haven't decided on the baby's name."

Voices rose from the downstairs of the two-story log house near Shadow Mountain Lake. Moments ago, someone else had arrived, and Rachel hoped the visitor hadn't blocked her van in the circular driveway. After guiding Sarah through five hours of labor, aiding in the actual birth and taking another two hours with cleanup and postpartum instruction, Rachel was anxious to get home. "It's time for me to go. Should I invite whoever is downstairs to come up here?"

"Jim's mother." Sarah pushed her hair—still damp from the shower—off her forehead. "I'd like a bit more time alone. Would you mind introducing the baby to her grandma?"

"My pleasure. If you need anything over the next few days, call the Rocky Mountain Women's Clinic. I'll be on vacation, but somebody can help you. And if you really need to talk to me, I can be reached."

Sarah offered a tired smile. "I apologize in advance for anything Jim's mother might say."

"That sounds ominous."

"Let's just say there was a reason we didn't want Katherine here during labor."

Rachel descended the staircase and handed the baby girl to her grandmother, who had positioned herself in a rocking chair beside the moss rock fireplace. With her bright red hair and sleek figure, Katherine seemed too young to be a granny.

After a moment of nuzzling the baby, she shot Rachel a glare. "I wasn't in favor of this, you know. In my day, this wasn't the way we had babies."

Really? In your day, were babies delivered by stork?

Katherine continued, "Sarah should have been in a hospital. What if there had been complications?"

"Everything was perfect." Jim Loughlin reached down and fondly stroked his baby's rosy cheek. His hands were huge. A big muscular guy, Jim was a deputy with the Grand County sheriff's department. "We wanted a home birth, and Rachel had everything under control."

Skeptically, Katherine looked her up and down. "I'm sorry, dear, but you're so young."

"Thirty-one," Rachel said.

"Oh, my, I would have guessed eight years younger. The pixie hairdo is very flattering with your dark hair."

Her age and her hairstyle had nothing to do with her qualifications, and Rachel was too tired to be tactful. "If there had been complications, I would have been prepared. My training as a certified nurse-midwife is the equivalent of a master's degree in nursing. Plus, I was an EMT and ambulance driver. I'm a real good person to have around in any sort of medical emergency."

Katherine didn't give up. "Have you ever lost a patient?"

"Not as a midwife." A familiar ache tightened her gut. Rescuing accident victims was a whole other story—one she avoided thinking about.

"Leave Rachel alone," Jim said. "We have something else to worry about. The baby's name. Which do you like? Caitlyn, Chloe or Cameron?"

His mother sat up straight. "Katherine is a nice name. Maybe she'll have red hair like me."

Rachel eased her way toward the door. Her work here was done. "I'm going to grab my coat and head out."

Jim rushed over and enveloped her in a bear hug. "We love you, Rachel."

"Back at you."

This had been a satisfying home birth—one she would remember with pleasure. Midwifery was so much happier than emergency medicine. She remembered Katherine's question. *Have you ever lost a patient?* Though she knew that not everyone was meant to survive, her memories of victims she couldn't save haunted her.

As she stepped outside onto the porch, she turned up the fur-lined collar of her subzero parka. Vagrant snowflakes melted as they hit her cheeks. She'd already brushed the snow off the windshield and repacked her equipment in the back of the panel van with the Rocky Mountain Women's Clinic logo on the side. Ready to roll, Rachel got behind the steering wheel and turned on the windshield wipers.

Heavy snow clouds had begun to blot out the sun. The weatherman was predicting a blizzard starting tonight or tomorrow morning. She wanted to hurry home to her condo in Granby, about forty-five minutes away. Skirting around Katherine's SUV, she drove carefully down the steep driveway to a two-lane road that hadn't been plowed since early this morning. There were other tire tracks in the snow, but not many.

After a sharp left, she drove a couple hundred yards to a stop sign and feathered the brakes until she came to a complete stop.

From the back of the van, she heard a noise. Something loose rattling around? She turned to look. A man in a black leather jacket and a ski mask moved forward. He pressed the nose of his gun against her neck.

"Do as I say," he growled, "and you won't be hurt."

"What do you want?"

"You. We need a baby doctor."

A second man, also masked, lurked behind him in her van.

The cold muzzle of the gun pushed against her bare skin. The metallic stink of cordite rose to her nostrils. This weapon had been recently fired.

"Get out of your seat," he ordered. "I'm driving."

Fighting panic, she gripped the steering wheel. "It's my van. I'll drive. Just tell me where we're going."

From the back, she heard a grumble. "We don't have time for this."

The man with the gun reached forward and engaged the emergency brake. "There's a woman in labor who needs you. Are you going to turn your back on her?"

"No," she said hesitantly.

"I don't want you to know where we're going. Understand? That's why you can't drive."

"All right. I'll sit in the back." Her van was stocked with a number of medical supplies that could be used as weapons—scalpels, scissors, a heavy oxygen tank. "I'll do what you say. I don't want any trouble."

"Get in the passenger seat."

Still thinking about escape, she unfastened her seat belt and changed seats. Her purse was on the floor. If she could get her hands on her cell phone, she could call for help.

The man with the gun climbed into the driver's seat. She noticed that his jeans were stained with blood.

His partner took his place between the seats. Roughly, he grabbed her hands and clicked on a set of handcuffs. Using a bandage from her own supplies, he blindfolded her.

The van lurched forward. Only a moment later, they stopped. The rear door opened and slammed shut. She assumed that the second man had left. Now might be her best chance to escape; she was still close enough to the cabin to run back there. Jim was a deputy and would know how to help her.

She twisted in the passenger seat. Before her fingers touched the door handle, the man in the driver's seat pulled her shoulders back and wrapped the seat belt across her chest, neatly and effectively securing her into place.

"Who are you?" she demanded.

He said nothing. The van was in motion again.

She warned, "You won't get away with this. There are people who will come after me."

He remained silent, and her tension grew. She'd been lying about people looking for her. Tomorrow was the first day of a week vacation and she'd already called in with the information about Jim and Sarah's baby. Rachel lived alone; nobody would miss her for a while.

The blindfold made her claustrophobic, but if she looked down her nose, she could see her hands, cuffed in her lap. Helpless. Her only weapon was her voice.

She knew that it was important to humanize herself to her captor. If he saw her as a person, he'd be less likely to hurt her. At least, that was what the police advised for victims of a kidnap. *Am I a victim?* Damn, she hoped not.

An adrenaline rush hyped her heart rate, but she kept her voice calm. "Please tell me your name."

"It's Cole," he said.

"Cole," she repeated. "And your friend?"

"Frank."

Monosyllables didn't exactly count as a conversation, but it was something. "Listen, Cole. These cuffs are hurting my wrists. I'd really appreciate if you could take them off. I promise I won't cause trouble."

"The cuffs stay. And the blindfold."

"Please, Cole. You said you didn't want to hurt me."

Though she couldn't see him, she felt him staring at her.

"There's only one thing you need to know," he said. "There's a pregnant woman who needs you. Without your help, she and her baby will die."

As soon as he spoke, she realized that escape wasn't an option. No matter how much she wanted to run, she couldn't refuse to help. The fight went out of her. Her eyes squeezed shut behind the blindfold. More than being afraid for her own safety, she feared for the unknown woman and her unborn child.

Cole McClure concentrated on the taillights of Frank Loeb's car. The route to their hideout was unfamiliar to him and complicated by a couple of switchbacks; he didn't want to waste time getting lost.

The decision to track down the midwife had been his. It was obvious that Penny wasn't going to make it without a hell of a lot more medical expertise than he or any of the other three men could provide.

Cole glanced at the blindfolded woman in the passenger seat. Her posture erect, she sat as still as a statue. Her fortitude impressed him. When he held the gun on her, she hadn't burst into tears or pleaded. A sensible woman, he thought. Too bad he couldn't explain to her that he was one of the good guys.

She cleared her throat. "Has the mother been having contractions?"

"Yes."

"How far apart?"

"It's hard to tell. She was shot in the left thigh and has been in pain."

She couldn't see through the blindfold, but her head turned toward him. "Shot?"

"A flesh wound. The bullet went straight through, but she lost blood."

"She needs a hospital, access to a surgeon, transfusions. My God, her body is probably in shock."

Cole couldn't have agreed more. "She won't let us take her to a doctor."

"You could make her go. You said she was weak."

"If she turns herself in at the hospital, she won't be released. Penny doesn't want to raise her baby in jail. Can you understand that, Rachel?"

"How do you know my name?"

In spite of her self-possessed attitude, he heard a note of alarm in her voice. He didn't want to reveal more information than necessary, but she deserved an explanation.

"When I realized that we needed a midwife, I called the women's clinic and pretended to want a consultation with a midwife. They gave me your name and told me that you were with a woman in labor."

"But they wouldn't tell you the patient's name," Rachel said. "That's a breach of confidentiality."

"Frank hacked their computer." The big thug had a sophisticated skill set that almost made up for his tendency toward sadism. "After that, finding the address was easy."

When they discovered that Rachel had been sent to the home of Sarah and Jim Loughlin, it seemed like luck was finally on Cole's side. The cabin was only ten miles away from their hideout.

Frank Loeb had wanted to charge inside with guns blazing, but Cole convinced him it was better to move with subtlety and caution. Every law enforcement man and woman in the state of Colorado was already on the lookout for them. They didn't need more attention.

"You're the casino robbers," she said.

"I wish you hadn't figured that out."

"I'd be an idiot not to," she said. "It's all over the news. How much did you get away with? A hundred thousand dollars?"

Not even half that amount. "If you're smart, you won't mention the casino again."

He regretted dragging her into this situation. If Rachel could identify them, she was a threat. There was no way the others would release her unharmed.

Chapter 2

Though the blindfold prevented Rachel from seeing where they were going, the drive had taken less than twenty minutes. She knew they were still in the vicinity of Shadow Mountain Lake, still in Grand County. If she could figure out her location, she might somehow get a message to Jim, and he could coordinate her rescue through the sheriff's department.

The van door opened, and Cole took her arm, guiding her as she stumbled up a wood staircase. Looking down under the edge of the blindfold, she saw it had been partially cleared of snow. The porch was several paces across; this had to be a large house or a lodge.

She heard the front door open and felt a gush of warmth from inside. A man ordered, "Get the hell in here. Fast."

"What's the problem?" Cole asked.

"It's Penny. She's got a gun."

Rachel stifled a hysterical urge to laugh. Penny had to be every man's worst nightmare: a woman in labor with a firearm.

Inside the house, Cole held her arm and marched her across the room. He tapped on a door. "Penny? I'm coming in. I brought a midwife to help you."

As Rachel stepped into the bedroom, she was struck by a miasma of floral perfume, antiseptic and sweat. Cole wasted no time in removing the blindfold and the handcuffs.

From the bed, Penny stared at her with hollow eyes smeared with makeup. Her skinny arm trembled with the effort of holding a revolver that looked as big as a canon. A flimsy nightgown covered her swollen breasts and ripe belly, but her pale legs were bare. The dressing on her thigh wound was bloodstained.

"I don't want drugs," Penny rasped. "This baby is going to be born healthy. Hear me?"

Rachel nodded. "Can I come closer?"

"Why?" Her eyes narrowed suspiciously. "What are you going to do?"

"I'm going to help you have this baby."

"First things first," Cole said. "Give mc the gun."

"No way." Penny's breathing became more rapid. Her lips pulled back as she gritted her teeth. Her eyes squeezed shut.

Even wearing the ski mask, Cole looked nervous. "What's wrong?"

"A contraction," Rachel said.

A sob choked through Penny's lips. Still clutching the gun, she threw her head back, fighting the pain with every muscle in her body. She stayed that way for several seconds. Instead of a scream, she exhaled a gasp. "Damn it. This is going to get worse, isn't it?"

"Here's the thing about natural childbirth," Rachel said as she moved closer to the bed. "It's important for you to be comfortable and relaxed. My name is Rachel, by the way. How far apart are the contractions?"

"I'm not sure. Eight or ten minutes."

"First baby?"

"Yes."

Experience told Rachel that Penny wasn't anywhere near the final stages of labor. They probably had several more hours to look forward to. "Can I take a look at that wound on your leg?"

"Whatever."

Rachel sat on the bed beside her and gently pulled the bandage back. In her work as an EMT, she'd dealt with gunshot wounds before. She could tell that the bullet had entered the back of Penny's leg— probably as she was running away—and exited through the front. The torn flesh was clumsily sutured and caked with dried blood. "It doesn't appear to be infected. Can you walk on it?"

Defiantly, Penny said, "Damn right I can."

"I'd like you to walk into the bathroom and take a bath. Treat yourself to a nice, long soak."

"I don't need pampering." Her raccoon eyes were fierce. "I can take the pain."

Rachel looked away from the gun barrel that was only inches from her cheek. She didn't like Penny, didn't like that she was a criminal on the run and definitely didn't like her attitude. But this woman was her patient now, and Rachel's goal was a successful delivery.

"I'm sure you're tough as nails, Penny." Rachel stood

and stepped away from the bed. "But this isn't about you. It's about your baby. You need to conserve your strength so you're ready to push when the time comes."

Cole approached the opposite side of the bed. "Listen to her, Penny."

"Fine. I'll take a bath."

Rachel went to the open door to the adjoining bathroom. As she started the water in the tub, she peered through a large casement window, searching for landmarks that would give her a clue to their location. All she saw was rocks and trees with snow-laden boughs.

Penny hobbled into the bathroom, using Cole's arm for support. As he guided her through the doorway, he deftly took the revolver from her hand.

"Hey," she protested.

"If you need it, I'll give it back."

Hoping to distract her, Rachel pointed to the swirling water. "Do you need help getting undressed?"

Penny glared at both of them. "Get out."

Before she left, Rachel instructed, "Leave the door unlocked so we can respond if you need help."

With Penny disarmed and bathing, Rachel turned to Cole. "I need fresh bedding and something comfortable for her to wear. It'd be nice to have some soft music."

"None of these procedures are medical," he said.

She leaned toward him and lowered her voice so Penny couldn't hear from the bathroom. "If I'd come in here and wrenched her knees apart for a vaginal exam, she would've blown my head off."

He blinked. His eyes were the only part of his face visible. "I guess you know what you're doing."

"In the back of my van, there are three cases and an oxygen tank. Bring all the equipment in here." She stripped the sheets off the bed. "And you can start boiling water."

"Hot water? Like in the frontier movies?"

"It's for tea," she said. "Raspberry leaf tea."

Instead of leaving her alone in the bedroom, he opened the door and barked orders. She tried to see beyond him, to figure out how many others were in the house. Not that it mattered. Even if Rachel could escape, she wouldn't leave Penny until she knew mother and baby were safe.

She went to the bathroom and opened the door a crack. "Penny, are you all right?"

Grudgingly, she said, "The water feels good."

"Some women choose to give birth in the tub."

"Naked? Forget it." Her tone had shifted from maniacal to something resembling cooperation. "Is there something else I should do? Some kind of exercise?"

Her change in attitude boded well. A woman in labor needed to be able to trust the people around her. Giving birth wasn't a battle; it was a process.

"Relax," Rachel said. "Take your time. Wash your hair."

In the bedroom, Cole thrust the fresh sheets toward her. "Here you go."

"Would you help me make the bed?"

He went to the opposite side and unfolded the fitted bottom sheet of soft lavender cotton. He'd taken off his jacket and was wearing an untucked flannel shirt over a long-sleeved white thermal undershirt and jeans with splotches of blood on the thigh.

She pulled the sheet toward her side of the bed. "We're probably going to be here for hours. You might as well take off that stupid mask."

He straightened to his full height—a couple of inches over six feet—and stared for a moment before he peeled off the black knit mask and ran his fingers through his shaggy brown hair.

Some women would have considered him handsome with his high cheekbones, firm chin and deep-set eyes of cognac-brown. His jaw was rough with stubble that looked almost fashionable, and his smile was dazzling. "You're staring, Rachel. Memorizing my face?"

"Don't need to," she shot back. "I'm sure there are plenty of pictures of you on Wanted posters."

"I said it before, and I'll say it again. I'm not going to hurt you."

"Apart from kidnapping me?"

"I won't apologize for that. Penny needs you."

Rather than answering her challenge, he had appealed to her better instincts. Cole was smooth, all right. Probably a con man as well as a robber. Unfortunately, she had a bad habit of falling for dangerous men. *Not this time.*

"Don't bother being charming," she said. "I'm going to need your help with Penny, but I don't like you, Cole. I don't trust a single word that comes out of your mouth."

He grinned. "You think I'm charming."

Jerk! As she smoothed the sheets, she asked, "Which one of the men out there is the father of Penny's baby?"

"None of us."

Of course not. That would be too easy. "Can he be reached?"

"We're not on vacation here. This is a hideout. We don't need to invite visitors."

But this was a nice house—not a shack in the woods.

Finding this supposed "hideout" that happened to be conveniently vacant was too much of a coincidence. "You must have planned to come here."

"Hell, no. We were supposed to be in Salt Lake City by now. When Penny went into labor, we had to stop. The house belongs to someone she knows."

The fact that Penny had contacts in this area might come in handy. Rachel needed to keep her ears and eyes open, to gather every bit of information that she could. There was no telling what might be useful.

By the time Penny got out of the tub, Rachel had transformed the bedroom into a clean, inviting space using supplies from her van. The bedding was fresh. A healing fragrance of eucalyptus and pine wafted from an herbal scent diffuser. Native American flute music rose from a CD player.

Before Penny got into bed, Rachel replaced the dressings on her leg wound, using an antiseptic salve to ease the pain. In her work as a nurse-midwife, she leavened various herbal and homeopathic methods with standard medical procedure. Basically, she did whatever worked.

Though Penny remained diffident, she looked young and vulnerable with the makeup washed off her face. Mostly, she seemed tired. The stress of labor and the trauma of being shot had taken their toll.

Rachel took her blood pressure, and she wasn't surprised that it was low. Penny's pulse was jumpy and weak.

When her next contraction hit, Rachel talked her through it. "You don't have to tough it out. If you need the release of yelling—"

"No," she snapped. "I'm not giving those bastards the satisfaction of hearing me scream."

Apparently, she was making up for her weakened physical condition with a powerful hostility. Rachel asked, "Should I send Cole out of the room while I do the vaginal exam?"

"Yes."

He was quick to leave. "I'll fetch the tea."

Alone with Penny, Rachel checked the cervix. Dilation was already at seven centimeters. This baby could be coming sooner than she'd thought. "You're doing a good job," she encouraged. "It won't be too much longer."

"Is my baby okay?"

"Let's check it out."

Usually, there was an implied trust between midwife and mom, but this situation was anything but usual. As Rachel hooked up the fetal monitor, she tried to be conversational. "When is your due date?"

"Two days from now."

"That's good. You carried to full term." At least, there shouldn't be the problems associated with premature birth. "Is there anything I ought to know about? Any special problems during your pregnancy?"

"I got fat."

Rachel did a double take before she realized Penny was joking. "Are you from around here?"

"We lived in Grand Lake for a while. I went to high school in Granby."

"That's where I live," Rachel said. "Is your family still in Grand Lake?"

"It's just me and my mom. My dad left when I was little. I never missed having him around." She touched her necklace and rubbed her thumb over the shiny black pearl. "Mom gave me this. It's her namesake—Pearl.

She lives in Denver, but she's house-sitting for a friend in Grand Lake."

They weren't too far from there. Grand Lake was a small village—not much more than a main street of shops and lodging for tourists visiting the scenic lakeside. "Should I try to contact your mother?"

"Oh. My. God." Penny rolled her eyes. "If my mom knew what I was up to, she'd kill me."

Her jaw clenched, and Rachel talked her through the contraction. Penny must have had some Lamaze training because she knew the breathing techniques for dealing with the pain.

When she settled back against the pillows, she said, "If anything happens to me, I want my mom to have my baby."

"Not the father?"

"Mom's better." She chewed her lower lip. "She'll be a good grandma if I'm not around."

Considering a premature death wasn't the best way to go into labor. Rachel preferred to keep the mood upbeat and positive. "You're doing fine. Nothing bad is going to happen."

"Do you believe in premonitions? Like stuff with tarot cards and crystal balls?"

"Not really."

"My friend Jenna did a reading for me. Hey, maybe you know her. She lives in Granby, too. Jenna Cambridge?"

"The name isn't familiar."

"She's kind of quiet. Doesn't go out much," Penny said. "Every time I visit her, I try to fix her up. But she's stuck on some guy who dumped her a long time ago. What a waste! Everybody falls. The trick is to get back on the bicycle."

Though Rachel wasn't prone to taking advice from a pregnant criminal who didn't trust the father of her baby, she had to admit that Penny made a good point. "Doesn't do any good to sit around feeling down on yourself."

"Exactly." She threw up her hands. "Anyway, Jenna read my cards and told me that something bad was going to happen. My old life would be torn asunder. Those were her words. And she drew the death card."

Her friend Jenna sounded like a real peach. Pregnant women were stressed enough without dire warnings. "The death card could mean a change in your life. Like becoming a mom."

"Maybe you're right. I have changed. I took real good care of myself all through the pregnancy. No booze. No cigs. I did everything right."

Except robbing a casino. Rachel finished hooking up the monitor and read the electronic blips. "Your baby's heartbeat is strong and steady."

When Cole returned with the raspberry tea, Rachel moved into the familiar pattern of labor—a combination of her own expertise and the mother's natural instincts. Needing to move, Penny got out of the bed a couple of times and paced. When she complained of back pain, Cole volunteered to massage. His strong hands provided Penny with relief. He was turning out to be an excellent helper—uncomplaining and quick to follow her instructions.

When the urge to push came, Penny screamed for the first time. And she let go with a string of curses. Though Rachel had pretty much heard it all, she was surprised by the depth and variety of profanity from such a tiny woman.

Cole looked panicked. "Is this normal?"

"The pushing? Or the I-hate-men tirade?"

"Both."

"Very typical. I bet you're glad you took the gun away."

"Hell, yes."

A mere two hours after Rachel had arrived at the house, Penny gave birth to an average-sized baby girl with a healthy set of lungs.

Though Rachel had participated in well over two hundred births, this moment never failed to amaze her. The emergence of new life gave meaning to all existence.

Postpartum was also a time that required special attention on the part of the midwife. Penny was leaking blood onto the rubber sheet they'd spread across the bed. Hemorrhage was always a danger.

Rachel held the newborn toward Cole. "Take the baby. I need to deal with Penny."

Dumbstruck, he held the wriggling infant close to his chest. His gaze met hers. In his eyes, she saw a reflection of her own wonderment, and she appreciated his honest reverence for the miracle of life. For a tough guy, he was sensitive.

Her focus right now was on the mother. Rachel urged, "You need to push again."

"No way." With a sob, Penny covered her eyes with her forearm. "I can't."

She had to expel the afterbirth. As Rachel massaged the uterus, she felt the muscles contract, naturally doing what was necessary. The placenta slipped out. Gradually, the bleeding slowed and stopped.

Cole stood behind her shoulder, watching with concern. "Is she going to be okay?"

"They both are."

Penny forced herself into a sitting position with pillows behind her back. "I want my baby."

With Cole's help, Rachel clipped the cord, washed the infant and cleared her nose of mucus. The rest of the cleanup could wait. She settled the new baby on Penny's breast.

As mother and child cooed to each other, she turned toward Cole in time to see him swipe away a tear. Turning away, he said, "I'll tell the others."

"Whoa, there. You're not leaving me with all the mess to clean up."

"I'll be right back."

Rachel sank into a chair beside the bed and watched the bonding of mother and child. Though Penny hadn't seemed the least bit maternal, her expression was serene and gentle.

"Do you have a name?" Rachel asked.

"Goldie. She's my golden child."

From the other room, she heard the men arguing loudly. Catching bits of their conversation, Rachel got the idea that they were tired of waiting around. *Bad news for her.*

When the gang was on the run again, they had no further need for a midwife. She was afraid to think of what might happen next.

Chapter 3

In the bedroom, Cole stood at the window and looked out into a deep, dark forest. Fresh snow piled up on the sill. He could hardly believe that he was considering an escape into that freezing darkness. He lived in L.A. where his only contact with snow was the occasional snowboarding trip to Big Bear Lake. He hated the cold.

A month ago, when the FBI office in Denver tapped him for this undercover assignment, he'd tried to wriggle out of it. But they'd needed an agent who was an unfamiliar face in the western states. The operating theory was that someone inside the FBI was connected to the spree of casino and bank robberies.

He stepped away from the window and began repacking Rachel's medical equipment in the cases from her van. Both of the women were in the bathroom, chatting about benefits of breast-feeding and how to use the pump. As he eavesdropped, he marveled at how normal their conversation sounded. For the moment, Penny wasn't a hardened criminal and Rachel wasn't a kidnap victim. They were just two women, talking about babies.

And he was just an average guy—shocked and amazed by the mysteries of childbirth. He didn't have words to describe how he'd felt when Goldie was born. He forgot where he was and why he was there. Watching the newborn take her first breath had amazed him. Her cry was the voice of an angel. Pure and innocent.

In that moment, he wanted to protect Penny instead of taking her into FBI custody.

And then there was Rachel. Slender but muscular, she moved with a natural grace. Her short dark hair made her blue eyes look huge, even though she wasn't wearing any makeup. He felt guilty as hell for dragging her into this mess. Top priority for him was to make sure Rachel escaped unharmed.

From the bathroom, he overheard her say, "Your body needs time to recover, Penny. You should spend time in bed, relaxing."

"Don't worry. I'm not going anywhere."

"Will the men agree to let you sleep tonight?"

"They'll do what I say," Penny said airily. "They can't leave me behind."

"Why not?" Rachel asked.

"Because I'm the only one who knows where the money is hidden."

Cole feared that her confidence might be misplaced. Frank and the other two were anxious to get going. No doubt, they could force Penny to tell them about the stash from five different robberies in three states.

Rachel seemed to be thinking along the same lines. "What if they threaten you?"

"They wouldn't dare. My baby's father is the head honcho. The big boss. If anybody hurts me, they'll answer to him."

Cole held his breath. *Say his name, Penny.* He needed to know the identity of the criminal mastermind who controlled this gang and at least five others. They referred to him as Baron, and he was famous for taking bloody revenge on those who betrayed him. Cole's reason for joining this gang of misfits was to infiltrate the upper levels of the organization and get evidence that could be used against Baron.

Rachel asked, "Does he know about Goldie?"

"Don't you remember? I told you all about Baron, about how we met. Damn, Rachel. You should learn to pay attention."

"Sorry," she murmured.

"He loves me. After this job, he promised to take me home with him, to raise our baby."

"Is that what you want?"

"You bet it is." Penny giggled. "Want to know a secret? A little while ago, I called Baron and told him about Goldie. He's coming here. He ought to be here any minute."

Not good news. Cole might have been able to convince the others in the gang to release Rachel. These guys weren't killers, except for Frank. Baron was a different story; he wouldn't leave a witness alive.

From the bathroom, he heard Rachel ask, "How does he know where you are? Cole said this house wasn't a scheduled stop."

"Simple," Penny replied. "This is Baron's house."

That was all Cole needed to hear. He could find Baron's identity by checking property records. As far as he was concerned, his undercover assignment was over. He reached into his jeans pocket, took out his cell phone.

This wasn't an everyday cell. Though Cole didn't need a lot of fancy apps, he'd used the geniuses at the FBI to modify his phone to suit his specific needs.

The first modification: he could disable the GPS locator. Unless he had it turned on, he couldn't be tracked. His handler—Agent Ted Waxman in L.A.—wasn't thrilled with the need for secrecy, but Cole needed to be sure his cover wouldn't be blown by some federal agent jumping the gun.

Second, his directory of phone numbers couldn't be read without using a five-digit code. His identity was protected in case somebody picked up his phone.

Third and most important, his number was blocked to everyone. Waxman couldn't call him with new orders and information. Cole, alone, made the decision when he would make contact and when he needed help.

Now was that time. He activated the GPS locator to alert Waxman that he was ready for extraction. Response time was usually less than an hour. Cole intended to be away from the house when that time came.

He slid the phone into his pocket and called out, "Hey, ladies, I need some help figuring out how to pack this stuff."

Rachel came out of the bathroom. Right away, he could see the change in her demeanor. No longer the self-assured professional, she had a haunted look in her eyes. Beneath her wispy bangs, her forehead pinched with worry. She whispered, "What's going to happen to me?"

Now would have been a good time to flash a badge and tell her that he was FBI, but he wasn't carrying identification. "I'll get you out of here."

Her gaze assessed him. During the hours of Penny's labor and the aftermath, a bond had grown between them. He hoped it was enough to make her cooperate without the reassurance of his credentials.

She asked, "Why should I trust you?"

"You don't have much choice."

Penny swept into the room and went to the travel bassinette where her baby was sleeping. "Be sure that you put all the baby stuff in the huge backpack so I can take it with me."

"Like what?" Cole asked.

"Diapers," Rachel said. "There's a sling for carrying newborns. And you'll need blankets and formula."

"But I'm breast-feeding. My milk already came in. Does that mean my boobs are going to get small again? Jenna said they would."

"Your friend Jenna doesn't have children. She doesn't know." Rachel's hands trembled as she sorted through the various baby items. "I don't have a car seat I can leave with you. You'll need to buy one as soon as possible."

Cole saw an opportunity to get Rachel alone. He wanted to reassure her that help was on the way. He asked her, "Don't you have a baby seat in your van?"

"I want it." Penny climbed onto the bed and stretched out. Her pink flannel robe contrasted her wan complexion. "Get it for me."

Rachel said, "I need that car seat for emergencies. If I have to transport a child to a hospital or—"

"Don't be stupid, Rachel. You're not going to need

that van anymore. You're coming with me. I need you to help me with Goldie."

Rachel recoiled as though she'd been slapped. "I have a job."

"So what? You'll make more money with me than you would as a midwife." Penny propped herself up on one elbow. "Come here and help me get these pillows arranged."

Rachel did as she'd been ordered, then she turned toward Cole. "I'll help you get the car seat out of the van. The straps are complicated, and I don't want you to break it."

From the bed, Penny waved. "Hurry back. I want more tea."

He grabbed Rachel's down parka from the bedroom closet and held it for her. She hadn't said a word, but he knew she'd made a decision to stick with him. Not surprising. Trusting Penny to take care of her would be suicidal.

Rachel didn't have a plan. Trust Cole? Sure, he'd shown sensitivity when the baby was delivered. The whole time he was helping her, he'd been smart and kind, even gentlemanly. But he also had kidnapped her and jammed a gun into her neck.

All she needed from him was her car keys.

When they stepped outside through the side door of the house, he caught hold of her arm and pulled her back, behind the bare branches of a bush and a towering pine. Edging uphill, he whispered, "Duck down and stay quiet. Something isn't right."

The night was still and cold. Snowflakes drifted lazily, and she was glad for the warmth of her parka and hood. Behind them was a steep, thickly forested hillside. Peeking around Cole's shoulder, she saw the side of the house and the edge of the wooden porch that stretched across the front. Since she'd been sequestered in the bedroom with Penny and hadn't seen the rest of the house, she hadn't realized that it was two stories with a slanted roof. To her right was a long, low garage. Was her van parked inside? She couldn't see past the house, didn't know if there was a road in front or other cars.

Through the stillness, she heard the rumble of voices. There were others out here, hiding in the darkness.

She whispered, "Can you see anything?"

"A couple of shadows. No headlights."

Mysterious figures creeping toward the hideout might actually be to her advantage. She prayed that it was the police who had finally tracked down the gang. "Who is it?"

"Can't tell." His voice was as quiet as the falling snow; she had to lean close to hear him. "Could be the cops. Or it could be Penny's boyfriend."

"Baron." He sounded like a real creep—much older than Penny and greedy enough to want his pregnant girlfriend to participate in a robbery. "Penny said this was his house. Why wouldn't he just walk inside?"

"Hush."

For a moment, she considered raising her hands above her head and marching to the front of the cabin to surrender. It was a risk, but anything would be better than being under Penny's thumb.

Gunfire from a semiautomatic weapon shattered the night. She heard breaking glass and shouts from inside the house.

She wasn't a stranger to violence. When she was

driving the ambulance, she'd been thrust into a lot of dicey situations, and she prided herself on an ability to stay calm. But the gunfire shocked her.

Shots were returned from inside the house.

There was another burst from the attackers.

She clung to Cole's arm. "Tell me what to do."

"We wait."

The side door they'd come through flung open. Frank charged outside. With guns in both hands, the big man dashed into the open, firing wildly as he ran toward the garage.

He was shot. His arms flew into the air before he fell. His blood splattered in the snow. He didn't attempt to get up, but she saw his arm move. "He's not dead."

"Don't even think about stepping into the open to help him," Cole whispered. "The way I figure, there are only two shooters. Three at the most. They don't have the manpower to surround the cabin, but they have superior weapons."

Though her mind was barely able to comprehend what she was experiencing, she nodded.

He continued, "We'll go up the hill, wait until the shooting is over and circle back around to the garage."

Taking her gloved hand, he pulled her through the ankle-deep snow into the surrounding forest. Behind them, gunfire exploded. Anybody living within a mile of this house had to be aware that something terrible was happening. The police would have to respond.

Crouched behind a snow-covered boulder, Cole paused and looked back. "We're leaving tracks. They won't have any trouble following us. We need to go faster."

Her survival instinct was strong. She wanted to make

a getaway, but there was something else at stake. "We can't leave Penny here. Or the baby."

A sliver of moonlight through clouds illuminated his face. In his eyes, she saw a struggle between protecting the innocent and saving his own butt. "Damn it, Rachel. You're right."

Sadly, she said, "I know."

They retraced their steps to the house. Instead of using the door, Cole went to the rear of the house. He stopped outside a window. Inside, she saw the bathroom where she and Penny had been talking only a little while ago.

He dug into his pocket, took out her car keys and handed them to her. "If anything happens to me, get the hell out of here. Hide in the forest until you can get back to the garage."

The car keys literally opened the door to her escape. Her purse was in the van. And her cell phone.

When he shoved the casement window open, she said, "All those windows were latched."

"I opened it hours ago," he said. "I expected to be escaping from the inside out. Not breaking in."

Walking into a shoot-out was insanity. But the alternative was worse. She couldn't leave a helpless newborn to the mercy of these violent men.

Cole slipped through the window, and she got in position to follow.

"No," he said. "Stay here."

There wasn't time to argue. He needed her help in handling Penny and the baby. She hoisted herself up and over the sill.

As soon as she was inside, she heard the baby crying. In the bedroom, Cole knelt beside Penny's body on the floor. She'd been shot in the chest. Her open eyes stared sightlessly at the ceiling.

Rachel reached past Cole to feel Penny's throat for a pulse. Her skin was still warm, but her heart had stopped. There was nothing. Not even a flutter. Penny was gone. After her heroic struggle to bring her baby into the world, she wouldn't live to see her child grow. Fate was cruel. Unfair. *Oh, God, this is so wrong.*

From the front of the house, the gun battle continued, but all she heard was the baby's cries. If it was the last thing she ever did, Rachel would rescue Goldie. Moving with purpose, she took the baby sling from the backpack. When she snuggled Goldie into the carrier, the infant's cries modified to a low whimpering.

Cole grabbed the backpack filled with baby supplies. They went through the bathroom window into the forest.

They were only a few steps into the trees when he signaled for her to stop. He said, "Do you hear that?"

She listened. "It's quiet."

The shooting had ended. The battle was over. Now the attackers would be coming after them.

Chapter 4

Cole went first, leading Rachel up the forested hill and away from the house. The cumbersome backpack hampered his usual gait. He hunched forward, moving as quickly as possible in the snow-covered terrain. Even if there had been a path through these trees, he wouldn't have been able to see it. Not in this darkness. Not with the snow falling.

His leather jacket wasn't the best thing to be wearing in this weather, but he wasn't cold. The opposite, in fact. He was sweating like a pig. Though breathing hard, he couldn't seem to get enough wind in his lungs. After only going a couple of hundred yards, his shoulders ached. His thigh muscles were burning. This high elevation was killing him. He estimated that they were more than eight thousand feet above sea level. What the hell was a California guy like him doing here? His natural habitat was palm trees.

He picked his way through the rugged trunks of pine trees and dodged around boulders. After he climbed over a fallen log, he turned to help Rachel. She had the baby in the sling, tucked inside her parka.

She ignored his outstretched hand and jumped over the log, nimble as a white-tailed deer.

"Careful," he said.

"I'm good."

Her energy annoyed him. Logically, he knew that Rachel lived here full-time and was acclimated to the altitude. But he wanted to be the strong one—the protector who would lead her and the baby to safety.

Hoping to buy a little time to catch his breath, he asked, "How's Goldie?"

Rachel peeked inside her parka. "Sleeping. She's snuggled against my chest and can hear my heartbeat. It probably feels like she's still in the womb."

They needed to find shelter soon. It couldn't be good for a newborn to be exposed to the cold.

"I have a question," she said. "Why are we going uphill?"

"Escape."

"If we go down to the road, we'll be more likely to find a cabin. Or we could flag down a passing car."

He looked down the hill. The lights from the house were barely visible. "We're going this way because we can't risk having the guys who attacked the house find us. They'll be watching the road."

"They'll be looking for us? Why?"

If the gunmen worked for Baron, they wouldn't leave without the boss man's baby. If they were Baron's enemies, the same rationale applied. Goldie was a valuable commodity. "It's not us they're after."

Her arm curled protectively around the infant. "The police ought to be here soon. Somebody must have reported all that gunfire."

It was too soon to expect a response from his GPS signal, but he trusted that the FBI was closing in on this location. "Nothing would please me more than hearing cop sirens."

"You can't mean that." Her earnest gaze confronted him. "You'll be taken into custody."

He'd almost forgotten that she still didn't know his identity. As far as Rachel was concerned, he was the guy who kidnapped her at gunpoint. An armed robber.

"If I got arrested, would you be heartbroken?"

She exhaled a puff of icy vapor. "No."

"Maybe a little sad?"

"Let me put it this way. I wouldn't turn you in."

Her response surprised him. He had her pegged as a strictly law-abiding citizen who'd be delighted to see any criminal behind bars. But she was willing to make an exception for him. Either she liked him or she had a dark side that she kept hidden.

He turned to face the uphill terrain. "We'll keep moving until we know we're safe. Then we can double back to the road."

The brief rest had allowed him to recover his strength. He slogged onward, wanting to put distance between them and the men with guns. In spite of the burn, his legs took on a steady rhythm as he climbed. Coming through a stand of trees, he realized that they'd reached the highest point on the hill. He maneuvered until he was standing on a boulder and waited for Rachel to join him.

"This is a good lookout point. Do you see anything?"

Together, they peered through the curtain of trees. The snowfall was thick. Heavy clouds had blocked out the light from the moon and stars.

"There." She pointed down the hill.

The beams of a couple of flashlights flickered in the darkness. They weren't far away. Maybe eighty yards. He and Rachel were within range of their semiautomatic weapons.

He ducked. She did the same.

The searchers were too close. His hope for escape vanished in the howling wind that sliced through the tree trunks. He and Rachel had left tracks in the snow that a blind man could follow. Peering over the edge of the boulder, he saw the flashlights moving closer. There was only one way out of this.

He slipped his arms out of the backpack. "Take the baby and run. Get as far away from here as you can."

"What are you going to do?"

"I'll distract them."

Going up against men with superior firepower wasn't as dumb as it sounded. Cole had the advantage of higher ground. If he waited until they got close, he might be able to take out one of them before the other responded.

"There's something you haven't considered," she said.

"What's that?"

"Snow."

While they'd been climbing, the full force of the impending blizzard had gathered. The storm had taken on a fierce intensity.

She grabbed his arm and tugged. "They won't be able to see us in the blizzard. The wind will cover our tracks."

Great. He wouldn't die in a hail of bullets. He'd freeze to death in a blizzard.

"Come on," she urged. "I need you. Goldie needs you."

He shouldered the pack again. Going downhill should have been easier, but his knees jolted with every step. At the foot of the slope, they approached an open area where the true velocity of the storm was apparent. The snow fell in sheets. His visibility was cut to only a few yards, but he figured they could cover more distance if they went straight ahead instead of weaving through the trees.

When he stepped into the open, he sank up to his knees. His jeans were wet. His fingers and toes were numb.

"Stay close to the trees," Rachel said. "It's not as deep."

At the edge of the forest, the snow was over his ankles. He trudged through it, making a path for her to follow. One minute turned into ten. Ten into twenty. Inside his boots, his feet felt like frozen blocks of ice. The snow stung his cheeks. So cold, so damned cold. If he was this miserable what was happening to Goldie? Fear for the motherless newborn kept him moving forward. He had to protect this child, had to find shelter.

But he'd lost all sense of direction in the snow. As far as he could tell, they might be heading back toward the house.

Trying to get his bearings, he looked over his shoulder. He doubted that the bad guys were still in pursuit. Any sane person would have turned back by now.

As Rachel had predicted, the snow was already drifting, neatly erasing their tracks.

He couldn't tell how far they'd gone. It felt like miles,

endless miles. Needing a break, he stepped back into the shelter of the forest. His chest ached with the effort of breathing. His eyes were stinging. He squeezed his eyelids shut and opened them again. Squinting, he looked through the trees and saw a solid shape. A cabin. He blinked, hoping that his brain wasn't playing tricks on him. "Rachel, do you see it?"

"A cabin." Her voice trembled on the edge of a sob. "Thank God, it's a cabin."

He helped her up the small embankment, and they approached the rear of the cabin. No lights shone from inside.

The front door was sheltered by a small porch. Cole hammered against the green painted door with his frozen fist. No answer. Nobody home.

He tried the door handle and found it locked. He was carrying lock picks, but it was too cold to try a delicate manipulation of lock tumblers. He stepped back, prepared to use his body as a battering ram.

"Wait," Rachel said. "Run your hand over the top sill. They might have left a key."

"We need to get inside." He was too damned cold and tired to perform a subtle search. "Why the hell would anybody bother to lock up and then leave a key?"

"This isn't the city," she said. "Some of these little cabins are weekend getaways with different families coming and going. Give it a try."

He peeled off his glove. His fingers were wet and stiff, but he didn't see the whitened skin indicating the first stage of frostbite. When he felt along the ledge above the door, he touched a key. It seemed that their luck had turned.

Shivering, he fitted the key into the lock and pushed

open the door. He and Rachel tumbled inside. When he shut the door against the elements, an ominous silence wrapped around them.

Rachel discarded her gloves and hit the light switch beside the door. The glow from an overhead light fixture spilled down upon them. They had electricity. So far, so good.

She unzipped her parka, glad that when she left the house this morning—an eternity ago—she'd been smart enough to dress for subzero weather. This jacket might have saved her life…and Goldie's, as well. She looked down at the tiny bundle she carried in the sling against her chest. The baby's eyes were closed. She wasn't moving. *Please, God, let her be all right.*

Cole hovered beside her, and she knew he was thinking the same thing.

Rachel slipped out of her jacket. Carefully, she braced the baby in her arms and adjusted the sling. *Please, God.*

Goldie's eyes popped open and she let out a wail.

Rachel had never heard a more beautiful sound. "She's okay. Yes, you are, Goldie. You're all right."

Looking up, she saw a similar relief in Cole's ruddy face. He'd torn off his cap and his hair stood up in spikes. His lips were chapped and swollen. Moisture dripped from his leather jacket. In spite of his obvious discomfort, he smiled.

Grateful tears rose behind her eyelids, but she couldn't let herself fall apart. "Are we safe?"

"I'm not sure," he said. "Tell me what Goldie needs."

The interior of the cabin was one big open room with a couple of sofas and chairs at one end and a large wooden table at the other. The kitchen area formed an *L* shape. A closed door against the back wall probably led into the bedroom. The most important feature, in her mind, was the freestanding propane gas fireplace. "See if you can get that heater going."

She held Goldie against her shoulder, patting her back and soothing her cries. The poor little thing had to be starving. There was powdered formula in the back-pack of supplies, but they needed water.

In the kitchen, Rachel turned the faucet in the sink and was rewarded with a steady flow. This simple, little cabin—probably a weekend getaway—had been well-prepared for winter. No doubt the owners had left the electricity on because the water pipes were wrapped in heat tape. The stove was electric.

Cole joined her. "The fireplace is on. What's next?"

He looked like hell. Hiking through the blizzard had been more difficult for him than for her. Not only did he go first, but his jacket and boots also weren't anywhere near as well-insulated as hers. She wanted to tell him to get out of his wet clothes, warm up and take care of himself, but she didn't want to insult his masculine pride by suggesting he wasn't in as good a shape as she was.

"Help me get stuff out of the backpack."

Near the cheery blaze in the propane fireplace, they dug through the baby supplies and put together a nest of blankets for Goldie. When Rachel laid the baby down on the blankets, her cries faded. Goldie wriggled as her diaper was changed.

Cole frowned. "Is she supposed to look like that?"

"Like what?"

"Like a plucked chicken. I thought babies were supposed to have chubby arms and legs."

"Don't listen to him." Rachel stroked Goldie's fine, dark hair. "You're gorgeous."

"Yeah, people always say that. But not all babies are beautiful."

"This is a golden child." She zipped Goldie into a yellow micro-fleece sleep sack. "She's beautiful, strong and brave—not even a day old and she's already escaped a gang of thugs and made it through a blizzard."

The baby's chin tilted, and she seemed to be looking directly at Cole with her lips pursed.

He laughed. "She's a tough little monkey."

"Newborns are surprisingly resilient." She held Goldie against her breast and stood. "I'm going to the kitchen to prepare the formula. Maybe you want to get out of those wet clothes."

"What about you?"

Her jeans were wet and cold against her legs, and her feet were cold in spite of her lined, waterproof boots. "I'd love to take off my boots."

"Sit," he ordered.

Still holding the baby, she sank onto a rocking chair. The heat from the fireplace was making a difference in the room temperature. She couldn't allow herself to get too comfortable or she'd surely fall asleep. This had been the longest day of her life; she'd attended at two birthings, been kidnapped and escaped through a blizzard.

Cole knelt before her and unfastened the laces on her boots. He eased the boot off her right foot, cradled her heel in his hand and massaged through her wool sock. His touch felt so good that she groaned with pleasure.

"Your feet are almost dry," Cole said. "Where do I get boots like this?"

"Any outdoor clothing and equipment store." Anyone who lived in the mountains knew how to shop for snow gear. "You're not from around here."

"L.A.," he said.

This was the first bit of personal information he'd volunteered. She'd entrusted this man with her life even though she knew next to nothing about him. "What's your last name?"

"McClure." He pulled off the other boot. "And I'm not who you think I am."

Chapter 5

Rachel gazed down at the top of Cole's head as he removed her other boot. Much of his behavior didn't fit with what she expected from an armed robber. He was too smart to be a thug but dumb enough to get involved with killers. *Who is he?* In the back of her mind, she'd been waiting for the other shoe to drop. Literally, this was the moment.

He'd said that he wasn't who she thought he was. What did that mean? Did he have superpowers? Was he actually a millionaire? She refused to be seduced by excuses or explanations. Rachel knew his type. He was a tough guy—dangerous, strong and silent...and sexy.

"You know what, Cole? I don't want to hear your life story."

He sat back on his heels. "Trust me. You want to know."

"Trust you?" Not wanting to upset Goldie, she kept

her voice level. Inside, she was far from calm. "You don't deserve my trust."

"That's not what you said when I was saving your butt."

"I didn't ask for your help."

"Come on, Rachel. I could have left you in the middle of a shoot-out. I'm not a bad guy."

"If you hadn't hidden in the back of my van and kidnapped me—" she paused for emphasis "—kidnapped me at gunpoint, I wouldn't have been in a shoot-out."

"There were circumstances."

"Don't care." Right now, she was supposed to be on vacation, relaxing in her cozy condo with a fragrant cup of chamomile tea and a good book. "I want this nightmare to be over. And when it is, I never want to see you again."

"Fair enough." He stood and stretched. "Take care of Goldie. I'm going to make sure we're secure."

"Go right ahead."

Cole opened the cabin door and stepped onto the porch. The brief moment of warmth when he'd been inside the cabin made the cold feel even worse than before. The blizzard still raged, throwing handfuls of snow into his face. The icy temperatures instantly froze his bare hands. In his left, he held his gun. In his right, the cell phone. His intention was to call for help. Shivering, he turned on the phone. His power was almost gone. He had no signal at this remote cabin. Holding the phone like a beacon, he turned in every direction, trying to make a connection. *Nada. Damn it.* He hoped the GPS signal was still transmitting his location to his FBI handlers.

The windblown snow had already begun to erase their tracks. Drifts piled up, nearly two feet deep on one side of the log cabin walls. In this storm, visual surveillance was nearly impossible. He couldn't see past the trees into the forest. All he could do was try to get his bearings.

In front of the house was a turn-around driveway. Less than thirty feet away, he saw the blocky shape of a small outbuilding. A garage? There might be something in there that would aid in their escape.

The wide front door of the garage was blocked by the drifting snow, but there was a side entrance. He shoved it open and entered. The interior was unlit, but there was some illumination from a window at the rear. The open space in the middle seemed to indicate that this building was used as a garage when the people who owned the cabin were here. Under the window, he found a workbench with tools for home repair. Stacked along the walls was a variety of sporting equipment: cross-country skis, poles and snowshoes.

He'd never tried cross-country skiing before, but Rachel probably knew how to use this stuff. She was a hardy mountain woman. Prepared for the snow. Intrepid. What was her problem, anyway?

He'd been about to tell her that he was a fed and she had no more reason to fear, but she'd shut him down. Her big beautiful blue eyes glared at him with unmistakable anger. She'd said that she didn't give a damn about him.

He didn't believe her. Though she had every reason to be ticked off, she didn't hate him. There was something growing between them. A spark. He saw it in her body language, heard it in her voice, felt it in a dim flicker inside his frozen body. Maybe after they were safe and she knew he was a good guy, he'd pursue that attraction. Or maybe not. He had a hard time imagining Rachel in sunny California, and he sure as hell wasn't going to move to these frigid, airless mountains.

Leaving the garage, he tromped along the driveway to a narrow road that hadn't been cleared of snow. No tire tracks. Nothing had been on this road since the beginning of the storm.

He looked back toward the house. Though the curtains were drawn, he could still see the light from inside. If anyone came looking for them, they wouldn't be hard to find.

Cradling the baby on her shoulder, Rachel padded around in the kitchen in her wool socks. She heard the front door open and saw Cole stumble inside. He locked the door and placed his gun on the coffee table. *And his cell phone.*

"Why didn't you tell me you had a phone?" she asked.

"It's almost dead. And I can't get a signal."

Warily, she approached the table. "Who were you trying to call?"

"Somebody to get us the hell out of here."

"Like who?" She wasn't sure that she wanted to be rescued by any of his friends. *Out of the frying pan into the fire.*

"I'm not trying to trick you." He tossed the phone to her. "Go ahead. See if you can get the damn thing to work."

She juggled the phone and waved it all around while he went through the door to the bedroom. He hadn't been lying about the lack of signal, but that didn't set her mind at ease.

Returning to the kitchen, she focused on preparing the formula—a task she'd performed hundreds of times before. Not only was she the third oldest of eight children, but her responsibilities at the clinic also included more than assisting at births. She also made regular visits to new moms, helping them with baby care, feeding and providing necessary immunizations.

The water she'd put into a saucepan on the stove was just beginning to boil. Since she had no idea about the source of this liquid, she wanted to make sure germs and bacteria had been killed. Ten minutes of boiling should be enough. A cloud of steam swirled around her. From the other room, she heard doors opening and closing. She hoped Cole was changing out of his wet clothes. He looked half-frozen.

His well-being shouldn't matter to her, but she'd be lying if she told herself she wasn't attracted to him. All her life, she'd been drawn to outsiders and renegades. There was something about bad boys that always sucked her in.

Her first serious boyfriend had owned a motorcycle shop and had tattoos up and down both arms. He definitely hadn't been the kind of guy she could bring home to meet her stable, responsible, churchgoing parents, which might have been part of her fascination with him. She'd loved riding on the back of his Harley, loved the way he'd grab her and kiss her in front of his biker friends. He hadn't been able to keep his hands off her. He'd called her "baby doll" and given her a black leather jacket with a skull and a heart on the back.

On the very day she'd intended to move in with him,

she'd discovered him in bed with another woman, and she'd heard him tell this leggy blonde stranger that she—the blonde bimbo—was his baby doll.

Even now, ten years later, that memory set Rachel's blood boiling. Before she'd departed from motorcycle man's house, she'd gone into his garage, dumped gasoline on her leather jacket and set it on fire.

After that ride on the wild side, she should have learned. Instead, she'd gone through a series of edgy boyfriends—daredevils, rock musicians, soldiers of fortune. Like an addict, she was drawn to their intensity.

Cole was one of those guys.

True, he had risked his life to rescue her and Goldie. He wasn't evil. But he wasn't somebody she wanted to know better.

Using a dish towel, she wiped around the lid of the container before she opened the powdered formula. There was food for Goldie, but what about them? Searching the kitchen, she found a supply of canned food and an opened box of crackers. There was also flour and sugar and olive oil. If they got snowed in for a day or two, they wouldn't starve to death. *A day or two?* The idea of being trapped with Cole both worried and excited her.

One-handed and still holding the fidgeting baby, she measured and mixed the formula. "Almost done," she murmured to Goldie. "You'll feel better after you eat."

One of the reasons Rachel had moved to the mountains was to get away from sexy bad boys who would ultimately hurt her. As a midwife, she didn't come into contact with many single men and hadn't had a date in months. *Fine with me!* She preferred the calm warmth of celibacy to a fiery affair that would leave her with nothing but a handful of ashes.

Bottle in hand, she returned to the living room just as Cole stepped out of the bathroom, drying his dark blond hair with a towel. He'd changed into a sweatshirt and gray sweatpants that were too short, leaving his ankles exposed. On his feet, he wore wool socks.

"Did you take a shower?" she asked.

"A hot shower. They have one of those wall-hanging propane water heaters."

She gazed longingly toward the bathroom. "Hot water?"

He held out his arms. "Give me the baby. I'll feed her while you shower and change out of those wet jeans. There are clothes in the bedroom."

That was all it took to convince her. She nodded toward the rocking chair. "Sit. Do you know how to feed an infant?"

"How hard can it be?"

"You haven't been around babies much, have you?"

"I was an only child."

Another piece of personal information she didn't need to know. "Here's how it's done. Don't force the nipple into her mouth. Let her take it. She's tired and will probably drop off before she gets enough nourishment. Gently nudge with the nipple. That stimulates the sucking reflex."

She placed Goldie in his arms and watched him. His rugged hands balanced the clear plastic bottle with a touching clumsiness. When Goldie latched onto the nipple, Cole looked up at her and grinned triumphantly. He really was trying to be helpful. She had to give him credit.

"What did you find when you went outside?" she asked. "Is it safe for us to stay here?"

"The men who were after us must have turned back. If they were still on our trail, they would have busted in here by now."

"The blizzard saved us."

"They won't stop looking. Tomorrow, we'll need to move on."

She turned on her heel and went into the bedroom. There was only one thing she needed Cole for: survival. The sooner he was out of her life, the better.

Like the rest of the cabin, the bathroom was well-equipped and efficient. Quickly, she shed her clothes and turned on the steaming water. As soon as the hot spray hit her skin, a soothing warmth spread through her body, easing her tension. She ducked her head under the hot water. One of the benefits of short hair was not worrying about getting it wet. She would have liked to stand here for hours but wasn't sure what sort of water system the cabin had. So she kept it quick.

As soon as she was out of the shower and wrapped in a yellow bath towel that matched the plastic shower curtain, Rachel realized her logistical dilemma. No way did she want to get back into her damp clothes. But she didn't want to give Cole a free show by scampering from the bathroom to the bedroom wearing nothing but a towel.

Her hand rested on the doorknob. *I can't hide in here.* Rachel prided herself on being a decisive woman. No nonsense. She did what was necessary without false modesty or complaint. And so she yanked open the bathroom door and strode forth, *decisively*. She had nothing to be ashamed of.

As she walked the few paces in her bare feet, she boldly gazed at him. In his amber eyes, she saw a flash of interest. His mouth curved in a grin.

She challenged him. "What are you staring at?"

"You."

Her bravado collapsed. She felt very, very naked. He seemed to be looking through the towel, and she had the distinct impression that he liked the view.

Despite her determination not to scamper, she dashed into the bedroom, closed the door and leaned against it. Her heart beat fast. The warmth from the shower was replaced by an internal flush of embarrassment that rose from her throat to her cheeks. If he could decimate her composure with a single glance, what would happen if he actually touched her?

In spite of the burning inside her, she realized that the temperature in the bedroom, away from the propane fireplace, was considerably cooler than in the front room. The double bed was piled high with comforters and blankets. Would she sleep in that bed with Cole tonight? As soon as the question formed in her mind, she banished it. Sleeping with the enemy had no place on her agenda.

Inside a five-drawer bureau, she found clothing— mostly long underwear and sweats—in several sizes. It was easy to imagine a family coming to this weekend retreat for cross-country skiing or ice skating or snowmobiling. When this was over, Rachel fully intended to reimburse the cabin owners and thank them for saving her life.

After she slipped into warm sweats and socks, she eyed the bedroom door. Cole was out there, waiting. Physically, she couldn't avoid him. But she could maintain an emotional distance. She remembered motorcycle man and the flaming leather jacket. Any involvement with Cole would lead inevitably to that same conclusion.

She straightened her shoulders. *I can control myself. I will control my emotions.*

She opened the door and entered the front room. Cole was still sitting in the rocking chair. Without looking up, he said, "I think Goldie's had enough milk."

"How many ounces are left in the bottle?"

He held it up to look through the clear plastic. "Just a little bit at the bottom."

"Did you burp her?"

"I do that by putting her on my shoulder, right?"

"Give me the baby," she said.

When he transferred the swaddled infant to her, their hands touched. An electric thrill raced up her arm, and she tensed her muscles to cancel the effect.

He took a step back. His baggy gray sweatsuit didn't hide the breadth of his shoulders, his slim torso or long legs. His gaze assessed her as though deciding how to proceed. Instead of speaking, he went to the front window and peered through the gap in the green-and-blue plaid curtains. "It's still snowing hard."

"This morning they predicted at least a foot of new snow." A weather report wasn't really what was on her mind.

"It's mesmerizing. I didn't actually see snow falling from the sky until I was nine years old."

"Not so pretty when you're caught in a blizzard." She did a bouncy walk as she patted Goldie on the back.

"I never want to do that again."

"Tomorrow morning, we shouldn't have to walk too far. All we need to find is a working telephone."

Then they could call for help. She and Goldie would be safe. Cole was a different story. When the police came to her rescue, he'd be taken into custody. Would he turn himself in without a fight? Or would he run?

"It's ironic," he said. "This is the first time in years that I've been without a working cell phone."

Had he planned it that way? She needed to clear the air of suspicions. "Cole, I—"

A shuffling sound outside the front door interrupted her, and she turned to look in that direction.

The door crashed open. A hulking figure charged across the threshold. His shoulders and cap were covered with snow. His lips drew back from his teeth in an inhuman snarl.

He had a gun.

Chapter 6

Frank Loeb! Cole barely recognized him. The man should have been dead. He'd been shot. Cole had seen his blood spattered in the snow. How the hell had he made it through the blizzard? Some men were just too damned mean to die.

Frank raised his handgun.

Cole's weapon was all the way across the room on the table. No time to grab it. No chance for subtlety or reason. He launched himself at the monster standing in the doorway. His shoulder drove into the other man's massive chest.

With a guttural yell, Frank staggered backward onto the porch. He was off balance, weakened. Cole pressed his advantage. He shoved with all his strength. His hands slipped against the cold, wet, bloodstained parka. The big man teetered and fell. Cole was on top of him. He slammed Frank's gun hand on the floor of the porch.

Frank released his grasp on the gun. He was disarmed but still dangerous. Flailing, he landed heavy blows on Cole's arms and shoulders. The snow gusted around them. Icy crystals hit Cole's face, stinging like needles.

He drew back his fist and slammed it into Frank's face, splitting his swollen lip. He winced. Blood oozed down his chin.

Cole hit him again. His fingers stung with the force of the blow.

"Wait." Frank lay still. The fight went out of him.

With his arm still cocked for another blow, Cole paused. He knew better than to let down his guard. He'd seen Frank in action. When the big man caught one of the other guys in the gang cheating at cards, Frank broke two of the cheater's fingers. And he smiled at the pain he had inflicted.

"The shooters," Frank said. "They were feds."

That wasn't possible. Though Cole had put in a call for backup, the shooters had appeared within minutes. Even if the FBI had been tracking his movements, the violent assault on the house wasn't standard procedure, especially not when they had a man on the inside. "I don't believe it."

"They were after you." His tongue poked at his split lip. "I heard them talking. They said your name."

"What else did you hear?"

"They reported to somebody named Prescott."

Wayne Prescott was the field agent in charge of the Denver office—the only individual Cole had met with in person. "How did you find us?"

His eyes squeezed shut. Clearly, he was in pain. "Wasn't looking for you."

"The hell you weren't."

"On the run. Just like you," he mumbled. "Went across a field. Saw the lights from the cabin."

Rachel stepped out on the porch. She took a shooter's stance, holding his gun in both hands and aiming at Frank. "Don't move. I will shoot."

There was no doubt that she meant what she'd said. Her voice was firm and her hand steady. She positioned herself far enough away from Frank that he couldn't make a grab for her ankle.

"You're a medic," Frank said. "I need your help."

Cole noticed a flicker of doubt in her eyes. Her natural instinct was to save lives, not threaten them. Even though he wasn't inclined to help Frank, he couldn't justify killing the man in cold blood.

He stood, picked up Frank's gun and aimed for the center of his chest. "Get up."

Moving slowly and laboriously, Frank got to his knees. Then he heaved himself to his feet and stood there with blood dripping down his chin onto his wet black parka.

Cole instructed, "Rachel, go inside. Keep your distance from him. If he makes a move toward you, shoot him."

After she was safely in the house, Cole escorted his prisoner into the cabin. He saw Goldie sleeping, nestled in blankets on one of the sofas. He had to protect that innocent baby. If Frank wasn't lying, Cole's hope for a rescue from the FBI was disintegrating fast. Agent Wayne Prescott was connected with the men who opened fire on the house. *Houston, we have a problem.*

With the gun, he gestured toward the bedroom. "In there."

Rachel wasted no time closing the front door. Frank had broken the latch, and she had to pull a chair in front of it to keep it shut.

In the bedroom, Cole ordered, "Take off the parka."

Frank peeled off his jacket. A swath of gore stained the left side of his plaid flannel shirt and the left arm. It looked like he'd been shot twice. It was a miracle that he'd made it this far.

The question was whether or not to treat his wounds. They didn't have medical supplies, but Rachel could probably do something for him. Cole hated the idea of her getting close to this dangerous criminal.

Frank groaned. "You had me fooled, man. I thought you were just some punk from Compton. But you've got the feds on your tail. You must have pulled something big-time."

Cole was aware of Rachel standing behind him, listening. He glanced toward her. "Find something to tie his hands and feet."

"We need to clean those wounds," she said. "He could still be losing blood."

"Listen to her," Frank said. "I don't want to die."

"Why should I help you? You crashed through the door with a gun."

"But I didn't shoot."

A valid point. Frank had caught them unawares but hadn't opened fire. What did he want from them?

Cole asked Rachel, "How would you treat him?"

"He needs to go into the bathroom, strip down and get out of his wet clothes. Then he should clean his wounds with soap. Once I can see the extent of the damage, I'll tell you what else is necessary."

"I still want you to find something to tie him up."

He turned back to Frank. "Here's the deal. Do exactly as she says, and I won't kill you."

He nodded. This willingness to cooperate was out of character. Maybe he was intimidated by his new idea of Cole's reputation. Maybe the loss of blood had weakened him.

Cole stood in the bathroom door and watched as the big man sat on the toilet seat and pulled off his boots, socks and wet jeans. His skin was raw. His feet had white streaks, indicating the start of frostbite, but the more serious physical problem became evident when he removed his shirt. Blood caked and congealed on his upper chest and left arm. When he turned his back, Cole didn't see an exit wound.

"You need treatment in a hospital," Cole said. "The bullet is still in your chest."

"I'm not going back to prison."

"Jail is better than a coffin."

"Not for me."

After Frank had pulled on a pair of sweatpants and dry socks, he washed the wounds. His left arm wasn't too bad, but the hole in his upper chest was ragged at the edges and slowly bleeding. It had to hurt like hellfire. Cole had never been shot, but he'd nursed a knife wound for three hours without treatment.

Still holding his gun, he tossed Frank a towel. "Press this against your chest, and come into the kitchen."

Frank shuffled forward obediently. His heavy shoulders slouched. His head drooped forward, and his long hair hung around his face in strings. He reminded Cole of an injured grizzly, willing to accept help but still capable of lethal violence.

After he was seated in a straight-back chair, Rachel went into the bathroom to look for first-aid supplies.

"How did you get away?" Cole asked.

"I lay still, played possum. They thought I was dead. When they all went inside, I got up and ran. Two of them went after you and Rachel. They had flashlights."

"You were following them?"

"I was going parallel up the slope behind the house. I thought for sure they'd hear me."

The wind and the fury of the oncoming blizzard had masked the sounds from desperate people climbing through the forest. "You had a gun."

"Nothing like the kind of heat they were packing. Damn feds. They've got the primo weapons."

Not always. "When did they turn back?"

"Didn't even make it to the top of the hill." Frank grimaced. "I kept going. Picked up your trail. Then I got to an open field. The snow was coming down hard. Couldn't see a damn thing. Man, I thought I was going to die out there in the field. Frozen stiff." He barked a laugh. "A stiff. Frozen. Get it?"

Rachel returned with an armful of supplies, which she placed on the table. "I found antiseptic, gauze and surgical tape. I think I can make this work."

When she approached Frank and touched his shoulder, Cole's gut clenched. Though she showed no sign of fear, he knew how dangerous Frank could be. If the big man took it into his head to attack her, Cole couldn't risk shooting him. Not while Rachel was so close. He holstered his gun and took a position behind Frank's right shoulder, preparing himself to react to any threatening move.

Focused on first aid, Rachel lightly probed the wound on Frank's chest.

He inhaled sharply. The muscles in his chest twitched. "What are you doing?"

"Feeling for the bullet," she said. "I'm afraid it's deeply embedded."

"Cut it out of me."

"That's a painful process, and we've got no anesthetic. Not even booze. Plus, you've already lost a lot of blood. If I open that wound wider, you could bleed to death."

"I can take the pain," Frank said.

"But I can't give you a transfusion. For now, I'm going to patch you up and get the bleeding stopped. Later, you can deal with surgical procedures."

"Just do it."

Quickly and efficiently, she dressed the wound on his arm and wrapped it with strips of cotton from a T-shirt she'd shredded. "We're going to owe the people who own this cabin a whole new wardrobe," she said. "All this stuff is saving our lives."

"But no booze," Frank muttered.

She peeled the wrapper off a tampon and removed it from the casing. "I'm going to use this to plug the hole in your chest. It's sterile. And the absorbency will stop the bleeding."

Cole had heard of using feminine products to staunch blood flow but had never seen it done. Frank would owe his life to a tampon. Cole kept himself from smirking.

Frank turned his head away as she packed the wound. "You got to be pretty good friends with Penny," he said.

"We talked." A frown pulled Rachel's mouth.

"What did you talk about?"

"Anything that would take her mind off the labor pains," Rachel said. "Her childhood. Her dreams."

"Her baby's daddy? Baron?"

"I know you guys work for him and think he's a big deal, but I think he's a jerk. Sending his pregnant girlfriend to rob a casino?" She finished taping and wrapping the wound. "What kind of man does something like that?"

Frank's right hand shot forward. He held Rachel's jaw in his grip and pulled her face close to his. "Where did Penny hide the money?"

Cole reacted. He broke Frank's grasp and yanked his arm behind his back. The damage had already been done.

When he looked at Rachel, he saw fear written all over her face. Frank had achieved his objective. He'd showed her that he was someone who would hurt her if she didn't do as he said. Cole hadn't protected her; she'd never trust him now.

Chapter 7

After checking one more time to make sure Goldie was sleeping peacefully, Rachel sat at the end of the long table in the cabin. She slouched, head bent forward. With her fingernail, she traced the grain of the wood on the tabletop. The unidentifiable aroma of something Cole was cooking on the stove assaulted her nostrils.

Though she tried to focus on simple things, Rachel couldn't dismiss her rising fears. When Frank grabbed her, she hadn't been bruised. But she could still feel the imprint of his fingers. His grip had been ferocious—strong as a vise squeezing her jawbone. He could have killed her. With a flick of his wrist, he could have broken her neck. He'd forced her to look into his dark, soulless eyes. His split lip had sneered when he asked where Penny hid the money.

She hadn't expected the big man to lash out. Not

while she was helping him by dressing his wounds. Her mistake had been letting down her guard and getting too close to him. The warmth of the cabin had imbued her with false feelings of security.

She wasn't safe. Not by a long shot.

Trusting Cole was out of the question. His subtle charm was more potentially devastating than a blatant assault. She'd heard Frank say that the FBI was chasing Cole. Those men with guns who came to the house had been after Cole.

He placed a bowl of the canned chili he'd been heating in front of her. Though she should have been starving, Rachel didn't have an appetite. As she picked a kidney bean from the chili with her spoon, she felt Cole watching her.

"You don't have to worry about Frank," he said. "I've got him tied down in the bedroom."

Though Frank scared the hell out of her, she didn't want to mistreat him. "He should eat something."

"I'm not going to feed him. He'd probably bite my hand off. Besides, he's fallen asleep."

"Or gone into a coma," she said.

"I don't want him to die," Cole said. "I wouldn't wish death on anyone. But I've done all I intend to do for Frank Loeb."

At least he was being honest. She dared to lift her gaze from the chili and look into his face. His cognac-colored eyes gleamed. The color had returned to his roughly stubbled cheeks. It wasn't fair for him to be so handsome. The evil he might have done wasn't apparent in his features.

She shoveled a bite of chili into her mouth. The taste was bland and the texture gooey, but she swallowed and took another bite. If she was going to survive, she needed her strength.

Cole said, "Not the world's best dinner. Would you like a stale cracker to go with it?"

She shook her head, not wanting to get into a conversation with him. Given half a chance, he'd seduce her with his smooth-talking lies.

"You might be wondering," he said, "about some of the things Frank said."

"Not at all." She forced herself to swallow more chili.

"There are a couple of things you need to know, starting with—"

"Stop." She held up her hand. "I don't want to hear it."

"Five words," he said. "Give me five words to explain myself."

"All right. And I'm counting."

"I'm. An. Undercover. FBI. Agent." He shrugged. "Maybe FBI ought to count as more than one word. But you get the idea."

She dropped her spoon. *I didn't see this coming.* "Why should I believe you?"

He grinned. "Are you willing to hear more?"

Not if he was lying. "I want the truth."

"Until tomorrow when we talk to the police, I can't prove my identity," he said. "The mere fact that I'm willing to turn myself in to the cops ought to tell you something. My handler works out of the Denver field office. I contacted him after the shoot-out at the casino, and he told me to stick with the gang."

"Even though Penny was wounded and pregnant?"

"I thought the gang would make a clean getaway. She seemed okay. And I didn't expect her to go into labor."

"But she did. Wasn't it your duty to protect her and her baby?"

"That's why I got you."

"And put me in danger." If he really was an undercover agent, he was utterly irresponsible. "A real FBI agent wouldn't put a civilian in harm's way."

"Think back," he said. "I was doing my best to keep you safe. I kept you from seeing the other members of the gang so they wouldn't think you could identify them. Damn it, Rachel. Before the shoot-out started, I was taking it to your van, helping you escape."

Some of what he was saying backed up his claim to be an undercover lawman, but all she could see when she looked back was Penny, lying dead on the floor after delivering her baby. "She didn't deserve to die."

"I never thought Penny would be harmed. She was the mother of Baron's child. That should have been a guarantee of safety." His smile had disappeared. "But you're right, Rachel. Her death—her murder—was my fault. I failed. I can tell myself that there was nothing I could have done to save her, but it doesn't change what happened. Somehow, I'll have to find a way to live with that."

His regret seemed real. Did she dare to believe him? From the start, she'd sensed that he was a dangerous man. As an undercover agent, that was true. Even if he was on the right side of the law, he had that renegade edge. "Why didn't you tell me before? We were alone in my van when you kidnapped me. You could have told me then."

"If you'd known I was undercover, you would have been in even more danger."

Again, his reasoning made sense. But she couldn't

allow herself to be drawn in to this improbable story. "Frank said the FBI was after you. Not the other way around."

"And that could be a big problem." He glanced toward the closed door to the bedroom where Frank lay unconscious. "Usually, I'd dismiss anything Frank said as a lie, but he came up with a name that makes me think twice."

"I'm listening."

"Let me start at the beginning." Ignoring his chili, he leaned back in his chair and stretched his long legs out in front of him. "It was a month ago, give or take a couple of days. The FBI had an opportunity to infiltrate Baron's operation. They recruited me from L.A. because they suspected there was an FBI agent working with Baron. None of the agents in the Rocky Mountain area know me."

"Except for your handler."

"His name is Wayne Prescott. That's the name Frank heard. One of the shooters at the house mentioned Prescott."

"The shooters were from the FBI?"

"I don't think so. Attacking the house with guns blazing isn't the way we do things, especially not when the shooters knew they had an agent on the inside. Before they opened fire, they would have negotiated and offered a chance to surrender."

"Is that always the way they work?"

"In my experience, yes."

His gaze was steadfast and unguarded. His posture, relaxed. He didn't seem to be lying, but an expert liar wouldn't show that he was nervous. "Well, then. How do you explain what happened at the house?"

"The shooters know Prescott, but they have to be Baron's men. Penny told us that he owned the cabin and knew the location. Baron has a reputation for cruelty. During the casino robbery, our gang screwed up by getting into a shoot-out and attracting attention. My guess is that he wanted us all dead rather than in custody."

"All of you? Even the mother of his child?"

"I've been undercover a lot, and I still don't understand the criminal mind. A lot of these guys seem perfectly normal. They have wives and kids. They live in houses in the suburbs and drive hybrids. But they don't think the same way that we do. They don't follow the same ideas of morality. Baron might have a moment of sadness about Penny and Goldie, but he won't let their death stop his master plan."

"Even if he loved her?"

"A guy like that?" Cole leaned forward, picked up his spoon and dug into the chili. "He's not capable of love."

Penny had certainly thought differently. During the time she was in labor, she'd talked about her relationship with Goldie's father. They'd known each other since she was a teenager. Not that they were the typical hand-holding high school sweethearts. Baron was older than she was—much older. The way they'd met wasn't clear to Rachel, but he was somehow connected to her high school.

Penny had talked about the way he swept her off her feet. He drove an expensive car and gave her presents and took her to classy restaurants.

The thought of this older man taking advantage of Penny disgusted Rachel, but she'd kept her opinion to herself. When a woman was in the midst of labor, she didn't need to have a serious relationship discussion.

She asked, "Why did Frank think I knew where Penny hid the money?"

"Do you?"

"She mentioned the hidden cash. It was her insurance policy to make sure the gang wouldn't kill her. But she never said where it was, and I didn't really know what she was talking about."

"It's complicated," he said.

"Explain it." She leaned back in her chair. "We've got time."

Cole took one more bite of chili before he responded. "Baron runs five gangs—maybe more—throughout the Rocky Mountain region. He does the prep work—figures out the site of each robbery and the timing. The gang goes in, makes the grab and gets away fast."

"Always at casinos?"

"Usually not. Casinos generally have better security than banks. The typical target is a small bank. The heists are nothing clever. Just get in and get out. Then comes the genius part of Baron's scheme."

In spite of her skepticism, she found herself being drawn into his story. "How is it genius?"

"A lot of robbers get caught when they start to spend the money. Sometimes, it's marked. Passing off hundred-dollar bills isn't easy. And the robbers can't exactly take their haul and deposit it in a regular bank account."

"Why not?"

"Think about it," he said. "If somebody like Frank strolls into a bank and wants to open an account with hundred-dollar bills, a bank teller is going to get suspicious."

She nodded. "I see what you mean."

"Baron has a designated person—in our gang, it was

Penny—who puts the cash into a package and mails it to a secure location."

"What do you mean by secure location?" she asked. "It seems like Baron would want the money sent directly to him."

"But that would mean that his location could be traced."

"Okay, I get it," she said. "Then what?"

"After a couple of weeks when the heat is off, the designated person either picks up the money and hand delivers it. Or they give Baron the location and he arranges for a pickup. He launders the cash and keeps half. The gang gets paid a monthly stipend, just like a real job."

She could see why the FBI wanted to shut down Baron's operation. "How much money are we talking about?"

"Five gangs pulling off two or three jobs a month. The take ranges from a couple thousand to twenty. I figure it's more than a hundred thousand a month."

"I can't believe all these gangs keep getting away with it," she said.

"You'd be surprised how many bank robberies there are," he said. "Last year in Colorado alone, there were over a hundred and fifty. Most of the time, they don't even make the news. Especially when there's not a huge amount of cash involved and no one is injured."

She finished off her chili while she considered what he'd told her. Baron's scheme sounded far too complicated for Cole to have made it up, but that still didn't prove that he was working undercover for the FBI.

His behavior while she'd been held captive was more convincing. During the whole time Penny was in labor, he'd been a gentleman. Like he said, he'd kept her separate from the other gang members. And he had been helping her escape when the shooters attacked.

She shivered from a draft that slipped around the edge of the front door. Though they'd pushed a chair against it and blocked the air with towels from the bathroom, the door didn't fit exactly into the frame after Frank burst through it.

Rising from the table, she carried her bowl to the kitchen and looked out the uncurtained window. "Still snowing."

"That's a good thing." He reached around her to put his bowl in the sink. "The blizzard will keep anybody from searching for us."

Though they weren't alone in the cabin, she felt as if they were sharing a private moment in the kitchen. Outside the wind rushed and hurled icy pellets at the window, but they were tucked away and sheltered.

When she turned toward him, he didn't back away. Less than two feet of space separated them. "Why did you tell me all this?"

"I wanted you to know. I'm one of the good guys, and I'm not going to hurt you."

She'd heard that promise before. Other men had assured her that they wouldn't break her heart. The smart thing would be to step away, to put some distance between them. But they were awfully close. And he was awfully good-looking.

Arms folded below her breasts, she tried to shut down her attraction to him. Diffidently, she asked, "Why do you care what I think?"

"I like you, Rachel."

He could have said so much more, could have called

her his baby doll and told her she was beautiful. "Is that all you have to say?"

"I like you...very much."

And she liked him, too. In spite of her resolution to steer clear of dangerous men, she unfolded her arms. Gently, she reached up and rested her hand on his cheek. His stubble bristled under her fingers. Electricity crackled between them.

His hand clasped her waist as his head lowered. His lips were firm. He used exactly the right amount of pressure for a perfect kiss.

She pulled away from him and opened her eyes. His smile was warm. His eyes, inviting. *Perfect! Of course!* Guys like Cole—men who lived on the edge—made the best lovers. Because they didn't hold back? Because they took risks in everything?

"That was good," she said.

"I can do better."

He stepped forward, trapping her against the kitchen counter, and encircled her in a powerful embrace. Through the bulky sweatsuits, their bodies joined. This kiss was harder and more demanding. If she allowed herself to respond, she didn't know if she could stop. In minutes, she'd be tearing off his clothes and dragging him onto her and...

His tongue slid into her mouth, and her mind went blank. Sensation washed through her, sending an army of goose bumps marching along the surface of her skin. She felt so good, so alive. Though she was unaware of moving a muscle, her back arched. Her breasts pressed against his chest, and the sensitive tips of her nipples tingled with pleasure. Her feet seemed to leave the floor as though she was weightless. Floating. Drifting through clouds.

When the kiss ended, she lightly descended to earth. *Oh, man, that was some kiss!* A rocket to the moon.

Still holding her, he leaned back and gazed down at her. She stared up at his face, watching as his lips pulled into a confident smile. He knew his kiss had affected her. He knew that he was in control.

In spite of her dazed state, Rachel realized that she needed to pull back. She'd have to be crazy to make love to him tonight. It wasn't possible. Not with baby Goldie sleeping nearby. Not with psychopathic Frank tied up in the bedroom.

She couldn't manage a single coherent word, but he must have sensed her reticence because he loosened his grasp and stepped back.

"I want to make love to you, Rachel." His voice was low and rough. "I want you. Now."

"Uh-huh."

"But the time isn't right."

She nodded so vigorously that she made herself dizzy. "Not tonight."

"You're a special woman. I want to treat you right."

"Uh-huh."

"And I want you to trust me."

"Okay."

He took her hand and squeezed. "When we're safe and this is over," he said with the sexiest smile she'd ever seen. "It won't be over between you and me. That's a promise."

Chapter 8

After Cole converted one of the sofas into a double bed and got Rachel and Goldie settled down to sleep, he stretched out on the other sofa on the opposite side of the cabin. Between his side of the front room and Rachel's the gas fireplace blazed warmly. His gun rested on the floor beside him, easily reachable. Though the sofa was too short for his legs, this wasn't the worst place he'd gone to bed. His undercover work meant he sometimes didn't know where he'd be sleeping or for how long.

Over the years, he'd trained himself to drop easily into a light slumber. Never a deep sleep. Not while on assignment. Even while resting, he needed to maintain vigilance, to be prepared for the unexpected threat.

As soon as he closed his eyes, he became aware of aching muscles from their hike and bruises from his fight with Frank. Ignoring the pain, he concentrated on letting go of his tension, keeping his breathing steady and lowering his pulse rate.

He tried to imagine a blank slate. Soft blue. Peaceful. But his mind raced, jumping from one visual image to another. He saw Penny in a pool of her own blood. Saw Frank being gunned down, throwing his arms into the air before he fell. He saw snow swirling before his eyes. Then through the whiteness, Rachel's face emerged. Her startling blue eyes opened wide. He saw Goldie in Rachel's arms. The baby reached toward him with her tiny hands.

No matter what else happened, he had to make sure Goldie and Rachel got to a safe place—a task that should have been easy. He should have been able to make one phone call and rest assured that the FBI would swoop in for a rescue. But he was wary of his connections, and he'd learned to trust his instincts. If he smelled trouble, there was usually something rotten. Special Agent Wayne Prescott?

Cole had only met with Prescott once at a hotel in Grand Junction for a briefing before his assignment. Though dressed in casual jeans and a parka, Agent Prescott had presented himself as a buttoned-down professional with neatly barbered brown hair and a clean-shaven chin. An administrator. A desk jockey. He had passed on the necessary information in a businesslike manner.

Cole had refused his offer of a cell phone with local numbers already programmed in. By keeping his own cell phone, Cole had more autonomy. Not only did his private directory have phone numbers for people he trusted, but his phone also had the capability of disabling the GPS locator so he couldn't be found.

Though his handlers didn't agree, Cole found it necessary at times to be completely off the grid. His current situation was a good example. If Prescott could track his location, they might be in even more danger.

Cole's eyelids snapped open. Though his body was exhausted, his mind was too busy for sleep.

Leaving the sofa, he went toward the kitchen table where he'd left his phone. Shortly after Frank mentioned Prescott's name, Cole had turned off the GPS. But was it really off? His boss in L.A., Agent Waxman, hadn't been pleased about having his undercover agent untraceable. Had Waxman programmed in some kind of tracking mechanism?

If Frank had been awake and hadn't been a psycho, Cole would have turned to him for help in analyzing his phone's capabilities. Frank had expert skills with electronics.

For a moment, Cole toyed with the idea of destroying his cell phone. Then he decided against it. Tomorrow when the blizzard lifted, they could use his phone to call for help. *Yeah? And who would he call? Who could he trust?*

Through the kitchen window—the only one without a curtain—he saw the snow continue to fall. His visibility was limited. He couldn't tell if it was letting up—not that it mattered. There was nothing they could do tonight. Trying to fight their way through the blizzard and the drifts in the dark would be suicide. They had to wait until morning. Until then, he needed to sleep, damn it. His body required a couple of hours' solid rest to replenish his physical resources.

He headed back toward his sofa but found himself standing over Rachel. She lay on her back, covered up to her chin with a plaid wool blanket. The light from the gas fireplace flickered across her cheeks and smooth forehead. Her full lips parted slightly, and her breathing was steady.

Hers was an unassuming beauty. No makeup. No frills. No nonsense. Her thick, black lashes were natural, as were her dark eyebrows that matched the wisps of hair framing her face.

Looking down, he realized that she was the real reason he couldn't sleep. He'd made her a promise, told her that they'd have a relationship beyond this ordeal. That was what he wanted. To spend time with her. To learn more about this complicated woman whose livelihood was bringing new life into the world.

He admired her strength of character and wondered what caused her defensiveness. Until she had melted into his arms, she'd been pushing him away with both hands. But she'd kissed him with passion and yearning. No way had that kiss been a timid testing of the waters. She'd committed herself. She'd responded as though she'd been waiting for him to strike a spark and ignite the flame.

He reached toward her but didn't actually touch her cheek. He didn't want to wake her; she needed her sleep. *I didn't lie to you, Rachel.*

But he hadn't been completely honest. A man in his line of work changed his identity the way other people changed their socks. He never knew how long he'd be on assignment and unable to communicate with a significant other. Bottom line: he couldn't commit to a real, in-depth relationship.

Tearing his gaze away from her, he went back to his sofa and lay down. This time, he fell asleep.

It seemed like only a few minutes later that he heard Goldie's cries. He bolted upright on the sofa. His gun was in his hand.

Rachel was already awake. "It's okay," she said. "Don't shoot."

After a quick scan of the cabin, he lowered his weapon. "What's wrong with her?"

"She's hungry." Rachel opened the blanket she used to swaddle the infant and picked her up. Immediately—as if by magic—the wailing stopped. Rachel bent her head down to nuzzle Goldie's tummy. "Most babies wake up a couple of times at night."

He knew that. A long time ago, he had a female partner with a newborn baby boy. She was always complaining about not getting enough sleep. "Anything I can do to help?"

"I'll handle this."

She got no argument from him. Through half-closed eyes, he watched her taking care of the baby. Her movements were efficient but exceedingly gentle as she changed the diaper. Even though Goldie wasn't hers, it was obvious that Rachel cared deeply for this infant. He understood; babies were pretty damned lovable.

As she walked to the kitchen she bounced with each step and made soft, cooing sounds. Her voice soothed him. So sweet. So tender. He closed his eyes and imagined her lying beside him, humming and—

"Cole." Frank's shout tore him out of his reverie. "Damn you, Cole. Get in here."

Cole groaned. He would have much preferred changing diapers to dealing with a wounded psychopath. With his gun in hand, he crossed the room and shoved open the bedroom door. In this room away from the fireplace, the temperature was about ten degrees cooler and it was dark. Cole turned on the overhead light. "What?"

"Untie me. I've got to pee."

The restraints Cole had used on Frank were a combination of twine, rope and bungee cords. There was enough play in the ropes that fastened his wrists to the bed frame on either side of him that he could get comfortable. The same went for his ankles, which were attached to the iron frame at the foot of the bed. Setting him free involved a certain amount of risk. Frank could turn on him; he needed to be handled with extreme caution.

Cole was tired of dealing with men like Frank. Always trying to stay two steps ahead. Never letting his guard down. He didn't like what his life had become.

He came closer to the bed and unzipped the sweatshirt stretched across his chest. The wound near his shoulder showed only a light bloodstain. Rachel's tampon plug had done its job in stopping the bleeding.

"Here's the deal, Frank. If you give me any trouble, I'll shoot. No hesitation. No second thoughts. Understand?"

"Yeah, yeah, I get it."

One-handed, he unfastened the cords. All the while, he kept his weapon trained on the big man. Once he was free, Frank stretched his arms and winced in pain. He hauled his legs to the edge of the bed. Slowly, he lumbered to the bathroom, where Cole stood watch. Not a pleasant experience for either of them.

When they returned to the bedroom, Frank sat on the bed and reached for the water glass on the bedside table. He swallowed a few gulps and licked his lips. "I'm hungry."

"Too bad."

"You don't have to tie me up, man. I'm not going to—"

"Save it." Cole wasn't taking any chances. Not with Rachel and Goldie in the other room.

With his finger, Frank touched his split lip. "As soon as the snow stops, we should move on. Those feds are still after you."

"Lie down. Arms at your sides. Legs straight."

"You need me. When those guys catch up to you, you're going to want somebody watching your back. Come on, man. I'm a good person to have on your side in a fight. You know that."

There were a few things Cole knew for certain. The first was that Frank enjoyed inflicting pain. The second, he was a bully who couldn't be trusted. Number three, he was smarter than he looked. "You can lie down. Now. Or I'll knock you unconscious. Your choice."

With a low growl, Frank stretched out on the bed. "I've been lying here, thinking. I know what you're up to. You've got leverage. A couple of bargaining chips."

Cole fastened the cords on his ankles. "You just keep thinking, Frank."

"You're going to use the baby to deal with Baron. I mean, Baron is as mean as they come, but he's not going to kill his own kid, right?"

While Cole dealt with the bonds on Frank's wrists, he pressed the nose of his gun into the big man's belly.

"And Rachel," Frank said. "She's going to take you to where Penny sent the loot. Oh, yeah, I got it all figured out. But there's something you don't know."

"What's that?" Cole finished securing the ropes and stepped back. "What don't I know?"

"If I tell you, I'm giving up my own bargaining chip."

As far as Cole was concerned, Frank could keep his information to himself. Tomorrow, after he and Rachel were far away from this cabin, he'd call the local police and give them the location. The cops could take Frank into custody.

Cole turned toward the door.

"Hey," Frank called after him. "I can tell you why the feds attacked. You want to know that, don't you?"

Clearly, Frank was grasping at straws, trying to play him. In other circumstances, Cole might have been interested in his information, but he was weary of these games. "Whether you tell me or not, I don't give a damn."

He wanted to get back to a semblance of normal life, to take Rachel home to California with him and show her his favorite beach. He hadn't seen much of her body, except when she stepped out of the bathroom in a towel, but he thought she'd look good in a bikini.

"It's about the money," Frank said. "Penny told me that she was keeping the place she'd sent the last three packages a secret from Baron. That's got to be close to seventy thousand bucks. Just sitting there. Waiting to be picked up."

"I don't believe you. Penny wouldn't try a double cross on Baron."

"She said that she wasn't going to steal from him. She just wanted to see him. And she knew he'd come for the money."

Though the idea disgusted him, Cole understood Penny's reasoning. Baron wouldn't come to see his pregnant girlfriend or his newborn child. But he'd make an effort for the money. "So what?"

"I'm betting Rachel knows where it is. She and Penny were getting real chummy." He gave a grotesque wink. "We can make her tell us where the money is hidden."

"Go back to sleep."

He closed the bedroom door and stepped into the front room, where Rachel sat in the rocking chair feeding Goldie by the golden light from the gas fireplace. Cole felt as if he'd entered a different world. A better place, for sure. The energy in this room nurtured him and gave him hope.

When Rachel met his gaze and smiled, he wanted to gather her into his arms and hold her close. He needed her honesty and decency. She was the antidote to the ugly life he'd been living.

"How is Frank doing?" she asked.

"I checked the wound. There's very little bleeding."

"He needs to get to a hospital tomorrow."

He wanted to tell her that tomorrow would bring a solution to all their problems. But he couldn't make that promise.

In the dim light of dawn, Rachel stepped onto the porch of the cabin and shivered. The furry bristles of her parka hood froze instantly and scraped against her cheek as she adjusted Goldie's position inside the sling carrier under her parka.

The blizzard had dwindled to a sputtering of snow, but the skies were still blanketed with heavy gray clouds. Cole joined her on the porch and held up his cell phone.

"Still no signal," he said.

"We shouldn't have to go too far." She pointed with her gloved hand toward a break in the trees. "It looks like a road up there. There ought to be other cabins. We should be able to find somebody with a working phone."

From inside the cabin, Frank yelled out a curse at Cole and threatened revenge. His voice was hoarse and rasping. She knew they couldn't trust Frank but felt guilty for leaving him tied to the bed.

As Cole fastened the broken front door closed with a bungee cord, she asked, "We're going to get help for Frank, aren't we?"

"When we talk to the cops, we'll give them the location of this cabin. Frank won't be happy about being rescued and arrested at the same time."

"I almost feel sorry for him."

"Don't."

Before they'd left the cabin, she'd made a final check on Frank's wounds. The bleeding had stopped, and he wasn't in imminent danger. Though the cabin wasn't cold, he'd told her that he was freezing and asked her to cover him up with his parka. She figured it was the least she could do for him.

She fell into step behind Cole. The oversize backpack on his shoulders blocked the wind. Though this area had been sheltered from the full force of the storm by trees, the new-fallen snow was well over her boots—probably a foot deep. On the north side of the cabin, the drifts reached all the way to the windowsill.

Cole led the way to a log structure that looked like a garage. He shoved the door open and ushered her inside.

"Which do you prefer?" he asked. "Cross-country skis or snowshoes?"

"What are you thinking?" He claimed to be one of the good guys but he acted like a thief. "We can't just walk in here and help ourselves. We've already destroyed the front door on the cabin, made a mess and eaten their food."

"Don't worry. It hasn't escaped my attention that this well-equipped little cabin saved our lives. I fully intend to pay the owners back."

"Did you leave a note?"

"It kind of defeats the purpose of being undercover if I start handing out my address."

"How about money?" she demanded. "Did you leave cash?"

"I'm sending people back here for Frank. If I left cash, somebody else would pick it up. Don't worry, I'll pay for the damages."

In an unconscious gesture, he patted the left side of his jacket then pulled his hand away. She was beginning to understand the sneaky undercover side to his personality. Every twitch had a meaning. She asked, "What's in your pocket? Are you hiding something from me?"

"Do you have to know everything?"

"Yes."

"Fine," he said. "I've got nothing in my pocket, but there's a pouch with cash, a switchblade and a new identity sewn into the lining."

"Impressive."

"In spite of this disaster, I'm good at my job. The hardest part of an undercover op is getting out in one piece." He sorted through the array of skis and snowshoes. "What's best for moving through the snow?"

She still didn't want to steal the equipment. If somebody took her cross-country skis, she'd be furious. "Why can't we just hike up to the road? Even if it hasn't been cleared recently, the snowplows will be coming through."

"We aren't taking the road."

"Why not?"

He held a set of snowshoes toward her. "The shooters—whether they're FBI or Baron's men—are going to be looking for us."

His gaze met hers. Even in the dark garage, she could see his tension. If they were found, they'd be killed. Normal rules of conduct didn't apply. She pulled off her gloves and took the snowshoes.

Chapter 9

After a bit of trial and error, Cole figured out how to walk in the snowshoes with minimal tripping over his own feet. Even using the ski poles for balance, he'd fallen twice.

From behind his back, Rachel called out, "You're getting the hang of it. Don't try to go backward."

He muttered, "It's like I've got tennis rackets strapped to my shoes."

"That's still better than plowing through two feet of new snow."

Or not. The winter sports he enjoyed involved speed—racing across open terrain on a snowmobile, streaking down a slope on downhill skis or a snowboard. A clumsy slog through deep snow was the opposite of fun—another reason to hate Colorado. After last night's blizzard, he'd lost any appreciation he might have had for the scenic beauty of a winter wonderland.

All this pristine whiteness depressed the hell out of him. Never again would he take an undercover assignment in the mountains. A tropical jungle filled with snakes and man-eating lions would be preferable.

Though they weren't on the road, he stayed on a trail through the forest that ran parallel to it. The worst thing that could happen now was to get lost in this un-populated back country. They'd been hiking on snow-shoes for nearly half an hour—long enough for him to freeze the tip of his nose—and they still hadn't sighted a cabin.

The dawn light was beginning to brighten, and the snowfall lacked the fury of the blizzard. On the opposite side of the road, he could see the outline of a tall ridge through the icy mist. What lay beyond? He'd lost all sense of direction.

"Hold up." He laboriously maneuvered his snow-shoes to face Rachel. "Do you have any idea where we are?"

"Let me check my GPS. Oh, wait, I don't have a GPS. Or a map. Or a satellite photo."

He preferred her snarky attitude to fear. It was better for her not to know how much danger they might be in. "I want to get a general idea. When I picked you up, what was the closest town?"

"We were near Shadow Mountain Lake. There are a couple of resorts there but nothing resembling a town until Grand Lake."

"In terms of miles, how far?"

With her glove, she brushed a dusting of snow off her shoulder. "Hard to say. As the crow flies, only about five miles or so. But none of these roads are straight lines."

They could be winding back and forth for hours and making very little progress. "I hate mountains."

"A typical comment from a Southern California boy."

"Yeah? What have you got against palm trees and beaches?"

"Real men live in the mountains."

Though tempted to yank her into his arms and show her that he was a real man, he took his cell phone out of his pocket. Miracle of miracles, he had a signal!

"What is it?" Rachel asked.

"The phone works. Finally." He peeled off his glove, accessed his directory and called Agent Ted Waxman in Los Angeles. California was an hour earlier and it was before seven o'clock here, but his primary FBI handler was available to him 24/7.

Waxman's mumbled hello made Cole think the agent was still in bed, warm and cozy under the covers.

"It's Cole. I need to come in from the cold. Literally."

"Where are you?" Waxman's voice had gone from drowsy to alert. "Do you have your GPS locator turned on?"

He wanted to believe he could trust Waxman. They weren't buddies; undercover agents didn't spend much face time inside the bureau offices. But Waxman had been his primary contact for almost four years.

Cole's phone didn't have much juice; he didn't waste words. "Give me an update. Fast."

"Turn on the GPS and go to a road," Waxman instructed. "We'll find you."

His suspicions about Agent Wayne Prescott and his possible involvement with the shooters from last night warned against giving away their location. "Who's looking for us?"

"Every law enforcement official in the state of Colorado, especially the FBI."

"Why? Give me the 4-1-1. What's going on?"

His pause spoke volumes. Waxman was a by-the-book agent who followed orders and trusted the system. If he'd been given instructions to withhold info, it would go against his nature to disobey. At the same time, he was Cole's handler, and it was his duty to protect his agent.

"Turn yourself in," Waxman said, "and we'll get this straightened out."

Turn myself in? That sounded like he was wanted for committing a crime. "The last time I contacted anybody was after the casino robbery. Prescott told me to stick with the gang. What's changed since then?"

Another pause. "Activate the damn GPS, Cole."

While he was at it, maybe he ought to paint a bull's-eye on his back. "Give me a reason."

"Don't play dumb with me. Three people are dead. And you're on the run with two of the gang members. You're considered to be armed and dangerous."

That description justified the use of lethal force in making an arrest. Cole saw their chances of a peaceful surrender disappearing. "Two other gang members?"

"One male and one female."

Somehow Rachel had been labeled as part of the gang. "You've got that wrong. The woman with me is—"

"Damn it, Cole. You kidnapped a baby."

The worst kind of crime. Violence against children. Cole was in even more trouble than he'd imagined. "Here's the true story. I'm close to identifying Baron, and he's running this show. Don't ask me how, but he's got people inside the Denver FBI office."

"A newborn infant." Waxman's voice rasped with anger. "You're using a baby as a hostage."

There would be no reasoning with him. Cole ended the call and turned off the phone, making sure the GPS wasn't on.

Rachel stared at him. Her eyes filled with questions. He didn't have the answers she'd want to hear.

Rachel listened with rising dread as Cole recounted his conversation with Agent Waxman. They were the subjects of a manhunt? Considered to be dangerous? The FBI thought they had kidnapped Goldie?

"No," she said firmly. "People around here know me. They'd know those accusations are wrong. As soon as they heard my name—"

"It's not likely that they've identified you."

"If they show my picture—"

"They won't."

In normal circumstances, she'd be missed at work. But this was her vacation; nobody would be looking for her. "The van," she said. "When I don't return the van to the clinic, the women I work with will know that something's wrong. I can contact them and get this all cleared up."

"Not a good idea."

"Why not?"

His face was drawn. His eyes were serious. "You saw what those men did last night at the house. It's best if we don't get anyone else involved."

"Are you saying that they'd go after my friends? My coworkers?"

"Not if they don't know anything."

She'd been cut off from anything resembling her normal life. The only person she could turn to was Cole, and she barely trusted him. "What's going to happen to Goldie?"

"We need to get her to a safe place. If we can find a cabin with reliable people, we'll leave her in their care."

She peered through the trees at the surrounding hillsides, which were buried in drifts and veiled in light snowfall. "We can turn ourselves in at the same time."

"It's not safe for us to be in custody. Not until we know who's working with Baron."

Inside her parka, she felt Goldie shift positions. The most important thing was to get the baby to safety. "Grand Lake. We need to go to Grand Lake. Penny told me that her mother was staying there. We'll take Goldie to her grandmother."

Cole reached out with his gloved hand and patted her shoulder. "You're a brave woman, Rachel. I'm sorry I got you into this mess."

"As long as you get me out of it, I'll be fine." She nodded toward the path ahead of them. "Make tracks."

She followed him, tramping through the snow on the path through the forest. The crampons on the snowshoes gave her stability, but the hike was exhausting. Though she couldn't see the incline, she knew they were headed uphill because of the strain on her thighs. Still, she was glad for the physical exertion. If she slowed down, she'd have to face her fear.

As an EMT, she'd worked with cops. She knew what "armed and dangerous" meant. She and Cole wouldn't have a chance to explain or defend themselves. The people looking for them would shoot first and ask questions later.

They approached a crossroads with open terrain on each side. The road was barely discernable under the mounds of snow, but a wooden street sign marked the corner.

Cole halted and squinted at the sign. "The road we're on is Lodgepole. The other is Lake Vista. Ring any bells?"

"Please don't ask me for directions." Grand County was huge, nearly two thousand square miles. Her condo was in Granby, which was forty-five minutes away from here. "I don't know this territory. I've only been to Grand Lake five or six times."

He looked over his shoulder at her. "It makes sense that the Lake Vista road will lead to water. We'd be more likely to find cabins at lakeside."

"But the other road goes uphill," she pointed out. "It offers a better vantage point."

She tilted back her head, looked up and glimpsed a hint of blue through the pale gray clouds. Good news: the snowfall was ending. Bad news: they were more exposed to the people who were searching for them.

"Do you hear that?" Cole asked.

"What?"

He sidestepped deeper into the forest. "Get back here."

Though she didn't hear anything, she did as he said, remembering how he'd sensed the attack at the house before the shooting started. She shuffled forward, taking cover behind the trunk of the same tree he stood behind.

Cole shifted his feet in the snowshoes so he was facing her. Quickly, he shed the huge backpack from his shoulders and moved closer to her.

She heard the sound of a vehicle. *They were coming.*

A black SUV crested the hill above the crossroads and ploughed a trail through the snow that covered the road. There were no markings on the vehicle; it wasn't a police car. She held her breath, waiting for them to pass.

The SUV drove past them, headed toward the cabin.

Cole took his cell phone from his pocket. Quickly, he dialed.

She heard his end of the conversation. "Waxman, this is Cole. There's a wounded man in a cabin on Lodgepole Road. He's tied down, helpless. The cabin isn't far from the house where we stayed last night."

He ended the call and put away his phone.

If the men in the SUV were the same shooters who attacked last night, Frank didn't stand a chance. Last night, she'd patched him up. Today, he could be murdered.

When she looked up at Cole, she felt a tear slip from the corner of her eye. "I wish things were different."

"There's nothing we can do for Frank." With his ungloved hand, he stroked her cheek and wiped away the tear. "They're close, Rachel. They'll be able to follow our tracks through the woods. We need to move fast."

There was no time for regret or recrimination. All her energy focused on pushing forward. They stayed in the trees, avoiding the road, but the forest was beginning to thin. Many of these trees had been lost to the pine beetle epidemic. The bare branches looked like gnarled fingers clawing at the snowy mist.

Rounding a boulder, Cole stopped so suddenly that she almost ran into him. She peered around his shoulder and saw the frozen expanse of Shadow Mountain Lake. Untouched, white and spectacularly beautiful, it was covered with snow, and the drifts swirled like vanilla frosting on a cake. Heavy clouds prevented her from seeing all the way to the opposite side.

"How wide is the lake?" Cole asked.

"It varies."

"How far from the town?"

"At the north end, it's only about a mile and a half farther to Grand Lake."

"If we cross it, we've got no cover," he said. "But we're running out of path. As soon as they pick up our trail, they'll know we're following the road."

She assumed the lake was frozen solid, but she didn't know for sure. If they broke through the ice, it would be over for them. And for Goldie. She imagined the dark, frigid waters beneath the pristine surface—waters that could suck them down to a terrible death.

Cole made a turn-around on his snowshoes and looked down at her. His eyes were warm. "We can do this."

"Or we could keep looking for a cabin." Hiking through a blizzard was one thing. Walking on a frozen lake—even when it appeared to be solid—was a risk. "I'm not sure this is safe."

"It's our best chance, Rachel."

He was right. She swallowed hard and nodded. "You go first."

They climbed down the incline leading to the frozen lake. As Cole stepped onto the surface, his snowshoes sank three or four inches into the snow. She clenched her jaw and listened for the cracking sound of ice breaking.

He strode ten feet onto the lake, breaking a path for

her to follow. He turned back toward her and held out his gloved hand. "It's all going to be all right."

"How do you know?"

"I'm taking a leap of faith."

Cautiously, she stepped onto the lake. The snow sank beneath her snowshoes, and she caught her breath. Was it solid? Would it hold?

Cole caught hold of her gloved hand and squeezed. "Stay close."

"Do I have a choice?"

Lowering her head, she concentrated on putting her shoes in his tracks. One foot after the other, she followed. With every step, she prayed that the ice would hold.

For what seemed like an eternity, they made their way forward. Without the shelter of the forest, the fierce wind bit the exposed skin on her face. Inside her parka, she was warm. Goldie was protected by her body heat.

"I can see the other side," Cole said.

Looking back over her shoulder, she saw the long trail they'd left in the snow. The point where they'd started was barely visible through the snowy mist.

She saw something else.

A volley of gunfire exploded behind them.

Chapter 10

The shooters had found them. The bursts from their semiautomatics boomed across the frozen landscape. Cole estimated they were over four hundred yards away on the other side of the lake—out of range unless they had a sniper rifle with a high-tech scope. Even with a more accurate weapon, their visibility would be hampered by the icy mist.

As he watched, the SUV lurched off the road. They were driving onto the lake.

He drew his handgun, ready to make a stand even though he was outmatched in terms of men and firepower. "Rachel, keep going."

"I can't leave you here."

"You need to get Goldie away from here."

Her internal struggle showed in her eyes. She didn't want to desert him, but the SUV was coming closer. The baby's safety came first.

"Don't die," she said. "I wouldn't be able to stand it if you—"

"Just go."

In her snowshoes, she rushed forward. The shoreline was so damned close. She had to make it into the forest. The bare limbs of trees reached toward her with the promise of shelter.

He looked back toward the SUV. They were coming closer, but their forward progress was slow. The heavy vehicle sank down into the new snow. The drifts piled up higher than the hubcaps.

One of the gunmen leaned out a window and fired off another round—a sloppy tactic typical of a drive-by shooter who figured if he sprayed enough bullets he'd eventually hit something. These guys weren't trained to attack in open terrain, and they sure as hell weren't FBI.

These were Baron's men. Lethal. Bent on murder.

Cole shrugged off his huge backpack and dropped it onto the snow in front of him. The canvas pack and lightweight aluminum frame wasn't enough to stop a bullet, but it was something. Not taking off his snowshoes, he ducked behind the pack and waited. When they got closer, he'd aim for the windshield on the driver's side. If he could take out the man behind the wheel, he might slow them down long enough to make his escape.

The engine of the SUV whined as the tires failed to gain traction on the ice. Snow had accumulated in front of the SUV. The driver had to back up in his own tracks and push forward again.

From the trees, Rachel called to him. "I made it."

"Go deeper into the forest."

"Not without you."

The SUV jerked forward and back. The wheels were stuck. Two men emerged from the vehicle and staggered through knee-deep snow to the front bumper, where they started digging.

The weight of the SUV had to be close to two tons. Heavy enough to break through the ice? That was too much good luck to hope for.

For now, he should take advantage of the situation. They were distracted by being stuck. He might have enough time to make his escape before they started shooting again.

He slung the pack onto his shoulders, grabbed his ski poles and rushed along the trail Rachel had made through the snow. He reached the forest. Gunfire erupted. Cole dodged behind a boulder, where she stood waiting.

Breathing hard, he rested his back against the hard granite surface.

"We're good," Rachel said. "Even if they get themselves dug out, there's no access to a road on this side."

The muscles of his face tightened as he grinned. They just might make it to safety. "We got lucky."

"It's more than that."

"Yeah, those guys are idiots."

"And we were prepared," she said. "After all your complaining, I'll bet you're glad you have those snowshoes."

"Hell, yes. I'm thinking of having them permanently attached to my feet."

"You might be a real mountain man, after all."

Another wild blast of gunfire reminded him that they needed to keep moving. Even idiots were dangerous when well-armed. He shoved away from the rock.

"When we get to the town, do you know how to find Penny's mother?"

"I do, indeed."

Until now, Rachel had been hesitant about giving directions. "What makes you so certain?"

"Penny called her mom after the baby was born and got the address, which she repeated several times."

"Why didn't she know her own mother's address?"

"Her mom doesn't actually live in Grand Lake. She's house-sitting for a friend who has a business in town. The house is around the corner from her friend's shop on the main street."

They'd be marching through the center of town. With every law enforcement officer in the state of Colorado looking for them, this might be tricky. "What kind of shop?"

"One that's closed in the winter," she said. "An ice cream parlor."

Their trek into Grand Lake went faster than Rachel expected. It was still early, and the locals were just beginning to deal with the aftermath of last night's blizzard. A few were out with shovels. Others cleared their driveways and sidewalks with snowblowers. None of them paid much attention as she and Cole hiked along the road in their snowshoes.

The main tourist area was a rustic, Old West boardwalk with storefronts on either side. She spotted Lily Belle's Soda Fountain and Ice Cream Shop with a neatly lettered sign in the window: Closed for the Season.

In minutes they'd be at the house where Penny's mom was staying. Rachel was glad to be dropping Goldie off with someone who would care for her, but she wasn't looking forward to telling Penny's mom what had happened.

A young man with a snowblower finished clearing the sidewalk leading up to a two-story, cedar frame house. He turned toward them and waved. She waved back and yelled over the noisy machine. "Does Pearl Richards live here?"

He nodded and continued along the sidewalk to dig out the next house on the street.

Cole gave her a glance. "Penny's mother is named Pearl?"

"Pearl, Penny and Goldie," she said. "I guess they're all material girls."

Standing on the porch, they took off their snowshoes and knocked. A woman with curly blond hair pulled back in a ponytail opened the door a crack and peeked out. "Do I know you?"

"Penny gave me your address," Rachel said.

She pulled the door open, revealing a brightly colored patchwork jacket over jeans and a turtleneck. Though it was early, Pearl was fully dressed and wearing hiking boots as though she was prepared for action.

Pearl stepped back into the dim recesses of an old-fashioned looking parlor with drawn velvet curtains, an Oriental rug and an uncomfortable looking Victorian sofa with matching chaise. Pearl went to a claw-footed coffee table and picked up her revolver. Like Penny, she was a small, slight woman who needed both hands to aim her weapon.

Rachel should have been alarmed, but this greeting was so similar to the way she'd met Penny that she almost laughed out loud. Apparently, the women in this family routinely said hello with a gun.

"Close the door," Pearl said. "Young man, take off that backpack and that ridiculous leather jacket. You're dripping all over the floor."

As Cole removed his jacket, he said, "I'm armed."

"I expected as much." Pearl leveled her gun at the center of his chest. "Using your thumb and forefinger, place your weapon on the floor and step away from it."

Though Rachel suspected that this wasn't the first time Pearl had confronted an armed man, she still wasn't afraid. Either she was growing accustomed to having her life threatened or she sensed a basic goodness in this curly haired woman who didn't look like she was much older than thirty.

"Both of you," Pearl said, "come through here to the kitchen. No sudden moves."

Rachel did as she was told. The huge kitchen, painted a sunny-yellow, had professional quality appliances and gleaming marble countertops. In no way did it resemble the antique parlor.

"The gun isn't necessary," Rachel said.

"I'll make that decision, missy. My daughter got herself tangled up with some bad folks. I'm not taking any chances."

"I'm a midwife," Rachel said. "I helped Penny deliver her baby."

Pearl's big brown eyes softened. "Goldie."

"She's right here." Rachel unzipped her parka and took it off to reveal the sling holding the infant. "And she's hungry."

"My granddaughter." Pearl's gun hand faltered. "But where's... Oh, no. Penny's dead, isn't she?"

"I'm sorry," Cole said.

He stepped forward, smoothly took the gun from

Pearl and helped her into a chair at the kitchen table where she sat, stiff as a rail. Her unseeing eyes stared at the empty space opposite her.

"I knew this day would come." Pearl's voice dropped to a whisper. "Penny was always wild. Careless. I encouraged her to be a free spirit and to express herself, but she should have had more controls, more rules."

"I'll get you a glass of water," Cole said.

"Make it orange juice."

"Orange juice it is."

"With a shot of vodka. The booze is in the cabinet over the sink."

While he went to do Pearl's bidding, Rachel lifted Goldie out of the sling and set her down on the countertop to take off the purple snowsuit. The baby waved her arms, kicked and cooed. She was full of life, deserving of a chance at happiness.

Rachel hoped Pearl would be able to care for her granddaughter. "Penny said you were house-sitting. Where do you live?"

"I have a studio in Denver."

"You're an artist?"

"I do some painting. And I design jewelry. For a while, I had a shop in Grand Lake. When Penny was in her teens, I moved up here. I wanted to get her away from bad influences in the city." She paused. "That didn't work too well."

"I only knew Penny for a short time," Rachel said. "No matter how many unfortunate decisions she might have made in her life, she did the right things during her pregnancy. She wanted to give birth without drugs, wanted the best for her baby."

"I had natural childbirth, too. I was only eighteen."

A thin smile played on Pearl's full lips. "I wasn't ready to settle down, drifted from place to place, fell into and out of love. But I always did right by my daughter. She was more precious to me than air. That's not to say we didn't fight. The last time I saw her, I was so angry."

"Did you know what she was doing?"

"I knew it wasn't good. The fellow with her was a thug. I believe his name was Frank. He's not the father, is he?"

"No," Rachel said quickly.

"Thank God." Pearl slowly shook her head. "I went looking for my daughter. Found her at a casino in Black Hawk. She stood there in the middle of all those slot machines with her belly bulging. I wanted to take her home with me, but she refused. I had hoped that when she was a mother, she'd understand."

"I believe she did. When she saw Goldie for the first time, she glowed from inside. It was as though she'd swallowed a candle."

Cole placed the vodka and orange juice on the table. "Penny couldn't stop smiling. She was beautiful."

Pearl lifted the glass to her lips and took a sip. Thus far, she had avoided looking at her grandchild. Glass in hand, she stood and snapped at Cole. "Come with me into the other room. I want to know what happened to Penny. Tell me everything."

They left the kitchen, but Cole returned almost immediately with the backpack. "You need to get Goldie changed and fed. I don't think we can leave her here."

"Penny wanted her mother to take the baby."

"I'm not sure Pearl can handle an infant."

An aura of sorrow veiled his features, and she knew that he was feeling guilt for Penny's death. Rachel understood. Logically, he'd know that her murder wasn't his fault. He hadn't pulled the trigger. He hadn't put Penny in danger. But he'd take responsibility the same way she'd blamed herself when she lost a patient.

He stood and straightened. When he walked back to the parlor, he looked stoic as though preparing to face a firing squad. His conversation with Pearl was going to be difficult, but it had to be done.

She looked down at Goldie and smoothed the fringe of downy brown hair that framed her round face. "What are we going to do with you?"

The baby gurgled in response. Her shining eyes fixed on the light from the window above the yellow café curtains.

Dragging this darling infant all over the frozen countryside simply wasn't an option. They'd been lucky so far; Goldie had stayed safe and warm, snuggled against her chest. But so many things could have gone wrong. If Penny's mother couldn't take the baby, they'd have to risk going to the police and handing Goldie to them.

As Rachel went through the procedures of preparing formula, she tried to imagine what would happen if they turned themselves in. Cole was in far more danger than she was. As soon as her identity was verified, she ought to be all right. After all, she had an alibi for the time when the gang was on the run. She'd been delivering a baby. *Jim Loughlin's baby.*

She caught her breath. Oh, God, why hadn't she thought of this before? Big Jim Loughlin was a deputy. She could call on him to help her.

The yellow phone hanging on the wall by the kitchen cabinets beckoned to her. Though she didn't know the Loughlins' phone number off the top of her head, information would have it. But if she used this phone, it would pinpoint her location. Other people could track them down to this house.

Deputy Loughlin was the answer to all their problems. She couldn't wait to tell Cole.

When he returned to the kitchen with Pearl, Rachel was glad to see that the vodka and orange juice had barely been touched. The older woman came directly to her. "I'm ready to meet Goldie."

Rachel placed the baby in her grandmother's arms. The bonding was instantaneous. The pained tension on Pearl's face transformed into adoring tenderness, and she exhaled in a sweet, soft hum.

Rachel exhaled a sigh of relief. Goldie was going to be just fine with her grandma.

Chapter 11

While Pearl settled down on the parlor sofa to feed Goldie her bottle, Rachel took Cole into the kitchen. She kept her voice low, not wanting to disturb the moment of bonding between grandma and baby. But she felt like singing. Their problems were all but over.

She beamed at Cole. In his black turtleneck and still-damp jeans, he looked big, rough and intimidating, until he smiled back and she saw the warmth in his eyes. He came closer. With his thumb, he tilted her chin up, and she thought he was going to kiss her again.

His voice was a whisper. "What's going on? You look like you just found the pot of gold at the end of the rainbow."

"Jim Loughlin," she said. "Deputy Jim Loughlin. He'll help us."

"Why do you think so?"

"Don't you see?" Excitement bubbled through her. "This is the perfect solution."

He rested his palm on her forehead. "That's funny. You don't feel feverish."

"I'm not delusional." She took a step back. "Once I contact Jim, we'll be in the clear. In fact, the police will probably thank us."

"Before you schedule our ticker tape parade, take a breath. Sit down."

"Why are you being so negative?"

"Start at the beginning. Who's Loughlin?"

She plunked into a chair at the kitchen table. "The house I was at before you kidnapped me belongs to Jim and Sarah Loughlin. Jim happens to be a deputy sheriff. If I call him, he can arrange for us to turn ourselves in."

"You believe that you trust him."

"One hundred and ten percent," she said confidently. "Jim would do anything for me. I just went through the labor-and-birthing process with him and his wife. They think I'm pretty terrific."

"Which you are."

"Thank you."

He wasn't responding with the enthusiasm she'd expected. As he took a seat beside her, his forehead furrowed. His cognac-brown irises turned a deeper, darker shade. "Let's think about it before you call him."

"What's to think about? We turn ourselves in, and he calls off the manhunt."

"After which," Cole said, "your friend will be ordered to turn us over to Wayne Prescott and the FBI."

"Not necessarily."

"It's his job. Even if Loughlin thinks you walk on

water, he can't go against orders. Prescott is calling the shots."

She hadn't thought that far ahead. "But the Loughlins know I'm innocent. They're my alibi. I was with them when you were on the run. They know I'm not a criminal."

"Neither am I." Gently, he took her hand. "But Prescott has somehow managed to turn my FBI handler against me."

"I still want to call Jim," she said. "Your cell phone doesn't have GPS tracking, right?"

He took it out of his pocket and placed the phone on the table. "Give it a shot. Put the call on speaker so I can hear."

She'd already used Pearl's phone to call information and get the home number for the Loughlins. She punched it into Cole's cell. *This plan will work. It has to work.*

As soon as Jim answered, she said, "This is Rachel. How's the baby doing? Do you have a name yet?"

"Caitlyn," he said. "She's beautiful."

"And Sarah?"

"I didn't think it was possible to love my wife more than the day we were married, but I'm in awe of this woman—the mother of my child."

He was the kind of guy who renewed her faith in the goodness of humanity. She felt guilty about intruding on his happiness with her problems. "What have you heard about the casino robbers?"

"There's a big-deal manhunt. Everybody on duty is looking for the three that got away. They've got roadblocks set up. They were trying to monitor the on-the-road cameras, but a lot of them got messed up by the snow. Why do you ask?"

"The woman fugitive," she said. "The supposed woman fugitive is me."

There was a silence. He cleared his throat and his deep voice dropped all the way into the cellar. "What are you talking about?"

"After I left your house, I was kidnapped by the robbers to help a woman in the gang deliver her baby. You must have suspected something. My van was at the house where the three people were killed."

"I haven't heard anything about your van. As far as I know the three victims were found by the FBI in a clearing right before the blizzard hit."

"Not in a house?"

"No."

A cover-up. She should have expected as much. Penny had told her that the house belonged to Baron; he wouldn't want to be associated with them.

Quietly, Cole said, "Tell him you have an address."

She spoke up, "I can give you the location of—"

"Is somebody with you?" Jim asked.

"Yes." She wouldn't lie. "I'm with a man who was part of the gang, but he's really an undercover FBI agent. A good guy. He saved my life. And the baby's."

"You have the baby with you," Jim said.

"If we'd left her behind, they would have killed her. You have to believe me."

"Where are you, Rachel?"

She looked at Cole, who shook his head. Sadly, she agreed with him. If she told Jim where she was, the police would be at the door, and they'd be handed over to the people who wanted them dead.

"I can't tell you. There's a conspiracy going on that's too complicated to explain. If I'm taken into FBI custody, I'll be arrested or made to disappear. Or killed."

"Is that what this undercover fed told you? Rachel, you have to get away from him. He's no good."

"Deputy Loughlin," Cole said with calm authority, "you know Rachel isn't a criminal. She's a healer. To protect her, it's imperative that you tell no one about this phone call."

"Don't tell me about protecting Rachel." Jim's voice rumbled. "I'd do anything for her."

"I'm counting on your silence," Cole said. "I'm going to give you an address. It's the house where the murders took place. Even if the blood has been cleaned up, there will be evidence of a shoot-out. Check the property records and find the name of the owner. Tell no one what you're doing."

"I won't help you. That's aiding and abetting."

"Please," Rachel said. "I need your help, Jim."

Cole gave him the address. "We'll call you back."

As he disconnected the call and slipped the phone into his pocket, Rachel felt her high hopes come crashing to the ground. She couldn't trust anyone. Not even Jim.

Cole pulled open the heavy velvet drapes in the front parlor and looked outside. Above the snow-laden rooftops, he saw the clouds breaking up and the sky turning blue. Sunlight glistened on mounds of snow piled beside the sidewalks. Kids in parkas and snow hats were having a snowball fight. People waved to each other. A four-wheel-drive vehicle bounced along the plowed street in front of the house.

His undercover work generally led him into rat-infested back alleys and strip joints. Not here. Not to small town America, where you couldn't see the criminals until they held a knife to your throat.

He turned away from the window.

The scene inside the house was equally charming. Rachel and Pearl sat beside each other on the fancy Victorian sofa. Their heads bent down; the curly blond bangs on Pearl's forehead almost touched Rachel's sleek dark hair as they fussed over the baby.

There wasn't time for cooing infants and cozy musing after the storm. He and Rachel had managed to find Penny's mother without too much difficulty. Sooner or later, Baron's men would do the same. They could be surrounding the place at this very moment.

"Ladies," he snapped.

Pearl looked up at him. Though her lips smiled, her expression was flat. Something inside her had died. When he'd talked to her earlier, she had demanded the truth about her daughter's death. He'd tried to be gentle, but as he spoke, he'd seen the cold embrace of despair and sorrow squeeze the light from her eyes.

Beside her, Rachel had slipped into an attitude of outward calm that masked her internal tension. She'd looked the same way when she directed Penny through the last stage of labor.

These two women weren't kidding themselves. No matter how unflustered they looked, both were aware of the tragedy and the danger. They needed him to point the way.

"Here's what we're going to do," he said. "First we get Pearl and Goldie to safety."

"Agreed," Pearl said. "I can't stay here. Too many people in town know that I'm house-sitting."

"Deputy Loughlin said there were roadblocks and surveillance cams, but they won't be looking for you. Take Goldie and get onto the highway as soon as possible."

"You need a car seat," Rachel said.

"Not a problem. The woman who owns this house has a couple of car seats in the closet of the guest bedroom for when her grandchildren come to visit in the summer." She looked down at the sleeping baby on her lap. "Don't worry, little one. Grammy Pearl is going to take good care of you."

"You shouldn't return to your home in Denver," he said. "Not until we know it's safe."

When she nodded, her curly blond ponytail bounced. "Maybe I can stay with a friend in Granby. She was Penny's favorite teacher in high school. Taught economics and history."

"Does she still teach there?" Rachel asked. "I might know her. I do health programs at the high school."

"Jenna Cambridge."

"A teacher?" Rachel lifted an eyebrow. "Penny talked about Jenna as though she was more of a friend."

"That boundary might have gotten a bit fuzzy. Jenna was new in town and lonely. Plain as dishwater. She liked to go out with Penny." Her lip trembled. "My daughter attracted attention wherever she went."

Though Cole had known Penny for less than a month, he had to agree. Even nine months pregnant, Penny was a firecracker. "Did Jenna know Penny's boyfriends?"

"More than I did." Pearl swiped a tear from the corner of her eye. "Penny didn't tell me much about the guys she dated."

Gently, Rachel said, "One of them might be Goldie's father. Penny said they started dating when she was in high school. He was an older man."

"How much older?"

"He took her to a classy places, bought her expensive gifts." Rachel circled her wrist with her fingers. "A diamond tennis bracelet."

"Those were real?"

"According to Penny."

"How could I miss that? I'm a jewelry designer." Pearl's features hardened. Anger was beginning to replace her sadness. "Not that I work with precious gems. Amethyst is about as fancy as I get. And pearls, of course."

He noticed that she was wearing silver teardrop earrings and a ring with three black pearls. Her only bit of artistic flamboyance was her colorful patchwork jacket. He liked her flair and her earthy sensibility.

Rachel cleared her throat. "Does the name Wayne Prescott mean anything to you?"

She frowned as she considered. Her hand absently patted Goldie's backside. "I don't know him. Is he the father?"

"I don't know."

"Tell me more about this older man."

"Penny didn't actually say how they met, but I got the idea that he was somehow connected to her school. Not a teacher, though. Maybe the father of another student. She said that Jenna told her he was Penny's Mister Big—the man she'd spend the rest of her life with."

"Jenna knew? All of a sudden, I don't want to see her or talk to her. Why wouldn't she tell me?"

"Penny probably asked her not to."

"I never guessed that Penny was dating an adult man. She was only seventeen when she waltzed through the door with that bracelet." She shot a hard glance at Cole. "If she was sleeping with him, that's rape, isn't it?"

He nodded. "This older man is the mastermind behind the gang and the robberies. They call him Baron."

Still holding Goldie, she surged to her feet. "And he's the father."

"Yes."

"I want you to catch this bastard."

Cole had come to the same conclusion. He and Rachel couldn't run forever. The only way they'd be able to turn themselves in to the cops would be if they had solid, irrefutable evidence against Baron. They needed to go on the offensive.

"We can start by talking to Jenna," he said. "She might know Baron's real name."

"I'll make the call," Pearl said as she handed the sleeping baby to Rachel.

In the kitchen, Cole went over a few things Pearl needed to avoid mentioning. Obviously, she couldn't tell Jenna about him or Rachel. And it was best not to mention that she had Goldie with her. Penny's high school teacher had already kept one secret from Pearl. "She's not entirely trustworthy."

"You can say that again." Pearl gave a brisk nod. "Listen, Cole. I'm a pretty good actress. Just tell me what to say."

"You want to get the father's name. That's number one."

"Got it."

"Pretend that you never saw us. Say that you had a call from Penny and she had her baby." He glanced at the clock on the stove. "It's after nine. Will Jenna be at work?"

"Not today. The kids are out of school because of the blizzard."

He handed Pearl his cell phone, which had been recharging for the past hour. "Make the call. Put it on speaker."

Jenna answered on the third ring. Her greeting was overly effusive—as giggly as the teenagers she taught. "I haven't seen you in ages, Pearl. How are you?"

"I'm worried," she said. "Penny called last night and said she had her baby, but I haven't been able to get in touch with her. Did she call you?"

"Boy or girl?"

"Girl. Her name is Goldie," Pearl said.

"Congratulations, grandma. You must be so happy."

"Must be." Sadness tugged at the corners of Pearl's lips, but she kept her voice upbeat. "I sure wish I knew the baby's daddy. I think it was somebody she dated in high school. Did she mention him to you?"

"Penny has so many boyfriends. I can't keep track."

"This one was special. He gave her that sparkly tennis bracelet."

"Sorry. I don't remember."

Cole didn't believe Jenna. Penny would have been sure to brag about her diamonds, and she'd told Rachel that Jenna was her confidante.

Pearl said, "She called him Mister Big."

"Like *Sex and the City*." She giggled. "I guess Penny is the Granby version of high fashion."

"Are you sure," Pearl said, "that you don't remember him?"

"Not at all, but I'll let you know when Penny contacts me. I'm sure she'll turn up. Like a bad penny."

"Why?" Pearl's voice betrayed her rising frustration. "Why are you so sure she'll contact you?"

"For one thing, we're friends. For another, she's been sending me these mysterious packages to hold for her."

Jenna was the contact.

Penny had been using her high school teacher as the drop-off person after the robberies. She'd been sending Jenna bundles of loot.

Chapter 12

As hideouts went, the office in the back of Lily Belle's Soda Fountain and Ice Cream Shop was okay. At least, Rachel thought so. She would have preferred staying in the house, but too many people knew Pearl was living there. Lily Belle's was empty, closed for the season and it had an alarm system.

She and Cole would stay here until nightfall. According to his FBI training, the first twenty-four hours were considered to be the most crucial in a manhunt. After that, the intensity would let up, and they'd make their move.

Rachel slipped off her parka and lowered herself onto the mint-green futon. After sending Pearl on her way with Goldie and the massive backpack filled with baby supplies, she felt unencumbered and a hundred times less tense. All she had to worry about was her own safety and Cole's.

After closing the office door and placing their food supplies on the coffee table in front of the futon, he prowled around the windowless, peach-colored room. The top of the cream-painted desk was empty except for a day-by-day calendar, a pencil jar that looked like an ice cream cone and a couple of framed photographs of smiling, blue-eyed kids. Lily's grandchildren, no doubt. A row of three-drawer cabinets in pastel colors lined the back wall. Bouquets of fake flowers in matching pastel vases sat atop them. A light coat of dust covered every surface. Otherwise, the office was clean. The lingering scent of vanilla and buttery cream hung in the air.

"Too cutesy," he muttered.

"Like Willie Wonka. But with ice cream."

He checked the thermostat. "Good thing we brought blankets. It's set at fifty-two degrees."

"Sounds about right. Warm enough to keep things from freezing but not wasteful. Nobody is supposed to be here until the summer season."

He sank onto the futon beside her. "Take off your shoes."

"Why?"

"We should explore this place, and I don't want to leave wet footprints in case somebody looks through the front window."

With a groan, she wiggled her butt deeper into the futon cushion and stretched her legs out in front of her. Her thigh muscles ached after their crack-of-dawn trek across Shadow Mountain Lake in snowshoes. "What's the point of looking around? Nobody knows we're here. We're safe."

"Are we?"

"Please let me pretend—just for a moment—that crazy people with guns aren't trying to kill us."

"That's not your style," he said. "You're realistic. Practical. You don't delude yourself."

His snap analysis was pretty much on target, but she didn't want him to get cocky. "What makes you think you know me?"

"I'm a trained observer."

She supposed that was true. "In your undercover work, I guess you need to be able to figure out how people are going to act. To be thinking one step ahead."

"That's right."

"But that's on the surface. On a deeper level, you don't know me at all."

He dropped his boots onto the pink-and-green patterned area rug. "I've had a chance to observe your behavior in high-stress situations. I know how you'll react."

"But you don't know why," she said. "You can't tell what I'm thinking. You don't know what's going on inside my head."

He turned toward her and stared—stared hard as though he could actually see her brain working. The two days' growth of stubble on his chin and his messy hair made him look rough, rugged and sexy. Her gaze shifted from his eyes to his lips.

The corner of his mouth twitched into a grin. Then he came across the futon and leaned in close. The suddenness of his kiss took her breath away.

Without thinking, she wrapped her arms around his torso and pulled him against her. His mouth worked against hers. His tongue pushed through her lips.

In spite of her exhaustion, her body responded with a surge of excitement. She didn't feel the chill in the room, didn't look for an escape, didn't want to do anything but prolong this contact.

Ever since their kiss in the cabin, she'd been waiting for this moment—a time when they were finally alone. She had every intention of making love to Cole, but she didn't want to give in too fast. She wanted him to work for it.

Abruptly, she ended the kiss and pulled away from him. But only a few inches away. His face filled her field of vision, and she was captivated by the shimmer in his light brown eyes.

He murmured, "Is that what you were thinking?"

Was she that obvious? Did she radiate a vibe that told him she was a single, thirtysomething woman who needed a big strong man? "You tell me."

"You kissed me back," he said.

"Just being polite."

"Here's what I know about you," he said. "You're smart, competent and pretty. You're at a good place in your life, and you love your work."

"I sound good," she said. "You're lucky to be in the same room with me."

"You're brave. But you're also scared."

Apparently, the compliment train had come to an end. The gleam in his eyes sharpened as he assessed her. He said, "You've been hurt."

"Who hasn't?"

As smoothly as he'd pounced on her, he adjusted his position so he was sitting beside her. "Who hurt you, Rachel? What happened?"

She thought of the men who had passed through

her life, ranging from motorcycle man to a rocker with more tattoos than brains. That array of losers wasn't her greatest hurt.

"A six-year-old boy," she said.

She had never talked about this. *Never.* The memory was too painful, too devastating. Her memory of that boy sucked the air from her lungs.

"His name," she said, "was Adam."

He held her hand. "Go on."

"I'd rather not."

After this crisis was over, she didn't honestly expect to see him again. He would go back to California and be an undercover fed. She'd stay here and continue with her midwife career. They were like the proverbial ships passing in the night—if ships were capable of stopping at sea and having hot sex. Bottom line: she didn't need to reveal the dark corners of her soul to him.

He squeezed her hand. "Do you want to talk about what happened with Adam?"

"You're not going to give up on this, are you?"

"No pressure." He sat back on the futon and turned his gaze away from her. His profile was relaxed and calm. He was waiting; his message was clear.

If she wanted to talk, he'd listen. If not, she could keep her secrets buried. It certainly would be less complicated to grab him and proceed with the passion they were both feeling, but the words were building up inside her. If she didn't speak, she might explode.

"I'd been working as an EMT for a year and a half," she said. "I'd seen a lot. Traffic accidents. Heart attacks. Gunshot wounds. The work was getting to me. I was on the verge of a burnout."

She remembered the sunny summer day in Denver—

the kind of day when you should be taking a puppy on a walk through a grassy green park. "We got the call and responded. It was a fire and an explosion in an apartment complex."

"Meth lab?"

"I don't know how it happened. Somebody probably told me, but the facts went out of my head."

The details blurred in her memory, but she felt a stab in her gut as she recalled the scene in a central courtyard with three-story buildings on all four sides. The smell of grit and smoke and blood came back to her.

"When we got there, rescuers were pulling people out of the buildings. Other ambulances had already arrived, and a senior EMT had taken charge. He assigned me to triage the wounded while my partner loaded the ambulance and took the more serious burn victims to the nearest hospital."

In minutes, her uniform had been covered in greasy soot and blood as she tended to the survivors. First-, second-and third-degree burns. Wounds caused by the shrapnel from the explosion. Someone had fallen down a flight of stairs.

"That's when I met Adam. A sweet-faced kid. He was lying on a sheet on the ground, and he didn't seem to be badly injured. His head was bleeding. The laceration didn't appear to be deep. When I started working on him, he looked up at me and smiled. He told me his name, and he promised he'd be all right. His exact words were… I'm not going to die."

A swell of emotion rose up inside her. She told herself that not everyone could be saved, but that truth did little to assuage the pain of her sorrow. She'd been hurt. God, yes, she'd been hurt. Not by a person but by life.

When Cole wrapped his arm around her and pulled her close, she didn't object. Her cheek rested against his chest; his solid presence comforted her.

In a whisper, she continued, "I left Adam. Went to deal with other victims. A woman with a broken leg called out Adam's name. His mother. Somehow, they'd gotten separated. She was frantic."

Rachel hadn't wasted time trying to calm Adam's mother. She'd gone back to the boy. His injuries had seemed less traumatic. She'd thought she could carry him and reunite the boy with his mother. "He was dead."

She'd tried to resuscitate the child. CPR. Straight oxygen. Mouth-to-mouth. Nothing worked. "I couldn't bring him back."

"Is that when you changed jobs?"

"Shortly after that." She shrugged. It wasn't necessary to talk about the months of debilitating depression and anger. The important thing was that she'd fought her way through to the other side. She'd learned how to cope. "You asked me what I'm afraid of, and this is it. I'm scared of losing someone I care about."

"Given that fear," he said, "you don't fall in love easily."

"No, I don't." She lifted her chin. "You?"

"Not so much." He kissed the tip of her nose. "Let's get moving. I want to check this place out. Your shoes."

She appreciated the lightning-quick change of subject. After baring her soul to him, the last thing she wanted was to wallow in grief. She'd said her piece. Time to move on.

When she caught his gaze, she wondered if Cole had

known this would be her reaction. God, she hated being predictable. "What about my shoes?"

"Take them off."

She raised a questioning eyebrow. "Only the shoes?"

"Later, I'll take your socks, your hat and your belt. I'll unbutton your shirt. Unsnap your jeans." He rose from the futon. "For now, just the shoes. We'll take a look around."

In her stocking feet, she padded behind him on the concrete floor of the kitchen area in the back of the ice cream parlor. Like the office, there weren't any windows. When Cole turned on the overhead light, she saw an array of shelves, drawers, stainless steel counters and a commercial-sized sink, as well as machines of varying size and shape.

"Lily must make her own ice cream," she said. "What's your favorite flavor?"

"Rocky Road," he said.

"That figures."

He opened the door to a pantry. The shelves were all cleaned out. Likewise for the freezer unit. A closet by the back door was filled with cleaning supplies.

She asked, "Is there something special we're looking for?"

"I'm visualizing. If somebody breaks in here, I want to know where I'm going."

"There's a burglar alarm," she reminded him. "We'll have time to escape."

"Not if the alarm is short-circuited."

She folded her arms and leaned against a counter. "It must be a drag to always focus on the worst-case scenario."

"Yeah, yeah, poor me. Living the hard life of an undercover agent. When you walk into a room, you always look for the exits. You check out everybody you meet, looking for concealed weapons."

"You sound bored with it."

"I'm ticked off. Usually, I'm on my own. Making my own decisions and deciding my own actions. I get a lot of grief for being a lone wolf. And now, when I call on my handler for help, Waxman turns his back on me."

The front area of Lily Belle's was a typical ice cream parlor and soda fountain with sunlight pouring through the front windows onto the white tile floor. The color scheme was—surprise, surprise—pastel. And the far wall was decorated with a fanciful painting of an animal parade. Pink lion with a top hat and baton. A lavender bear in a tutu. Green and blue squirrels blowing bubbles from their trumpets.

Wrought-iron white chairs and tables were stacked against the walls. Padded stools lined up at a typical soda fountain counter, and there was a long row of empty coolers where the ice cream would be stored in the summer.

"FYI," he said, "if we get attacked, come this way. There's room to hide behind the counter and the coolers. If worse comes to worst, you can bust through the windows. In the back, there's only one exit."

"Lovely." She smiled at him. "You know what makes me really sad?"

"What's that?"

"Looking at all this, I'm dying for some ice cream. Maybe a fudge sundae with whipped cream on top."

"Sounds like you need a little sweetness."

He slung his arm around her waist and yanked her

toward him with such force that her feet came off the floor. He pressed her tightly against him and kissed her hard. There was nothing tentative about his approach; the idea of making love was a foregone conclusion. He was aggressive, fierce, demanding.

And she liked it.

Chapter 13

The creamy pastel ambience in the office contrasted the hot red fire of their passion. Rachel felt like she ought to turn the desktop photographs of Lily Belle's grandchildren facedown so they wouldn't be traumatized. Her spirits rose and her excitement soared as Cole tore off her panties.

Breathing hard, she wrapped her arms around his neck and clung to him. Her right leg coiled around his, and she pressed herself against his erection.

His hand grabbed her butt and held her in place. He arched his neck and tilted his head back. For a moment, she thought he might start howling like a wolf. Then he lowered his head and consumed her with a kiss. His hands explored her body with rough caresses.

She felt herself turning into a quivering mass of jelly, unable to stand. They slid to the floor. On the pink-and-green patterned carpet, he straddled her and sat back, looking down.

His body amazed her. Muscular arms. Lean torso. Smooth chest. When she reached toward him, he cuffed her wrists in his grasp.

"No fair." She gasped. "I want to touch."

"How bad do you want it?"

She tried to pull her hands free, but he held her wrists firmly. He was in complete control. Or so he thought.

She widened her eyes and softened her voice. "Please, Cole. You're hurting me."

Concern flashed in his eyes. Immediately, he released his grasp.

And she took advantage. She rose up and twisted her body, throwing him off balance. Now she was on top. "Gotcha."

"You win."

He lay on his back with his arms sprawled above his head while she fondled, stroked and pinched. Her fingers glided along the ridges of his muscles. Leaning down, she nuzzled his chest and torso. Her excitement was building to a fever pitch. She didn't want to wait for one more second.

"Condom?" she asked.

"Wallet."

She crawled across the carpet to where he'd discarded his jeans. Was it really necessary to stop for a condom? Of course, it was. She gave lectures on the importance of protected sex. She had to do this.

After clumsy fumbling, she held the tiny see-through package in her hand. "It's blue."

"The only ones they had in super, gigantic, extra-large."

He took charge again, and she let him. When he plunged into her, she gave a sharp cry. Her last coherent thought was that this was the best sex she'd ever had. Then she abandoned herself to the sheer physical pleasure of their lovemaking.

When it was over, she was shivering from head to toe. Not because it was fifty-two degrees in the room. This was a sensual release that had been building in her for years.

For the first time, she wondered if there might be a future for her and Cole.

Cole wanted to spend the rest of the day making love to Rachel. Their hideout in the office of the ice cream parlor seemed insulated from the rest of the world. After he converted the futon into a bed and spread out blankets, they were cozy and comfortable.

He lay on his back, and she snuggled her head against his shoulder. Cuddling had never been one of his favorite things, but he was betting that this cuddle would lead to something more.

"I only had the one rubber," he said.

"That could be a problem." She rose up on an elbow and looked down at him. "I'm guessing that Lily Belle doesn't keep a condom supply in her desk."

He looked up at her, memorizing every detail. Until now, she'd been so bundled up in turtlenecks and sweaters that he hadn't been able to appreciate her. From the neck down, she was firm but not too muscular and surprisingly graceful from the arch of her back to the crook of her elbow. Her throat was as smooth as ivory. He liked her short hair; it suited her face. Her high forehead balanced a strong, stubborn jaw. And her eyes? Those big blue eyes sparkled with humor and excitement.

He already wanted her again. "Would it help if I told you I recently had a physical, and I'm clean?"

"I give health lectures about bad boys like you. You wouldn't believe the stories high school boys come up with when they're trying to get their girlfriends to say yes."

"Actually, I'm familiar with those stories."

She traced a line down his nose and across his lips. "You and me? We're not in high school. Nothing you could say would convince me. It's my decision whether or not I take a risk."

They had bigger threats to worry about than unprotected sex. Armed killers could burst through the door at any given moment. He needed to deal with that situation.

Reaching toward the coffee table, he picked up the cell phone and turned it on. "I want to check in with Pearl and see how she's doing."

"Put it on speaker," Rachel said.

Pearl answered right away on her hands-free phone. Her voice was chipper. "I got on the highway with no problem. The snowplows have been out, and I'm making good time."

"Any roadblocks?"

"None that I've seen. But there were a whole lot of police cars on the road when I was leaving Grand Lake."

"Are you headed to Jenna's house?"

"Certainly not. I'd rather camp in the forest than see that lying little snake again. I'm staying with a friend in Denver. She has a penthouse condo in a secure building. We ought to be safe."

He was glad to hear that Pearl was taking the threat seriously.

Rachel piped up, "How's Goldie?"

"Sleeping in the car seat, snug as a bug. I might have to stop and give her a bottle, but I want to get out of the high country. There's more bad weather coming in."

"How bad?" he asked.

"Another eight to ten inches. On the radio, the ski areas are whooping and hollering about great conditions."

More snow presented an obstacle. He wanted to drive to Granby tonight, to talk with Jenna Cambridge and take possession of the packages Penny had sent to her. "Take care of yourself, Pearl. We'll call again later. Don't tell anyone else where you are."

"I understand."

"Give Goldie a hug," Rachel said.

He disconnected the call and looked toward her. She was sitting up on the futon, wide-awake and alert, with a blanket around her shoulders to keep warm. He asked, "How are you at driving in snow?"

"Better than you, California boy."

"I'm good in a high-speed chase."

"What about black ice?"

"Have I mentioned how much I hate the mountains?"

"Seriously," she said, "the highway ought to be okay. The real problem will come when we get to Granby. Side roads don't get cleared too often. Since Pearl took the four-wheel drive SUV that belongs to Lily Belle, we're driving her little compact—not the best vehicle for deep snow."

"Do you think we can make it?"

"I don't know," she said. "If we run into trouble, we're caught."

It wouldn't be too bad to stay here overnight. He and Rachel could find plenty of ways to amuse themselves. "Let's call your cop buddy and see what he's found out."

Like Pearl, Deputy Jim Loughlin was quick to pick up. Had he been hovering by the phone, waiting for their call? Cole wanted to trust this guy because Rachel did, but he was realistic about the responsibilities of a law enforcement officer. At some point, Loughlin would have to obey orders. His tone was anxious. "Are you all right? Can you tell me if you're all right?"

"I'm good." She gave Cole a sultry smile. "Better than you'd expect."

"I went to the address you gave me," Loughlin said. "You were right. There was blood all over. Bullet holes. Looked like a semiautomatic weapon."

"Did you report it?" she asked.

"I should have, but I didn't." He grumbled, "I couldn't figure out how to tell the sheriff without mentioning that I'd been in contact with you."

"Sorry to put you in this position," Cole said.

"Not your fault. There's something about this manhunt that just doesn't ring true. For starters, Rachel, you're obviously not a criminal."

"Thanks," she said. "What else bothers you?"

"The sheriff stopped by to see the baby. By the way, Sarah appreciates those instructions you left behind about breast-feeding. My mom kept telling her that the bottle was better, but Sarah won't hear of it."

"Good for Sarah."

Cole told himself to be patient while the deep, rumbling voice of Deputy Loughlin talked about being a new daddy. His chat about breast-feeding made a strange counterpoint to the massacre of the gang, but it was best to let Rachel's friend take his time.

"Anyway," Loughlin said, "there was an FBI agent with the sheriff. A guy by the name of Prescott."

Son of a bitch. Cole could think of only one reason why Prescott would be there. He knew about Rachel and wanted to get a lead on her whereabouts. It was looking more and more like Agent Wayne Prescott was a link to Baron.

Rachel asked, "What did Prescott want to know?"

"Here's the funny thing about him. He claimed that he doesn't know this area, but he used the names of local landmarks. Things like Pete's Pie Shack and Hangman's Tree. Stuff you wouldn't find on a map."

"You thought he was fishy?"

"Something about him didn't smell right," Loughlin said. "Then he asked me about you and the clinic. He mentioned your vacation and asked if we knew where you were going. But he never identified you as the female fugitive. The only name that's been given is Cole Bogart."

She shot him a questioning glance. Bogart wasn't the name he'd told her; that was his undercover identity.

Loughlin continued, "You're both described as being armed and dangerous based on the murders of those three people. But if you killed them, how did you remove the bodies? And why?"

"Somebody wants to keep the house where they were killed a secret," Cole said. "Did you check the records to find the owner?"

"It's a corporate group called Baron Enterprises. The

primary name is Xavier Romero, who happens to be the owner of the Black Hawk casino that got robbed."

Cole knew that name, knew it well. Xavier Romero had been a small-time operator in the Southern California gambling scene. He was also a snitch—a likable old guy but shifty as a snake. Cole hadn't known that Romero owned the casino they hit.

Deputy Loughlin cleared his throat. "This just doesn't add up. Why would the gang hide in a house that belongs to the guy they robbed?"

Xavier Romero had to be in on the plot. Cole asked, "How much does Romero claim was stolen?"

"Over a hundred thousand."

Cole shook his head. "It wasn't half that much."

"The robbery report stated the higher amount," Jim said, "which means the insurance company will pay out the hundred thousand to the casino."

"Unless we can prove fraud," Cole said. "We need to find that money."

"We're talking about a lot of cash." The deputy's voice took on a note of suspicion. "I've never met you, Cole. I'm putting a lot of trust in you based on what Rachel says. Don't let me down."

"I won't," he promised.

"Thank you, Jim," Rachel said. "We'll be in touch as soon as we know anything else. Give Caitlyn a kiss from me."

She ended the call and turned to him. "Is that the answer you were looking for? Is Xavier Romero really the Baron?"

"Not possible. Romero is close to seventy. A potbellied old man with thinning white hair and thick glasses.

His hands look arthritic, but he can make the cards dance when he's dealing poker."

"He must be Baron's associate. They're part of the same group that owns the house. And it sounds like he intends to commit insurance fraud with Baron's help."

"Right on both counts, partner."

She shook her head. "I'm not your partner in crime. Or crime solving. I'm not cut out for this undercover life."

"It's a gift," he said.

"Is it, Mister Bogart?"

"That's my undercover name. Cole Jeremy McClure is the name on my birth certificate."

"You didn't lie to me." She snuggled down beside him. Her flesh molded to his. "That makes me feel good."

He pulled her close. There were a number of things he ought to be thinking about: logistical problems in driving through another damn blizzard to Granby at night and the usefulness of calling Waxman with the new information about Xavier Romero. But his brain was clouded by her nearness. The scent of her body made him stupid. And happy.

He brushed his lips across her forehead and looked into her eyes. "How do you feel about making love *sans* condom?"

"I'm for it," she said.

"What if you get pregnant?"

"This is something I never thought I'd hear myself say. Never. Do you understand? Never."

"I get it."

"But the truth is that I wouldn't mind getting pregnant. At this point in my life, I'm ready to have a baby."

His heart made a loud thud. His pulse stopped. He was lying naked with a woman who wanted a baby. *Danger, danger, danger.* "Excuse me?"

She laughed. "I've never seen the blood drain from someone's face so fast. Are you going into shock? Should I start CPR?"

"I'm cool."

"If I should happen to get pregnant, I wouldn't saddle you with any responsibilities. Being a single mom isn't my first choice. But I'm in my thirties, and I want kids. I love kids. And it's entirely possible that I'm not cut out for the whole marriage thing."

"Marriage?" He choked out the word. Was she trying to give him a heart attack?

"Don't worry, Cole. I'm not looking for a relationship with you. How could I? You live in California. And you have an incredibly dangerous job. Frankly, I wouldn't marry you on a bet."

His mood swung one hundred and eighty degrees. Because she said she'd never marry him, he had an urge to propose. "Are you giving me a preemptive rejection?"

"Absolutely. Long-distance relationships hardly ever work. And your undercover work scares me."

"Doesn't seem fair," he muttered.

"Don't feel bad. I consider you to be an excellent sperm donor. You're intelligent, and you seem to be healthy. There aren't any weird genetic diseases lurking around in your DNA, are there?"

"Not that I know of."

She slipped her fingertips down his chest. "I don't think we need to worry about not having a condom."

When he kissed her, he was thinking of more than her slim, supple body. In his mind, he visualized a home with Rachel. She'd be wearing his grandmother's wedding ring and holding his baby in her arms. Not a typical fantasy for making love. But he found the thought of being with her—long-term and committed—to be intensely arousing.

Chapter 14

Though Rachel didn't want to get dressed, she shoved her arms into her sleeves and pulled on her turtleneck. Hours had passed since they'd entered the windowless office behind the ice cream parlor, but the time had gone faster than the blink of an eye. She wished these moments could stretch into days, months, years.

In a way, it felt like she'd known Cole forever. There was something so familiar about him. In spite of being opposites, they were well-matched, like a hook and an eye. A bolt and a screw. She chuckled to herself. Best not to think about screws or she'd never get her clothes on.

Their passion was wild. It was crazy. And she knew better. She was an adult—a thirtysomething woman who had her life on track. Why had she abandoned all restraint? Was it the intensity of being chased? Did she cling to him because she was terrified that she wouldn't survive this ordeal?

Reluctantly, she zipped her jeans. Maybe the answer was Cole himself. He was different from all the other bad boys she'd known. True, he had an edge. The man earned his living by deception. But he also made her laugh. And he was capable of incredible tenderness.

He smacked her butt and said, "Get your jacket on. If it's not snowing too hard, we need to get on the road."

She was praying for a blizzard. "I don't want to go."

He yanked her into his arms and held her tightly against him. She liked the rough-and-ready way he handled her. He treated her as an equal, not a porcelain figurine that might shatter and break.

"Rachel, beautiful Rachel." His voice dropped to a low, intimate level. "If we had a choice, I'd keep you here forever. I'd burn your clothes so you could never get dressed."

The way she'd burned motorcycle man's leather jacket? "Do you ride motorcycles?"

"Only Harleys."

"Figures."

Pulling away from him, she shrugged into her parka. The superwarm coat felt empty without the added burden of Goldie snuggled against her chest. "Do you think Pearl is okay?"

"We checked with her an hour ago. She was at her friend's condo, feeding the baby."

"That's not what I meant."

He nodded. "It's going to be a long time before she's okay. She lost a daughter and gained a granddaughter. In the space of a day, her whole life got turned upside down."

Like mine. "I'm dressed. What's next?"

"Come with me." He took her hand. "I'm not going to turn on any lights. Somebody might notice."

A shiver trickled down her spine. "Do you think they're watching?"

"Don't know."

They left the office, and he closed the door behind them. For a moment, they stood in the kitchen area and waited for their eyes to become accustomed to the darkness. The empty area with stainless steel fixtures felt cold, even with her parka. She held Cole's hand as he moved toward the front of the shop.

The glow from a streetlight fell softly through the wide, snow-splattered front windows. They circled the serving counter and crossed the white tile floor until they stood at the glass, looking out.

Though it was only nine o'clock, there was no traffic on the main street running through Grand Lake. Snow piled up three feet high at the curb, and a car parked at the side of the road was completely buried. The sidewalk had been cleared enough that two people could walk abreast. On the opposite side of the street, the storefronts were all dark. The town had closed down early.

The light snowfall disappointed her. She'd been hoping for a raging storm that would force them to cancel their plan.

"Looks peaceful," Cole said.

"These blizzards can be real deceptive. I vote to stay here until morning."

He stepped behind her and slipped his arms around her waist. She leaned back against his chest, feeling cozy and protected in his embrace.

"It's pretty," he said. "Maybe your mountains aren't so bad, after all."

She closed her eyes and thought about spending time with him in a ski lodge with paneled walls, a fireplace and a mug of hot buttered rum. "There's nothing as beautiful as a blue sky day with the sun sparkling on champagne powder snow."

"A full moon on a white, sandy beach," he said.

"Mountain streams."

"Palm trees waving in the breeze." He hugged her. "When this is over, I want to take you to California. You can vacation with me."

Her heart took a happy little leap. *He wants to spend more time with me.* Immediately, she pushed the thought aside, not wanting to get her hopes up. "You're just trying to convince me that we should make this drive tonight."

"We'll exit through the back. Then we'll head down the street to the garage behind Pearl's house." He kissed the top of her head. "If everything goes well, this could be over in a matter of hours."

With a sigh, she gave in and followed him through the door at the front of the ice cream parlor into the darkness of the kitchen area.

Cole came to a sudden halt. She couldn't see what he was doing, but she sensed his movement as he raised his gun.

"What's wrong?" she asked.

"The green light on the alarm box is off."

"It must be a malfunction."

"Let's hope so."

They hadn't heard the alarm go off. Though she couldn't see far into the darkness, she surely would have sensed the presence of another person. "There's nobody else in here."

"It's too dark back here," he muttered. "We'll go out the front entrance."

She turned and retraced her steps. He stayed with her, close enough that she felt his arm brush against hers. As she reached the open doorway, the light through the front windows gave her more visibility. She glanced over her shoulder and saw Cole facing backward, toward the kitchen.

When she passed the doorway, she looked toward the front counter to her right. And she froze. The dark silhouette of a huge broad-shouldered figure stood out against the pale pastel of the wall.

His arms flung wide. "He-e-e-re's Frankie."

He charged toward her, more stumbling than deliberate. His hands slid under her arms and he lifted her off her feet. His forward momentum carried her beyond the counter toward the far wall.

She kicked hard. Her foot tangled with his legs, and she could feel him losing his balance. If he fell, he'd land on top of her with his full weight. He'd crush her.

The instant her boots touched the floor, she threw her weight toward his left. His left shoulder was the one that was injured—the weaker shoulder. The bullet was still in there, probably turning septic.

Frank crashed to the floor, pinning her legs. She struggled to free herself. Frank sat straight up, grabbed her arm and yanked her around so she was sitting in front of him on the floor. Light reflected off the barrel of his gun.

"Don't move," he said. "Neither one of you."

Cole stood only a few feet from them, looking down. His gun aimed at Frank's forehead. "Let her go."

"Yeah? Then you'll drill a hole in my head?"

"If I wanted to kill you," Cole said, "I would have done it back at the cabin."

"You left me there." He coughed. Phlegm rattled in his throat. "Left me to die."

His stench—stale sweat, blood and grit—turned her stomach. A feverish heat emanated from him, and he was shaking. It was clear to her that he was feeling the effects of the gunshot wounds, loss of blood, shock and exposure. He was weakened and losing control. That made him even more dangerous.

Keeping the fear from her voice, she said, "You need a doctor, Frank."

"I need for you to shut the hell up." He pressed the nose of his gun against her temple. "I can't see a damn thing in here. Turn on the lights, Cole."

"Will the light be a signal for your friends? The murderers you hooked up with at the cabin?"

"I ditched those guys as soon as I got into town."

A spasm shook Frank's body. His gun hand twitched. She was afraid he might kill her by accident. Rachel said, "Do as he says."

"That's right," Frank growled. "I'm in charge."

Cole backed up a few paces, heading toward the light switch by the door. "How did you find us?"

"I met Penny's mom in Black Hawk at the casino. Pearl Richards. She said she was living in Grand Lake. I asked around. Found her house. Went inside. And then… I don't remember. It was warm. Must have gone to sleep."

His grip on consciousness was fading. She wanted to

keep him calm and placated. "Finding Pearl was smart, Frank. Why don't you put the gun down and—"

"I'm a hell of a lot smarter than you know," he said. "Ask Cole. I'm good with electronics. Disconnected the alarm to this place. No problem."

"Why did you come here? To the ice cream parlor?"

"Found a business card. I got inside. Easy does it. Then I got dizzy. Shhhhh." He slurred, "Had to s-s-s-sleep."

From the corner of her eye, she saw the gun drooping in his hand. He was on the verge of passing out.

"Let me bring you something to drink," she said gently. "Something nice and cool. You'd like that, wouldn't you?"

His body stiffened as he forced himself awake. "Turn on the damn lights."

When Cole flicked the switch, light flooded the room. The cheerful, pastel décor mocked the hopelessness of her situation. Two men with guns faced each other, and she was in the middle.

Frank shook her arm and ordered her to stand up. "Slow. Move real slow."

She was tempted to bolt. Frank was suffering; his reactions would be slowed. She remembered what Cole had told her earlier. If attacked, hide behind the counter.

"Move," Frank barked.

She did as he said, and he maneuvered into position behind her, using her as a shield. He held her left arm to keep her from running. His gun jabbed her ribs.

When she flinched, Cole reacted. His movements were slight, not enough to spook Frank. But she saw the tension in his jaw and noticed that he had moved a few inches closer.

Like her, he kept his tone level and calm. "You don't want to hurt Rachel. She's the one who's going to lead you to all that money."

"Penny sent the cash here to her mom," Frank said. "It's close. I can smell it."

"You're wrong," she said. "But I'm sure you already know that. You must have searched in the house before you came here."

"Where is it?"

She looked toward Cole, who gave her a nod. Then she said, "Penny sent the money to a friend in Granby. We have to drive to get there."

"If you're lying, I'll kill you." He poked her again. "Cole, put your gun on the floor and step back."

She could guess what would happen if Cole disarmed himself. Frank was desperate, half crazed. He thought he needed her to lead him to the money, but he had no further use for anyone else. He'd shoot Cole in a minute.

She couldn't stop herself from crying out. "No, Cole. Don't do it."

Frank dragged her by the arm. He edged toward the windows as though he was planning to walk out the front door. Was it unlocked? Had he entered through that door?

"Listen to me, Frank. We'll take you with us," Cole said. "We'll drive together and take you to the money."

"Drop your weapon. Or I'll shoot her in the gut."

"You need her. She's the only one who—"

"Drop it."

Cole placed his gun on the floor.

"That's real good," Frank said. "Kick it over here."

She watched in horror as the automatic weapon slid across the white tile floor into the corner under the painting of the dancing lavender bear in a tutu. This shouldn't be happening. Not here. Lily Belle's Ice Cream Parlor wasn't the place for a showdown.

With a satisfied grunt, Frank pulled the gun away from her side and aimed at Cole. Though his hand wobbled, he couldn't miss from this distance.

She didn't plan her move. All Rachel knew was that she had to do something. She bent forward from the waist. Before Frank could yank her back into an upright position, she flung her head back as hard as she could. Her skull banged against Frank's wounded left shoulder.

He screamed in pain. His grip on her arm released.

She made a frantic dash.

Chapter 15

The gutsy move by Rachel gave Cole the chance he needed.

There wasn't time to reach his gun. Every second counted. He took two quick steps and launched himself in a diving tackle. His shoulder hit the solid mass of Frank's chest, and the big man went down with a thud. Still, he managed to fire two shots. He didn't lose his grip on the weapon.

On the floor, Cole struggled for the gun. From the corner of his eye, he saw Rachel dive across the countertop. She was out of sight. Out of range. Good.

With a yell and a ferocious surge, Frank threw Cole off him and staggered to his feet. He braced his legs, wide apart. His shoulders hunched as he groped the empty air. He squinted. His eyes seemed unable to focus. Like a wounded beast, he swung his long arms, waving the gun back and forth.

Cole squared off with him. A one-two combination to the gut drove Frank backward. Cole flicked a stinging blow to the center of Frank's face, snapping his head back.

His arms flew wide. His fingers loosened. The gun clattered to the floor. This fight was all but over.

Frigid air rushed into the ice cream parlor as the front door opened. A man with a gun entered. Frank had brought backup, and Cole couldn't handle two of them.

Following Rachel's example, he pivoted and leaped across the soda fountain counter, where he found her crouched on the floor in a tight little ball. "Are you all right?"

She nodded. "You?"

"Been better."

Three gun shots erupted.

Cole peered over the edge of the counter. Frank sprawled on the floor. His blood splattered the white tile floor.

The gunman flipped back the hood of his parka and said, "It's over. You can come out."

Agent Wayne Prescott.

Slowly, Cole stood. When he'd been looking down the barrel of Frank's gun, he felt less threatened than when Prescott came toward him and extended his hand. There was every reason to believe that this man had betrayed him and put him in lethal danger. Should he shake that hand? Why not just stick his arm down a wood chipper?

"Agent McClure," Prescott said, "you're a hard man to find."

"You've got me now." There was no choice but to play nice. He reached across the soda fountain counter and gripped the traitor's hand. In spite of his years as an undercover operative, he couldn't force himself to return Prescott's smile. "Rachel, this is Agent Wayne Prescott."

His supposedly disarming smile extended to her. "I apologize, Ms. Devon. It's unfortunate that you were caught up in this situation. I assure you that this isn't the way the FBI does business."

Her lips pressed tightly together. With wide, unblinking eyes, she stared at Frank's body. "Is he dead?"

"He's not going to hurt anybody."

Cole knew that her EMT training and instincts wouldn't allow her to ignore a victim. He wasn't surprised when she straightened her shoulders, walked around the counter and knelt beside Frank.

Watching her check for a pulse gave Cole a renewed respect for her. She valued human life—even the miserable existence of someone like Frank Loeb, a man who had tried to kill her. Rachel was a good woman. The best.

She looked up and shook her head. "No need to call for an ambulance."

When Prescott moved closer to her, Cole vaulted over the counter and inserted himself between them. Even though Prescott had holstered his gun, he couldn't be trusted. He looked like one of the good guys with his barbered black hair and clean-shaven jaw. His manner was calm. His expression showed no emotion, typical of a trained agent. Pulling information from him wasn't going to be easy.

Cole helped Rachel to her feet and guided her to one of the padded turquoise stools in front of the counter.

When she was seated, he turned toward Prescott, waiting for him to speak first.

Unfortunately, Prescott employed the same negotiating tactic. He stood beside Frank's body as though he was a hunter with a fresh kill waiting to have his photograph taken. The corner of his mouth twitched. Cole could tell that there was something Prescott wanted to know, a burning question that would break his silent facade.

"The baby," Prescott said. "Is the baby all right?"

Cole hadn't expected him to ask about Goldie. If he was right about Prescott working with Baron, the first question should have been about the money.

Rachel answered, "Goldie is doing very well. She's with Penny's mother."

"Where?" Prescott demanded.

Before Rachel could answer, Cole said, "In a safe place."

"I need to see the baby before I can call off the search."

"That doesn't make a hell of a lot of sense," Cole said. "You know we're not armed and dangerous fugitives. You shook my hand. Apologized to Rachel. You put your gun away."

"I'm not the one who made the call for a manhunt," Prescott said. "Somebody higher up said you'd lost it. You know how often that happens with undercover ops."

"Not with me."

"There were three dead bodies. One of them, a woman who had just given birth."

"Who called for the manhunt?"

"The director gave the order. I don't know who talked to him."

A lie? Prescott had jammed his hands into the pockets of his parka so he wouldn't betray any nervousness with his gestures. His forehead pulled into a frown that might indicate concern or confusion. Or else he was hiding something. His dark eyes were steady, but his lips thinned. *Was he lying?*

"You called me in on this investigation," Cole said. "You suspected someone in your office of working with Baron."

"I still do."

Cole continued as though he hadn't spoken. "Then you show up here with Frank."

"Hold it right there. Frank Loeb and I weren't working together. I was following him." He paused. "I didn't know Frank was so skilled at electronics. It didn't take him ten minutes to bypass that burglar alarm."

There was something cruel about discussing Frank's skills while the man lay dead at their feet. Though Rachel was no stranger to violent death, he wanted to get her away from this horror.

Less than an hour ago, they'd been lying in each other's arms. The world had been sweet. He had been happy. No more.

His life didn't have room for a normal relationship. He lived on the razor's edge.

"Call Waxman," Cole said. His handler needed to be apprised of the situation.

Prescott's scowl deepened. "Waxman might be the one who betrayed you. When he assigned you, he warned me that you were a loose cannon. He said that when you go undercover, you cut all ties."

That policy had served Cole well. If Prescott had been able to track him with GPS, he and Rachel would have been caught. "You're saying that Agent Waxman is the traitor."

"I'm not accusing anybody."

But he was pushing suspicion away from himself, which seemed like a blatant ruse. Cole needed to be careful in dealing with this guy. If Prescott had been working with Baron, he had a lot to lose. Not only would his payoff money stop coming, but he'd also lose his job, his reputation and his freedom. The feds dealt harshly with those who conspired against them.

"Think about it, Cole." Prescott's hands came out of his pockets. He held them open, showing that he had nothing to hide. "I'm not the bad guy. If I wanted you dead, I could have killed you when I walked through this door."

A threat? "Don't underestimate me."

It had been a while since he'd killed a man with his bare hands. The years had taught him patience. He was smarter now than when he first started.

"Here's the deal." Prescott's hands went back into his pockets. "If I call off the manhunt, I have to take you and Rachel into custody."

He looked toward her. She hadn't made a peep. Until now, she hadn't been shy about making her needs and desires known. What was going on behind those liquid blue eyes?

He glanced at Prescott. "Excuse us for a moment."

Taking her arm, he led her toward the door into the rear of the shop. He stood just inside, where he could keep an eye on Prescott while they held a whispered conversation. "Why so quiet?"

"I was watching you," she said. "When you're negotiating, you become a different person."

"How so?"

She lifted her hand as though she wanted to touch him. But she held back. "You know how much I like a bad boy. That element of danger is… Well, it's a turn-on. But you're not the same man who made love to me all day."

"I'm not?"

"You're more like the guy in the ski mask who kidnapped me in my van and stuck a gun in my face."

Though he wanted to give his full attention to Rachel, his gaze focused on Prescott, who stood at the window, staring out at the snow. "That was my undercover identity. You know, like an actor playing a role."

"Actors don't carry real guns."

"True," he conceded.

He wasn't an actor following a safe little script that led to the inevitable happy ending. When he went undercover, he took on another identity. From the way he combed his hair to the way he handled his weapons, he was different. He couldn't risk showing a single glimpse of himself, and he never knew how it would all end.

"You're scaring me, Cole. You're so closed off, so tough, so cold. Your eyes don't even reflect the light. You're dangerous. And it's a real danger, the kind that got Penny killed."

He could feel her pulling away as though she was walking backward into a mist, fading into a memory. "I don't want to lose you."

"I'm not blaming you. It's your job. It's what you do."

He'd work this out with her later. "We have to make a decision. Do we turn ourselves in?"

"Is it safe?"

"I'd feel better if I knew Baron's identity. I'd have a bargaining chip."

Thus far, his undercover assignment was shaping up to be an unmitigated failure. Four people, including Penny and Frank, were dead. And he was only a few inches closer to finding the mastermind who caused those deaths and engineered a chain of robberies throughout the west.

"You hate to quit," she said.

"Right, again."

"And you promised Pearl that you'd find the man responsible for Penny's murder."

He nodded. "The only way we'll really be safe is when Baron is found, and the traitor in the FBI is identified."

A grin lifted the corners of her mouth. He knew she wasn't trying to be sexy, but that energy emanated from her. "I say the hell with Prescott."

"I've never wanted to kiss somebody so much in my life."

"Kiss me later. Right now, we need to get away from here."

As they returned to the front of Lily Belle's ice cream parlor, a plan was already taking shape in his mind. He confronted Prescott. "Where were we?"

The pinched eyebrows and the scowl had become a permanent fixture on Prescott's face. "I want an update on your investigation."

"You'll have to wait."

Prescott glared and looked him straight in the eye in an attempt to assert his authority as the higher ranking agent. "You need to start cooperating with me. Tell me what you've learned about Baron."

Cole had two options: keep quiet or dribble out just enough information to get a response. This was a chess game played with hubris and cunning. Spending years undercover gave Cole the clear advantage; he knew how to manipulate people to get information.

He made the first move, starting with the truth. "Baron is the baby's daddy."

Without admitting or denying, Prescott asked, "Will DNA confirm that relationship?" It was a sideways move.

"Penny named him. She grew up in this area."

Prescott's nod was a signal of confidence. "I have background on her. She went to high school in Granby."

"Is that how you tracked her mother?"

"Finding Pearl Richards didn't take any complicated sleuthing." Prescott moved toward bragging. Clearly, he thought he was winning this game. "She had her mail forwarded to the house in Grand Lake."

Cole shot him down. "But you didn't know that the owner of the house also owned the ice cream parlor."

"No, I didn't."

"But you're familiar with the Grand County area," Cole said, remembering what Deputy Loughlin had told them.

"I've been up here a couple of times. I used to be the information liaison for the FBI in Colorado."

A piece of new information. How did it fit? "You did public relations?"

"Checking in with the locals. Giving Q-and-A talks. Creating an FBI presence. In some of these remote areas, weirdo militia groups can take root. It's good if the local people have someone they've met and can talk with."

"So you know people around here." That could be a useful attribute if he was working with Baron. Cole pushed with a more aggressive move. "Is there a more personal reason you've spent time around here?"

"No."

Prescott had hesitated slightly before answering; Cole knew that he'd hit a nerve. The game shifted to his advantage. "Ever owned property in Grand County?"

"This isn't about me." An edge of anger crept into his voice.

"I think maybe it is."

"Damn it, McClure. I offered you a deal to go into custody. I'll take care of you. Trust me."

"I never trust anybody who uses those words."

"My actions speak louder." A red flush colored Prescott's throat. He was getting angry, losing control. "I'm here to help. I didn't kill you when I had the chance."

"You never had that chance." He gestured for Rachel to stay back, out of harm's way.

"Get real, McClure. Frank was charging after you like a wounded grizzly. I had a gun, and you were unarmed."

It was time to take Agent Wayne Prescott down. This was the endgame.

Since they'd both had the same FBI training in H2H, hand-to-hand combat, Cole decided to avoid a real fight. His plan wasn't to hurt Prescott. Just to show him who was boss.

A pat on the shoulder and a light slap on the ear distracted Prescott enough for Cole to slip his gun from the holster and drop it on the floor. Likely, Prescott was carrying other weapons. Probably had a knife in those pockets where he kept hiding his hands. And an ankle holster.

He blocked a punch with his forearm and waded in closer. Cole ducked. When he popped up, he spun the agent around and pulled off his jacket. He had him in a choke hold.

The whole altercation took less than a minute.

"Here's the deal," Cole said. "I want your vehicle."

"Why?"

Cole released him. "You have to stay here and deal with poor old Frank. And I have someplace to go."

"I'm urging you to turn yourself in. I can't call off the manhunt. Every cop in the state is looking for you, and they are authorized to use force."

"I'm not walking away from this assignment until it's done," Cole said. "Now it's time for you to trust me."

When Prescott leaned down to pick his parka off the floor, he reached for his ankle holster.

Anticipating the move, Cole already had the gun he'd slipped from Prescott's holster pointed in his face. *Checkmate.*

Chapter 16

Fat snowflakes splatted against the windshield of Prescott's four-wheel-drive SUV. A nice vehicle for driving in the snow; Cole understood why Prescott was willing to fight instead of handing over the keys.

As soon as they got into the car, he'd searched the glove box and found nothing but a neat packet containing registration and proof of insurance. Prescott was a careful man. A career agent. He hadn't given up any information, except the part about him being a liaison and knowing people in the area. Somehow that had to be useful.

Though this storm was nowhere near as violent as the blizzard, Cole hated driving through it. He gripped the steering wheel with both hands, willing the tires not to slip on the snow-packed road leading away from Grand Lake. On the plus side, the bad weather was keeping cars off the road. If anybody followed them, the tail-lights would be easy to spot.

Rachel held his cell phone but hadn't yet dialed. "I don't want to drag Jim Loughlin into this mess. Cole, it's getting worse and worse. You assaulted a federal officer."

"I *am* a federal officer," he said. "A damn better one than Prescott. And we need your friend to help us."

"Why?"

"I'm pretty sure this nice SUV has GPS. Prescott can track our location."

His plan was to drop off Prescott's car at the house where they were attacked. Like it or not, the feds and the cops would be forced to look at that house and to realize the murders had been committed there. Even a rudimentary crime-scene analysis would show evidence of a major assault. Their investigation would take a different direction—leading *away* from them.

Unfortunately, when the cops checked the property records, they'd see the connection between Xavier Romero and Baron. If Cole wanted to get information from Romero, he needed to contact him before Prescott and his men closed in.

Rachel asked, "What do you want Loughlin to do?"

"Ask him to meet us at the house. He's already been there so he knows the location. I want him to give us a lift."

"Where to?"

"How much he wants to be involved is up to him. Make the call, Rachel. The alternative is another hike through the snow." He dared to take his eyes off the road for an instant to glance at her. "You don't want that, do you?"

As she made the call, he followed the route that he vaguely remembered from the first time the gang went to the house where three of them had died. Navigating in the mountains on these twisting roads that were half-hidden by snow took 90 percent of his concentration. With the other 10 percent, he figured out what they should do next.

Initially, he'd thought they would find Penny's friend, Jenna Cambridge, in Granby and pick up the bundles of cash to use as evidence. Now, it was more imperative to hightail it over to Black Hawk to see Xavier Romero. In the past, the old snitch had helped Cole out with information. Romero might be able to cut through the crap and give him Baron's name.

It was becoming obvious that the only way Cole would end this assignment successfully was to apprehend Baron by himself and turn him over to the cops.

"Okay," Rachel said, "Loughlin will meet us at the house."

"Good." He made a left turn. Was this the route? He wished like hell that he was driving on a clean, paved, well-marked California freeway.

"What's going to happen next?"

"I'm going to have a talk with Xavier Romero."

"In Black Hawk? You can't ask Loughlin to drive all the way to Black Hawk."

"I'm hoping he'll loan us his car."

"That's a lot to ask," she said. "He could be charged with aiding and abetting fugitives."

"If we were criminals, he'd be in trouble. But we're not. Remember? We're the good guys."

"I'm an upstanding citizen, but I'm not so sure about you."

That wasn't the way she'd felt when they were lying in each other's arms. She'd snuggled intimately beside him. They were one. Not anymore.

In the real world—the one where she lived in snow-ridden Colorado and he resided in sunny California—he and Rachel were very different people. He lived by deception, and she couldn't tell a lie to save her life. He was no stranger to violence; she was a healer. Different.

And yet, there was a level where they matched perfectly. He didn't quite understand the connection. In a way, she filled in the places where he was lacking. And vice versa.

She gave him a solid grounding. He gave her…excitement. She'd never admit it, but he'd seen the fire in her eyes. Every time they'd been at risk, she had risen to the challenge. He wanted her with him, didn't trust her safety to anyone else, not even Loughlin. But he couldn't ask her to continue on this dangerous path. He needed to do what was right for her.

When he recognized a road sign, he almost cheered. They were headed in the right direction. "This might be a good time for you to take shelter. When I go to Black Hawk, you could stay with the Loughlins."

"Are you trying to get rid of me?"

"I'm trying to keep you safe. Think about it."

Their tire tracks blazed the first trail through the new snow piling up on the road. He would have worried about being followed if that hadn't been his intention; he wanted the cops to come to this house.

"I'm thinking," she said. "If I stay with the Lough-lins, I'm putting them in danger. Those guys who attacked the house are still out there."

"The odds are in your favor. Nobody has reason to suspect you'd be with a deputy sheriff."

"But if they guess…" She exhaled a sigh. "This isn't about being safe and smart. Here's the truth. I want to come with you."

He didn't understand, but he liked her decision. "Because?"

"Are you going to make me say it?"

"Oh, yeah."

"I care about you, Cole. I can't imagine being apart from you, sitting around and worrying. Too much of my life has been wasted with sensible decisions. I'm going to follow my heart and stick with you."

He couldn't remember another time when he'd been a heartfelt choice. "I care about you, too."

"Besides," she said, "I can help. You need a partner."

"I've always worked alone."

"Things change."

He made the last turn into the driveway outside the house, put the car in Park but left the engine running. He turned toward her. In the dim illumination from the dashboard, he saw her smile. "Clearly, you've lost your mind."

"Clearly."

He unfastened her seat belt and pulled her toward him. "I'm so damn glad."

When Jim Loughlin pulled up in his four-wheel-drive Jeep, Rachel made a quick introduction. Cole sat in the passenger seat, and she got into the back. During their time on the run, she'd grown accustomed to the way they looked. Their clothes were filthy, bloodstained and torn from catching on branches. Cole's stubble was turning into a full beard. They might as well have the word *fugitive* branded across their foreheads.

Loughlin glanced over his shoulder at her and shook his head. "Hard to believe you're the same woman who helped my sweet Caitlyn into this world."

A lot had changed since then. "How's she doing? Is Sarah okay?"

"They're both great, especially since my mom went home." He put the Jeep in gear and pulled away from the house where the killing had taken place.

Cole said, "I appreciate your help."

"I'd do just about anything for Rachel." He expertly swung onto the road. "She seems to like you. That makes you okay in my book. But I'm hoping you've decided to turn yourselves in and end this."

"I'd like to pack it in," Cole said, "but we're still not safe. There's a traitor in the FBI network. He's working with Baron, and he's not going to let us live. We know too much."

From the backseat, Rachel said, "We need a favor. You don't have to say yes. I'm only asking."

Loughlin drove for a long minute in silence while he considered. She knew this was a hard decision for him. On one hand was his duty as a deputy. On the other was his innate sense of what was right and wrong. Did he believe in her enough to go along with them?

In his deep rumbling voice, Loughlin said, "Name it."

"We need to get to Black Hawk," she said. "We have to talk to a man who—"

"Don't tell me why. I don't want to know." He held up his hand to forestall further conversation. "I can't take you there on account of I need to stay with Sarah and the baby. But you can use my car."

"There's one more thing," Cole said. "We need clothes."

"You're right about that," Loughlin said. "When we get to my house, I'll pull into the garage. You stay here in the car, and I'll bring some stuff down to you. I haven't told Sarah about any of this, and I don't intend to."

"Thanks," Cole said. "I'd be happy to pay you."

"Don't want your money," he grumbled. "Use it to make a donation to Rachel's clinic."

She unhooked her seat belt, leaned forward and gave Loughlin a kiss on the cheek. "You're a good guy."

"Or a crazy one."

She grinned. "There seems to be a lot of that going around."

Settling back into her seat, Rachel realized that she was feeling positive. Crazy? Oh, yeah. Ever since Cole kidnapped her, she'd been caught up in a sort of madness—an emotional tempest that plunged to the depth of terror and then soared. Their passion was unlike anything she'd ever experienced. She wanted to be with him forever, to follow him to the ends of the earth, in spite of the peril. *The very real peril.* She couldn't let herself forget that they were still the subjects of a manhunt, not to mention being sought by Baron's murderous thugs. And they were on their way to chat with a snitch.

None of the other bad boys she'd dated came close to Cole when it came to danger. Why was she grinning?

She only halfway listened to the conversation from the two men in the front of the Jeep. Cole was telling Loughlin about Prescott's role as an FBI liaison.

"He claimed," Cole said, "that he'd met a lot of people in Grand County."

"I recall that some years back there was an FBI agent who talked at a couple of town councils when we had a problem with militia groups setting up camp in the back country."

"Can you think of any other connections he might have?"

"Maybe church meetings. Or Boy Scouts. The idea is to give folks a face—a real live person they can call at the FBI. We do the same thing at the sheriff's department. Right now, we've got a program to get teenagers off their damn cell phones when they're driving."

Rachel had a brain flash. "The high school."

"What's that?" Cole asked.

"Prescott could have given an informational talk at the high school. I do those programs all the time. The teachers love it when I show up. It gives them a free period."

If Prescott had come to Granby High School when Penny was a student there, he could have met her. Through Penny, he might have linked up with Baron.

In deference to Loughlin's wishes not to know any more about what they were doing than absolutely necessary, she said nothing more, but her mind kept turning.

As soon as they were parked in Loughlin's two-car garage and she was alone with Cole, she said, "What if Prescott met Penny at the high school? Then she introduced him to Baron."

"Interesting theory. But I don't think Penny was a teenage criminal mastermind."

"From what she told me and what her mother said, she was wild. The kind of kid who gets into trouble."

Instead of pursuing her line of thinking, he grinned. "They say it takes one to know one. Were you a wild child?"

"I had my share of adventures," she admitted. "And really bad luck with the guys I dated."

"Bad boys. Like me."

He left the passenger seat and came around to open her door. In the glare from the overhead light, she realized how truly ratty and beat up his clothes were. In spite of the grime and the scruffy beard, she liked the way he looked. One hundred percent masculine.

She slid off the seat and into his arms. Looking up at him, she said, "You're not a bad boy. Dangerous? Yes. But not bad."

His long, slow kiss sent a heat wave through her veins. Definitely not bad.

Before their kiss progressed into something inappropriate, Loughlin returned to the garage with fresh clothing. He set the pile of coats, shoes and clothing on his cluttered workbench against the back wall and turned to Rachel. "Could I talk to you in private?"

She went with him through the garage door into a back hallway. "What is it?"

He took both her hands in his and leaned down to peer into her eyes. In a low whisper, he asked, "Is this really what you want? To go with Cole?"

"Yes."

"Rachel, you could get hurt."

"It's worth the risk. *Cole* is worth it."

"You just met this man a couple of days ago," Loughlin said. "You've only known him for a matter of hours."

But she wanted to believe that Cole was the man she'd been looking for all her life. She'd gone through a string of losers—so many that she'd almost given up on men altogether. If she didn't take this chance, she'd regret it. "I'm sure."

He pulled her into a bear hug. "I trust your instincts, girl. Try to be careful."

"I will." His concern touched her. He and Sarah and their baby were like family to her. "Your friendship means a lot."

"Just don't wreck my car. Okay?"

She returned to the garage to find Cole dressed in fresh jeans and a cream-colored turtleneck. Though Loughlin was heavier than Cole, they were the same height. The new outfit was a decent fit.

"A major improvement," she said. "Except for the scruffy beard."

"I thought you liked the rugged mountain-man thing."

"But you're not a mountain man. You're a clean-shaven dude from California."

"Apparently, your friend thinks so, too." He held up an electric razor. "I'm not sure if I should shave. The cops have probably circulated ID photos of me. I don't want to be recognized. On the other hand, a beard could attract closer scrutiny. It's an obvious disguise."

She hadn't considered photos. "Will they have a picture of me?"

"It's possible. But, as you pointed out before, a lot of people in this area know you. If they saw your photo, they'd suspect something was wrong with the manhunt."

"I hope you're right. There's nothing I can do with my short hair except put on a wig or a hat."

He held up a wool knit Sherpa hat with ear flaps. "Ta da."

"I love these." She grabbed it and put it on. "Mmm. Warm."

"Warm and damn cute." He gave her a grin. "I was thinking about your theory of Prescott meeting Penny at the high school."

"And?"

"What was the first thing he asked when he found us?"

He had wanted to know about Goldie, wanted to know that she was safe. His concern for the infant was apparent. "The baby."

"Why? Why would that be his first question?"

"He could be the father."

Agent Wayne Prescott might be Baron.

Chapter 17

As they drove to a lower elevation, they left the snowstorm behind. Rachel gazed through the passenger-side window at pinprick stars in the clear night sky. Leaning back in the comfortable seat, she listened to the hum of the Jeep's tires on clear pavement. The only sign of the blizzard that had paralyzed Grand County was a frosting of white on moonlit trees and the rocky walls of the canyon leading to Black Hawk.

The more temperate weather had an obvious effect on Cole, the California guy. His mood was more contemplative. His death grip on the steering wheel had relaxed. The worry lines across his forehead smoothed, and he was almost smiling. With his left hand, he massaged his clean-shaven jaw. Losing the beard made him appear less ferocious and more handsome.

Jim Loughlin had been right when he said she didn't know much about Cole. Even when they were making love, he hadn't talked about his past. Did she want to know? Did she really want to see Cole as more than a casual affair?

Connecting to him on a deeper level was dangerous. He hadn't represented himself as relationship material. Sure, there were the occasional hints that he'd like to see more of her. But nothing he'd said—not one single word—resembled a commitment.

On the other hand, she had taken the ultimate risk when she had unprotected sex with him. Caught up in the whirlwind of their passion, she'd made that decision. Maybe not the smartest thing she'd ever done. Didn't she give lectures to high school classes on exactly this topic? No condom means no sex.

She'd broken her own rule.

For the first time.

Wow.

With other boyfriends, even men she thought she was in love with, she had never once taken that chance. Clearly, there was something special about Cole and she needed to know more about him.

Clearing her throat, she asked, "Did you grow up in California?"

"Mostly."

Not a very revealing answer. She'd have to be more specific. "Where were you born?"

"Vegas."

Now they might be getting somewhere. Cole was in his thirties. When he was born, Las Vegas had been more decadent and edgy than it was now. "Did your parents work in the casinos?"

"Nope."

Another one word response. *Great.* "How long did you live there?"

He turned his head toward her. Moonlight through the windshield shone on the sculpted line of his jaw. "There's no need for you to go on a fishing expedition. If there's something specific you want to know about me, just ask."

"I'm curious," she said. "I want to get an idea of where you came from. How did you grow up to be an undercover FBI agent? What were you like as a kid?"

"I always played with guns." He grinned. "My mom wouldn't let me or my younger brother bring our violent toys into the house. She was a pacifist. A grade school teacher."

"And your father?"

"Dad was a preacher in Vegas—a reformed gambler who started his own church. I can't remember the name of it, but there was a lot of 'repent and be saved' going on."

"You were a preacher's kid." She wouldn't have guessed that background. "If the stereotypes hold true, that means you were either annoyingly perfect or a holy terror."

"I didn't have time to get settled into either personality. I was only five when my parents split up. Marrying my mother and having kids went along with Dad's preacher identity. But it didn't last."

"He went back to gambling," she guessed.

"It turned out that he had a lot of loyal followers, and they donated bundles of cash to build a new rec hall for the church. Dad thought the Lord might help him find a greater contribution in the casinos. Apparently, God was looking the other way."

"He lost the money."

"Not all of it, but a significant portion. The crazy thing was that he admitted what he'd done, and his followers forgave him. Mom wasn't so easy to con. She divorced him and moved us to Los Angeles."

"Did your dad stay in Vegas?"

"For a while. After he paid back the money, he handed over the church to his assistant and devoted himself full-time to gambling. He does okay. He paid child support and stayed in touch with the family. Whenever he showed up, he always had big extravagant presents."

She was beginning to have a context for understanding Cole. "Were you more like your dad or your mom?"

"I've got a bit of the con man in me," he admitted.

"Which is why you're so good at going undercover."

"But I get my sense of fair play and loyalty from my mom. I never once heard her say a bad thing about my father. She remarried several years ago and moved to Oregon."

"And your brother?"

"He's a fireman. Happily married with two little girls whom I love to spoil."

"By showing up with big extravagant presents?"

He shot her a glance. "I never thought of it that way. Maybe I'm more like my dad than I realize."

"Do you gamble?"

"I'm a hell of a good poker player, but I don't have the sickness. I hate losing too much."

They were on the last curving stretch of road through the canyon that led to Black Hawk. The roads were pristine—well-maintained by casino and hotel owners who wanted to make the trip easy and smooth.

"What we're doing right now is a gamble," she pointed out. "You're taking a chance on being recognized at a casino where you committed a robbery."

"I was wearing a ski mask. Nobody saw my face."

"What if the police put out a photo of you?"

"I've got new identification from the papers I had sewn inside my leather jacket." He shrugged. "If somebody thinks they saw me before, I can talk my way around it."

She wished she had half his confidence. If somebody accused her of being one of the fugitives the FBI was looking for, she'd fall apart. "And what should I do?"

"Say as little as possible. I'm going to introduce you as my associate, even though most FBI agents tend to wear more conservative attire."

The clothing she'd borrowed from Sarah Loughlin was a size too small. The jeans hugged her bottom, and the pink knit top stretched tightly across her breasts. Even the lavender parka was fitted at the waist. Rachel missed her oversize practical parka. "Too cutesy?"

"Not if you put on the cap with the ear flaps."

"Then I would definitely be too dorky," she said. "Should I have a different name? Can I be Special Agent Angelina?"

"It's better if you have a name you can relate to. Do you have a nickname?"

"My youngest brother calls me Rocky."

"Short for Rachel. I like it. For the last name, let's use the street where you lived as a kid."

"Logan. Call me Special Agent Rocky Logan."

He grinned. "Xavier thinks my name is Calvin Spade. I met him a long time ago, probably eight years, when he was involved in an illegal gambling operation in Culver City. I went in as a card shark, and I did okay in a couple of tournaments. Then I recruited Xavier as a snitch."

She was beginning to feel apprehensive. "I've never been good at lying. Maybe my identity should be something more familiar. Like a nurse."

He reached over and stroked her cheek. "Don't try to play a role. Just be yourself. Go along with whatever I say."

"Roll with the punches."

"Let's hope it doesn't come to that."

The lights of Black Hawk glittered against the dark slopes and the surrounding forest. Extralarge new casinos and parking structures bumped up against the older buildings that had been part of the historic town before limited stakes gambling was legalized here and in neighboring Central City.

Xavier's casino—the Stampede—was at the quiet end of town away from the new casinos. Cole parked at the far end of the half-full lot. On a weekday night at eleven o'clock, there weren't many cars.

He killed the headlights and turned to her. "If you want, you can stay in the car. I don't expect this to take too long."

Pulling off an undercover identity was daunting, but she wanted to do it. The best way to understand Cole was to see him in action. "I'm ready. Let's go."

As they walked through the crisp night to the casino that appeared to be in a renovated barn, she noticed his sense of humor falling away from him. His posture shifted. His shoulders seemed wider. His height, more impressive.

Trying to match his cool attitude, she narrowed her eyes to a squint. *Agent Rocky Logan is on the job. Bad guys, beware.*

The interior of the casino was similar to an Old West saloon. Rows of slot machines blinked and made clinking noises as though money was pouring out of them. In truth, there were only a few people at the slots. Most of the patrons were huddled around the poker tables.

Cole strode up to the bar. He ordered a couple of beers and asked the bartender—who sported an old-fashioned handlebar mustache—where he could find the old man, Xavier Romero. "Tell him Calvin Spade wants to talk."

The bartender left his post and went through an un-marked door at the rear of the casino. Her apprehension was turning into full-blown anxiety. Her hand trembled as she lifted the beer to her lips. What if Xavier was calling the cops? What if Baron's armed thugs charged out of the back room?

Cole gave her arm a nudge. When she looked up at him, she saw a flash of the familiar Cole—the guy she knew and trusted. He gave her a wink. "It's going to be all right."

She wanted to believe him, but she'd used those very words often when she was dealing with a difficult labor. *It's going to be all right.* An empty reassurance. The pain always got worse before it got better.

When the bartender returned, a short man with white hair and black-rimmed glasses trotted at his heels. He was solidly built but light on his feet. He came to a stop in front of Cole and did a two-fisted handshake. When he smiled, she saw the gleam of a gold tooth.

"It's been a long time." Xavier's voice was a whisper. He swung toward her. "Who's the broad?"

"My associate, Rocky Logan," Cole said. "This is Xavier Romero."

He took her hand and raised it to his lips. "Charmed. When he says 'associate' does he mean you're—"

"We work at the same place," Cole said. "I want to talk to you in private."

Xavier stepped back and gave them both a golden

grin. "Take a look around, buddy boy. Finally got my own place. And it's legit."

"The Stampede," Cole said drily. "I never figured you for a cowboy-themed casino."

"Yippee-ki-yay."

Cole said, "I didn't come to talk about the decor."

"We had some good times, you and me. Remember that Texas Hold 'em tournament in Culver City? When I was dating that sweet little redheaded dealer?"

"Didn't come to reminisce, either."

"You were always impatient. Good things come to those who wait. I'm living proof. Seventy years old, and my dream finally comes true."

If she hadn't known that Xavier was involved with Baron and in the midst of a scheme to defraud his insurance company, she would have liked the old man.

Cole pushed away from the bar. "We'll go to your office. Giddyap."

Though she thought he was being unnecessarily rude, Rachel fell into step behind him. There wasn't enough room between the tables and the slot machines to walk side by side. Xavier hustled to the front of their little parade. He used a key card to open the door and ushered them into a wide hallway with paneled walls and framed sepia photographs of old-time Black Hawk and the gold rush prospectors who populated the town.

The door to his office was open, and Xavier guided them inside. In addition to his cluttered desk, there were a couple of leather sofas and an octagonal poker table covered in green felt. The scent of cigar smoke hung in the air, and she suspected that smoking wasn't the only law that had been broken in this room.

The overhead light, unlike the dimness of the casino, showed a road map of wrinkles on Xavier's face.

He sat at the poker table and picked up a deck of cards. "Have a seat."

Cole positioned himself facing the door. "Tell me how you know Baron."

Xavier shuffled the cards with stunning expertise. "Let's play a little five-card stud. No reason we can't be civilized while we talk."

"The last time I played you," Cole said, "I won."

"Give me a chance to get even. If you win again, I'll tell you whatever you want to know."

Cole took the cards from his hand and passed them to her. "Rocky deals."

She knew how to play poker but wasn't an expert. If Cole was expecting her to cheat and give him winning cards, he'd be sorely disappointed. She cut the cards twice and palmed the deck. "Five cards, facedown."

Xavier fixed her with a steady gaze. "Have you been with Calvin long?"

Calvin? Oh, yeah, that was Cole's alias. "Long enough," she said as she dealt.

He tapped his gold tooth with the tip of his index finger. Unlike his weathered face, his hands were smooth. His fingernails, buffed to perfection. "I'm surprised," he said, "to see Calvin with a partner. He usually works alone."

"Things change," Cole said.

"Indeed." Xavier chuckled. "I used to be a petty crook. Now I'm a casino owner."

"Hard to believe that a wheeler-dealer like you is completely legit." He glanced at his cards and turned them facedown on the table. "How did you put together the money to open this place?"

"I know people."

"Baron?"

Xavier checked his cards, pulled out two and slid them toward her. "Hit me."

Cole held up his hand, indicating that he didn't need any more cards. "I'm thinking that you might have used property for collateral to raise cash. A house near Shadow Mountain Lake."

"Or maybe I gambled big in the big game, the stock market. And maybe I was smart enough to get out before the crash." Xavier's wrinkles settled into an expressionless poker face. "If you win this hand, I'll tell you one fact. Then we can play for another and—"

"All or nothing," Cole said. "You don't have much time. All I want is information on Baron. The feds that are going to show up here after me won't be so gentle."

"You? Gentle?" He shook his head. "If I win this hand, you tell me what you know. Then get the hell out."

"I don't lose." Cole's hands on the table were steady. His deep-set eyes radiated confidence. "I'll tell you this for free. Your house near Shadow Mountain Lake was being used as a hideout. People were killed there."

Xavier blinked. "The idiots who robbed my place?"

"The gang was at your house. Not even the dumbest pencil-pushing fed is going to believe that was a coincidence. You were in on the robbery."

"This isn't happening." The old man shook his head slowly. "You're lying. Trying to bluff me."

"Not this time."

Cole turned over his cards. Full house, jacks over tens.

Chapter 18

The only sure way to win at poker was to cheat, and Cole had been learning card tricks from his less-than-holy father before he could read and write. When he'd taken the deck from Xavier, straightened the edges and passed it to Rachel, he'd palmed the cards necessary to play a winning hand.

A simple move. Cole assumed Xavier had been planning to deal himself a winner from the bottom of the deck, so he took those five cards. Voilà! A full house.

Winning was convenient, but he didn't really need that nudge. Xavier was ready to talk; the threat of an FBI investigation into his connection to known criminals had already loosened his lips. He readily admitted that he'd been in touch with Baron when he set up his initial financing. Further, he said that he'd agreed to the casino robbery, knowing that he could claim his missing cash from the insurance company.

"Then everything went wrong," Xavier said. "One of my moron security guards—a guy who's usually asleep in a back room—got trigger happy. Somebody else pulled the alarm."

Cole knew how badly the robbery had been botched. He'd been there. "On the surface, the shoot-out makes it look like you double-crossed Baron."

"It wasn't my fault. I swear it."

Having experienced Baron's wrath when his men peppered the Shadow Mountain Lake house with bullets, Cole was surprised that Xavier wasn't already dead. "There's another piece to the robbery. You're running an insurance scam of your own. You put in a claim for double the amount that was stolen."

"What?"

"You heard me."

Xavier's poker face crumpled. "There's only one way you could know how much was stolen. You were part of the gang."

In order to extract information, Cole needed to balance truth with deception. He had to apply the right amount of pressure and not show his own disadvantages.

Leaning across the table toward Xavier, he said, "You weren't surprised to see me when I walked in the door. You already knew I was one of the robbers. The feds have already sent you my mug shot."

A twitch at the corner of Xavier's mouth confirmed the statement. *He knew.*

Cole continued, "I infiltrated the gang. I was working undercover."

Though confident in his ability to manipulate the old man, Cole had a weak spot, and her name was Special

Agent Rocky Logan. Rachel had already told him that she was a lousy liar. He couldn't predict what she'd say.

Apparently, Xavier realized the same thing. He turned toward her and glared through his thick glasses. "What about you, pretty lady? Where do you fit in?"

She narrowed her big blue eyes to a squint—an expression that she probably thought made her look tough. Cole thought she was adorable.

"I advise you to listen to my partner," she said. "He's trying to help you."

"Is he?"

Cole said, "I've got a soft spot when it comes to you, Xavier. A long time ago, you pointed me in the right direction. Do the same thing now. Tell me about Baron."

Xavier leaned back in his chair. "I've never met the man in person. I couldn't ID him if he walked through the door right now. And I don't know where he lives. When I talked to him on the phone, the calls were untraceable."

"It's hard to believe you set up complicated financial dealings without a meeting."

"His secretary handled the paperwork."

Secretary? "You met the secretary?"

"Sure did, but I can't give you a good description. She was wearing a wig and a ton of makeup. Nice breasts, though. She showed plenty of cleavage."

The makeup sounded like Penny. She applied it with a trowel. "How about her age?"

"The older I get," Xavier said, "the younger the ladies look to me. I'd guess that she was in her thirties."

"When did you see her last?"

"A couple of weeks ago. She was with a pregnant woman."

Therefore, the secretary was *not* Penny. Then who? Cole had been part of the gang at that time, but he'd never come to Black Hawk with Penny. A memory clicked in the back of his mind: Pearl had mentioned meeting her daughter here.

Was Penny's mother working for Baron? He didn't want to believe that he'd been so blinded by guilt about Penny's murder that he'd handed over the baby to another crook. When he'd looked into Pearl's eyes, he hadn't seen a hint of deception. She'd been heartbroken about her daughter's death and ecstatic about her new grandbaby. "Did she wear jewelry? Maybe a string of pearls."

Rachel gasped. If she hadn't been thinking of Pearl, she was now.

Xavier pointed to his nicely manicured hands. "Just an engagement ring. A diamond. Not too flashy."

That didn't sound like Penny's mother. She hadn't been wearing an engagement ring when they saw her. Who was this mystery woman? Finding her was the key to finding Baron.

"I played square with you," Xavier said. "What are you going to do to help me?"

"I suggest you call your insurance company and tell them you made a mistake about the amount of money stolen. They haven't made a payout yet. They might let you off the hook."

"Or refuse to pay." Behind his glasses, his eyes darkened. "I need that money to keep going. The whole gang is dead except for you. If you could see your way clear to—"

"Can't do it," Cole said. "We have the loot."

The lie slipped easily off his tongue. But Rachel wasn't so calm. She fidgeted.

And Xavier noticed her nervous move. He zeroed in on her. "Do you? Have the money?"

Before she could stammer out an unconvincing answer, Cole rose from the green felt table. "We're going."

Rachel dropped the cards and stood. Her hands were trembling.

"You don't have the cash," Xavier said. "Baron's procedure is to get the money away from the robbers as soon as possible so they won't get greedy."

"We know where it is," Rachel said. "In a safe place."

The old man sprang to his feet with shocking agility for a man of his years. "Take me with you. If I can turn in the money and prove that I'm working with the good guys, I could get out of this okay."

"Not a chance," Cole said.

"For old times' sake," he pleaded. "We've got history together. I know your friends. Whatever happened to your buddy from Vegas? That old guy named McClure?"

Moving swiftly and deliberately, Cole came around the table and took Rachel's arm. As soon as he touched her, he knew he'd made a mistake. Xavier would see that his relationship to her was more than a professional association.

He rushed her toward the door. To Xavier, he said, "I'll take care of you."

Instead of making their way through the tables and slot machines in the front of the casino, Cole went to the rear. He pulled Rachel with him through a back door, setting off a screeching alarm.

They ran to Loughlin's Jeep, dove inside and pulled

out of the parking lot. As they were driving away, he saw the local police converge on the Stampede casino.

Rachel held her breath as Cole eased out of the casino parking lot with his headlights dark. How could he see? Moonlight wasn't enough.

Sensing a turn, he whipped onto a side road that led past a row of houses. He turned again and headed uphill. The headlights flashed on. He took another turn and another, still climbing. Without snow on the road, his driving skills were expert but scary. She averted her gaze so she couldn't see the speedometer as he fishtailed around a hairpin turn and started a descent. He flew down the narrow canyon road as fast as an alpine skier on the last run of the day.

Across an open field, he drove into forested land. The tall pine trees closed around them, and he slowed.

She exhaled. "How many times in your life have you made dramatic getaways?"

"Often."

Her heart thumped so furiously that she thought her rib cage might explode. Her fingers clenched in a knot. Her skin prickled with an excess of adrenaline. Clearly, she wasn't cut out for undercover work.

Not like Cole. He didn't show the least sign of nervousness. Not now. And not in the casino. The whole time he'd been baiting Xavier, his aura of cool confidence had been unshaken. "How do you do this?"

"Not very well," he muttered.

"You're kidding, right? You were like an old-time riverboat gambler. Sooooo smooth. Always one step ahead, even in that weird poker game. You cheated, right?"

"Yeah."

"If I wasn't familiar with the facts, I wouldn't have known when you were lying and when you were telling the truth. How did you learn to bluff like that?"

"Blame it on genetics. When I first joined the FBI, one of the shrinks told me that I was uniquely suited to undercover work because of my innate behavioral makeup. He gave me a battery of tests, including a lie detector, which I faked out."

"Not surprised," she muttered.

"It seems that I'm a natural born risk-seeker. Most people are risk-averse, more cautious."

"That would be me," she said.

"Not from what you've told me about your boy-friends."

"Okay, maybe I have a risk-seeking lapse when it comes to men. But I'm careful in every other area."

"Being an EMT? Riding in an ambulance?"

"I left that work." Because she couldn't stand the pain of failure. "In every other way, I'm careful."

"And yet, you're riding in a getaway car. You could have backed out at the Loughlins', but you chose to come with me."

She had to admit that he had a point. They weren't total opposites but definitely not peas in a pod. For one thing, she couldn't tell a convincing lie to save her life. "The way you handled Xavier was amazing. You played him."

"But I slipped up," he said. "When we were leaving the room, I took your arm. That's not the kind of gesture I'd use with another FBI agent. And you can bet that Xavier saw that I wanted to protect you. He's no dummy. The old guy knows you're important to me."

"And that's a bad thing?"

"It's a tell," he said. "Like in poker. You never want your opponents to know what you're thinking. I let him see that you're important to me."

In a way, she was touched. In spite of the con, he couldn't keep himself from responding to her. She looked down at her lap and pried her fingers apart. Then she reached toward him. When her hand touched his smoothly shaven cheek, he glanced toward her and grinned.

In that instant of eye contact, she saw his defenses slip away. He really did care about her. She whispered, "What are we going to do for the rest of the night?"

"There are plenty of hotels in Black Hawk and Central City, but they're well-run and organized. The desk clerks might have my photo posted in front of their computers, especially after our escape from the Stampede."

"Right." She frowned. "Why exactly did you rush me out the back door?"

"I had an edgy feeling. When we first saw Xavier, he seemed to be stalling. Maybe he called somebody."

"But when we left, he wanted to come with us."

"I changed his mind," Cole said. "For tonight, I'm thinking of a small motel, a mom-and-pop operation."

Though she was glad that he wasn't planning to drive straight through to Granby and confront Jenna Cambridge, she asked, "Should we go after the money tonight?"

"Too tired. My slip with Xavier showed me that I'm not at the top of my game. I've got to be sharp when we go back to Granby."

Granby. Her home base. She would have loved to take him to her comfy condo, but she was well aware that her home was dangerous. The hunt for them was still active.

"I'm thinking," he said, "that Jenna might be Baron's mysterious secretary."

The same idea had occurred to Rachel. "It makes sense. Penny said that she met Baron at the high school where Jenna teaches."

"If she's the secretary, we could be walking into a trap at her house. Tomorrow is Friday. Jenna will be at the high school, and we'll have a chance to search her place for evidence without interference."

When Penny had talked about her supposed friend, she'd never mentioned a connection with Baron. Though Rachel hated to think ill of the dead, Penny hadn't been very perceptive. She'd cast Jenna in the role of a homely girl who needed advice on makeup and clothing—a nonentity, a sidekick.

The pattern was familiar. A flashy blonde like Penny always seemed to have a dull-as-dishwater friend tagging along. An accurate picture?

Penny's mother also considered Jenna to be a friend, until she found out that Jenna encouraged her daughter's relationship with Baron.

Cole cleared his throat. "There's another woman I suspect."

"Pearl."

Rachel hated that alternative. "If Pearl was working with Baron, why wouldn't she have told him we were hiding at Lily Belle's? We were there all day. His thugs could have attacked us at any time."

He nodded. "My gut tells me Pearl is innocent. But that might be wishful thinking. I've got to believe that Goldie is safe."

"Pearl won't hurt the baby," she said with certainty. "As soon as she took Goldie into her arms, she was in love, and there's nothing stronger than the bond that forms with an infant."

"I'll call her tomorrow morning," he said. "If she's working for Baron, I'll find out."

"How?"

He shrugged. "It'll come to me."

In other words, he would come up with a convincing lie. His talent for deception and manipulation was a bit unnerving; she couldn't be certain of anything he said to her. "Can you teach me how to lie?"

"Why would I do that? I like your honesty."

She wasn't so sure. The truth might be her downfall.

Chapter 19

The adobe-style motel with a blinking vacancy sign promised low rates for skiers. Since nearby Eldora was one of the closest ski runs to Denver, not many people stayed in the area overnight. There were only four other vehicles parked outside the twelve units.

When Rachel entered room number nine, she felt oddly shy. Though she and Cole had spent the afternoon making passionate love, staying at a motel was different—not because there was a comfortable-looking bed or a shower with hot water. Tonight was planned; they intended to sleep together, and she couldn't claim that she'd been carried away by the drama of the moment. Being here with him represented a deliberate choice. A decision she'd regret?

Every step closer to him deepened the feelings that were building inside her, and it was hard to keep those emotions from turning into something that resembled love. She couldn't make that mistake. Cole wasn't made for a serious relationship. Ultimately, he'd go back to California and leave her in the mountains. They had no future. None at all.

While she opened a greasy bag of fried chicken they'd picked up at a drive-through, Cole did a poor man's version of surveillance and security. He checked the window in the small but clean bathroom to make sure they had an escape route. Then he shoved the dresser in front of the door.

"What if the bad guys climb in through the bathroom window?" she asked as she pulled out a bag of fries and a deep-fried chunk of white meat.

"They won't," he said. "The lock on the front door is so pitiful that a toddler could kick it open."

"Hence the dresser blockade."

He posted himself at the edge of the front window curtain to watch the parking lot. "Pass me a thigh."

"I had you figured for a breast man."

"I start with the thigh and savor the breast." He tossed her a grin. "But you already know that."

Earlier when they'd made love, she noticed that he paid particular attention to her breasts. The memory tickled her senses. "Have you always been that way? I mean, with other women?"

"You're starting again with the questions." He mimicked her tone and added, "Do you always give men the third degree?"

She washed down a bite of chicken with watery soda. "In the normal course of events, I don't jump into bed with somebody I've only known for a couple of days.

There's a period of time when we talk and become familiar with each other."

"Is that so?"

"You might have heard of the concept. It's called dating."

"Touché."

Even though he spent a lot of time undercover, it was hard to believe that a good-looking, eligible guy like Cole hadn't gotten himself hooked once or twice. She asked, "Have you ever had a serious girlfriend? Someone you lived with?"

"You mean like settling down? It's not my thing."

"You must have a home base. A bachelor pad."

"I pay rent on an apartment, but I hardly ever spend time there. It took me over a year to hang pictures on the walls."

She knew exactly what he was talking about. One of her brothers was the same way. He lived in a square little room with a beat-up futon and used pizza boxes for a coffee table. "Sounds lonely."

"Sometimes." He peeked around the edge of the curtain and sighed. "I wish I could have a dog."

Great! His idea of a long-term commitment was canine. "What kind of dog?"

"Border collie," he said without hesitation. "They're smart and fast. And would come in handy if I ever wanted to herd sheep."

Dragging information from Cole was like trying to empty Grand Lake with a teaspoon. "Is that a secret fantasy? Being a shepherd?"

"There are times when I wouldn't mind having a ranch to tend and a couple of acres. Not heavy-duty farming but a place away from the crowds. A quiet place. Peaceful. Where I could raise…stuff." He gnawed at his chicken and avoided looking her in the eye. "Someday, I want to have a family. When I hang out with my nieces, I get this feeling. An attachment."

She remembered his look of wonderment when Goldie was born and his gentleness when he fed the baby her bottle. Maybe this undercover agent wasn't such a confirmed loner, after all. If so, she was glad. Cole was a good man who deserved the comforts of home—a safe haven after his razor-edge assignments.

But was that what he really wanted? A niggling doubt skulked in the shadows of her mind. He might be lying, saying words he knew she wanted to hear. Deception was second nature to him, innate.

Fearful of probing more deeply, she changed the subject. "How long are you going to stand at the window?"

He checked his wristwatch. "Another twenty minutes. There was a sign posted in the office—Open Until Eleven. If they turn out the lights and go to bed, I reckon we're safe until morning."

She finished off her chicken and retreated to the bathroom. Not the most modern of accommodations but the white tile and bland fixtures were clean. She shed Sarah Loughlin's clothes, turned on the hot water and stepped into a bathtub with a blue plastic shower curtain.

The steaming hot water felt good as it splashed into her face and sluiced down her body. Warmth spread through her, and the tension in her muscles began to unwind. She closed her eyes. The bonds of self-control loosened as she relaxed.

Big mistake. As soon as she let her guard down, her mind filled with images she didn't want to remember.

Too many bad things had happened. They played in her head, one after another. Gruesome. Horrible. Sad.

Her eyelids popped open. She tried to focus. Through the plastic shower curtain, the bathroom was a blur.

When she held her hand in the shower spray, she imagined crimson blood oozing through her fingers. Frank's blood when he lay on the floor of the ice cream parlor. The blood that came when Goldie was born. Penny's blood when her life was taken.

More blood would spill before this was over. They were getting closer to Baron. The threat was building. Danger squeezed her heart. Not Cole's blood, she couldn't bear to lose him. Not like that.

A sob crawled up her throat, and she realized that she was crying. Her tears mingled with the hot, rushing water. If only she could wash her memory clean and erase her fears.

Her knees buckled, and her hand slid down the white tile wall. With a gasp, she sat down in the bathtub. The shower pelted down on her. The steam clung to her pores.

She heard the bathroom door open. Cole asked, "Are you all right?"

Had she been weeping out loud? "I'm fine."

"The lights in the office are out."

"Great. Close the door."

She didn't want him to see her vulnerability. So far, she'd done a pretty good impression of somebody who could keep it together no matter what. She didn't want him to know that she was afraid. Or needy. That was the worst.

He closed the door but didn't leave the bathroom. "Rachel? Talk to me. You can say anything."

The tenderness in his voice cut through her like a knife. She doubled over into a ball with her head resting on her knees. "Go away."

He eased open the shower curtain. Humiliated by her weakness, she refused to look up at him.

"It's okay," he murmured. "You're going to be okay."

He turned off the shower and draped a towel around her shoulders. The cool air made her shiver. She wanted to move, to pull herself together. But she couldn't pretend that she was fine and dandy. She'd witnessed murders, had been attacked and pursued. Right now, it felt like too damn much to bear.

"You need to get into bed," Cole said as knelt on the floor beside the tub. "Under the covers where it's warm."

"Leave me alone."

His arm circled her back. With a second towel, he dried her face. She batted his hands away.

"Let me help you, Rachel. You're always helping others. It's your turn." His low voice soothed her. "When you're with a woman in labor, you guide her through the pain. That's your job, and you're good at it."

"So?"

"This is my job. The violence. The lies. The fear. And the guilt. It's not easy. If you take my hand, I can help you through it."

She allowed him to guide her into the bedroom, where she slipped between the sheets. Fully dressed except for his boots, he lay beside her and held her.

Though she snuggled against him, she was afraid to close her eyes, fearful of the memories that might return in vivid color. How would she sleep tonight without nightmares?

"I'll tell you a story," he said. "A long time ago, almost ten years, I went on my second undercover assignment. Shouldn't have been complicated, but things went wrong. Some of it was my fault, my inexperience. Anyway, the situation turned dangerous. A man was killed and—"

"Stop." She shoved against his chest. "I really hope this isn't your idea of a cozy bedtime story."

"There's a happy ending," he promised.

"Get to it." She ducked her head under the covers. Her hair was still wet from the shower and she was dripping on him and on the pillow.

"After the assignment, I fell apart. Couldn't sleep. Didn't want to eat. Every loud noise sounded like gunfire. And there were flashbacks. I shed some tears, but mostly I was angry. Unreasonably angry."

"But you're always so cool and controlled."

"I lost it. This little two-tone minivan stole my space in a parking lot, and I went nuts. Slammed on my brakes, grabbed my tire iron. I charged the van, ready to smash every window. Then I saw the driver— a petite lady with panic in her eyes. There were two toddlers in car seats." He shuddered. "Probably scared those kids out of a year's growth. I got back in my car and drove directly to a shrink."

"You got help."

"Yeah." He pulled her closer. "Having a reaction to what you've been through in the past couple of days is natural. It's all right to cry or yell."

Or curl up in a fetal position in the shower? She appreciated his attempt to let her know she wasn't crazy, even though she still felt like a basket case. "When do we get to the good part of your story?"

"Eventually, you learn to live with it."

"What kind of happy ending is that?" She drew back her head so she could look him in the eye. "I want sunshine and lollipops."

"The truth is better."

"That's my line," she said. "I'm the big stickler for the truth."

His mouth relaxed in a smile. "If you want to cry, go ahead. I understand. And if you want to hit somebody, I can take it."

"Are you sure about that? I hit pretty hard."

"There's no need for you to put up a front, Rachel. You're brave. You're smart. There's nobody I'd rather have for a partner."

As she gazed at him, she realized that she didn't need to explode with tears or screams. She wanted him. To connect with him. To make love.

When she leaned down to kiss him, she dared to close her eyes. She wasn't afraid. Not right now.

His caresses were gentle at first. He tweaked her earlobe and traced the line of her chin. His hand slid down her throat. He cupped her breast, teased the nub, lowered his head and tasted her.

A powerful excitement crackled through her veins, erasing every other emotion. She was torn between the desperate need to have him inside her and a yearning to prolong their lovemaking for hours. Somewhere in between, they found the perfect rhythm. He scrambled out of his clothes and their naked bodies pressed together.

This was the kind of happy ending she'd been looking for.

When she first came to bed, Rachel hadn't thought she'd be able to sleep. The bloody culmination of everything that had happened to them haunted her, and she was afraid of the nightmares that might come.

But after making love, her fears dissipated and exhaustion overwhelmed her. She had slipped into a state of quiet unconsciousness.

She awakened gradually. Last night, she and Cole had once again made love without a condom. Her hand trailed down her body and rested on her flat stomach. Had his seed taken root inside her? Was she pregnant? Other women had told her that they knew the very moment of conception, but she didn't feel any different.

The thought of having a baby—Cole's baby—made her smile. For her, it was the right time. Even if he wasn't the right mate, even if she never saw him after Baron was in custody, she'd be glad finally to be a mother.

She rolled over and reached across the sheets, needing to feel him beside her. But he was gone. "Cole? Cole, where are you?"

"Here."

She saw him standing at the edge of the front window—his sentry position, where he kept an eye on the parking lot outside the motel. The thin light of early morning crept around the curtain and made an interesting highlight on his muscular chest.

"What are you doing all the way over there?"

He sauntered back to the bed and returned to his place beside her. When they touched, her heart fluttered. In spite of her independence, she never wanted to be apart from him.

"I called Waxman," he said.

The last time he talked to his handler in Los Angeles, the man had thrown them under the bus, refusing to help and telling them to turn themselves in. "What did he say?"

"He's coming around." His voice was bitter. "After working with me for years, it finally occurred to Waxman that he could trust me."

"That's good news, right?"

"Not entirely. Without solid evidence, there's nothing Waxman can do about the local feds. Prescott is still running this circus." He ruffled her hair. "Do you like road trips?"

"It depends on where I'm going."

"California," he said. "I want to pick up the loot from Jenna's house, drive to Denver, get a rental car and go home, where Waxman can offer us real protection."

He wanted to take her home with him. She loved the idea. "I'm ready for a trip to the beach."

Chapter 20

"In other developments," said the TV anchorman on the early morning local news, "the police in Grand County are still on the lookout for two suspects in the Black Hawk casino robbery."

Cole groaned as his mug shot flashed on the motel room television screen.

The anchorman continued, "If you see this man, contact the Grand County Sheriff's Department. And now, let's take a look at sports. The Nuggets…"

Using the remote, Cole turned off the TV. Apparently, the manhunt was still active but didn't rate headline status. He figured the Grand County cops were plenty busy, processing the crime scene at the Shadow Mountain Lake house and investigating Frank's death—a murder that Prescott would undoubtedly try to pin on him.

Rachel emerged from the bathroom looking fresh

and pretty. He liked the way her wispy hair curled on her cheeks when it was damp. Her blue eyes were bright and clear. For the moment, she seemed to have recovered from last night's meltdown, but he knew it would take more time for her to fully cope with the trauma of the past couple of days—trauma that was all his fault, one hundred percent. He'd kidnapped her and dragged her into this mess.

Somehow, he had to make it better.

She'd seemed pleased when he mentioned the road trip. While they were in California, he'd take real good care of her. They'd go for walks on the beach. Or surfing. Or a sailing trip. Or maybe they'd visit his brother. His nieces would love Rachel. He'd show her why living near the ocean was preferable to these damned mountains.

She rubbed her index finger across her teeth. "I brushed with a washcloth and soap. Disgusting."

"As soon as we're on the road, we'll buy toothpaste."

"Or we could stop at my condo when we get to Granby. I actually own a toothbrush. Might even have a spare for you."

He pulled her close and gave her a kiss. Her mouth tasted like detergent, but he didn't complain. "We can't go to your condo. That's the most obvious place for Prescott to arrange for surveillance. And the cops are still looking for us. I just saw my picture on TV."

"What about me? Was I on TV?"

He shook his head. "No mug shot."

"I'm kind of surprised. When the sheriff's men went to the Shadow Mountain Lake house, they must have found my van in the garage. They've got to know my identity."

"They might consider you a hostage." He urged her toward the door. "When we're on the road, you need to turn up your collar and wear the hat with earflaps to hide what you look like. Never can tell where traffic cams might be located."

He was glad to be driving away from the motel. Though the owner hadn't recognized him last night, the guy might remember after seeing the photo on the news. And he might be suspicious if he noticed that Cole had transposed two digits on the license plate when he checked in. He hadn't wanted to leave a record of Loughlin's car being here; no point in getting Rachel's friend in trouble.

In the passenger seat, she stretched and yawned. "It's early."

"Not a morning person?"

"But I am," she said. "I like to start the day with the sun. Look at that sunrise."

To the east, the sky was colored a soft pink that reminded him of the inside of a conch shell. Overhead, the dawn faded to blue with only a few clouds. The morning TV news program had said the weather throughout the state was clear.

He wasn't looking forward to returning to the mounds of snow left behind by the blizzard in Grand County. "How long do you think it'll take us to get to Granby?"

"A couple of hours," she said. "Jenna probably leaves for school around nine. We'll get there a little after that."

Morning was a busy time in most neighborhoods with people going to work and getting started with their day. Since they were going to break into Jenna's house, he preferred to wait until after ten when people had settled into their routines. "We've got about an hour to kill."

"What should we do?"

"Lay low." On the road, they risked being seen on cameras. If he went into a diner or a store, he might be recognized.

"My picture wasn't on TV," she said. "Pull into the next store that's open, I'll run inside and get supplies. Then we find someplace secluded and park until it's time to go."

As good a plan as any.

After a quick stop in Nederland at a convenience store, he left the main road and drove to a secluded overlook that caught the morning sun. One positive about the mountains: it was never hard to find solitude.

Rachel passed him a coffee cup and opened her car door.

"What are you doing?" he asked.

"Come with me."

Grumbling, he unfastened his seat belt and left the warmth of the car. The mountain air held a sharp chill, but he couldn't retreat without looking like a whiner. At least, there wasn't much snow—only pockets of white in the shadows.

He followed her as she climbed onto a flat granite rock and walked to the edge. Stepping up beside her, he took a sip of his hot black coffee.

She inhaled the cold air and smiled as she looked down from their vantage point. The sun warmed her face. She was beautiful, at peace with herself and the world. No hidden motives roiled inside her. Seldom had he known anyone who lived with such honesty. When Rachel was scared, her fear came from a natural response to a threat. When she laughed, she was truly amused. The woman spoke her mind.

Being with her was the best time he'd had in his life.

Resting his arm on her shoulder, he accepted her vision. Jagged, rocky hillsides filled with trees spread before them. They could see for miles. Sunlight glistened on distant peaks that thrust into the blue sky. Her mountains. Beautiful.

Rachel leaned her back against his chest as she drank her coffee. She said nothing, and he appreciated her silence. No need for words. The experience was enough.

In this moment, he knew. There was no denying the way he felt. He loved this woman.

Before they headed into the high country, Cole needed to make one more phone call. There was, after all, the possibility that they ought to go to Denver instead of Granby. He'd been operating under the theory that Jenna Cambridge was Baron's secretary, but there was another woman in the picture.

He leaned against the driver's side door and punched numbers into his cell phone. She answered on the fourth ring.

"Hello, Pearl," he said. "How are you doing?"

"Dog tired. I forgot how much work it was to take care of an infant. Goldie was up twice last night for feedings. If she wasn't the most adorable creature in the whole world, I'd be really mad at her."

"We had some trouble at Lily Belle's." His vast understatement didn't begin to describe Frank's attack on them and his murder. "The feds might try to contact you."

"Well, then, I'm not going to answer the phone unless it's you. Nobody knows where I'm staying."

"It's smart to keep it that way."

Her instinct to avoid law enforcement reassured him. If Pearl had been Baron's secretary, she'd know about the traitor in the FBI, and she'd use that contact to keep herself out of trouble.

"I miss Penny." Pearl's voice cracked at the edge of a sob. "I keep telling myself that she's an angel in Heaven, looking down and smiling. But she's not here. It's not fair."

"It's not," he agreed.

"You said you'd get the man responsible for my daughter's murder. I'm holding you to that promise."

He wanted nothing more than to see Baron pay for his crimes. "I need to ask you about the last time you saw Penny in Black Hawk. Was there a woman with her?"

"Not that I noticed. That big thug was hanging around, but nobody else."

"What casino were you at?"

"The Stampede. That's the one that got robbed."

Though Cole didn't think Xavier's description matched Pearl, he had to ask about the engagement diamond. "Were you wearing any jewelry?"

"I always wear jewelry. It's free advertising for the stuff I design. But I don't recall what I had on. A couple of rings, some earrings."

"A diamond?"

"Definitely not. I don't use precious gems in my designs."

He switched topics. "Have you ever noticed Jenna wearing an engagement ring?"

"Jenna." She growled the name. "That girl isn't married and is never likely to be. She called me last night, and demanded to know why I hadn't come to her house with the baby. Let me tell you, I gave her a piece of my mind. She should have told me about the older man Penny was dating."

"Did she say anything about him?"

"Not a word. She said she didn't want to betray Penny. I never should have allowed my daughter to spend time with her. It was inappropriate. Why would a high school economics teacher want to hang out with one of her students?"

Why, indeed. "Jenna seems to have a lot of secrets."

"I never thought so before, but you're right. She threatened me on the phone, told me that I wouldn't get custody of Goldie because the baby belongs with her father. That's not true, is it?"

Not if the father was Baron, a criminal mastermind. "I don't think you'll have a problem keeping Goldie."

He passed the phone to Rachel so the two women could talk about the wonderful world of baby care. The fact that Jenna had checked up on Pearl gave him cause for worry. Was she acting for Baron? Was he looking for his child?

No way in hell would Cole allow that bastard to touch one precious hair on Goldie's head. Her survival was a miracle. She had to be kept safe.

When Rachel finished talking, she handed him the phone and gave him a familiar kiss on the cheek. "Pearl and Goldie are okay."

"For now," he said.

She stepped back and regarded him. Her head cocked

to one side. Her fists planted on her hips. "Why so ominous?"

"Baron might take it into his head that he wants Goldie. Think about it. The first thing Prescott asked about was the baby. Now Jenna wants to get her hooks into Pearl."

"We can't let that happen." Rachel shuddered. "We have to end this now."

They got back into the Jeep and drove. Though he was glad for the beautiful clear skies, the weather provided nothing in the way of cover. They were exposed. But no one knew they were driving Loughlin's car. With their collars turned up and hats pulled down, he doubted there would be facial recognition on traffic surveillance cams.

When he turned onto U.S. 40, Rachel said, "I have a theory about the engagement ring."

"I'm listening."

"Penny told me that Jenna referred to Baron as Mister Big. A powerful man. An attractive man. Maybe Jenna is more than a secretary. What would you call it? A secretary with benefits? She might be having an affair with Baron, and the ring is wishful thinking."

"If that's true, she would have hated Penny."

"Exactly," Rachel said. "She might be the one who sent those guys to shoot up the house near Shadow Mountain Lake."

Her theory was sound until she got to the shoot-out. "She wouldn't go against Baron. He's vicious with people who don't follow his orders."

"Then why?" she asked. "Why would he send his men to kill the gang at the hideout?"

"The gang screwed up. Almost got caught."

Baron ran his organization according to strict rules: do as you're told, and you'll profit. Make a mistake, and you'll pay.

"But he almost got his own child killed," she said. "He must have cared something for Penny and she was murdered."

"Collateral damage."

He didn't expect Rachel to understand the workings of a criminal mind. A man like Baron made up his own rules. Penny's murder sent a powerful message to the other people who worked for him. Nobody—not even his pregnant lover—got in his way.

"When you're around someone like that," she said, "how do you keep yourself from showing your emotions?"

"It's my job."

He couldn't explain why he was good at undercover work or why he could beat a lie detector test without breaking a sweat. The FBI shrinks called it a skill. Cole was beginning to think he was cursed.

"Okay." She shrugged. "What do you think about my theory? That Jenna is in love with Baron?"

"I like it." He grinned. "You're one smart detective, Special Agent Rocky Logan."

"It's about time I did something to prove my worth."

"You're the most valuable part of my investigation. Without you, I could never have saved Goldie. It was your connection with Loughlin that got us this transportation. You've helped me. More than you will ever know."

She leaned back against her seat. "This is turning into quite a vacation for me. I can't wait to get to California."

"I have plans for what we'll do when we're there."

In general, Cole considered himself to be good at interrogation and not so much when it came to small talk. But he went at length, telling her about the places he would take her to see and the foods they would sample. "And a sailboat ride on a balmy night. There's nothing like making love at sea."

For once, she didn't counter with a comparison about how the mountains were better. Instead, she beamed a smile. "I know I'll love it."

The long drive into the snow passed quickly. Before he knew it, they were entering the Granby area. He clammed up. Time to put his game face on.

As he drove along the street where Jenna's house was located, Rachel pointed to the address. "That's a nice little place. If I stay in Granby, I might look for something like that."

"If you stay?"

"I'm keeping my options open."

Jenna's cedar frame house with a two-car garage in front was nothing spectacular. An evergreen Christmas wreath hung on the door, and Jenna hadn't yet taken down the string of lights that decorated the eaves.

Cole would have preferred a more secluded location. The house stood on the corner in a residential area with large lots, but the house across the street had a window looking directly at Jenna's front door. The sidewalk and driveway were shoveled, but there was no way they could sneak up on the house through the mounds of snow left behind by the blizzard.

He braked for the stop sign, and then drove on. Though there were no other cars on the street, he had the sense that they were being watched.

"What's the plan?" Rachel asked.

"I'm not sure yet."

He'd rather not risk being seen, but there didn't seem to be any approach other than parking in the driveway and marching up to the door. If she didn't have an alarm system, he could pick the lock.

Circling the block, he checked his mirrors. Two blocks away, he saw a truck cross an intersection. Nothing else seemed to be moving in this quiet neighborhood. Still, he decided to retreat and consider their next move.

Several blocks away, he backed into a parking space in a lot outside a supermarket. The snow that had been cleared from the lot made an eight-foot-high pile at the far end. Damn this Colorado snow.

He passed his cell phone to Rachel. "Call Jenna and make sure she didn't stay home from work."

"You think we might be walking into a trap."

"Something isn't right."

"I trust your instincts," she said. "I still remember how you sensed the attack on the hideout before a single bullet had been fired."

Before she could make the call, a red SUV pulled up in front of them, trapping them in the parking space.

The back door swung open, and Xavier stepped out. His heavy-duty parka was as red as his vehicle. Stealth had never been his strong point.

He opened the back door to their Jeep and climbed in.

"Hi, kids." His gold tooth flashed when he smiled. "Did you miss me?"

Chapter 21

Wearing her hat with the earflaps, Rachel doubted she could pull off her supercool undercover identity as Special Agent Rocky Logan. She turned around in her seat and glared at Xavier. "How did you find us?"

"A good poker player never tells his secrets."

Without turning around, Cole growled, "He must have planted a GPS tracker."

"Where?" she demanded. "How?"

Xavier chuckled. "Under your collar, sweetheart."

Leaning forward, he patted her shoulder, slid his hand up toward her neck and detached a tiny circular object from her parka. Like a magician, he held it up so she could see. "Ta da!"

Though she didn't remember him touching her at the casino, the evidence was there. He had bugged her parka.

She drew the logical conclusion. "That's why we

didn't see you tailing us. You knew where we were all the time."

Xavier pocketed the device. "If I'd thought you two were going to stop for the night at a motel, I could have arranged for classier accommodations. But then, you might be seen and recognized. Other people wouldn't be as understanding as I am about harboring a fugitive."

"What do you want?" Cole muttered.

"To get my money back. The insurance company isn't going to be understanding about my losses in the robbery, and I can't afford to be out forty-two thousand bucks."

"Is that right?" She heard the anger in Cole's voice. "Why should I do you any favors?"

"For old times' sake. We go back a long way, buddy boy. You know things about me that nobody else does. And vice versa."

"You don't know squat."

"Come on, now. There's no need to be hostile."

Cole stared through the windshield at the red SUV, and she followed his gaze. The driver was visible through the front window, but she didn't see anybody else. "How many men did you bring with you?"

"Only two. It was never my intention to overpower you. I've seen you in action, and I'm too old to recover from a busted kneecap." Xavier turned to Rachel. "He can be a dangerous fellow. Are you aware of that?"

Since he wasn't treating her like an FBI agent, there was no reason for her to try to outbluff this canny old man. "I know him well," she said. "He's only dangerous with people who need to be taken down."

Behind his glasses, his beady little eyes narrowed.

"Be careful about standing too close to the flame, my dear. You might get burned."

Cole turned in his seat to face Xavier. "I don't like the way you followed us. And I'm not making any promises about what happens to the money. But the truth is, I could use some backup."

The old man massaged his chin while he considered. Then he said, "Fine. I scratch your back and you—"

"Here's the deal," Cole said. "Rachel and I are going to break into a house. You and your men wait outside. If we don't come out in ten minutes, it means we need your help."

"I'll do it, and we'll settle up afterward. Aren't you lucky that I turned up when I did?" Xavier opened the car door. "You never appreciated all that I did for you back in the day. It takes guts to be a snitch."

"Guts and greed," Cole said. "Follow us and don't be too obvious."

"By the way." A wide grin split the old man's wrinkled face. His gold tooth gleamed. "How's your wife?"

His wife?

The inside of her head exploded.

Cole was married?

She watched Xavier scamper to his red SUV like an evil leprechaun. She couldn't trust a word he said. He wanted to get back at Cole, to cause him strife.

Desperately wanting to believe that Xavier had been lying, she turned her gaze on Cole. His cognac eyes held a seriousness that she had never seen before.

"Rachel," he said, "I've never lied to you."

That wasn't an answer. She'd asked him dozens of questions about his prior girlfriends and relationships, but she had never actually asked if he had a wife. "Are you married?"

"I can explain."

He hadn't denied it, and she didn't want to be sucked into whatever deceptive ruse he was playing. The man lied for a living. He changed identities every other day. "Yes or no?"

"It's a technicality. No big deal."

She repeated, "Yes or no?"

"Yes."

Anger and hurt knotted in her gut. A flush of heat crawled up her throat and strangled her. Once again, she'd fallen for a bad boy—another man in the long line of dashing, sexy, handsome jerks who ultimately betrayed her. "Don't say another word. I don't want to hear your phony explanations. Let's get this over with and say goodbye."

"Is that what you want?"

"Damn right."

She held up his cell phone and tried to remember how to contact Jenna Cambridge. Pearl had given them the phone number. Was it in the memory? She thrust the phone toward Cole. "Get Jenna on the line."

"I should make this call," he said.

"Because I'm not a natural born liar like you? Because you don't think I can pull it off?"

He grasped her arm near the wrist and pulled her closer, forcing her to confront him. "Settle down, Rachel. If we're going to get through this in one piece, you need to concentrate."

"Don't tell me what I need."

She locked gazes with him. His eyes were intense,

volatile. He was nearly as angry as she was, and that was just fine with her. She was done with him and his lies.

With a strength born of fury, she yanked her arm away from him. "Go ahead and call her. I don't care."

While he made the call, she stared through the windshield at Xavier's red SUV. She could see the old man's face in the window of the backseat. He was laughing and she knew the joke was on her.

Cole drove into Jenna's quiet, residential neighborhood where every sidewalk was shoveled. No one was outside. Nothing seemed to be moving. Beams of sunlight glistened and slowly melted the snow.

He hadn't been able to reach Jenna on the phone, but he'd called the high school and been informed that she was teaching her senior economics seminar and couldn't be disturbed. She wasn't at home; that was all he had to know.

There were still obstacles to breaking into her house. She might have an alarm system or a guard dog or a lock he couldn't pick. *Logistics.* He needed to concentrate on logistics. In normal circumstances, that wouldn't have been a problem. He was good at honing in with sharp focus, doing what had to be done. But Rachel had distracted him.

He glanced over at her. In defiance, she'd torn the cap with earflaps off her head, and her short hair stood up in spikes. A feverish red flush colored her throat and cheeks. Anger sizzled around her like static electricity.

Later, he'd explain about his alleged wife. He should have said something before, but he wasn't accustomed to baring his soul. Damn Xavier for bringing up his wife and making him out to be a liar. Or an unfaithful husband.

Why the hell had Rachel jumped to the worst possible conclusion? It was almost as though she'd been looking for a reason to cut him off at the knees and end this thing that was growing between them. They had a connection, a relationship.

Oh, hell. He might as well face it. He loved her. And she loved him back. But she was as scared of commitment as he was. Why couldn't she understand? He wasn't like all the other creeps she'd dated. He was one of the good guys, damn it.

He shook his head. For now, he had to maintain a single-minded objective. *Get into Jenna's house and find the money.*

In the rearview mirror, he saw the red SUV following them. Tersely, he said, "You should stay outside with Xavier. I'm not sure what I'll find in the house."

"I'm going with you."

"It could be a trap."

"Do you really think so?"

He considered. The evidence connecting Jenna to Baron was largely circumstantial. The only thing they knew for certain was that Penny had sent Jenna the bundles containing the haul from the casino robbery. "Even if she is Baron's secretary, she has no reason to suspect that we're coming after the money."

"So we ought to be fine," Rachel said. "And I'm coming with you to search. Two sets of eyes are better than one."

He pulled into Jenna's driveway and parked. "I go first. If I tell you to run, do it. No questions."

"You're the boss."

"I'm not kidding around," he said.

"You don't need to remind me about the danger." She kept her head averted as though she couldn't stand the sight of him. "I've seen Baron's men in action."

They got out of the car and followed the shoveled path through the snow to the front porch. He saw no indication of an alarm system, but that didn't mean much. Most of these systems were invisible. "We've got five minutes to get in and out. If she has a silent alarm that rings through to a security company, it'll take that long for them to get here."

He pressed the doorbell and listened for any sound coming from inside the house.

Rachel moved along the porch to the front window. "I can't see inside. The drapes are closed."

"Any of the windows open?"

She shook her head. "Triple pane casement windows. They're sealed up tight."

The lock on Jenna's door was a piece of cake, but she also had a dead bolt, which could be a pain in the butt. He squatted so he was eye level with the door handle and went to work.

"Of course," she said, "you carry a lock pick."

"My version of a Swiss Army knife."

He had the lower lock opened in a couple of minutes. When he pushed on the handle, the door swung open. Jenna hadn't bothered with the dead bolt.

"Five minutes," he reminded her as he took his gun from the holster and stepped inside. "You go left. I'll go right."

He was only halfway down the hallway to the bedrooms when he heard her call out. "Cole."

Something had gone wrong. He whipped around,

raising his gun to shoot. A man with a shaved head held Rachel by the throat. His gun pointed to her head.

Cole sensed someone behind his back. A deep voice with a Western twang said, "Drop your weapon or she dies."

If he'd been alone, he might have taken his chances with these two. But he couldn't risk Rachel's life. He set his weapon on the floor and raised his hands. "We're not going to cause trouble."

"Too late," the guy behind him said. "We've been chasing you two all over the damn mountains. We halfway froze to death."

If these were the same guys who chased them onto Shadow Mountain Lake, they'd talked to Frank. What had he told them? Cole had to come up with a story that would convince these guys to let them go. Was it better to tell them he was a fed, and the full force of the law would be after them? Should he act like he was still a loyal member of the robbery crew? His mind raced.

He came up with…nothing. No bargaining chip. No leverage. No believable threat. Nothing. Nada. His entire focus was on Rachel. He had to get her out of here. Somehow, he had to save her.

The man behind him shoved him against the wall in the hallway, yanked his arms down and cuffed his hands behind his back. Then, he did a thorough pat down. When he was satisfied that Cole had been disarmed, he stepped back. "Turn around and walk into the bedroom. I'd advise you not to make any sudden moves."

Cole rooted himself to the floor. No matter what happened to him, he wouldn't leave Rachel alone with these two. "She comes with me."

"Don't you worry none. She's going to be with you. Until death do you part."

The man holding Rachel moved toward them. His arm at her throat was tight.

They went through Jenna's bedroom into the master bathroom. As soon as they were inside, the door closed.

They weren't alone.

Agent Prescott curled up on the floor beside the freestanding bathtub. When he heard them, he opened his eyes and struggled to sit up. Blood from a head wound caked in his hair.

He croaked out one word. "Sorry."

Chapter 22

Rachel's nurturing instinct should have sent her running across the bathroom toward Prescott. The man was clearly in need of first aid.

But she wasn't a paramedic anymore. She was the one in imminent danger. She turned toward Cole and placed the flat of her hand on his chest. *Until death did them part?* They weren't going to get out of this alive. The guys who nabbed them were the same merciless bastards who mowed down the gang at the Shadow Mountain Lake house. "Why didn't they kill us when we walked in the door?"

When he looked down at her, his gaze was so warm and full of caring that her heart ached. "Murder leaves a mess," he said. "That's why we're in a bathroom. If they kill us here, they can swab down the tiles and get rid of the evidence."

"That can't be right."

"Why not?"

How could she be discussing the circumstances of her own death? With ridiculous calm, she said, "There'd still be evidence. The CSI shows on TV always find traces."

"I seriously doubt the Grand County Sheriff's Department has a mass spectrometer or instant DNA analysis."

"But you and Prescott are FBI. You guys have all the forensic goodies."

He gave her a sad smile. Then he looked at Prescott. "You're in the Denver office. Do you think they're good enough to figure out who killed us?"

Using the edge of the tub, Agent Prescott forced himself to stand. His breathing was shallow. Even from a distance, she could tell that his pupils were dilated. "You're in shock," she said. "You're probably concussed and should be in a hospital."

He reached up and touched the wound on his head. His fingers came away bloody. "Tell me about Goldie. Is my baby girl safe?"

His baby? "You're Goldie's father?"

"Son of a bitch," Cole muttered. "I underestimated you, Prescott. I thought you were nothing more than a scumbag traitor, but I was wrong. You're the big man himself. You're Baron."

Prescott wiped his bloody hand across his mouth, leaving a streak of crimson. "Not by choice."

Cole looked down at her. "Get the lock picks from my jacket pocket and put them in my hands. I need to get out of these cuffs."

Moments ago, she'd been complaining about the fact

that he carried tools for a break-in. Now, she was glad. "Tell me how to do it. I can help."

"It's faster if I handle it myself. This isn't the first time I've been in this position."

When she reached inside his jacket, her physical connection with him was immediate and intimate. She couldn't deny their chemistry. Not that it mattered. Even if she forgave his deception and admitted how much she cared about him, they were going to be dead. "What's going to happen to us?"

Prescott answered, "They'll load us in a car, drive to the mountains, kill us and bury our bodies. We won't be found until the spring thaw. By then, Jenna will be long gone."

She placed the picks in Cole's hands and turned toward Prescott. He seemed to be regaining strength. From experience, she knew that head wounds were unpredictable. He might have a surge of coherence, might even appear to be making a recovery. Or he might collapse into a coma.

"You're Baron," she said. "Why can't you stop them?"

"I don't call the shots. Jenna is in charge. She's always been the boss. Ever since I first met her."

"Was that when you came to the high school in Granby to lecture about the FBI?"

"Before that." He winced. "Jenna lived in Denver. We were engaged."

That explained the ring she still wore. "After you broke up, she moved to the mountains."

Rachel understood the need for a change of scenery. She'd done much the same thing when she joined Rocky

Mountain Women's Clinic as a midwife. Like Jenna, she'd been searching for a place to start over.

Prescott said, "She invited me to Granby to talk to her class. That's when I met Penny. Poor, sweet Penny. I was attracted to her right away, but she was a high school kid. Too young. I wooed her. Gave her presents."

"A diamond tennis bracelet," Rachel said.

"I picked it up at a pawn shop, but she didn't know that. She thought I was her true love, her soulmate. All that lovey-dovey crap. And here's the funny part." He inhaled and straightened his shoulders. "I felt the same damn way. I waited until she was ready. I swear to God, I didn't make love to her until she was eighteen."

"Real decent of you," Cole muttered. "How did you get hooked up with Jenna again?"

"She pretended to be my friend. And Penny's. But she was scheming. Spinning her web. Like a spider. A black widow spider. A poisonous creature who..."

His words faded, and she could see him slipping toward unconsciousness. If he passed out, there was a good chance he wouldn't wake up. She went toward him, grabbed his arm and shook him. "Stay with me, Prescott. Tell me about Jenna."

"She's smart. Cunning. Has a master's degree in economics. She put together the whole robbery and money-laundering scheme."

"Interesting," Cole said. "Her logistics were complicated but kind of genius. How did she pull it off?"

"Untraceable email. Throwaway phones. She pretended to be a secretary and invented a boss nobody saw. Baron."

"How did you get involved?"

"She needed to hide behind a frontman. So she set

me up with fake deposits to an account in my name. When we were engaged, she handled my bills, got my social security number, all my passwords. By the time she told me about it, there was enough evidence against me to destroy my career and my life."

"You should have turned her in," Cole said.

"I wanted to. But she had Penny on the hook. If I didn't do what Jenna said, Penny would pay the price."

The long confession seemed to invigorate him. Instead of growing weaker, his voice sounded determined. "When I found out that Penny was pregnant, I started making plans to run away with her. We could have had a decent life. Could have raised our baby. Could have—"

A burst of gunfire echoed from the other room.

Cole broke free. The cuffs dangled from his left wrist, but his hands were separated. "Let's get the hell out of here."

She didn't see an escape. The only window in the bathroom was glass bricks—the kind you can't break without a jackhammer.

"What's happening?" Prescott demanded. "Who's shooting?"

"We brought backup," Cole said. "But I don't trust them to be effective. We've got to get out of the bathroom. If those guys catch us in here, it'll be like shooting fish in a barrel."

He eased open the bathroom door. Over his shoulder, he whispered, "I don't see a guard."

If she'd had time to think, she would have been terrified, but everything was happening too fast. Cole grabbed her hand and pulled her behind him into Jenna's bedroom.

She scanned the room, looking for a place to hide.

Under the king-size four-poster bed? In the closet? There was a lot of large, heavy furniture in dark wood. Floor-to-ceiling curtains hung beside two windows. Both had decorative security bars on the outside.

Shouts and more gunfire echoed from the front of the house. Cole peeked into the hallway and came back to her. "If we go that way, they'll see us."

He pulled her into the walk-in closet and closed the door. The closet was as big as a bedroom. A scent of cedar and cinnamon hung in the air.

Cole turned on the overhead light. The closet system combined hanging racks, drawers and shelving. Against the back wall were shoes, hats and a shelf with three wigs—black, blond and auburn. Jenna's disguises. Nothing was out of place. Everything was meticulously organized.

It seemed almost sacrilegious when Cole scooped the clothes off a low rack and took the pole where they had been hanging. He did the same with another pole and handed it to her.

"Weapons," he said.

Wooden dowels wouldn't be much use against bullets, but it was better than nothing. He pulled her to a position beside the door and whispered, "I need to explain about my wife."

"Not now. It's not important."

"This might be the last thing I ever say to you, and I want you to know that I'm not a liar or a cheat. The marriage was years ago. I was investigating the illegal gambling scene in California, and I had a female partner. There were problems with our undercover identities. Somehow, we ended up going through a wedding ceremony and signing papers that I suppose are still legal. But there was never anything romantic between us."

"Why should I believe you?"

"I never had to mention this phony marriage to you. But I'm trying to be honest. To tell you everything."

"So, what happened with this partner of yours?"

"She transferred back east. Neither of us bothered with a divorce. I didn't see a need. There wasn't anyone else in my life. Not until now. Not until you."

She heard more gunfire from the other room. There was no way out of this mess.

"That's a mighty strange story," she said.

"It's the truth."

A fake marriage to a partner? An unconsummated marriage? Not bothering with a divorce? If she hadn't gone through the past days with Cole and seen how many twists and turns his life involved, she would have dismissed his story. But she knew his life was complicated. Crazy. Wild. "I believe you."

"I love you, Rachel."

Her arms closed around him. She wanted to be strong and brave, didn't want to cry. But tears spilled down her cheeks. "I love you, too."

This might be the last time they embraced. She'd found love only to lose it.

"When we get out of this," he said, "I'll get a divorce and marry you."

"That's a hell of a way to propose." She scrubbed the moisture from her face. "What if I say no?"

"That's not an option."

The shooting stopped abruptly. She heard voices from the other room.

Cole turned off the overhead light in the closet and

stepped in front of her. "Stay back," he said. "No matter what happens, stay in here."

The voices came closer. One was a woman. Jenna?

The closet door whipped open. Cole reacted. He swung hard with the dowel, striking the gun of the man who opened the door. He dropped his weapon. Cole dove, trying to reach the gun.

He was out of her line of sight. She heard shots being fired.

Then silence.

Panic roared through her. Without thinking, she charged through the open door with her dowel raised to strike.

The scene before her was a tableaux. Cole stood between Prescott and a mousy woman in a button-down shirt, striped vest and gray slacks. They both had their weapons aimed at him.

On the floor in front of Cole, another man lay bleeding.

"Drop your weapons," Prescott ordered. "Both of you."

Cole glanced at her and gave a nod as he dropped his dowel on the floor. "It's okay, Rachel."

"No." She refused to give up. "It's not okay."

"We can negotiate," Prescott said. "Nobody else has to die."

Rachel pointed her dowel at the woman. "I want to hear from her. Jenna Cambridge."

Jenna looked down her long nose. "Don't be stupid. I might decide to let you go after you've served your purpose as a hostage. I don't particularly want to kill you."

"Not like Penny?"

Jenna's dull brown eyes flicked nervously from

left to right, but her gun hand remained steady. "That shouldn't have happened."

"Convenient for you that it did," Rachel said. "With Penny out of the way, your former fiancé can come back to you."

"I told you once not to be a fool," Jenna said in a teacherlike voice. "I won't tell you again."

"You won't get away with this."

"I'm a good planner." She glanced toward Prescott. "We're going away together. We'll have a new life with enough money that we won't ever have to work again. I've worked hard and I deserve that much, don't I, darling?"

Prescott crossed the room and stood before her. "You deserve something."

"There's only one thing I've ever wanted," she said with a simpering grin. "Your love."

"Sorry, Jenna. I already gave my heart."

He shoved his gun against her rib cage and pulled the trigger. She gasped. And fell.

She was dead before she hit the floor.

He tried to turn the gun on himself, but Cole was too fast. He wrenched the weapon from Prescott's hand. With surprising gentleness, he guided the wounded agent to the bed.

Prescott sat with his head drooped forward. "She would have killed you. Couldn't let that happen."

Cole patted his shoulder. "You came through when I needed you. I won't forget that."

"My life is over."

"Not yet," Cole said. "You have a baby."

"Goldie." He lifted his head. "Penny's baby."

"You need to see her and hold her. But first, you've

got to get us out of this mess. The cops still think Rachel and I are fugitives."

"I'll take care of it." Prescott rose. He wavered for a moment before he straightened and walked toward the front of the house. "The police should be here any minute. As soon as I got out of the bathroom, I put in a call."

Eager to leave the carnage in the bedroom, Rachel followed him. She didn't get far. In the hallway, Cole caught hold of her hand and spun her around to face him. His hands rested at her waist.

He smiled down at her. "When you came charging out of the closet, you scared me."

"I think you have that backward. I was scared." She remembered how he'd told her that eventually the trauma would fade. "I guess our road trip to California is off."

"Hell, no. I'm not letting you out of my sight." He dropped a kiss on her forehead. "The world is a dangerous place. I need to protect my bride-to-be."

There were a million details to work out, but nothing seemed important. They were together. They were safe, and she wanted to keep it that way forever.

Epilogue

Nine months later, Rachel draped her wedding gown over her swollen belly. Turning sideways, she admired her profile in the full-length mirror in her bedroom. Pregnancy suited her well.

After a quick tap on the door, Cole slipped inside. She was too big for a normal embrace, but he managed to wrap his arms around her. "How's my bride?"

"Good." She'd felt a bit of cramping earlier. It might be a good idea to hurry. "And my groom?"

"Never better."

Given the fact that he was an uncompromising man, he'd been incredibly cooperative about making changes in his life. After the betrayal by his handler in California, Cole didn't want to return to the Los Angeles office of the FBI. He still loved the sun and the beach, but he decided that being a mountain man wasn't so bad.

Prescott's arrest had left an opening in the Denver office, and Cole stepped in to fill it. He still did undercover assignments, but much of his workload fell under the category of investigation. He was considered a rising star because he had not only put the Baron theft ring out of business but had also recovered the stolen cash.

She had also made concessions. Granby was too far from his work, so she moved closer to Denver and opened a new branch for the Rocky Mountain Women's Clinic. When they bought their house in Idaho Springs, Cole had one stipulation. Twice a year, they would vacation on a beach.

Everything seemed to be working out neatly. Except for the wedding. She'd wanted a small ceremony, but things had gotten out of hand. All of her huge family was there as well as Cole's brother's family, his mother and his silver-haired gambler father, who was one of the most charming men she'd ever met. Cole's dad was making quite an impression on Pearl, who had full custody of Goldie the Miracle Baby.

As they made plans, the guest list multiplied. They couldn't leave out the people she'd worked with and the parents of the babies she'd delivered. Nor could they ignore Cole's coworkers. And then there were friends, including Xavier, who had gotten off with little more than a slap on the wrist for his involvement with Baron. She didn't resent the casino owner. How could she? He and his men had provided the gunfire and distraction that had saved their lives.

She kissed Cole on the cheek. In his black suit and white shirt, he was so handsome. Was she really getting married to this gorgeous man?

"How's the crowd?" she asked.

"Restless," he said. "Most of them have already left for the church. I should be going, too. But I wanted to see you one more time before we say our vows."

"Having second thoughts?"

"Hell, no. I just wanted to tell you how much you mean to me. I never imagined I could be so happy. And that's the truth."

"I love you, Cole."

When she reached up to stroke his cheek, the ache in her abdomen became more intense, more prolonged. Rachel knew the signs; she was going into labor.

"Something wrong?" he asked.

"Everything is right." She looked up at her husband-to-be and smiled. "It's time."

For the first time since the moment they met, she saw sheer panic in his eyes. He gaped. He gasped. He ran to the door. Then back to her. "Are you sure?"

She nodded. "This is what I do."

He placed one hand on her belly, leaned down and kissed her. "It's going to be all right."

And it was.

* * * * *

Leona Karr loves to read and write, and her favorite books are romantic suspense. Every book she writes is an exciting discovery as she finds the right combination of romance and intrigue. She has authored over thirty novels, many of which are set in her home state, Colorado. When she's not reading and writing, she thoroughly enjoys spoiling her eight beautiful granddaughters.

Books by Leona Karr

Harlequin Intrigue

Shadow Mountain
Charmed
Stoneview Estate
Shadows on the Lake
A Dangerous Inheritance
Semiautomatic Marriage
Lost Identity
The Mysterious Twin
Innocent Witness
Mystery Dad

Visit the Author Profile page
at Harlequin.com for more titles.

SHADOW MOUNTAIN

Leona Karr

To my husband, Michael,
whose love and laughter inspire and enrich my life.

Chapter 1

The clock in the hall had already struck midnight when Caroline Fairchild pushed back from her home computer. Muttering an unladylike expletive, she rubbed the tense muscles in her neck. The discouraging financial printout told her what she already knew. Her newly launched decorating business in Denver was in the red. If she didn't get at least one lucrative contract this fall, she'd lose the investment of her late husband's life insurance and probably the house, too.

It wasn't just her future that was at stake. There was Danny, her six-year-old son. Growing up without his father was hard enough. She wanted him to have a full and happy life. Being a single parent presented more challenges than she had ever imagined.

Wearily, she turned out the lights on the lower floor and went upstairs to Danny's bedroom.

"I'll figure something out," she whispered as she bent over the child's bed and brushed back his light-brown hair from his forehead. He was a beautiful child and her heart swelled with the miracle that he was hers. Since she had no other family, she'd wanted to be a mother more than anything in the world. Now that she had lost her husband, having this darling little boy to raise made every day a special blessing.

Quietly, she crossed the hall to her bedroom and left the door open in case Danny called to her. Even though her husband, Thomas, had been dead two years, being alone at night was still the hardest part of being a widow. She'd given up wearing the sexy nightgowns and settled for old-fashioned flannel pajamas. Sometimes when she looked in the mirror, she wondered where her youth had gone. Even though she'd kept herself physically fit and her hair was still a rich dark brown and her blue eyes were 20/20, she thought she looked older than her thirty-two years.

She lay awake for a long time, her thoughts heavy with unanswered questions and decisions to be made. The tiny bedside clock had passed two o'clock before her tense body began to relax. She was finally on the edge of sleep when suddenly her nostrils quivered with the stench of burning wood. She sat up and clasped a hand over her nose and mouth.

Smoke!

She leaped from the bed and bounded into the hall. Clouds of black smoke rolled up the stairway. Somewhere on the floor below was a terrifying brightness and the sound of crackling flames.

"Danny!" Shouting, she ran into his room and grabbed him up from the bed. Half-asleep, he started to fight her. "No, honey no, the house is on fire! We have to get out."

He was a load to carry as she fled back into the hall, holding him tightly against her chest. They had to get out of the house. Frightened, Danny began to cough and struggle in her arms.

The only exits from the house were on the ground floor. As she froze at the top of the stairs, she could see tongues of red flames already licking at the stairs and banister. In moments the entire staircase would be in flames. Black smoke swirled around them.

"I can't see," Danny wailed.

As she wavered at the top of the stairs, the heat rose up to meet her, instantly parching her mouth and throat with a burning dryness. Her eyes were watering and the biting smell of scorched wood and cloth seared her nostrils.

A dancing brightness at the bottom of the stairway warned her that the entire first floor might already be a flaming furnace. Danny was coughing and crying as she plunged down the stairs through the swirling, thick haze.

Panic drove her through an encroaching ribbon of fire spreading along the bottom step. She leaped over it, almost losing her balance as she fled down the smoke-filled hall.

Fiery flames were devouring the dining-room curtains and spreading along the carpet runner leading to the front room. Danny bolted out of her arms with the panicked strength of a terrified six-year-old. He disappeared in the direction of the front foyer just as a thunderous crash vibrated through the depths of the house.

"Danny!" she screeched with parched lips and a

burning throat as she ran after him. He was already at the locked front door, pounding on it and whimpering when she reached him. Her eyes were watering so badly, she couldn't see the dead bolt. As her hands played blindly on the door seeking it, her fingers touched a hinge. She was on the wrong side of the door!

Danny had his face buried against her nightgown when she finally found the lock. Frantically, she turned it with one hand and jerked open the door with the other.

They bounded outside.

Coughing and gasping, they stumbled across the porch and down the front steps. The sound of falling timbers and radiating heat from leaping flames followed them across the yard.

Grabbing Danny's hand, she croaked, "Run."

At two o'clock in the morning all was quiet in the modest neighborhood in North Denver. The street was empty of people and cars. Only a few porch lights were on as they bolted across the cul-de-sac to the house of Betty and Jim McClure, her closest neighbors and long-time friends.

They stumbled up the steps and Caroline's frantic ringing of the doorbell and pounding brought Jim, disheveled and sleepy-eyed, to the door.

His eyes widened when he saw them. "Caroline! What on earth? What's happened?"

"Call 9-1-1! Fire. My house!"

When Jim looked across the street and saw the flames leaping out of the windows and roof, he spun on his bare feet and ran for the phone.

"What is it?" Betty called from the top of the stairs and hurried down.

Caroline tried to answer but a spasm of coughing choked her words.

"Our house is on fire," Danny whimpered.

All night crews from two fire trucks fought to control the flames. Caroline knew she never would forget the sound of the wailing sirens and the sight of firemen mobilizing to fight a dangerous enemy.

By sunup, their victory was small.

A stench of smoke, ashes and foul water floated through the whole neighborhood. The entire house had been gutted. The back was leveled. Most of the roof on the remainder had collapsed and water damage was everywhere.

As Caroline stared at the devastation, her lips quivered with disbelief. She and Thomas had bought the house when they were first married.

It had been the only real home she'd ever had. Her parents had been dryland farmers in eastern Colorado, moving from one acreage to another when times were bad—and they always were. Caroline was an only child and had been weighed down with responsibility and never-ending poverty as she grew up. Her parents had died within a year of each other when she was a senior in high school. She'd always been a hard worker and good student and her perfect 4.0 high-school record earned her a full scholarship to Colorado University.

She'd been working in the cafeteria when she met Thomas Fairchild, an older medical student doing his internship. Thomas always told her she was the prettiest girl with summer-blue eyes and soft brown hair that he'd ever seen. Their marriage had been a happy one, especially after Danny had become a part of their lives.

Now, she bit her lip to fight the ache in her heart as she walked across the street and stared at the shambles of their home. Most of the firemen had left, but the fire chief had remained. His expression was sympathetic as he walked over to her.

"I'm afraid there's not much left."

"But surely, I haven't lost everything?" she asked, biting her lip to control her emotions.

He avoided a direct answer. "Do you have any idea what started the blaze?"

She shook her head. "I can't imagine how it happened."

"Did you have any combustible material stored at the back of the house or in the kitchen?" he prodded.

"No. And nothing left on the stove. I always clean up after dinner and work a few hours in my office."

His eyes traveled over what was left of the house. "I'm afraid the damage is extensive."

"I'll need to go through and see what I can salvage," she said in a strained voice.

"Maybe tomorrow," he hedged. "You'll have to have one of the firemen go with you." He cleared his throat. "The cause of the fire is under investigation. We don't want any potential evidence destroyed. Arson is always a possibility."

The way his eyes narrowed suggested he was considering the idea that she'd set it herself.

She stiffened. "How long will the investigation take?"

"Hard to tell."

Caroline knew that meant the insurance company was absolved of any responsibility to write out a check for who knew how long.

* * *

Three days passed before she was finally allowed inside the house. In the company of a young fireman, she went through the painful process of salvaging what she could.

She was relieved that her important personal papers and a few old photos of her late parents were in a metal box that had survived the heat. Her office was destroyed.

Nothing in the upstairs rooms was salvageable. What hadn't burned was ruined by smoke and water. When all was said and done, she accepted the stark reality that all was gone.

She was grateful for the generosity of friends and strangers and, luckily, she had just taken some fall and winter clothes to the cleaners to get ready for the October weather. She had no choice but to use funds from her less-than-impressive bank account to buy necessities for her and Danny.

"What are you going to do, Caroline?" Betty asked as Caroline sat dejectedly in the kitchen, staring at a cup of tea. "I mean about your business? I know you've always worked out of your home but you're welcome to put in a desk at our furniture store."

Jim and Betty owned the McClure Furniture Outlet and it was through their referral of some of their customers that Caroline had secured several redecorating contracts.

"Maybe that way you'll pick up some decorating jobs from more of our customers," Betty encouraged. "And you and Danny can stay with us until things get settled."

"That's kind of you. I just don't know."

After the shock had worn off and reality set in, Caroline gratefully accepted both offers.

Danny had turned six the first week in October—after school had started, so he was in kindergarten.

Betty loaned Caroline a laptop and she set up her "office" in a corner of their store. Using the telephone, she prospected for viable clients and created a simple advertising brochure to hand out.

She had just hung up the telephone, batting zero for the morning, when Betty and an attractive woman approached her desk.

"Caroline, I want you to meet Stella Wainwright. She's from Texas and her brother-in-law has a mountain lodge in Colorado that he's decided to redecorate."

"Pleased to meet you." Caroline rose to her feet and held out her hand. "Caroline Fairchild."

The woman was fashionably dressed in gabardine slacks, a pink knit shell and a leather jacket. Her blondish hair was cut short around a tanned face and alert hazel eyes matched her steady expression. Caroline guessed her to be close to forty despite her youthful appearance.

"She tells me she's having trouble hiring a decorator willing to go and work in such an isolated place," Betty explained quickly. "I told her I didn't know whether you'd be interested—with your other commitments and all," she added with a straight face.

"The project sounds interesting," Caroline responded, smiling and playing the role of a successful, busy decorator.

With obvious satisfaction, Betty made her retreat, leaving the two women to talk.

"Please sit down." Caroline motioned to a nearby

chair and turned her desk chair in that direction. "Where is the lodge located?"

"At the foot of the San Juan Mountains on the western slope of Colorado," she answered, crossing her legs in a relaxed fashion.

"Near Durango?"

"North of there. Closer to Telluride."

"I see." Caroline had never been in that part of the state but she had a general idea of the area.

"His property is extensive and includes its own lake and encompasses hundreds of acres of mountain forest," Stella Wainwright continued. "The lodge is quite isolated and private."

Caroline mentally groaned. The nearby Rocky Mountains were great for an occasional recreational pastime, but working in a rugged, isolated area of the state with a six-year-old boy wasn't high on Caroline's preference list.

"I'm not sure," Caroline began.

"I know what you're thinking." The other woman gave a light laugh. "It's not that bad, trust me. The Wainwright family built Shadow Mountain Lodge as a welcome retreat for family and friends from hot, muggy Texas summer heat. My late husband, Delvin, loved it. He was Wes's younger brother and was killed in a private plane crash en route to the lodge."

"Oh, I'm sorry," Caroline said sincerely; she knew what it was like to lose a husband.

"My teenage son, Shane, and I still spend a good deal of time at the lodge. It's isolated and set on the slopes of Shadow Mountain. The surroundings are quite beautiful."

"I'm sure they are," Caroline replied evenly. Without even seeing the place, she was intimidated by the challenges such a job would present. The demands of acquiring materials and dependable labor to carry out a job there could be a living nightmare.

Before Caroline could put her refusal in polite terms, Stella Wainwright surprised her by reaching out and touching her hand. "I can assure you that Wesley Wainwright, heir to the family's oil empire, would financially make it worth your time and effort." In the next breath, she mentioned a figure that was ten times what Caroline had expected.

"For that amount of money, you could hire the very best—"

"I've tried," Stella replied shortly. "All the interior decorators I have on my list have refused for one reason or another. Maybe it's because I have very definite ideas about what I want done. Of course, sometimes those ideas change when I don't quite like the way they work out."

Uh-oh, enough said! Now Caroline understood! Stella Wainwright was looking for someone who would put up with her constantly changing her mind about what she wanted. A decorator's nightmare!

As if to verify Caroline's thoughts, Stella gave Caroline a measuring look and asked, "Do you think we could work together?"

The innocent question was loaded. Caroline knew it. If she accepted this job it would probably turn out to be pure hell. She'd bet there would be plenty of headaches with little satisfaction. Maybe even the loss of her own integrity included.

She wanted to say, "No thanks. I'll pass." But she didn't. There were too many things at stake, like securing an immediate income and having a place for her and Danny to stay without imposing on anyone. Her options were painfully limited. When it came down to it, she really didn't have a choice.

She straightened her shoulders and replied in a calm and rational tone, "Yes, I think we could work together nicely, Mrs. Wainwright."

"Call me Stella," the woman invited with a smile that sealed the matter. "How soon do you think you could begin?"

Wesley Wainwright had just come back to the lodge from a hike on Shadow Mountain when the phone rang. He was breathing a little heavily when he answered it. The climb was always a strenuous one, but his six-foot body had handled the muscular demands with ease and he felt as strong now in his thirties as he had in college. He loved being out in the mountain air, away from closed-in offices, board meetings and the ever-present demands of his financial responsibilities.

He sighed as he picked up the receiver. If it was his secretary in Houston, he was going to hang up.

"Hi, it's Stella."

His sister-in-law had been gone nearly a week and he'd rather enjoyed not having her around. Sometimes Stella's presence got a little tedious. He wasn't all that happy when she'd showed up at the lodge during his planned vacation away from work and family. Frankly, he'd been relieved when she'd left to spend time in Denver. She was one of those women who liked to manage everything and everybody—including him.

"What's happening?" he asked in a guarded tone. Stella's voice was laced with excitement.

"It wasn't easy but I did it. I found one."

"One what?"

"An interior decorator," she answered impatiently. "I found one who will come to the lodge. Last spring we talked about doing some redecorating at the lodge. Don't you remember?"

Wes's hand tightened on the receiver. "I thought that was in the future." *Way in the future,* he added silently. "I didn't know you were intending to carry out the idea so soon."

"I just haven't been able to find a decorator who would spend several months isolated in the mountains—until today."

"When is all of this going to start happening?" His sister-in-law was constantly testing his patience. If she hadn't been his late brother's widow, he wouldn't have put up with her being such a controlling force in his life.

"Since it's early October, everything will be just perfect for the Christmas holidays. I've arranged for the decorator to start next week. Her name is Caroline Fairchild and she'll be bringing her little boy with her." She paused. "I'm thinking of putting them in rooms on the second floor. She'll need another room close by to work in. Since your suite is at the far end of the corridor you won't be bothered. What do you think?"

He controlled an impulse to tell her exactly what he thought. "Yes, fine."

"Good. They'll arrive next week."

Wesley hung up the phone, muttering, "Well, so much for peace and quiet."

Having Stella show up had been bad enough but now she was arranging for some decorator and her kid to move in for God knew how long. Stella had been twenty-four years old when she'd married his nineteen-year-old brother, Delvin. Noticeably pregnant at the time, Stella eventually gave birth to a baby boy they named Shane. To her credit, since Delvin's death almost six years ago, Stella had been a conscientious single mother to her son.

Wes had tried to fill in the empty spot that his brother's death had left in the boy's life. Now seventeen, Shane loved spending time in Colorado. The young man had made it clear he'd rather forget about college and just enjoy life on the ski slopes and hiking trails. His mother disagreed, but Wes thought it might be a good idea for Shane to take a year off, to discover a few things about himself.

Wes always tried his best to accommodate Stella's ideas and plans when they were at the lodge but this latest decorating craze of hers was the limit.

He could imagine the frenzy the lodge would be in when the redecorating got into full swing. Well, he wasn't going to stick around to see it. He'd be long gone. There were plenty of spots in Colorado where a man could find peace and quiet.

He reached for some brochures and settled back to make plans for his escape.

Chapter 2

The Wainwright property on the southern edge of the Colorado San Juan Mountains was a seven-hour drive from Denver. A narrow road twisted through rugged shadowy slopes that reminded Caroline of pictures she'd seen of Germany's brooding Black Forest.

"Are we there yet?" Danny asked in a bored voice.

"Almost." She sent him a reassuring smile that faked the confidence she didn't feel.

"I'm tired."

"Me, too." She'd turned off the main highway hours ago and had no idea how close she was to the Wainwright lodge. Only vaulting wooded cliffs rose on each side, making a tunnel-like passage for the twisting mountain road. Signs of habitation were scarce and the pencil map Stella had drawn was of little help. She'd made an *X* to show where the lodge stood at one end of a small, private lake—but where was the lake?

Caroline's hands were tense on the steering wheel as she maneuvered a series of hairpin curves. Then, suddenly, without warning, there was a break in the view ahead and a startling vista opened up before her eyes. Nestled in the circle of the encroaching mountains was a meadow, a small lake and an access road posted with a wooden sign, Shadow Mountain Lodge.

"We're here," she said with a sigh of relief.

Danny peered over the front seat as best he could, straining against his seatbelt. "Where? I don't see nothing."

"Anything," she automatically corrected him. "See that building across the lake? That's where we're going."

He stuck out his lower lip the way he did when things weren't going his way. When they got closer, he said, "I hate it. It's ugly."

Caroline wasn't about to argue. Built of austere, dark wood, the mountain lodge was set in the depths of towering trees that hugged its square, unrelieved lines. A late-afternoon sun failed to lighten the blankness of recessed dormer windows crouched under a sharply slanted roof.

She remembered Stella had told her that her brother-in-law was a widower and had a six-year-old daughter named Cassie. Caroline hoped that Danny and the little girl got along. Her son was easygoing most of the time but when Danny set his mind against some thing or someone, a team of horses couldn't budge him.

She followed the road that bordered the lake and then rose sharply to the lodge set against the steep backdrop of a mountain. She continued past the lodge and parked in an open area which looked as if it might lead to some other smaller buildings like stables and bunkhouses set back in the trees.

Once released from his seat, Danny bounded out of the car like a young animal freed from a cage.

"Stay close," she ordered as she took out an overnight bag and decided to leave the rest of the luggage until later. The place looked deserted, but she could hear the neighing of a horse and spied a corral set back in the trees.

With Danny at her side, they walked around to the front of the lodge and climbed a flight of wooden stairs to a heavy, planked front door. A brass lion's head with its mouth open made a loud clanging sound as she dropped the knocker several times.

As they waited, she rested her hand reassuringly on Danny's shoulder but already the enveloping isolation was getting to her. Her mouth went dry.

What on earth am I doing here?

The massive door suddenly opened and Stella stood there, smiling at them. "Oh, good, I was hoping you'd get here before dark. Sometimes these mountain roads can be a little tricky at night."

Caroline silently added, *And in daylight*. It was some kind of miracle she'd found the place at all.

"Please come in. I'll send Shane to bring in the rest of your luggage."

They followed her inside and the interior of the lodge seemed just as dark and intimidating as the exterior. Beyond a shadowy vestibule, they entered a large room with a high ceiling and a monstrous chandelier made of elk horns suspended from a high rafter. Several tall windows allowed muted sunlight to slightly relieve the shadows of high ceilings and dark-panelled walls. A massive stone fireplace dominated the far wall and a variety of furniture, mostly leather and dark walnut, was scattered about. An area rug of faded green covered a small section of a wide-planked floor. Some framed black-and-white photographs hung on the wall. They were group pictures as far as Caroline could tell. She wondered if this was one of the rooms Stella wanted redecorated. If so, simply introducing some color would be a step in the right direction.

"I'll show you to your rooms first," Stella said motioning toward a massive staircase mounting a far wall. "You'll probably want to freshen up before meeting Wes. He was set to leave yesterday when one of his good friends, Dexter Tate, showed up unexpectedly. They're out target-shooting but should be back anytime. Wes's daughter, Cassie, is upstairs with her nanny, Felicia." She glanced at her watch. "I'd better see that some refreshment is ready."

As they mounted the steps to the second floor and walked a short distance down the hall, Stella said in a practiced hostess manner, "I hope you'll be comfortable here. There's a small sitting room, a bedroom with twin beds and a connecting bath. I've set up a workroom just down the hall. If there's anything I've missed, just let me know."

She opened the door and motioned them inside. They had just walked into the sitting room when Danny suddenly cowered beside her, hugging her leg.

"What is it?" She followed his frightened gaze to the walls of the room. Her breath caught. "Good heavens!"

Mounted on the walls were heads of wild animals—a fierce black bear, a threatening mountain lion and a snarling wildcat. She could tell from the raw fear in

Danny's expression that he thought they were alive and about to jump down on him.

"It's all right, honey," Caroline said quickly. "They won't hurt you."

"They're dead?"

"Yes. Somebody killed them."

"Why?" he demanded with childish bluntness.

"They're like trophies," Stella answered quickly before Caroline could. "Big men shoot them and then hang them on the walls to show how brave they are. I'm afraid you'll find them all over the lodge." Then she brightened. "But your mother and I are going to make some nice changes."

Caroline didn't say anything, but she wondered how easy that was going to be. Changing anything that had become a male tradition might be an uphill battle. If she were a gambler, she'd bet the mounted animals stayed despite Stella's best efforts.

Fortunately the small bedroom was spared any hunting decor. Several scenic pictures hung on the walls. One window had simple green draperies hanging from a brass rod. Caroline was delighted with the hand-crafted aspen bedroom furniture. She immediately visualized how a little color and fresh wallpaper would add a pleasant warmth to the room.

"If there's anything you need, just let me know," Stella said, preparing to leave them. "Please come downstairs when you're ready. There's a small social room just past the main stairs and down the hall. I know Wes will be pleased to meet you both. He has a little girl about your age, Danny. Her name is Cassie. I know you'll have fun playing with her while your mother and I are busy."

Danny's scowl plainly showed his reaction to the idea. Girls weren't his thing.

Caroline silently sighed. A belligerent little six-year-old was all she needed to make this whole experience a living nightmare. Her son's mood certainly didn't improve when she insisted on a hands-and-face washing, a quick change of clothes and a brushing of his tousled brown hair. He flopped down on one of the beds while she freshened up.

Stella had warned her they'd need warm clothes as well as walking shoes and boots. Caroline had followed her suggestions and found some bargains for her and Danny that she could afford.

She wanted to make a good first impression. After exchanging her jeans for a pair of tan slacks and her plain pullover for a variegated knit sweater in the red and orange colors of fall leaves, a quick glance in the mirror warned her she didn't look very professional. Somehow her two tailored outfits didn't seem right either. Besides, they were packed in the luggage she'd left in the car. She brushed her lips lightly with pink gloss, gave her short, wavy hair a quick combing and straightened her shoulders.

"I guess I'm ready," she said as she came out of the bathroom. When she saw that Danny had fallen asleep, she groaned. Now what? She couldn't leave him here asleep. If he woke up and was alone with all those animal heads, he'd freak out! But he'd be grumpy if he didn't have a nap.

Stella would probably be waiting impatiently, but she didn't have a choice. Caroline knew she'd have to wait at least a half hour before waking him.

As she looked at his sweet face, so angelic in sleep,

her chest was suddenly tight with emotion. He was so precious. Her whole life now. He'd been only two years old when she was left to raise him alone. Even though Thomas's medical career had dominated his time and energies, his unexpected heart attack and death had left her without any emotional support. There were no grandparents or close relatives to provide an extended family for either of them.

She turned away from the bed and walked over to the window to look out. Her view was of the wooded slopes behind the lodge. Already the sun had slipped behind craggy mountain peaks and she would have missed seeing the two horsemen moving through the trees if their movement had not caught her eye. Before she could get a good look at them, they disappeared beyond her view.

Wes Wainwright, no doubt, and the guest Stella mentioned who had gone target-shooting with him. She wondered what targets they'd chosen for their sport and doubted that she could even be polite to her Texas host after seeing the mounted heads.

She'd always had trouble controlling her temper when she encountered selfish, self-centered men. Bragging rich Texans who seemed to throw their weight around had never been very high on her list.

When she finally woke Danny, he was less than co-operative.

"When can we go home?" he said with a scowl as she brushed his hair once again.

"Not today," she said with false cheerfulness. She couldn't tell him when it would be because she really didn't know the answer. Everything depended upon Stella and her redecorating plans. If they were superficial and limited, the job would only require a few weeks. If the entire lodge was to undergo a coordinated redecoration, several months might be involved.

"I bet you're hungry." Caroline said brightly. "Let's go downstairs and have a nice dinner."

She was glad a bedroom door led into the hall so they didn't have to go through the sitting room with the overpowering animal heads. Danny needed time to adjust to this strange environment.

And so do I!

Their feet made a muffled sound on the bare steps as they descended the staircase to the main room. Someone had turned on a few scattered lights that played over the furniture, gloomy walls and stone fireplace. The bulbs on the ugly antler chandelier remained dark as it hung like a menacing threat overhead.

Following Stella's instructions, Caroline turned down a dimly lit hall and, with Danny hugging her side, passed a series of doors opening into various sized rooms. She couldn't tell what they were used for because they were all dark.

Caroline was beginning to wonder if she'd missed the right way when she heard the sound of voices and saw light spilling through double doors opening into the hall.

She tried for a composed smile when they entered the social room, as Stella had called it. Even though the decor was much the same as the main room's—paneled walls and brown leather furniture—the warmth and lighting in the room was a sharp contrast to the rest of the lodge. The room gave off a surprising cheerfulness.

She held Danny's tense little hand firmly as he started to pull back. She saw then he was staring at a black bear skin with an snarling, open mouth stretched out above the fireplace.

Stella immediately stood up from a chair next to a coffee table. "There you are. I was about to send someone after you. I want you to meet Wes."

Caroline could tell she was nervous. *Maybe as nervous as I am.* "I'm sorry, Danny took a little nap and delayed us."

Two men stood in front of a blazing fireplace with drinks in their hands. *Which one is the Texas tycoon?* Was it the overweight, round-faced fellow wearing leather trousers and a fringed jacket? The one doing all the talking and gesturing with his free hand?

The other man was taller, well-proportioned, wearing jeans and a denim shirt open at the collar and rolled up at the cuffs. A shock of brown hair with a glint of red hung low on his forehead and framed a strong, masculine face.

A slight frown creased his forehead as Stella brought Caroline across the room and introduced her. "Wes, this is Caroline Fairchild and her son, Danny. She's the decorator," she added as a reminder.

"Oh, yes. Pleased to meet you," he replied politely and Caroline sensed a decided lack of enthusiasm in his manner.

"Did you kill that?" Danny demanded, thrusting a pointing finger up at the mounted bear skin.

"Nope. My grandpa killed that one."

"Why?"

"Well, that old bear was looking around for something to eat. You can see his sharp teeth. Grandpa didn't want him to have his dog, Shep, for dinner. My little girl says he looks mean. What do you think?"

"I don't like him," Danny answered flatly.

"Smart boy." He nodded approvingly. "How old are you, Danny?"

"Six."

"Really? What do you know? I have a little girl the same age." He turned to Caroline. "They're a handful, aren't they?" She could tell he was forcing himself to be congenial so she smiled and nodded.

Obviously, he wasn't all that pleased about having an interior decorator under foot. Something warned her that she'd better tread softly and keep her distance. If he was going to pay her the exorbitant amount Stella had promised, she couldn't afford to antagonize him. She remembered Stella had said he had intended to be gone before she arrived. Caroline suspected that under those good looks there was probably plenty of barbed wire.

Despite Wes's lack of enthusiasm, Stella seemed to be determined to proceed full speed ahead with the project. "We'll be looking over the lodge and deciding where to begin—"

"Just leave my suite and the gun room alone." His tone brooked no argument. The lines and planes in his face suggested a firm control of his thoughts and feelings. Even when he smiled his eyes held a certain glint, as if his mind were functioning on many levels. He was worth millions and his casual attire didn't fool Caroline a bit. She suspected only a fool would judge him by outward appearances.

The robust man still standing by the fireplace chuckled as he took another drink from his glass. He must be the old friend Stella said had arrived unexpectedly. As the man's assessing eyes traveled over her, Caroline mentally stiffened against his open appraisal. They hadn't even met yet and she didn't like him.

At that moment, a little girl bounded into the room, blond pigtails flapping. She was wearing jeans and a plaid shirt. A red cowboy hat hung by a string down her back. When she saw Danny, she stopped short.

"Who's that?" she demanded, scowling.

Danny's little mouth tightened as he scowled back.

"This is Danny Fairchild, Cassie," Stella answered quickly in a warning tone. "He's going to be a guest at the lodge and you'll want to make him feel welcome."

"What if I don't like him?"

Oh, no, thought Caroline. *This could turn out to be a real nightmare.*

"What's not to like, honey?" her father asked as he motioned Cassie over to his side. "You've been complaining about not having anyone to go horseback-riding with you. How about it, son? Would you like to take a ride on one of Cassie's Shetland ponies?"

As Danny's scowl instantly faded, Caroline stiffened with sudden irritation. How dare this man make such an offer without knowing whether her son would be safe riding a horse—pony or otherwise.

Danny's eyes were already sparkling with anticipation as he looked up at her. "Mom…?"

"We'll see."

"Spoken like a true mother," quipped the man in leather trousers before Wes had a chance to say anything. As he stepped forward, he held out a pudgy hand. "Dexter Tate. Wes didn't warn me that we were going to have feminine company or I would have shaved for the occasion." He rubbed a growth of dark whiskers on his full cheeks and chin.

"Dexter thinks of himself as a ladies' man and we try to humor him," Wes said with a chuckle. Dexter took a playful swipe at him and they both laughed like good friends who enjoyed ribbing each other.

Cassie had moved closer to Danny. "You want to go see my ponies?"

"Not now, Cassie," her father said before Danny could respond. "It's almost time for dinner." He turned to Caroline. "I imagine it's been a long day. Traveling is never easy."

"Not unless you have a jet plane, helicopter and a slick foreign car," Dexter quipped and added with pointed emphasis, "Not that Wes ever travels alone."

"Cut it out, you two," Stella said quickly, obviously wanting to change the conversation.

A tall, lanky youth with a tanned narrow face and longish unkempt dark hair appeared in the doorway. He was wearing cowboy boots, a Western shirt and low-slung jeans held in place by a leather belt with a huge silver and turquoise buckle.

"Come in, Shane," Stella said with a wave of her hand.

"Cook says grub's on. Come and get it," he said as he ambled in with his hands in his pockets.

"Shane, that's no way to announce dinner. I want you to meet Mrs. Fairchild. This is my seventeen-year-old son, Shane."

"Nice to meet you," Caroline quickly responded. "This is my son, Danny."

Shane gave a quick bob of his head at the introductions and as if to ward off a lecture from his mother, he told Caroline, "I took your suitcases up to your rooms."

She quickly thanked him and was rewarded with a fleeting smile that didn't quite meet his light-brown eyes.

"Shane's a big help around here," Wesley said as he put his arm around the adolescent's shoulders.

Caroline could tell that Shane was pleased with the attention. He ducked his head and shuffled his feet as if a little embarrassed by his uncle's attention.

"Shane's only going to spend a year here in Colorado before going to college," his mother said quickly as if there might have been some heated discussion about it. "His late father would have wanted him to fill his shoes, being responsible and taking care of family business. That means some brain work and study."

Caroline could tell from Shane's expression that he'd heard this lecture before. His eyes darkened. The young man's suddenly stiff posture hinted at an explosive emotion close to the surface.

Wes murmured, "Easy does it."

There was something threatening and unsettling about Shane Wainwright. Caroline decided then and there to keep Danny as far away from him as she could.

Chapter 3

Caroline was relieved that dinner was a casual affair served in a square room that resembled a café more than a formal dining area. The walls were knotty pine and undressed windows with open shutters overlooked a rocky slope and the lake below. Small maple tables and chairs were scattered around the room with no sign of the traditional long table. She suspected the lodge's main dining room was closed off when so few people were in residence.

Stella had told Caroline that usually only relatives and close friends made use of the lodge, but Wes invited business associates and acquaintances to be guests a few times during the year.

Wes and Dexter had stayed behind to finish their drinks and the only occupant in the room when Caroline, Stella and the children entered was a woman with graying dark hair and strong Spanish features sitting at one of the tables. Her dress was a bright, exotic print with a matching fringed shawl and a stream of different colored beads hung around her neck. Large silver hoops dangled from her ears.

"Nanny, here's another kid," Cassie exclaimed as she bounded over to her. Pointing a finger at Danny, she added with a frown, "I don't like him much. Does he get to play with all my things?"

The woman slowly set down her cup and rose to her feet. She was tall with a rather regal posture. Caroline guessed her to be in her fifties.

"No, sit down, Felicia," Stella ordered, but the woman remained standing as Stella drew Caroline forward. "I spoke to you about Mrs. Fairchild and her son being with us for a few weeks. Well, this is Danny. He's the same age as Cassie."

Felicia's dark eyes narrowed and she seemed to stiffen as she looked at Danny. Caroline wondered if she had already decided that the boy's presence spelled trouble.

"I'm sure having someone for Cassie to play with will be a help," Stella told her.

Caroline spoke up rather defensively. "Danny's preschool teachers have found him easy to manage. He plays well with other children. If there's any problem, I'll want to know about it."

"Such beautiful brown eyes, round and clear," Felicia said, her expression softening as she looked at him.

Cassie shook her finger at Danny in a warning manner. "You have to do as she says."

Danny stuck his tongue out at the bossy little girl.

To Caroline's surprise Felicia laughed deeply, her earrings jingling as she nodded. Apparently, Danny's rejection of Cassie's bossiness amused her. "He's a nice boy. You bring him to my rooms. We'll all play and learn together."

"Good. That's settled then," Stella said, just as Wes and Dexter came into the room.

"Mmm. Smells good," Dexter said. "I'm hungry as a bear. Grrrr," he said patting his stomach as he made a play move for Danny. He laughed when Danny backed up and gave him a wide-eyed stare.

"That's enough, Dex," Wes said and motioned Caroline and Danny toward a built-in buffet along one wall. "We don't stand on formality here. We serve ourselves except for drinks."

"Wait for me at a table, Danny," Caroline told him. "I'll bring you a plate."

The choices were unbelievable and Caroline decided there were enough steaming dishes set out to feed a harvest crew. She had a choice of chicken, roast beef or barbecue pork ribs. There were several vegetable casseroles and potatoes oozing with butter. A platter of fruit was about the only thing that didn't shriek calories.

Caroline selected a piece of chicken, modest servings of two kinds of vegetables and sliced oranges for both her and Danny. Wes, Dexter and Shane were in line behind her, filling their plates to the fullest.

Stella and Cassie took their plates to the table where Danny was sitting and as Caroline followed, she noticed that Felicia had left. She wondered if it was the nanny's habit not to eat with the family.

As the two men and Shane sat together at another table, a murmur of conversation and laughter filled the small room. Almost immediately, as if there'd been some kind of signal to the kitchen, a rather plump, red-headed woman in slacks and T-shirt came into the room to serve the drinks.

"Trudie Benson, our housekeeper," Stella told Caroline. "Her husband, Hank, is our wonderful cook and the two of them keep the place going. They're recruits from the Texas ranch. Been with the Wainwright family for years. Wes brought them to Colorado when he was first married."

"How long ago was that?"

"Before I was born," Cassie piped up. "Daddy told me. Him and Mommy were lonesome until I came along. When she went to heaven, he was glad he still had me."

"My daddy went to heaven, too," Danny said as if he wasn't going to be outdone. "And my mom's glad she has me."

Both Caroline and Stella choked back smiles. Competitive natures, both of them.

Caroline begged off staying downstairs after dinner. It had been a long day and both she and Danny were tired. To her surprise, Wes invited her to have an after-dinner drink before retiring, but she politely refused. She knew better than to fraternize with the boss.

After they were settled in their beds and Danny had said his prayers, she wearily closed her eyes and courted sleep. None came. After an hour of turning and tossing, she was still awake. The dynamics of her new situation and the people she'd met kept her mind whirling.

Wes Wainwright certainly had perfected an image of devoted father and unpretentious millionaire. But was it just a facade? What was he like, really? She doubted that he'd stay around long enough for her to find out. Even if he did, she was pretty sure he'd make his presence scarce while the redecorating was going on.

And what about Stella and her son, Shane? Stella must have been much older than the younger brother, Delvin, to marry and have a son of seventeen. She wondered what Wes's wife had been like and what had happened to her. Caroline tossed all of this around in her mind until she finally fell into a restless sleep.

The room was filled with morning light when she came awake with a jerk. Danny was bending over her, his breath warm on her face. "Are you awake?"

"Almost," she said and smiled as she cupped his face with her hands and kissed his forehead. "Are you?"

"Can we go home, now?"

"Not today."

"When can we?"

"I'm not sure," she answered honestly. Taking one day at a time was the only way she could cope at the moment. She wasn't at all sure how this decorating job was going to play out. Stella's temperament was certainly a question mark. Conceivably, the woman could throw her hands up at any time and fire Caroline without much cause.

Obviously, her brother-in-law, Wes, had no emotional investment in the project. Caroline suspected he'd be glad enough to have the whole idea scrapped.

And then there was Cassie. If Danny got crosswise with her in any serious way, her father would promptly show them the door to keep her happy. And Felicia wasn't exactly the kind of nanny Caroline would have chosen. She didn't seem the type who easily related to children.

* * *

Wes was the only one in the room when they came down to breakfast. He watched as Caroline and Danny moved along the buffet. When she gave him a hesitant smile, he was glad he'd made the effort to come down early. He stood up and motioned for them to join him at his table.

He thought she looked trim and neat in light-blue slacks, matching jacket and simple white blouse. The first thing he'd noticed about her was her eyes. They were as blue and clear as a summer's sky. Her brunette, wavy hair was short, casual and carefree. He liked that. He couldn't stand women who were always fussing with their hair. His late wife, Pamela, had been the worst. She'd been a Texas beauty queen when he'd met and married her. Her appearance had always been uppermost in her mind. It got a little wearying at times.

As they sat down, Wes poured her coffee from a table carafe and offered Danny a carton of chocolate milk.

"I like chocolate best," Danny said with a happy grin.

"I thought you might," he said smiling as he poured it into a glass for him. He was a damn cute kid. Not as outgoing as Cassie, but he'd bet Danny was just as sure of himself in his own way. "Did you sleep well?" he asked Caroline as if the dark circles under her eyes weren't answer enough.

"So-so. I guess I had a few things on my mind."

As she sipped her coffee and looked at him over the rim of her cup, a feeling he hadn't experienced for a long time stirred within him. Her features were totally feminine and her full breasts and rounded hips invited the caressing touch of a man's hands. Her lips were moist and pink from the warmth of the hot coffee and he couldn't help but imagine what they would feel like pressed against his. As he felt desire begin to stir, he looked away quickly and gave his attention to his cinnamon toast.

"Lovely view," she said, looking out the window.

"This early in the morning the sun just brushes the tops of the trees," he told her. "The mountains look as if they've been painted against the sky. As far as I'm concerned, the Colorado Rockies have the kind of beauty that makes life worthwhile. I hope you can relax, Caroline, and enjoy yourself a little while you're here."

"Stella said you wouldn't be staying."

Wes couldn't tell from her tone whether it made the slightest difference to her one way or the other. He was used to women who welcomed his company and for some strange reason he wanted her to be one of them.

"I've changed my plans a bit—because of Dexter. I guess I'll have to keep him company for a few days at least."

The excuse was a lie. Dexter often spent time at the lodge or Wes's Texas ranch when Wes wasn't around. His old friend had been trying to make time with Stella for quite a while—without much luck. If Stella favored anyone it was Tim Henderson, the manager-caretaker of the property. Tim was a little older than Stella, quiet-spoken and didn't jump when she threw her weight around. Their relationship hadn't changed much through the years and Wes really didn't know if they had a private, intimate relationship going or not.

"I hope Dex and I won't be in your way," Wes added, blatantly fishing for an assurance his presence would be welcome.

"I'm not sure how extensive Stella's plans are," she replied evenly.

"You may have trouble putting a leash on Stella's wild ideas," he warned.

"That isn't my job. I've been hired to follow her wishes as best I can. My commitment is to please Stella and offer suggestions, but not implement my own ideas."

"Then heaven help us both," he said lightly. He was impressed with the firm way she set him straight. He liked that.

"More coffee?" he asked as he filled her cup.

Danny piped up. "Where's that girl?"

"You mean Cassie?"

Danny bobbed his head. "Yeah, her."

"She usually has breakfast and sometimes lunch with her nanny upstairs. They have a nice little kitchen apartment all their own. Maybe you'd like to join them sometime?"

Danny's expression clearly expressed his lack of enthusiasm for such a happening. "I don't like girls."

Wes chuckled at the child's display of disgust. Danny was all boy. Watching a son like that grow up would be a joy. Wes's heart tightened just a bit. He loved his daughter, but he couldn't help wishing he also had his own son to raise.

"Girls are a pest sometimes," he agreed solemnly. "It's too bad you're not interested though. Cassie has a playroom filled with all kinds of fun things. And then there're the ponies."

"I'm not sure that's a good idea," his mother said quickly. "Danny's never been around horses."

"Maybe this is a good time to give him that opportunity. One of my staff, Tim Henderson, is very good with youngsters. He rides with Cassie almost every day." Wes could tell she wasn't sold on the idea. "What about you? Have you done any horseback riding?"

Her laughter surprised him. "I've ridden bareback, saddled up my own mount and even mucked out a stable or two." She told him that her parents had been farm people.

"Well, I guess I'd better brush up on my own performance before asking you to go riding with me."

"We could all go," Danny popped up in a firm little voice.

Wes was beginning to like this kid more and more. "Good idea. How about this afternoon?"

"Oh, I don't know. Stella—" Caroline started to protest.

"Let's say four o'clock. She should be through with you by then."

"Please, Mama, please," Danny begged.

Wes could tell Danny's mother was hard put to deny his eager expression. "We ought to take advantage of the nice weather. October can be unpredictable, especially in the high country."

"All right, if Stella doesn't object."

"Good," Wes stood up and ruffled Danny's hair. "See you then, cowboy."

Caroline and Danny were just finishing their breakfast when Trudie Benson came in from the kitchen. She wiped her hands on an apron large enough to cover her rounded middle and asked, "Everything all right?"

"Great," Caroline assured her. "Thank you."

"No need for thanks. Hank and I are happy just to see people enjoying the food."

"Where is everybody?"

"The hired help eat early and the rest eat late. You're kinda in the middle. Felicia and Cassie are having breakfast upstairs."

"Could you tell me where their rooms are? I need to check with the nanny about looking after Danny while I work." Caroline ignored Danny's audible groan.

"Top of the stairs, turn to the right. Knock on the double doors at the end of the hall."

Caroline thanked her and they left Trudie busily checking the buffet and coffeepots.

Danny hung back and grumbled all the way up the stairs.

"It's going to be fun," Caroline assured him. "Like daycare and preschool…only better. Just the two of you to play with all the toys."

"Girls' stuff," he muttered.

"Did you notice her cowboy boots and hat? And she has her own ponies." She smiled to herself as his frown disappeared.

"I guess she's okay."

"You'll have your own special teacher, too. Felicia seems very nice. And this afternoon we'll go horseback riding—if you behave yourself." She wasn't above a little bit of bribery when the situation invited it.

She found Felicia's apartment on the second floor at the opposite end from their rooms. She knocked on the double doors. It opened slowly and Cassie peeked out. Her round eyes instantly fixed on Danny. "What do you want?"

"May we come in?" Caroline asked politely, ignoring the two children glaring at each other.

"We've already had breakfast," Cassie declared with

obvious satisfaction as she opened the door wider. "You can't be sleepyheads and eat with us."

"We already ate," Danny declared triumphantly.

The apartment's sitting room was quite spacious and light with the morning sun pouring through windows along one wall. Draperies, furniture throws and fringed gaudy lamps were various shades of red and purple. Artificial flowers were displayed on small tables covered with silk cloths and Caroline could smell an invading scent of potpourri coming from a cut-glass bowl.

Cassie pranced ahead of them into an adjoining room which was obviously the playroom of a very rich little girl. Even Danny's eyes widened as he looked around at the games, toys, paints, clay and inviting electronic gadgets he'd only seen in toy stores.

Cassie knocked on one of the doors at the far side of the room and called out loudly, "That boy's here."

The bedroom door opened almost immediately and Felicia glided into the room wearing a long multicolored robe that swept the floor. Her salt-and-pepper hair was held back by a braided band and fell freely halfway down her back. If Felicia was embarrassed by her less-than-formal appearance, there was no evidence of it.

"I hope we're not too early," Caroline quickly apologized.

"Not at all," she said smiling and in a formal tone, she said, "Good morning, Danny."

To Caroline's surprise, Danny responded with a preschool ritual. "Good morning, Miss… Miss…" He fumbled for the right name.

"Felicia. Fe…lis…e…a," she pronounced phonetically. When he repeated it, she nodded. "Very good."

Danny beamed. Caroline began to relax.

"Cassie, why don't you set up the race track for you and Danny? And let him have his choice of cars?" she prompted.

The car-racing game must have been a rare treat because Cassie's frown instantly changed in to a wide smile. Caroline blessed Felicia for recognizing a pivotal moment and handling it so beautifully. The two children happily busied themselves setting up the track and positioning their choice of cars.

"Would you join me in a second cup of coffee while the children get acquainted a bit?" Felicia asked Caroline.

"Yes, thank you." She doubted that Stella would be looking for her this early.

Felicia motioned toward the kitchenette. A small round table and chairs were in an alcove off the main room. Caroline didn't see any dishes in the sink or on the table.

"You must have breakfast early," she commented as Felicia brought cups and a coffeepot from an apartment-sized stove over to the table.

"Dawn is the best time to greet the world. Vibrations are at their highest then. All shadows of the night flee before the healing rays of the sun, you know," she said as she sat down opposite Caroline. "Of course, Cassie wakes up several hours later."

Caroline took a sip of coffee before responding to her unusual remarks. "I can imagine how a person could lose oneself in the grandeur of the surroundings. You must love being here."

"I'm always ready to go back to sunbaked earth, clear skies and warm nights. Texas is home."

"Have you lived there all your life?"

She nodded. "My parents worked on Wes's grandfather's ranch when they first came over the border. I grew up there. Sadly, Wes lost both of his parents while he was still in college but when he got married, he asked me to come and work for him."

Caroline wanted to know how she had liked Wes's wife, but she refrained from asking. Gossiping with the nanny wasn't exactly the wisest thing to do.

"I really appreciate your looking after Danny."

Felicia's forehead was suddenly creased with thoughtful lines. She didn't answer as she stirred her coffee.

She doesn't want to do it. Now what?

"Danny really isn't as difficult to handle as he might appear," Caroline quickly assured Felicia. "He has a lot of interests and he wouldn't demand a lot of time if he has something to do."

Felicia set down her spoon and sighed deeply. "It isn't that. He's a fine little boy, I can tell that."

"Then what?"

"Nothing," she said but her eyes betrayed her words. There was a haunted look about them.

Caroline was suddenly uneasy. She'd leave the lodge in a minute if she felt it wasn't safe leaving Danny in this woman's care.

"If there's something that might affect my son, I need to know it now. Tell me."

Felicia took another sip of her coffee, carefully holding the cup steady with both hands. Then, slowly, she set it down and took a deep breath.

"I'll let no harm come to your boy, I promise."

Whatever reservation Felicia had had in her own mind seemed to be resolved. In the weighted silence, they could hear the children squealing in the other room. Danny was cheering and Cassie was laughing deeply.

"It will be good for them to be playmates," Felicia said as she reached across and patted Caroline's hand. "You do your work and I will take good care of your son, I promise. I have taken care of Cassie since she was born. They trust me and so should you." Her dark eyes hardened. "You pay no attention to what anyone says. Today is not yesterday."

Caroline wasn't sure what Felicia meant by that cryptic remark, but she knew that she wouldn't rest easy until she found out.

Chapter 4

Caroline left Danny sitting on the floor, watching as a red racer careened around a track. He barely gave his mother a quick glance as she said, "I'm leaving now, Danny. You stay here with Cassie and Felicia."

"Okay." His face was flushed and his eyes bright. "I'm ahead of Cassie two laps."

"You're going to miss a curve going that fast," Cassie retorted as if she'd learned that lesson the hard way. "Wait and see! Then I'll catch up."

"No, you won't."

Felicia gave Caroline a reassuring smile as she eased down in a nearby chair and picked up her sewing basket.

"I'll be back before lunch," Caroline said. Everything seemed to be under control. She couldn't find any rational reason for a lingering apprehension. *Quit being an overprotective mother,* she told herself, but the lecture didn't do much good. She wished they'd never left home.

Her chest tightened. *What home?*

After leaving Felicia's apartment, she walked the length of the hall to her rooms and spent a few minutes making up the beds and putting things away. Because of her limited finances, she'd shopped for only enough clothes for about a week. One of her first challenges would be to find the laundry room.

After glancing at her watch, she decided she'd go downstairs and see if Stella was ready to give her the tour of the lodge that she'd promised and tell her what rooms she wanted redone.

The eating room was empty except for Trudie Benson who was clearing off the buffet. When Caroline asked about Stella, she nodded. "She had breakfast and I think she left to talk to Tim Henderson. He's the year-round manager-caretaker, you know."

Caroline remembered that Wes has mentioned Tim before.

"Well, you'll probably find them in his office. It's just down the hall at the back of the house. It has an outside entrance so Tim can come and go without having to traipse through the whole house. He spends half his time outside checking the property and overseeing the two stablemen.

"Maybe I shouldn't bother them."

Trudie waved away the objection with her chubby hand. "Tim doesn't stand on ceremony. Besides, if Stella isn't there, he'll probably know where she is."

Trudie's instructions seemed simple enough, but Caroline soon discovered that the hall didn't continue in a straight line but made several abrupt turns. She passed a couple of narrow stairways rising to the floor above. She hugged herself against a penetrating chill in the dank, shadowy hall. The only sound was her own steps vibrating on the planked floor.

When the silence was broken by a floating echo of Stella's laughter, Caroline let out a breath of relief. Quickening her steps, she reached a door that opened into a low-ceilinged room with one window and an outside door. The furnishings were meager: a desk, a couple of straight-back chairs and some gray metal file cabinets.

A muscular man of about forty, with a weathered face and sandy hair was half sitting on the corner of the old desk and smiling at Stella who stood close by.

Both turned quickly in Caroline's direction when she appeared in the doorway. From their startled expressions she couldn't tell whether she'd interrupted something personal or they were just surprised to see her.

Stella waved her in. "Come and meet Tim Henderson. He's the boss around here."

"Hardly," he objected with an easy smile.

"I told you about her, Caroline Fairchild. She's the decorator who's going to help me put a little class in this place. And about time, too," Stella added as if she'd fought more than one battle on this subject.

"Welcome to Shadow Mountain," he said, shaking her hand. From his slight Western drawl, Caroline assumed he was another Texan. "Reckon you gals are going to be pretty busy, all right."

"You better believe it. Maybe we'll start here." Stella gave him a teasing smile as she glanced around the packed office.

"Not on your life, honey."

"Oh, you men. Wes has already warned us to leave his suite and the gun room alone. You'll be sorry when you see how beautiful the rest of the lodge turns out."

She turned to Caroline. "I'll show you the lodge and we can decide where we'll start first."

Tim walked with them to the hall door. "I hope you can keep a rein on this gal. She can be a handful sometimes."

Caroline wondered if he was speaking from experience.

As they walked down the hall, Stella explained, "We have our own generator, water supply and telephone service via Telluride. Cell phones are useless here. And no house mail delivery. We order groceries from Telluride or go after them ourselves."

As they toured the main floor, Caroline was thoroughly frustrated with Stella's ambivalence about making any decisions about basic changes she wanted. They could end up with a hodgepodge of fabrics, colors and furnishings that completely lacked harmony and balance.

Caroline was ready to call a halt to the unorganized approach and suggested they spend the afternoon going over some basic plans.

"Oh, I can't," Stella said. "You're on your own for the rest of the day. We'll get together again tomorrow morning and go over some ideas."

Caroline swallowed back a protest. A myriad of initial decisions had to be made before they could proceed. Spending only half days working out the details could extend the project almost indefinitely.

Caroline would have made an issue of the matter if she hadn't already agreed to spend the late afternoon with Wes and the children.

"I'll show you the workroom and you can get set up there," Stella said as if she sensed Caroline's impatience. "I've made a collection of magazines, books and articles that offer some good suggestions. You could look them over and see what you think."

"That might be a place to start," Caroline agreed.

When Stella showed her the workroom and Caroline saw the pile of material stacked on a long work table, she silently groaned. It would take more than one day to go through that collection.

"I set up my laptop and printer." Stella motioned to a small table. "I thought that would be an easy way for you to make some notes. Anything else?" she asked.

"No, that's fine," Caroline lied. The woman hadn't given her any clues about what she had in mind nor any specific changes she wished to make in any of the rooms. Caroline was thoroughly frustrated. If Stella had already decided on some definite ideas, this would be the time to share them, but she left Caroline alone in the workroom without another word.

As Caroline sifted though a pile of books and a dozen magazines, all new, she didn't see any signs that Stella had gone through them. Usually clients marked specific ideas that they liked or turned down pages for easy reference.

Caroline leaned back in her chair, suddenly overwhelmed by the project ahead. How could she hope to please Stella when she didn't have a clue how to begin to shape her nebulous ideas?

When she left the workroom and returned to Felicia's apartment, Danny and Cassie were happily playing with clay. If her son had missed her, there was no outward sign of it.

"Time to go downstairs for lunch," she told him.

"I don't like that stuffy old dining room," Cassie said, wrinkling up her pert nose.

"Me, neither," Danny echoed.

"Why don't I fix the children something here?" Felicia offered.

"Yay," they said, almost in unison.

Caroline laughed. "All right. I'll be back after lunch to get you for your nap, Danny."

When he groaned, she reminded him that they were going horseback-riding later in the afternoon.

"Oh, I forgot."

"I don't want you to fall asleep on Cassie's pony."

"Blackie will keep him awake," Cassie promised with a grin.

On the way downstairs, Caroline realized she would much rather have stayed and had lunch with the kids. When she reached the dining room, she was even more regretful.

Dexter was the only one there. He was wearing burgundy leather pants and a plaid shirt that only emphasized his beefy build and pot belly.

"Hi there, pretty lady," he greeted her as she came in, immediately rising to his feet. He stayed at her elbow while she selected soup and salad from the buffet and then ushered her over to the table where he was sitting.

"Where's Wes?" she asked pointedly as he guided her chair to the table.

"Oh, he's holed up in his suite, working. The price of being rich, I guess. He has to keep on top of things no matter where he goes. No rest for the weary—or the rich," he added, grinning. "Wes has probably talked to a dozen big shots this morning, keeping the wheels of commerce moving, you know." His tone was tinged with something that might have been jealousy.

"It's too bad he can't relax when he's here," Caroline said, already impatient with the man's boorish manner.

"Oh, I think he does. This lodge has really been a godsend. It's one of the blessings his grandfather left the family. I doubt that Wes or his father would have built it. When his parents died Wes inherited all the family property and fortune held in escrow for the oldest living male Wainwright." Dexter gave Caroline a knowing wink. "Wes is quite a catch for any gal who plays her cards right."

Caroline forced herself to say lightly, "I imagine there are plenty of downsides. How many times has he been married?"

"Just once. He married a Texas beauty queen, Pamela Labesky. Wow, that gal could send any man's desire into orbit just looking at her. She was something else and once Pamela set her silver tiara for Wes, he didn't have a chance. Ruined him for any other woman, that's for sure." Dexter looked thoughtful as he speared a link sausage and popped it in his mouth. "Too bad Pamela only enjoyed her good fortune and Wainwright prestige for a few years. You know about the plane crash?"

"Only that Stella said she lost her husband in one."

"The same crash. Wes would have been with them if something hadn't come up at the last minute to keep him in Houston. Stella and Shane were already at the lodge. Wes pilots his own plane, you know. Anyway, Delvin and Pamela decided not to wait for him and they hired a pilot to fly them to Colorado. Bad decision. There's a dangerous downdraft when landing in these mountains. The pilot miscalculated."

"How awful."

"Wes took it pretty hard. The tragedy was tough on him, that's for sure."

"How long ago was that?"

"Cassie was only a few months old when the plane crashed. And then there was—" He broke off as Shane came into the room.

Apparently Dexter preferred gossiping when no one else was around. He quickly changed the subject and asked Caroline how the redecorating was going.

She made a non-committal answer then purposefully gave her full attention to her lunch.

Shane made no attempt to join them and slumped down at a window table by himself. He had the stand-offish air of an adolescent and the common belligerency that went along with it. Caroline finished her lunch as quickly as possible and wasn't pleased when Dexter left the dining room with her.

"Why don't you let me show you around the place?" he offered, trying to take her arm. "You haven't been down to the stables yet, have you?"

"The children and I are going riding with Wes this afternoon," she told him quickly. "I'm looking forward to it."

"I bet you are," he said with a slight smirk. "All the women enjoy Wes's company."

She refrained from making a caustic reply about his own apparent lack of charm in that area. Being trapped under the same roof with him was going to test her endurance for repulsive men. If Wes left the lodge, she hoped to heaven he took Dexter Tate with him.

After a long nap, Caroline and Danny made their way down to the social room to meet Wes. She'd changed into jeans and the bright sweater she'd worn the night before.

Danny wore a pair of new overalls and a denim jacket. She was glad she'd invested in boots for both of them.

The social room was empty. No sign of Wes nor of Cassie. Caroline felt an instant pang of disappointment. Maybe something had come up and Wes had changed his mind—or he'd forgotten.

No, Cassie wouldn't let him forget, Caroline decided. Not that willful little girl. Thank heavens she and Danny seemed to have taken to each other—at least for the moment.

As the minutes passed, she was beginning to think he'd completely forgotten their date when she heard Cassie's high-pitched chatter floating down the hall.

Caroline smiled at Danny. "Here they come."

The little girl darted into the room ahead of Wes. She was dressed like a movie-star rodeo queen. White fringed pants matched a fringed studded vest and white boots. Her cowboy hat was the same shade of red as her satin shirt.

She grinned from ear to ear as she put one hand on her hip and demanded, "Well, what do you think?"

Danny missed the nature of her question. "I think you're late."

"Spoken like a true man," Wes said, chuckling. "Sorry, I got held up by a telephone call. Anyway, I sent word ahead to the stable. The horses should be saddled up and waiting."

Cassie danced ahead of them down a worn path under a canopy of ponderosa pine trees. Danny followed at her heels. Wes fell into step beside Caroline and she realized that she was nervous and rather ill at ease.

Maybe she'd given him the wrong idea about her riding ability? After all, a farm horse wasn't in the same league as a prancing thoroughbred. What if she made a complete fool of herself?

At that moment, she realized how much she wanted to impress this rich, handsome Texan. Why, she didn't know. In a few days he'd be gone and most likely she'd never see him again. Still, her feminine vanity wanted him to remember her as a capable horseback rider.

When they reached the stable her misgivings were doubled. Wes nodded toward a restless sorrel mare all saddled up and tethered beside two small shaggy ponies, one black and one dark brown. Two middle-aged stablehands nodded at Wes and then went about their business in the barn.

Cassie immediately ran over to the ponies. "You can ride Blackie," she informed Danny. "He's kinda old. I like Cocoa best."

"They're both gentle," Wes quickly assured Caroline. "We bought them from a Texas breeder who specializes in Shetland ponies. They're a good mount for children. Strong and muscular, but rein-easy."

Caroline began to relax. The saddles, harnesses and stirrups were proportionate to the size of a small rider. This could be a wonderful chance for her son to experience his first horseback ride.

"I'll walk along beside Danny," Wes told her. "We'll follow the path around to the western end of the lake. You can ride ahead if you'd like and we'll catch up with you."

"Why don't I walk with Danny and you ride?"

"Because I want you to enjoy yourself," he replied flatly and his tone brooked no argument.

He cupped his hands and helped Cassie up into the saddle. As she took the reins in her little hands, she grinned at Danny. "Race you to the lake."

"Cassie! We'll have none of that," Wes said sharply and quickly helped wide-eyed Danny mount the other pony. "I'll keep the reins for a while, Danny," he said reassuringly. "We'll just go for a nice walk."

As Caroline led the sorrel mare out of the barn, Wes watched. There was an easy, confident stride in her movement that pleased him. Nothing about her was showy or pretentious. Deftly she arrange the reins in her hands and patted the mare's neck. As Wes watched her swing easily into the saddle, he smiled to himself.

She hadn't lied. She settled back in the saddle as if she were born to it.

Maybe they could go for a real ride before he left, he mused. He'd like to take her up one of the rugged trails and show her God's country from the top of a mountain ridge.

The path down to the lake was a twisting one, weaving in and out of thick stands of pine and spruces. Caroline and Cassie rode ahead while Wes walked in front of Danny's pony, leading it at a comfortable pace.

When they broke out of the trees at the edge of a meadow slanting down to the water, he stopped and handed Danny the reins.

"I'll stay by the horse's head while you guide him," he told the wide-eyed boy. "You hold the reins like this," he instructed as he put them in Danny's hands. "Now, when you pull back on them and say whoa, that tells Blackie you want to stop. Understand?"

Danny nodded his head vigorously.

"Okay. Now when you move the reins to this side and tighten them that turns his head and Blackie goes in that direction. When you put them on the other side he turns that way. Got it?"

Danny grinned and nodded.

"Good. Now give him a little kick and say geddy-up."

Wes smothered a chuckle at Danny's croaky little voice and his wide-eyed look as the pony moved forward. Looking at the shine on his little face tightened Wes's chest. Suddenly he was filled with an unexpected resentment that fate had cheated him of having a son to raise. He loved his little daughter with all his heart, but a son would have had a special place in his life. Watching him grow into manhood and take over the Wainwright financial holdings would have made all the challenges worthwhile.

"This is fun," Danny said, his eyes sparkling and his mouth curved in a broad smile.

"You're a real cowboy now," Wes told him, chuckling at the boy's enthusiasm.

As they reached the lake, he could tell that Caroline was anxious when she saw her son with the reins in his hands. Her short wavy hair was windblown and her face ruddy from the ride. Wes was all too aware of the way her slender body hugged the rounded contours of the horse.

As Danny reached her, he reined in his horse with a forceful, "Whoa!"

She laughed with such abandonment that Wes found himself laughing with her.

"You want to race?" Cassie challenged.

"Sure," Danny answered promptly with all the false confidence of a beginner.

"No way!" Wes said firmly. He pointed to a grassy knoll a short distance away. "Caroline, there's a nice view of the lake and alpine meadow from there. Shall we leave the horses here and take a look?"

Her smile was nearly as broad as her son's. "Yes, I'd like that."

Caroline quickly dismounted and tethered her mount to a nearby tree while Wes helped the children.

The children scampered like young goats up a slope of rocks that flattened out in a natural lookout above the lake. As Caroline and Wes followed, she was surprised he reached out and took her hand when they reached a rather steep mound of boulders. His clasp was firm and he kept his supple fingers interlaced with hers all the way to the top of the ridge.

She suddenly realized how much she'd missed sharing the simplest joys with someone else. Her son had become her whole life and she'd lost a part of herself just taking care of him and managing the necessities of life.

Nothing in Wes's manner was the least bit flirtatious and she chided herself for the warmth that flowed through her from his touch. She even toyed with the idea of missing a step just to see if he'd catch her. He radiated the kind of sensuality and masculine virility that made her feel utterly feminine.

He quickly dropped her hand when they reached the high plateau where the children were running wildly about near a drop-off ledge.

"Stop that!" he ordered in a no-nonsense tone. He motioned to a pile of flat stones a safe distance from the edge. "Sit down over there."

Cassie scampered over to the spot but Danny hung back.

Caroline could tell from her son's stubborn frown he was debating whether or not he had to obey Cassie's father.

Wes continued to watch him without saying anything more. Very slowly Danny shuffled his feet and moved over to the rocks where Cassie was sitting.

Wes turned around and as he winked at Caroline, she smothered a smile.

They walked over and joined the children. As the sun was beginning to set behind a high craggy mountain range, they made their way back down to the lake and the horses.

Caroline held out the reins of the mare to him. "You ride and I'll walk."

The way she took charge totally surprised him. Nobody flatly gave him orders. He'd grown up with the conviction that people should and would do his bidding whenever he expressed his wishes. Her steady unwavering look was one he wasn't used to seeing and there wasn't the slightest hint that she was open to negotiation. He decided to let her think he was amiable to her dictates—for now.

He let Cassie lead the way back on her pony.

Caroline came next, walking beside Danny's horse.

Wes followed on the sorrel mare, riding close enough to handle the unexpected if Danny suddenly lost control of the animal.

The Rocky Mountains were a treacherous playground. Unexpected threats like snakes and wild animals could send the most placid horse into a frenzy without warning. Even the most docile mount could get spooked by a situation that couldn't be anticipated.

Wes felt a swell of protectiveness and suddenly realized this woman and her son had engaged his emotions on a level that was both foolhardy and dangerous.

People he deeply cared about always seemed to end up dead.

Chapter 5

When they returned to the lodge, Wes suggested the four of them have dinner in his suite.

"That would be nice," Caroline replied, totally surprised. The thought of eating with Dexter, Stella and the others made acceptance easy.

"Goody." Cassie clapped. "Can we have a picnic? It's fun," she told Danny. "We sit on the floor and eat."

"Sorry, not tonight, Cassie," Wes said. "We'll sit at a table and mind our manners."

She puckered her lower lip. Danny frowned as if he didn't think much of Wes's idea either. Obviously, minding their manners was not high on either of the children's lists.

Caroline would have voted for the picnic herself. Her experience dining in private suites with the wealthy was lacking.

"My rooms are in the west wing of the lodge, second

floor at the end of the hall," Wes told her. "Shall we say six? I think Felicia likes to get Cassie to bed by eight."

"Sometimes I stay up 'til nine," Danny bragged in a tone that challenged Cassie's early hour.

"Me, too," the little girl quickly retorted. "Sometimes ten and eleven—"

"That's enough." Wes chuckled, obviously amused that the two of them were trying to upstage each other. "Maybe we can put both of you to bed early. What do you think, Caroline? Shall we plan some quiet time for ourselves?"

He'd never used that tone before and she didn't know what he was really asking. Was there a double meaning in the question? The thought crossed her mind that this whole dinner invitation might be only a smooth come-on. Rich, handsome and sexy, no doubt Wes Wainwright was used to having women fawn over him. Maybe she'd been sending the wrong signals? *Get rid of the kids and then what?* she wanted to ask. Even though his manner was totally friendly and seemed quite innocent, she was suspicious.

"All this fresh air and exercise will make me ready for an early bedtime, too," she replied quickly.

Later, when she had time to think about it, she suspected that she was flattering herself even thinking Wesley Wainwright might want to amuse himself with her company. He'd probably asked her to dinner because he was bored and, perhaps, wanted to avoid the others downstairs as much as she did.

At six o'clock, Wes answered Caroline's knock on the suite's door. He was pleased that she was punctual.

He hated being kept waiting and his usual experience with women sorely tested his patience in that respect.

"Are they here?" Cassie asked, running to the door.

Felicia had brought her up to the suite a few minutes earlier. "I'll wait up," she had told him.

"It won't be late. We'll all be turning in early."

He was a little chagrined that his suggestion of extending the evening beyond the children's bedtime had met with negative vibes from the attractive Ms. Fairchild. He couldn't remember when his offer to spend time with an attractive woman had been turned down. Apparently, he'd been too obvious about wanting to spend time with her without the kids.

Cassie looked quite the sweet, little princess with her hair hanging loose behind a pink ribbon, but a mischievous sparkle in her eyes warned him to keep a tight rein on her.

A subtle rivalry was quite evident between the two youngsters. It amused him the way they challenged each other. Having Danny around would be good for Cassie. She'd always had things go her way without any competition from someone her own age.

Trudie had sent up two barbecued beef dinners and two baked chicken meals, complete with drinks and apple tarts for dessert.

"Smells good," Caroline said, smiling.

"Me and Danny are having chicken," Cassie piped up. "And there's dessert." Then she whispered audibly to Danny. "Ask for two apple tarts. They're good. I snuck a bite."

"That's my daughter." Wes shook his head. "Danny, we'll have to make sure she gets the one with the bite out of it."

Danny giggled.

Caroline had changed into simple black slacks and a tailored white knitted sweater. He was glad he'd decided on tan cords and a casual dark green turtleneck pullover. Obviously, Caroline Fairchild wasn't a fancy dresser, but he could imagine a short party skirt swirling around those slim hips and long legs.

"Everything's ready," he said and motioned them into the spacious room where an expanse of windows framed a view of Shadow Mountain's craggy peak.

A night owl's lamenting cry sounded from a high perch in a ponderosa tree brushing its needled branches against the outside walls of the lodge. Twilight had already settled in the high valley and only the reflection of lights from the lodge lessened the invading darkness outside.

"Have a seat," Wes said, waving his hand toward a table that had been set for four at one end of the large room. "I'll bring in the food."

"Can I help?"

"Nope. But I could suggest a tip if the service is good," he quipped and winked suggestively.

When her cheeks flushed slightly, he realized she wasn't used to these kinds of glib sexual innuendoes. He'd been around uninhibited, anything-goes women for so long, he'd forgotten there were other kinds.

Caroline was surprised how relaxed she felt when they'd finished eating and all moved into the living room. Wes fixed a Scotch and soda for himself and a cream Kahlua for her.

Cassie went immediately to a large built-in cupboard and opened a bottom drawer. Impatiently, the little girl fished through a pile of toys until she found the game she wanted. Then she plopped down on the rug and motioned for Danny to join her.

As Cassie opened up a game board and set it between them, Caroline was surprised to see that it was a preschool Scrabble game. Although Danny had learned to read some simple words while watching *Sesame Street* and recognized beginning sounds, Caroline wasn't sure he was up to playing that kind of word game. She kept her eye on him as Cassie dealt out the letter tiles.

Wes must have picked up on her concern. "Don't worry. Cassie will play for both of them," he assured her. "She's not competitive about winning and she's used to Felicia helping her read words she doesn't know."

"I wish I'd had more time to work with Danny this past year," Caroline said regretfully, but much to her surprise Danny did very well.

When his score inched higher than Cassie's, he gave his mother a huge grin. She smiled back and gave him a thumbs-up sign.

"I envy you," Wes said and his tone made her look at him.

He was watching at Danny and his expression betrayed a deep emotion she hadn't seen before. She was startled by the sudden pain in his eyes. "I lost my son. He was just an infant, a month old. I never got to know him."

"Oh, I'm so sorry," Caroline said quickly.

His expression hardened and suddenly the set of his jaw spoke of a consuming anger. For the first time Caroline was aware of underlying fury behind his smooth, controlled manner. He was obviously still hurting and angry at a fate that had deprived him of his son. After taking a deep drink of his Scotch and soda, he put down the empty glass with a punctuating sound.

She was at a loss how to respond. Probing questions about his grief were not appropriate. For several minutes he visibly retreated into a private agony of his own and the children's chatter and laughter were the only sounds in the room.

She was uncomfortable in his strained silence and searched for something to say, but everything seemed too light and inappropriate in the face of his deep emotional turmoil.

When the children put aside the game and Cassie pestered Wes for another apple tart, he seemed to shake off his mood and assume his role of the genial host.

When Felicia came to collect Cassie, Caroline decided it was time for them to go, too.

"I'm sorry," he apologized as he walked them to the door. "I'm afraid I haven't been at my best tonight. Sometimes the past catches up with me."

She nodded. "I understand." She couldn't even begin to imagine what it would feel like to lose her precious Danny.

Caroline didn't see Wes at all the next day and spent most of her time going over the decorating books and magazines in the workroom.

Stella popped in from time to time, but Caroline's frustration grew. Despite all their conversations, nothing seemed to be moving them toward any concrete decisions.

Try as she would, Caroline failed to get a feel for Stella's overall intentions for the lodge. Was the woman only going to redecorate on a superficial level or was she thinking of making some basic changes—like combining some of the small rooms into larger living areas?

Caroline was puzzled. Even though Wes had apparently given Stella free rein to carry out her project, Caroline sensed a hesitation in the woman to act on her own. Perhaps she'd seen that angry, brooding side of her brother-in-law often enough to be wary.

Caroline was uneasy herself about seeing Wes again. Behind that easy smile of his, she'd glimpsed a tortured spirit. She was tempted to ask Stella for the particulars around the loss of Wes's son, but keeping everything on a business footing was important, especially while they lived under the same roof.

Late that afternoon, she received a telephone call from the Denver fire chief that put everything else out of her mind; he told her that their investigation had determined beyond a doubt that her house fire was definitely arson.

"We found empty containers of a flammable liquid in the alley and two broken windows in the basement, where the fire started."

"I can't believe it!"

"Do you know of anyone who would deliberately want to burn your house down and hurt you, Mrs. Fairchild?"

She was stunned by the question.

"No...no one..." she choked.

"Maybe an old enemy of your husband's? I understand he was a doctor. Maybe a former patient of his went off his rocker and wanted to get even."

"My husband has been dead for four years. Why would anyone wait until now—"

"Who knows?" he answered shortly. "The fact is

someone set the fire for a reason. I understand you have full fire coverage on the house and contents."

"Yes."

"A rather extensive policy. In cases like this, the homeowner comes under intense scrutiny."

"I did not burn down my own house," Caroline flared angrily. "And the police had better spend their time finding out who did."

"I'm sure you'll be hearing from them as the investigation proceeds. Are you going to remain at your present location for some time? If not, you should advise them of your whereabouts."

Caroline hung up the phone and brushed a hand across her forehead as she muttered, "I can't believe this."

"Bad news?"

She jerked her head up. Dexter was standing close to the alcove where the telephone was located on the main floor. She hadn't heard him come up behind her.

"Can I help?"

He certainly wasn't the person she would have chosen to unload on, but her exasperation made her explode. "They think I burned down my house for the insurance."

"Who's they?"

"The Denver police and fire department."

He let out a low whistle. "Well, I guess it happens like that sometimes. I mean, I've known cases—"

She brushed by him and headed up the stairs. If Dexter had followed her, glibly chattering, she might have happily tripped him.

Once inside her bedroom, she sat on the edge of the bed and stared at the floor. As she went over and over the telephone conversation, she tried to make some sense of it. The fact that someone had set the fire was a total shock, but having the suspicion fall on her was a double blow. She was angry and sick to her stomach at the same time.

Who could have done it?

She didn't believe for a minute that it had been an ex-patient of her husband. If anything, Thomas had been too concerned about every one of them. She couldn't think of a single case where there had been any kind of incident that would warrant revenge.

There had been some petty destruction in her neighborhood from time to time, but mostly kids' stuff. Nothing even as serious as broken car windows.

Pressing her fingers against her forehead, she struggled to make sense out of everything. It had to be vandals! A high school was only a few blocks away. Undoubtedly, the police would look there first. The arson could be gang-related. She'd heard of gang initiations where the newcomer had to prove his worth in order to join the group. Some hopeful could have been trying to show he was good enough to be in the gang.

As this thought took hold, the tension inside her began to ease. She went into the bathroom and after splashing her face with warm water and combing her hair, she straightened her shoulders and glanced at her watch.

Time to pick up Danny.

Felicia's door was open and the two children were playing some kind of treasure-hunt game and darting all over the apartment and the hall, looking for clues. Danny's were written in blue and Cassie's in red.

Felicia had cleverly used the primer words they knew

and drawn pictures to illustrate hiding places like a kitchen chair, a sofa pillow, a clock or cooking utensils. One clue led them to another and Caroline and Felicia laughed as they watched them racing to see who could find their treasure first.

Luckily, they both found their candy bars within seconds of each other. Cassie's was hidden behind a photograph and Danny's prize was inside the cookie jar.

"Good job," Caroline told both of them and complimented Felicia on her ingenuity. "What a great way to improve their reading skills. You're a wonderful teacher."

Felicia flushed as if she wasn't used to such compliments and quickly changed the subject. "I have some lemonade ready for the children. Would you like a cup of tea?"

"I'd love one," Caroline said honestly.

Danny's face glowed as he bit into his chocolate bar and his brown eyes sparkled with childish glee. A warm feeling poured over Caroline as she watched him. As long as her son was happy and safe, she could cope with anything.

While the children watched a cartoon video, the two women had some privacy in the breakfast nook. Caroline was never quite sure afterwards how the conversation had led around to Wes Wainwright, but found herself saying, "I was shocked when he told me about the tragic loss of his son."

Felicia set down her teacup with such force that the liquid spilled onto the table. Her eyes rounded. "He told you?"

"Yes, last night, when we had dinner in his suite."

Her dark eyes fixed on Caroline like someone waiting for an ax to fall. Her voice was ragged and her breath short. "He told you—everything?"

"Only that he'd lost an infant son. He didn't go into details but I could tell that he was still mourning the baby's death. What happened? How did he die?"

Caroline thought Felicia was going to leave the table without replying. Then she straightened her back and her eyes were moist as she pleaded, "You have to understand. It wasn't my fault. Everyone said it wasn't."

Felicia suddenly looked as tortured as Wes had the night before. Caroline wasn't sure she wanted to hear any more. The way the woman was defending herself indicated that she must have some guilt over the baby's death. But if Felicia was responsible in any way, why on earth would Wes have left Cassie in her care?

As quickly as she could, Caroline apologized for bringing up the subject. "I'm sorry, I didn't realize you suffered the infant's untimely death as well as the family. It's always traumatic to bury a baby."

"That's what makes it so awful." Felicia swallowed hard. "We didn't even have a baby to bury."

"I don't understand."

She sobbed, "Cassie was a twin. She had a twin brother. They were only a month old when it happened."

"What happened?"

"He was kidnapped."

Caroline felt as if someone had knocked the air out of her. In a strained voice, Felicia told Caroline how she'd taken a fussy Cassie to bed with her in a room adjoining the nursery. Near morning, when Felicia went to put Cassie back in her crib, the baby boy was gone. A demand for ransom was never made and all of the wealth and resources of the Wainwrights failed to find any trace of the kidnapped baby.

Felicia was crying now and Caroline bent over her, putting an arm around her shoulder. Her own mouth was dry and her chest tight.

Poor Wes. Her heart went out to him. And to Felicia. What an emotional burden for the two of them. Watching Cassie grow up must create a kind of never-ending torment for them.

If Felicia was really blameless...?

The thought was like a prick of barbed wire. If a baby had been kidnapped while it was under her care, could this woman really be trusted with Danny?

Chapter 6

When Caroline and Danny went downstairs for dinner, Stella and her son, Shane, were the only ones who came in while they were eating. Without an invitation, Stella sat down at their table and Shane followed. His pained look clearly indicated it wasn't his choice.

"I guess Wes and Dexter aren't back yet," Stella said. "They took the Jeep to Telluride to get some supplies."

Shane muttered audibly, "They probably ran out of beer."

"Maybe because someone else was helping them drink it," his mother countered sharply and added in a sarcastic tone, "I wonder who that might be."

Her son hunched over his plate without answering, but his scowl spoke volumes. Caroline shifted uncomfortably; she wasn't about to get involved in any family squabble.

Stella gave an exasperated sigh. "You give your life trying to make things good for your kid and what do you get? Nothing but grief. I found a half-dozen beer cans in Shane's room last night."

"The kind they show on TV?" Danny piped up. "You know, like those funny bears that laugh and sing?"

"I don't think Shane has a favorite," Stella answered coolly.

Caroline decided to take a sip of water and stay out of the conversation. A heavy silence followed, but the unspoken tension between Stella and her son was almost deafening.

Throughout the meal, it was obvious Stella was in a very bad mood and Caroline decided it wasn't her role to make pleasant dinner conversation.

As soon as possible, she excused herself and made a hasty retreat with Danny out of the dining room.

Instead of going upstairs to their rooms, Caroline decided to check out a small reading room she'd noticed when Stella gave her a tour of the lodge.

"I want to go play with Cassie," Danny complained loudly.

"Not tonight," she said firmly as she took his hand and led him down the hall. Maybe she was being foolish, but she intended to seek some reassurance from Wes about Felicia. She needed to know that his confidence in letting Cassie remain under the nanny's supervision was well-founded.

The reading room wasn't a library by any means. It was a small, square room with a few bookcases offering a variety of reading material. Some straight chairs were placed around a small table and an uncomfortable-looking couch that looked like a discard from a garage sale stood against one wall.

Caroline was disappointed. The reading room completely lacked warmth and comfort. She hoped it was on Stella's list to redecorate.

Once again a feeling of frustration swept over her. If she'd had any other clients waiting, she might have pushed Stella to make some decisions but as it was, unfortunately, Caroline had more time than anything else at the moment.

She spied some books on one of the lower shelves and was delighted to find they were children's picture books as well as classes such as *The Little Engine That Could* and *Are You My Mother?*

Danny grabbed them as if they were familiar friends. She smiled as he sat on the couch and eagerly turned the pages. Her trips to the library with him had paid off. She'd bet he was going to be a reader just like her.

She quickly surveyed the bookcases to see what she could find for herself. There were lots of books about wildlife, mountain-climbing and outdoor adventures.

Someone had made a collection of Westerns by Zane Grey and Louis L'Amour and she selected a couple of them to try. After all, when in Rome…

"Let's take the books up to our room, Danny. We can always come back down for more," she assured him.

As they were heading for the main staircase, Caroline heard Wes's voice at the front door. "Dexter, drive the Jeep around back. Tim will help you unload."

Caroline hesitated, trying to decide whether to go on up the stairs or turn around. He solved the problem for her.

"Hello there," he called as he hurried to catch up

with her. "We just got back from Telluride. We're later than I planned. Dexter had an agenda of his own, as always. That guy seems to collect buddies everywhere he goes. Anyway, we had dinner earlier. Did you have a good day?"

"Pleasant enough," she answered, sidestepping an honest answer. Complaining to him about Stella wasn't going to do any good. He'd already washed his hands of the whole decorating project.

"What about you, Danny?" Wes asked, putting his hand on the boy's shoulder as they mounted the stairs. "What have you got there?"

"Books. I can read 'em, too," he bragged. "Just like Cassie."

"I bet you can." Wes winked at Caroline. "Nothing like a little competition to speed things up. Did the two of them behave themselves today?"

She nodded. "Felicia had made a clever treasure hunt game for them. They ran all over the apartment looking for clues—"

"And I found my candy bar in the cookie jar," bragged Danny.

"Felicia is always thinking up creative, fun games. It's a good thing, too." He sighed. "I know Cassie is a challenge to her sometimes. I'm afraid my daughter's going to be a terror when she starts regular school."

"Has Felicia always been Cassie's nanny?" Caroline asked, a little ashamed of herself for trying to verify Felicia's sad story. She couldn't see Wes's eyes clearly in the dim light, but she thought there was a tightening at the corners of his mouth.

"Yes. She'd been employed by my late wife's family and when Pamela was expecting, Felicia came to live with us. I don't know how I would have managed Cassie as a single parent without her. Are you concerned about leaving Danny with her?"

"A little."

"Don't be," he said flatly. "There have never been any questions about her loyalty. Your son is safe with her."

Like your son was?

It was all she could do to keep from plying him with questions about the kidnapping. Remembering how intensely he'd been discussing his loss, she hesitated to bring up the subject. If he trusted Felicia with his only child, what more reassurance did she need?

"Would you like to go riding tomorrow afternoon?"

Surprised, she stammered, "Oh, I... I don't know—"

"We ought to take advantage of the nice weather before we get hit with winter and socked in with five-foot snowdrifts.

"You mean we might get snowbound in October?"

"It's been known to happen. Usually not this early, though," he reassured her. "Anyway, tomorrow's going to be chilly but clear. A great day for a horseback ride. What do you say?"

Danny piped up, "I'll go."

Caroline laughed. "Not this time, honey."

"Is that a yes?" Wes asked. The way he searched her face seemed at odds with his usual air of assurance and command. "About three o'clock?"

The thought of enjoying a lovely horseback ride without the children was very tempting. When she was growing up on the farm she'd loved riding a galloping horse with the wind blowing her hair and the strong muscles of her mount rising and falling beneath her.

How could she refuse an escape from the mounting pressures at the lodge?

"All right, if Stella doesn't object to a short workday."

"She won't," he flatly predicted. "Dress warmly. We'll be heading up the canyon and the wind coming off the high ridges can be a little chilly."

To Caroline's surprise, Stella informed her the next morning that she'd finally made some decisions.

"We'll start with the large main room."

"Good," Caroline replied, but her relief was short-lived; after asking Stella a few specific questions, she realized that the woman was still totally undecided about the effect she wanted to create.

They spent time discussing various options for minor renovations that would allow for more modern focus and design. They considered possible changes in furniture style, fabrics, wall hangings and floor coverings. Stella kept nodding as she listened to Caroline's advice, but continued to vacillate about making any definite selections. Caroline had the feeling she needed to be in charge but deep down didn't completely trust herself and would do anything to avoid admitting it.

By three o'clock Caroline was more than ready to escape the lodge. She'd been filled with a mixture of apprehension and excitement as she'd watched the clock all day.

It wasn't really anything like a date, she assured herself repeatedly. After her husband's death, even good friends like Betty and Jim had failed in their match-making efforts. She'd dated some very nice men but none of them had captured any serious interest. How ironic that she might finally be attracted to someone completely unavailable so far from home.

There wasn't any need for her to worry about what kind of an impression she might make. If there'd been any immediate feminine competition for his attention, she wouldn't be the one going horseback riding with a Texas tycoon.

She left Danny happily playing a video game with Cassie while Felicia sat in her chair, knitting. She exchanged her slacks for jeans, put a denim jacket over a long-sleeved blouse and slipped into her new boots.

Hurrying down the stairs, she was surprised to find Wes waiting there for her. He was wearing brown Western pants, a matching shirt, a leather jacket, a narrow-brimmed Stetson and cowboy boots. She could tell from his expression he was trying to control his impatience.

"I'm sorry," she quickly apologized. "Leaving Danny took a few minutes longer than I'd planned."

He eyed what she was wearing and nodded as if he was satisfied she'd followed his advice. Then, to her surprise, handed her a lady's white Western hat.

"One of our guests left it at the lodge." He eyed the way it looked when she'd put it on. "Looks better on you."

"Was she blonde or brunette?" Caroline inquired with teasing solemnity.

"I guess it depends upon which day of the week we're talking about," he countered. "Shall we get out of here before I'm trapped by business?"

As they walked to the stables, he said, "I thought we'd head up the canyon to Cascade Falls. You ride well enough to hold to the trail. The view is spectacular. You shouldn't miss it while you're here."

His meaning was plain enough. This kind of outing wasn't on his usual busy agenda. Since this might be the one pleasant memory she took back to Denver, she was determined to enjoy it.

"It'll take us about thirty minutes to reach the falls," he told her. "If we're lucky the clouds will hold off until then. The view is unbelievable when the setting sun hits the water. It's one of my favorite rides."

The horses were saddled and waiting. Wes nodded at the two stablemen. When he said something to them in Spanish, she realized they probably weren't fluent in English. She suspected he'd brought them here from his ranch in Texas.

Wes led the sorrel mare outside and held Caroline's stirrup as she lifted herself into the saddle. After she gathered the reins firmly in her hand, he went back in the stable and led out a black stallion.

"Beautiful!" Caroline exclaimed as the stallion raised dust with his prancing feet. "What's his name?"

"Prince."

"Fits him," Caroline readily replied.

"He was a wild one when we brought him in from the open range but we bonded from the beginning." Wes swung easily into the saddle and took command of the powerful animal with confidence.

Riding side by side, they passed the lake and headed west across a meadow cupped by surrounding hillsides. When they came to a narrow canyon bordered by high cliffs, Wes reined his horse to a slow walk.

"We'll have to go single-file from here. Let your mare have her footing. She'll follow Prince. We can turn back now if you don't want to go any farther. It's not going to be an easy—"

"Let's go," she said, interrupting him. "Didn't you say we didn't have time to waste?"

He gave her an approving smile. "That's what I thought."

As his stallion led the way up a rugged trail cut into the side of a mountain, it seemed to Caroline that they were climbing high enough to reach the top of encircling peaks etched across the skyline.

She heard the sound of rushing water even before they reached Cascade Falls. As they came through the trees, the ground leveled out and alpine grass softened the rough gray surface of a high precipice. They were only a short distance away from plunging cascades of white-foamed water falling from a rocky cliff high above.

After dismounting, they tied their mounts to trees whipped by the wind into grotesque shapes and walked to a spot which gave them a spectacular view of the falls.

Caroline caught her breath as cold mist sprayed their faces and a deafening roar rang in their ears. Streams of crystal water plunged hundreds of feet downward and then rose, spraying glistening gigantic boulders that lay below.

Unexpectedly, Wes put his arm around her shoulders as a late afternoon sun broke through the clouds and created a myriad of jewels in the sparkling waterfall.

The heavenly beauty defied description and Caroline shivered just looking at it.

"Are you cold?" he asked as he turned her around and held her in the warm circle of his embrace.

She was dismayed by the swell of emotion that flooded through her. Sharing this moment with him had created unexpected feelings she didn't understand. When his fingertips began to lightly trace the soft curve of her cheek, she willed him to stop but a stirring of unbidden feelings kept her motionless.

He lowered his mouth to hers and brushed her moist lips, gently at first, then he deepened the kiss until heat radiated throughout her whole body.

Frightened by her unbridled response to his kisses, she pulled away and searched his face. He was smiling at her in a way that made her think he'd expected this to happen.

Part of the tourist package offered by Shadow Mountain Lodge.

She pushed away from him and headed in the direction of the tethered horses. Indignation came to her rescue as she fought to regain her emotional balance. Undoubtedly, Wes Wainwright had brought many female companions to this very spot and would probably bring many more. Maybe kisses, caresses and promises of hot passion were always included.

She took off the white hat and flung it into the bushes. How often had he planted kisses on willing lips shaded by that brim?

"What's going on?" he demanded as he caught up with her.

"That's exactly what I was wondering."

"I don't get it," he said. "If I didn't know better I'd think you were pretending to be sweet sixteen and never been kissed."

She ignored the sarcasm. Undoubtedly he was used to feminine invitations and ploys that invited his amorous attention and he probably stayed clear of women who weren't pleasant, accommodating companions.

Obviously, his masculine pride was smarting over the whole incident.

"I'm chilled to the bone," she answered in a kind of double entendre.

He was silent for a moment and then said curtly, "I'll get you a saddle blanket."

On the ride back to the lodge, their previous, easy companionship was gone. Caroline was grateful for Wes's stony silence. She'd made enough of a fool of herself for one day.

By the time they reached the stables, the last rays of a setting sun had disappeared and shadows were deepening on wooded slopes of craggy high mountains.

They left the horses in the hands of the stablemen and when they entered the lodge through the front door, Caroline's thoughts were still on the afternoon ride that had gone wrong.

Felicia was just coming down the main staircase as they came in. She was alone and Caroline suddenly realized she hadn't thought about Danny in any way during the outing. Hurriedly, Caroline crossed the room and met Felicia at the bottom of the stairs.

"Where's Danny?"

Felicia stiffened and her dark eyes flashed. "The children came down to get more books. I was delayed slightly and they went ahead. They're waiting in the reading room. They ran out of things to do. Neither of them would settle down for a nap."

"I'm sorry," Caroline said quickly. "I'll have a talk with Danny."

"And I'll speak to Cassie," Wes promised.

Felicia frowned as if she didn't think talking would do a lot of good.

"I really appreciate your looking after him." Caroline said. A strained weariness was evident in the nanny's voice.

"The two of them play off the other. What one doesn't think up, the other one does." Sighing, she added, "They're precious children—but a handful."

"We'll look after them until bedtime," Wes said with obvious irritation.

Caroline was anxious to get Danny and escape from Wes's glowering presence.

The door to the reading room was open, but there was no sign of the children. No books lay on the floor. No chairs were out of place. Nothing indicated two youngsters had even been there.

"I told them to stay here until I came after them," Felicia said in an exasperated tone. "Now, where have they run off to?"

"Don't worry, we'll find them," Wes promised with a stern edge to his voice. "Go back to your rooms, Felicia. Maybe they went upstairs the back way and you missed them."

Mumbling to herself, she nodded and hurried out of the room.

"Let's check the social room," Wes said. "The kids probably got sidetracked, especially if there's any food or drink set out. Cassie's been known to help herself when she finds a snack anywhere around." He didn't seem worried, just irritated.

Caroline tried to ignore an unfounded tightness in her chest. She'd never thought of herself as an overanxious mother, but Danny had never been in strange surroundings like these before. And neither had she!

She kept pace with Wes's long stride and listened

for echoing laughter or high-pitched voices as they approached the room. When they went in they found it as silent and empty as the hall had been.

Where could they have gone?

Wes frowned as if he was asking himself the same question. "Maybe they decided to go to my suite and get some books, instead of the reading room. Cassie has a boxful in my front closet."

"You're probably right," Caroline agreed with instant relief. She'd seen all the stuff the little girl had pulled out. "They wouldn't even think about Felicia looking for them in a different place."

Quickly mounting the stairs to the second floor, they hurried down the long hall to Wes's suite.

"Cassie," he called as they went in.

No answer. The living room echoed with emptiness. A lack of clutter told them it wasn't likely that two wayward six-year-olds had been there.

Wes checked the bedrooms and bathroom. "They haven't been here."

"Maybe our rooms. Danny might have wanted to show Cassie the animal heads and they could have easily been distracted from going downstairs."

The hope died when they found her rooms as empty as Wes's suite.

"Okay, we'll go back downstairs and check the kitchen," Wes said impatiently. "Maybe they decided to hit Trudie up for a treat before getting the books. Cassie knows there's always something for her sweet tooth."

Caroline could tell Wes was still just irritated, not worried, and she tried to control her own uneasiness. After all, six-year-olds couldn't be expected to stick to any one plan for very long—especially if cookies or candy were in the offering.

Hank was busily tending to a roast that had just come out of the oven when they checked the kitchen. He shook his head when Wes asked if he'd seen Cassie and Danny.

"Nope. They didn't come in here. Better ask Trudie. She's been busy setting up the dinner buffet. They might have been pestering her. I thought Felicia was watching them?"

"They got away from her," Wes said.

Chuckling, Hank said, "I'd rather keep track of a couple of wild squirrels than those two."

When they asked Trudie if she'd seen them, she said, "Nope, haven't seen hide nor hair of them. And I spent the afternoon doing some spot cleaning both upstairs and down." She frowned. "Maybe you ought to ask Tim and Dexter. They've been in the game room most of the afternoon. The kids could have been watching them play pool."

Wes's growing impatience showed when they entered the game room and found Dexter sitting alone in one of the leather chairs drinking a can of beer. Signs of a recent pool game were on the table.

"Want to play a couple of games, Wes?" Dexter asked eagerly as they came in. "I'm all warmed up, buddy. Beat Tim three games in a row," he bragged.

"We're looking for Cassie and Danny," Wes answered shortly. "Have they been in here?"

"Nope. Haven't seen them all day. I thought they were upstairs with Felicia while you two were taking your romantic ride to the falls."

Caroline stiffened at his reference to a romantic ride and resented the smirk that accompanied it.

"The kids were supposed to be in the reading room," Wes said curtly. For the first time his manner radiated a growing concern that had not been there before.

"Tim might have seen them," Dexter offered with a shrug as if he didn't understand what all the rush was about tracking them down. "I think he's in his office."

Caroline wonder if it was anger or anxiety that pulled at the corner of Wes's mouth. "If they come in you keep tabs on them," he ordered.

He swung on his heel and Caroline had trouble keeping pace with him as he led the way toward the back of the house. She kept telling herself the children were safe somewhere in the lodge.

They had to be!

Tim wasn't in his office but Shane was unpacking some boxes in an adjoining storeroom. "If you're looking for my mom, she took off with Tim somewhere." His tone was full of resentment. "I didn't ask where."

"Have you seen Cassie and Danny anywhere around?"

"Not for an hour or so. They were playing some kind of stupid game. They asked me if I wanted to play," he added in a disgusted tone.

"What kind of game?"

He shrugged. "They were following some kind of a treasure map."

"Did you get a look at the map?" Caroline demanded before Wes could.

"Nope. But I think Cassie said something about hiking up to the hunting cabin—"

"And you didn't stop them!" Wes exploded. The fury

in his eyes made Shane take a step backward. "What in the hell were you thinking?"

"I'm not their babysitter," he snapped.

"Damn it, Shane!" Wes swore as he put his face just inches from his nephew's. "If anything happens to them, you'll answer to me! That's a rough climb for anyone in the middle of the day, let alone two kids when it's almost dark. There are a hundred places to miss your footing and fall." He swung around to Caroline. "You stay here and I'll go after them."

"Where is the cabin?" she demanded in a strained voice, staying at his heels as he left the lodge by the back door.

"At the top of the ridge."

Wes headed for a rugged path behind the lodge that led upward through a heavy drift of evergreen trees. He knew Caroline would have trouble keeping up with him. The climb was not an easy one and even though the path was fairly well defined, it rose steadily upward.

The lodge's two-room cabin had been built for use during the hunting season and could only be reached on foot because the terrain was not suitable for horseback riding.

Even in bright sunlight the footing was precarious and this late in the day shadows had begun to spread over the rugged terrain making the ground deceptive in places where the path narrowed, or dipped dangerously with loose rocks. Only a couple of hours of fading daylight remained.

Wes tried to remember how many times he'd taken Cassie up the mountainside with him. Not many. He'd held her hand all the way every time, making sure to steady her footing when the climb became arduous and dangerous.

Nervous sweat beaded his brow as he imagined what could happen to two unwary six-year-olds on such treacherous slopes and high precipices. If they slipped and fell—

He jerked his thoughts away from a horror that sent an icy chill down his spine. What in the hell was all this about a treasure map? Shane had said they were playing some kind of game.

Cassie was certainly capable of creating some childish fantasy and Danny would go along with it if only to prove he was as brave as any girl. If they got off the path, no telling where they would end up. They could easily get lost amongst the trees and fallen rocks.

He repeatedly called out their names as they climbed upward. "Cassie! Cassie! Danny!" They both held their breath as they strained to hear any responding cry.

Nothing!

The only sound was the rustling of wild birds in the high treetops. Wes knew that night predators would be on the prowl as soon as darkness claimed the mountainside.

He bounded upward at increasing speed until he heard Caroline's frightened gasp. He swung around.

She'd fallen and was sliding dangerously backward on a narrow ledge. Racing back down the path, he grabbed her and carefully helped her back to her feet. "Easy does it."

"I'm all right," she said, wiping the dirt from her cheek.

Even though he admired her stubbornness, he wanted to lash out at her for not staying at the lodge. As they labored up the steep mountainside, the path ahead was even steeper and darker where thick stands of pine and spruce trees hugged the rocky rim.

Wes knew they had to make it to the cabin before darkness settled in on the mountain. They'd never find it safely in the dark. Even now the gray light of a fading day was claiming its hold on Shadow Mountain.

"We're almost there," he assured her finally as they climbed the last steep incline. "The cabin is just ahead."

The words were barely out of his mouth when a whiff of smoke touched his nostrils.

"What the—"

As the cabin came into view, he could see a trail of black smoke rising against the evening sky.

Chapter 7

"Fire!" Wes plunged forward at a dead run over the rough ground. His breath was short at this high altitude and his hands and face were scratched by needled branches as he thrust them aside.

The pungent smell of burning wood was stronger as he ran toward the cabin but he couldn't see any flames. As he came closer, he realized the smoke was spiraling up from the chimney.

Relief was short-lived.

The fear that the children had never made it as far as the cabin was still with him as he reached the planked door and threw it open. The scene that met his eyes was so unexpected that for a long moment he just froze in the doorway.

Cassie and Danny were sitting on the floor in front of the fireplace sharing an open bag of potato chips.

"Whatcha doing here, Daddy?" Cassie greeted him with total innocence.

Danny went on munching the potato chips without showing any concern that an adult had showed up.

Wes swallowed hard. He'd never been so relieved— and so angry. When he heard Caroline's running footsteps, he turned around quickly.

"They're all right," he assured her as he stepped aside and let her enter.

"Danny," she gasped. "Thank God!" She threw herself down beside him and taking him in her arms, kissed him, stroked his hair and anxiously searched his face.

"Why is she crying?" Cassie asked, looking up at her father with innocent puzzlement.

"Because she was worried about him!"

"Were you worried about me, too, Daddy?"

"Damn right I was worried," he snapped.

"Then why aren't *you* crying?" she asked.

He took a deep breath as he eased down beside her. As he gave her a hug, he closed his eyes and let relief pour through every cell in his body. Then he said, "Honey, I'm not crying but I was scared, too. You must never do something like this again."

"Okay."

"I mean it. Don't you ever leave the lodge without my permission. Understand?"

"Don't be mad, Daddy. I wanted to tell you but you were gone." Cassie's petulant tone somehow put the blame on him.

"You both should have known better," Caroline said, looking Danny straight in the eyes.

"Nobody said we couldn't go," he argued.

"Did you ask anyone?" she countered sternly.

"Cassie knew the way. And the door was open," he added as if that made everything all right.

"Who lit the fire?" Wes asked. The last occupant of the cabin always left one log laid in the fireplace and there was a box of wooden matches on the mantel.

"I did." Cassie smiled proudly. "Felicia showed me how. She let me light one for her lots of times. First, you strike a match. Then quickly drop it in the middle on the paper and wood." Her eyes sparkled. "And then you have a fire."

"All right, but you know better than to play with matches," he lectured as he picked up the match box lying on the floor beside her.

"We were cold," Danny piped up.

"And it was getting dark," Cassie added, giving Danny a grateful look for his support.

"We couldn't find anything to eat 'cept these potato chips," Danny complained, getting into the flow of defending themselves.

"Well, you're safe. That's the important thing," Caroline said with a deep sigh of relief as she put an arm around her son and held him close.

Wes glanced out the window at the darkening landscape. Night was falling fast. Trying to return to the lodge could be a disaster. They'd have to spend the night here. When he'd arranged for the cabin to be made ready with provisions—bottled water, bedding and firewood for the approaching elk season—he'd never dreamed they'd be needed in such weird circumstances. As he glanced at Caroline, he felt uncomfortable in her presence. She was barely speaking to him. Somehow he'd completely misread the situation at the falls. He'd felt a strange harmony between them as they stood mesmerized by the power and beauty displayed before them.

When she'd looked at him with those deep, liquid blue eyes, her supple body had seemed to welcome his embrace and as his fingertips had traced the smoothness of her face and trembling lips, he couldn't help himself. An overwhelming urge to claim that sweet mouth had surged through him. He'd pulled her close and kissed her as an explosive sexual desire surged through him.

Then it had happened—total rejection! Her whole body had suddenly gone rigid and she'd forcibly shoved him away. Too late, he realized she was in a different space altogether. His romantic advances were totally unwanted. If they hadn't been swept up in this terrifying ordeal with the children, they probably could have successfully ignored each other and gone their separate ways.

In spite of her dishevelled appearance, she seemed totally relaxed now that Danny and Cassie had been found safe and sound. Thank heavens, she wasn't weeping and wailing and scolding her son and threatening punishment. He certainly didn't need a hysterical female on his hands.

As she sat in front of the fire, her lovely face glowing with relief, he promised himself that he'd make it clear to her that he wasn't the least bit interested in any unwanted romantic intimacy. Maybe he'd been around a different kind of woman too long. He couldn't think of one of his acquaintances who would have reacted the way she had. In fact, he was slightly indignant that Caroline Fairchild had made such an issue of a few harmless kisses.

Going into the kitchen end of the room, he opened

a cupboard and took down a kerosene lantern from a high shelf. The lighted lamp created a warm glow as he placed it on a small table in the center of the room near a long sofa covered by an Indian blanket. An assortment of scattered chairs included an old-fashioned rocker that matched with those in some old-time photographs hanging on the wall. Hikers and hunters who used the cabin weren't particular about the furnishings. An oak door beyond the fireplace opened into a second room which had a full-sized bed and a couple of cots.

"All right, kids," he said as he sat down again on the floor in front of the fire. "I want to know where you got the idea to come up here all by yourselves."

"It was Danny's idea," Cassie said quickly.

"Was not!"

"Was too!"

"That's enough." His stern gaze made both children squirm as he held up a hand to stop the volley of accusations. "What's this about a treasure map?"

Neither child answered. Their little mouths were clamped shut and their eyes rounded with apprehension. Obviously, they knew they were in deep trouble.

"It's all right," Caroline coaxed. "Show us the treasure map. Do you still have it?"

Slowly, Cassie stuck a hand in her jeans pocket, drew out a piece of rumpled paper and handed it to her father.

"I'll be damned," Wes swore.

Caroline moved closer to him. "Let me see."

In silence, they both studied it. The map was a very simple drawing. A rectangle with a roof was marked Lodge and the surrounding mountains were drawn as single arching lines. A line of arrows pointed the way from the Lodge along a path that zig-zagged upward to another simple drawing labeled Cabin with another arrow marked Treasure pointing to the door.

Wes's frown was a mixture of rage and disbelief. "What do you think of that?"

"It's amazingly easy to follow."

"Who drew it for you, Cassie?" Wes's tone warned his daughter he wanted a straight answer.

The little girl swallowed hard as if she were trying to think of an answer that would please him. Caroline reached out and squeezed the little girl's hand. "It's all right, honey. You can tell us. Who made the map?"

"I... I don't know," she finally stammered.

"I don't either," Danny echoed quickly.

"Where'd you get it, Cassie?" Wes asked as he tried for a softer tone. He knew he could be demanding and short-tempered when something frustrated him. It had never been easy for him to rein in his impatience. "Who gave it to you?"

"Nobody," Danny answered before Cassie could. "We found it. By her telephone. Didn't we, Cassie?"

She nodded.

"Are you making this up, Danny?" Caroline searched her son's face. "Cassie really has a telephone?"

"Not a real one," Wes explained quickly. "She has a little table with a pretend phone in the downstairs telephone alcove. She plays there sometimes when Felicia is busy making calls. Is that where you found the treasure map, Cassie?"

"Uh-huh. I wanted to show Danny the phone," she replied defensively as if she shouldn't have been anywhere near the alcove without an adult. "And there it was. Right on my desk."

"We were going to get books," Danny added, looking at his mother for approval.

"But you never went to the reading room, did you?" Wes said. Now he knew why. They'd stopped at the telephone and found the map.

Had someone deliberately left the map there for the kids to find?

Wes looked at Caroline and saw the same question in her eyes.

"Felicia has been making up games for them," Caroline told him.

He was surprised by the noticeable edge to her voice and hard speculative glint in her eyes. Surely, she didn't suspect Felicia of doing something so irresponsible? "She'd never do something like this," Wes replied flatly.

"Are you sure? Do you completely trust her?"

Her question made Wes wonder if Felicia had been talking to Caroline about the kidnapping. He knew the tragedy had rested heavily on Felicia's conscience all these years even though he'd done everything he could to show her that he trusted her completely with his remaining child. He'd always felt that her concern for Cassie that night by taking the baby into her own bed had saved his daughter from being kidnapped, too.

"Felicia would never put Cassie in jeopardy," he said firmly. "Nor Danny."

"She put the idea of hunting for treasure in their heads," Caroline insisted. "I know Felicia made up a game that sent them hunting for clues. They were running all over the place. This treasure map could be just another one of her ideas."

"She'd never send them on some dangerous hike like this one."

"Somebody did!" Caroline flared angrily.

"Yes, and I'll find out who," he promised. "At the moment, I'm inclined to think this is some of Shane's doing. Tim tries to keep a handle on him, but it's not easy. I think he has too much time on his hands. No doubt, he'd think it was a big joke to do something like this."

"He told us to save him some of the money," Cassie volunteered.

"But we're not going to give him any, are we, Cassie?" Danny said, giggling.

Wes just shook his head as he got to his feet. How could anyone talk sense into a couple of six-year-olds? "Come on, Caroline, I'll show you the rest of the cabin and we'll decide how to arrange things for spending the night."

At first, he thought she was going to refuse his extended hand to help her to her feet. She seemed hesitant about having any physical contact with him as she gave him her hand.

Her behavior irritated him. Out of some nebulous need to prove his masculine superiority, he held her hand slightly longer than necessary. Very slowly he let his fingers slide away from hers. As a flush rose in her cheeks, he wondered if it was caused by anger or something else she wouldn't admit to herself.

Maybe I'll have to find out.

As Caroline followed him into the other small room, she knew her limited experience with powerful men was pitifully inadequate to deal with Wes Wainwright. She suspected he'd used the cabin for more than one rendezvous with a lady of his choice.

Motioning around the small bedroom, he said, "As you can see, there's a full-sized bed and two cots. We always leave extra bedding in that large chest and a couple of bedrolls." His expression was innocent enough, but she had the impression that he was deliberately trying to embarrass her when he added, "There's a small bathroom. It's designed like those at isolated highway rest stops, so I'm afraid privacy is rather limited."

"I've been camping and was raised on a primitive farm," she briskly informed him. "I think the children and I can manage." Then she asked sweetly, "And where will you be sleeping?"

To her surprise, he chuckled. "You're something else, my dear Caroline."

"I don't know what you mean."

"Probably not, and that's what makes you such a challenge."

Before she could summon a cool reply, Danny and Cassie bounded into the room shouting in unison, "We're hungry."

"Okay. Okay." Wes quickly held up a hand to stop the chant. "Now, which one of you wants to be the cook?"

"Not me!" Cassie giggled.

"We don't know how to cook," Danny said solemnly as if Wes was dumb not to know it.

"Oh, that's too bad." Wes shook his head sadly. "I guess we don't eat."

"My mother cooks good," Danny volunteered quickly.

"She does?" Wes acted surprised. "Well, now, do you think she could fix supper for us?"

Danny looked up at her. "Could you, Mom?"

"I could try," she answered solemnly. "First, we'll need to get a fire going in that old stove."

"I think I could handle that," Wes replied

"I could show you how," she offered, unable to resist the temptation to tease him. After all, she was sure the task wasn't one listed in his portfolio.

"I bet you could." He chuckled. "Well, come on. Let's see what we can scare up to feed these hungry yahoos."

Wes built the fire while Caroline opened cans of baked beans, Vienna sausages and mixed fruit. The children filled their paper plates and sat cross-legged in front of the fire to eat.

Wes and Caroline sat at a small fold-down table in the kitchen area. Trying to keep the conversation on a nonemotional level she asked questions about the cabin. "Does it get a lot of use?"

"Usually just overnight. During elk season, mostly."

"You enjoy hunting then?"

"Your tone reveals where you stand on the matter."

"Yes, I guess it does," she admitted. "All those animal trophies at the lodge turn my stomach. I think it's a horrible sport."

"Sometimes hunting is not a sport but a necessity."

"Not in this day and age."

"That's where you're wrong," he said, leaning back in his chair. "Once this land belonged to the Indians. They lived off of it until the U.S. government moved them south onto dry, barren land. No more fresh venison or buffalo meat to feed their families." He looked grim. "We stole their livelihood from them. When I kill deer every year, it's not just for sport. We load up a freezer van and deliver the meat to Indian reservations in New Mexico."

She was embarrassed by her totally wrong assumption that he killed only for sport. "I'm sorry, I guess I jumped to the wrong conclusion."

His eyes took on a hard glint that startled her. "On the other hand, I'm sure I could kill someone who threatened my life or the welfare of my family."

She suddenly felt a chill that had nothing to do with the cold drafts seeping into the cabin. His pleasing outward persona was girded by an iron will that only the foolish would challenge. When he spoke of shooting someone who threatened his family, she wondered if he was thinking of the kidnapper who had robbed him of his son.

If things had been less tense between them she might have encouraged him to talk about the hideous crime. She certainly could sympathize with the heartbreak he'd endured.

As soon as Danny and Cassie had finished eating, they began to quarrel. Tired and fussy, they wouldn't do anything without an argument and bedtime was something of a challenge.

Wes made ready to sleep on the couch while Caroline settled Danny and Cassie on the cots.

At the last minute, she gave in to Danny's pleas to let him sleep in the big bed with her.

"That's not fair," the little girl protested with pouting lips.

"Is too," Danny argued. "She's my mom."

Caroline quickly intervened. "You can sleep in the big bed, too, Cassie. There's room for three of us. We'll all be warmer in the same bed, anyway."

She had just snuggled the little girl in on one side and Danny on the other when Wes appeared in the doorway. When he saw the three of them in bed together, he teased, "Isn't there room for me, too?"

"No, Daddy," Cassie answered sleepily. "You can use a cot."

"Thanks, but I think I'll stay with the couch," he said. "Sleep tight—"

"—And don't let the bedbugs bite," Cassie and Danny piped up in unison.

Laughing, he went into the other room, leaving the door ajar.

The children fell asleep almost immediately, but Caroline lay wide awake, staring at the rough pine ceiling. Emotional tension created by her fear for their safety lingered. Her muscles ached from the arduous climb and she couldn't get comfortable sandwiched between the children. Finally, she gave up and decided she'd move to one of the cots.

As she slipped out of bed she saw the flicker of light from the lamp coming through the half-open bedroom door. She had discarded her jeans and jacket and remained in her blouse and underwear for sleeping. Taking one of the blankets from a cot, she wrapped it around herself and boldly walked out into the living-room area.

Wes was sitting on the floor with his arms wrapped around his pulled-up legs as he stared at the fire. He looked up at her with a questioning frown.

"Something the matter?"

"Can't sleep."

"Join the club."

"I think I will." She eased down on the rug beside him.

After several minutes of silence, he said, "What we both need is a good strong drink."

He went to a kitchen cupboard and came back with a bottle of brandy and two shot glasses.

"Oh, I couldn't," she protested quickly.

Ignoring her, he poured out two drinks of equal amounts. "Hold this one," he ordered. "You don't have to drink it."

"Then why do I have to hold it?"

"So it can talk to you." He eased down beside her. "And if you don't drink it, I will."

She smiled. "Fair enough."

He resumed his former relaxed position on the floor and seemed content to ignore her as they gazed at the fire. The wind had come up and they could hear branches scraping against the outside walls.

She was surprised when he said, "I'm sorry about what happened at the falls. The moment just felt special. Hard to explain."

She took a sip of brandy and her voice was husky as she admitted, "I think the mistake was mine. Somehow I thought the kiss was part of your usual package deal. You know, an exhilarating horseback ride, a beautiful waterfall and a come-on kiss."

"I've been at Cascade Falls more times than I can count…and never a kiss. I just felt the two of us were sharing something special." He shook his head as if he didn't know quite how to put it into words. "But when I kissed you, something changed."

"I guess that's why it scared me."

"Why?"

"I hadn't been kissed like that in a very long time," she admitted.

"That's a shame," he murmured as he gently turned

her chin in his direction and brought his mouth tantalizingly close to hers.

A longing to feel his lips once again on hers challenged her pride. Was he manipulating her feelings again? She might have surrendered to the spiraling sexual attraction between them if the quiet of the night had not suddenly been shattered by raised voices in the bedroom.

"Move!"

"You're on my side of the bed."

"Am not."

"Are too!"

"Daddy!"

"Mommy."

Caroline sighed.

Wes grumbled. "What rotten timing."

Chapter 8

Sometime in the middle of the night, Wes got up, threw some more wood on the fire and then stretched out on the couch again and dozed until about daybreak.

When he sat up, he listened for some sign that Caroline and the children were awake but there was no hint of movement in the bedroom. They'd probably sleep for another hour or two.

Going into the kitchen area, he built a fire in the stove and set a coffeepot on the back burner. He knew there was dry cereal in a metal canister and some canned milk. The kids would probably turn up their noses but they'd have to forgo pancakes and chocolate milk this morning. As soon as they had breakfast, they'd start back down the mountain. The trail would be easier to follow in the daylight.

As he glanced out the window his heart lurched.

It was beginning to snow!

"Damn!" he swore. A heavy Colorado storm could sock them in with high drifts. He turned on his boot heels and headed for the bedroom.

"Everybody up," he ordered as he came through the doorway. "We're leaving!"

Caroline's head came up from the pillow. "What's... what's the matter?" she stammered.

"It's beginning to snow! No telling how long it would take us to dig out if the storm settles in. We've got to make it down the trail before it gets covered."

She was on her feet in an instant and reaching for her jeans but the children didn't even move.

Wes pulled back the blankets covering them. "Okay, buckeroos. On your feet."

When the cold air hit them, Danny and Cassie curled up even tighter without opening their eyes. Weary from their strenuous climb, they weren't ready to get out of bed this early in the morning.

"Wake up! Wake up," he urged and gently jostled them. With determined effort, he finally got them out of bed. Then he made sure the kitchen was safely secure.

After what seemed like a frustrating eternity to him, the kids were finally dressed and he grabbed some small blankets to wrap around them.

He'd found a large man's woolen coat that had been left in the cabin and tossed it to Caroline. "Put this on."

"What about you?"

"My leather jacket will be enough. Let's go."

When he opened the front door a swirl of wind and snowflakes hit him in the face. The air was frigid, but he was relieved to see that only an inch of whiteness had collected on the ground so far. If they could keep ahead of any heavy snowfall the trail would be visible most of the way.

He grabbed Cassie's hand and took the lead with Caroline and Danny following. They had left the clearing and started downward through a thick stand of pine trees when Wes realized the snow was coming down at a faster rate than when he had looked out the kitchen window. As they bent their heads against the increasing wind and whipping snow, they moved forward at an excruciatingly slow pace.

The children held them back. Several times they would have tripped and fallen if they hadn't been holding on to an adult's hand. Clutching their blankets, they were slow-moving, their steps uncertain on the rough ground.

Cassie whimpered when the flakes began to coat her face. Wes could hear Caroline trying to reassure Danny. He knew he could carry one of them but not both. Maybe he'd made a mistake, thinking they could make it down to the lodge before the storm really hit. Turning back now would mean they'd have to climb back up the steep incline and lose the progress they'd already made down the path.

As the minutes passed, the nightmare grew. Snow began to change trees, rocks and ground into an unfamiliar white terrain. The path began to disappear. The wind began to paralyze them with its biting cold.

Their steps were shorter and slower and Wes thought he was hallucinating when he glimpsed a movement on the trail below. Slowly, a figure came through the falling snow and Wes couldn't believe it when someone held up a hand and waved.

Tim Henderson!

Wes had never been so glad to see the big-boned,

soft-spoken Texan. He couldn't find the words to show his relief that help had arrived.

"We were pretty worried about you all," Tim told him. "When you didn't come back from the cabin by nightfall we decided you'd found the kids. Then, this morning, with the snow starting, I decided to check."

"Thank God you did."

"With the trail drifted over, you'd have to wait until the snowdrifts cleared."

"It's been rough going. The kids can't hack it. We'll have to carry them."

Tim nodded.

"You take the boy." Wes turned to Caroline. "I'll carry Cassie. You stay between me and Tim."

She nodded and he turned away quickly before he gave in to an absurd impulse to hold her close and brush the snowflakes from her eyelashes. As they started down the snow-covered trail again, he silently vowed to make someone pay for putting her through this hell.

Under normal circumstances, when the rough ground and shelves of rocks were clearly visible, the mountain trail was challenging enough. Now, in the growing storm needled boughs of overhanging trees sagged with the weight of collecting snow.

Every minute seemed like an eternity to Caroline. In the whipping wind and falling snow every rocky ledge or pile of boulders seemed like all the others. She just kept putting one foot in front of the other, matching her footsteps with the imprints of Tim's large boots. She had no idea how far below the lodge nestled against the rugged mountain slope.

With every treacherous step, she was relieved that

Danny was safe in Tim's strong arms as the man kept a steady, knowing pace ahead of her.

When the roof of the lodge became visible below through the snow-laden trees she heard Wes's chilled cry, "We made it!"

Relief caught in her own throat. She felt like shouting when Danny peered over Tim's shoulder and gave her a weak smile. He was safe. That was all that mattered.

They entered the lodge through the back door to Tim's office. No sign of a welcoming committee. The morning silence was undisturbed. Apparently, Tim was the only one who had risen at dawn to hunt for them.

As the men set the shivering children down, Wes said, "We need to get them into a warm bath and some dry clothes." Caroline covered her blue lips with her hands and blew on them before she stroked Danny's chilled face. "It's okay, honey. It's okay."

Wes took Cassie's hand. "Tim, alert Hank and Trudie to get a hot breakfast ready for us." Then he nodded at Caroline. "We'll take the back stairs."

Wes and Cassie led the way up the servants' stairway to the second floor.

When they came through a door that opened into the hall, they heard a loud high-pitched cry and jerking their heads in that direction they saw Felicia running down the hall toward them. The nanny was still in her nightclothes, her hair loose and flying like gray-black wings on her shoulders.

"I saw you coming from my window," she gasped when she reached them. "All night I kept candles and incense burning. Oh, my poor baby, my poor baby," she sobbed as she embraced Cassie. "Are you all right?"

"I'm hungry."

Felicia's hysterics were in sharp contrast to Cassie's flat reply and Caroline thought Wes's lips seemed to curve in a secret smile at his daughter's matter-of-fact response.

"She's fine, Felicia. Bring her down to breakfast after she has a warm bath and dry clothes." He nodded at Caroline. "Let's do the same."

When they reached her bedroom door, he opened it for her and Danny. She was about to follow her son inside when Wes put a detaining hand on her arm.

She searched his thoughtful expression. "What is it?"

"I just wanted you to know that if I had a choice of getting snowbound with anyone, it would be with you. I know you don't believe me but it's true. I've never met another woman who could have handled the situation with such courage."

He turned away before she had a chance to reply and disappeared down his end of the hall.

Later when she and Danny went downstairs for breakfast, she was still mulling over the surprising compliment. She knew there were too many hidden levels to Wesley Wainwright to take him at face value. At the moment, it seemed enough that a positive, fragile relationship might be in the making.

Even before she and Danny reached the dining room, she could hear raised voices. Pausing a moment in the doorway, she saw Wes and Stella standing at one end of the buffet, facing each other.

Stella was holding a full plate but Wes's hands were empty and clutched at his side. Their expressions verified that they were in a heated argument.

Caroline quickly led Danny to a table. She didn't want to be drawn into their confrontation by joining them at the buffet.

"I tell you, Shane didn't have anything to do with it," Stella insisted in a strident voice. "I can't believe you'd suggest such a thing."

"And I can't believe he didn't stop the kids," Wes retorted angrily. "He knows how dangerous that trail is. And he knew they were going to the cabin. They showed him the map."

"All right, I agree that he should have told someone what they were up to but he's a teenager living in his own world. Give him some slack."

"Someone deliberately drew that map," Wes countered.

"And you've already decided that it was Shane. Well, I have news for you. This whole situation reeks of your hunting buddy's brand of humor…and jealousy."

"What are you talking about?"

"In case you haven't noticed, you've been spending more time with Caroline and the two kids than you have with Dexter. Why don't you ask him about this whole fiasco?"

Stella set her plate back on the buffet and with her head held high and her back rigid she walked out of the room. She must have passed Dexter in the hall because he came in just seconds later.

Giving a pretend shiver, he walked over to Wes. "Brr, it's as cold inside as it is outside. What's up with Stella? Jealousy?"

"Don't be stupid, Dex," Wes replied shortly.

Dex just grinned. "Tim tells me you spent a cozy night in the cabin with our lovely decorating lady. How did you arrange that?"

Wes said something to Dexter that Caroline couldn't hear but Dexter's smile instantly disappeared.

"Wait a minute, Wes. I didn't know until this morning that you guys were even gone."

"Are you sure, Dex?" Wes asked. His eyes narrowed as he studied his friend.

"Damn sure! If you want to know, I drank my dinner last night. You know how I am sometimes. Too much Scotch and I have to sleep it off. Why don't you tell me what's going on?" His eyes slid knowingly to where Caroline was sitting. "I can't say that I blame you for using the cabin for more interesting things than a hunting party."

Heat surged up in Caroline's cheeks. She shoved back her chair. "Stay here, Danny. I'll get our breakfast."

Wes maneuvered Dexter over to one of the other tables. "Meet me in my suite after breakfast, Dex," he said abruptly and then walked back to Danny and sat down at the table beside him.

Caroline quickly filled two plates and was relieved when Dexter completely ignored her. He stayed at his table, drinking black coffee. No doubt about it, he looked like someone with a brute of a hangover.

Wes had already opened a carton of milk for Danny and poured two cups of coffee when Caroline returned to the table.

"Aren't you eating?" she asked as she sat down opposite him.

"I had something in the kitchen earlier. I wanted to quiz Trudie and Hank. They know pretty much what's going on most of the time."

"And—?"

He shook his head. "Hank said Tim made some telephone calls on the hall phone yesterday afternoon but Trudie didn't see anyone near Cassie's desk when she dusted earlier in the day."

"Do you think someone put the map there knowing that sooner or later Cassie would find it?"

"I believe Hank and Trudie when they say they didn't see it there," Wes answered. "Tim said he didn't know anything about the map. He heard about it from Shane last night."

Caroline frowned. "Have you talked to Shane?"

"No, I decided to talk with his mother first. You saw how that went over. Stella's always been too protective of Shane for his own good."

"Mothers are often like that," Caroline admitted as she glanced at Danny. Even though he was busily licking grape jelly off his toast, she knew her son was taking in the conversation at some level. More than once Danny had repeated with embarrassing results something he'd overheard. She certainly didn't want Wes to launch into any tirade about Stella's parenting skills that might be repeated. Working professionally with the woman was difficult enough without battling any emotional issues.

"Where's Cassie?" Danny piped up, his lips and fingers sticky with jelly.

"Having breakfast upstairs with Felicia as usual." Wes nodded at Caroline. "You can leave Danny whenever you're ready."

She answered as evenly as she could, "After what's happened, I may keep a short leash on him myself."

"Why is that?"

Wes's obvious trust and confidence in the woman puzzled Caroline. Surely, he must feel that the woman was responsible for a situation that had left his infant son vulnerable to kidnappers?

"She's the logical one to have drawn the map," Caroline replied evenly. "It fits in with the other games she created for the kids."

"You're not blaming Felicia for what happened, are you?"

"I don't know who to blame," she admitted. "Maybe Felicia made the map for some harmless activity. Someone else could have thought it would be a joke to place it by Cassie's telephone and see what the children did with it." Caroline sighed. "I don't know what happened, but Felicia was the one who was supposed to be looking after them."

"I agree she shouldn't have trusted them to go straight to the reading room, but she would never endanger their lives, I know that."

"Someone did."

"It couldn't have been intentional. Just bad judgment."

Caroline couldn't tell if he was trying to convince himself or her. There were deep creases in Wes's forehead when Dexter got up and left the room without looking in their direction.

"Have you known him a long time?" Caroline asked.

"I can't even remember when Dex wasn't hanging around," Wes admitted. "He was best man at my wedding. When we were young, he had more money to spend than I did and Dex was generous to a fault. When we were in college, our family fortunes changed. My father made wise investments and extended our financial holdings beyond our cattle ranch. Dexter's family didn't fare so well. I've tried to be there for him when he needs a friend."

"You don't think he'd do something stupid like draw that treasure map?"

Wes's jaw visibly tightened. "Sometimes Dex's sense

of humor gets out of bounds, I'll admit. His practical jokes have backfired more than once, but they've never presented any real danger to anyone."

"I don't like him," Danny said with childish solemnity.

Both Caroline and Wes were startled. "Why not?" Caroline asked quickly.

"He tickles."

"When does he do that?" She didn't know Dexter had been with Danny when she wasn't around.

"When he counts my ribs. And Cassie's, too. He says boys have one less rib than girls. Felicia tells him to get lost."

"I see," Caroline said, forcing a smile. "Well, I think I'll tell him the same thing."

Wes shoved back his chair and stood up. "I'll talk to him. Oh, I almost forgot. I promised Cassie that she and Danny could enjoy the Jacuzzi this afternoon. It'll warm them up." He paused. "You might want to join them, Caroline."

"Without a bathing suit?" she impulsively asked with mock solemnity.

"Especially without." His smile was an open challenge.

Wes worked through the noon hour taking care of matters referred to him by his various executive teams. His original plans to shorten his time at the lodge had been pushed aside for reasons he still couldn't quite define. The arrival of Caroline Fairchild shouldn't have changed his intent to leave—but it had. Now, this latest near tragedy demanded that he stay and make certain nothing like it happened again.

Standing at the window, he was looking out at heavy drifts of snow piling up around the lodge when Cassie arrived with Felicia.

"I'm ready, Daddy," she said as she pranced in wearing a pink bathing suit, terry-cloth robe and rubber thongs. Felicia had braided her blond hair and fastened the ends with pretty seashell barrettes.

"Wow, aren't you pretty," he said, hugging her. "You look ready for an afternoon at the beach."

"Why aren't you ready?" Cassie scowled at his sweater and slacks.

"It's just you and Danny today," he told her. He knew Stella might have a couple of bathing suits, but he doubted Caroline would ever borrow one.

"Do you want me to come, too?" Felicia asked as if feeling insecure about letting Cassie out of her sight after what had happened.

"No, I'll bring her back to your apartment in about an hour."

She nodded and gave Cassie one last look as if reassuring herself that all was well. Her soft slippers and full skirt made a whispering sound as she left.

"All right, let's go, my little mermaid," he said taking her hand.

"Daddy, I have feet," she corrected him as if he didn't know anything at all.

"So you do. And pretty ones at that."

A misty warmth greeted them when they entered the small Jacuzzi room and an inviting gurgle of bubbling water filled their ears. The sunken Jacuzzi was recessed in a tiled floor and a couple of chairs and one reclining lounge were set nearby.

No sign of Danny or Caroline. Maybe she'd changed

her mind about coming, Wes thought and was startled by the wave of disappointment that went through him.

Cassie quickly kicked off her thongs and threw off her robe. Wes stood by as she carefully descended the stairs and began bobbing in the water and trying to splash him.

He wasn't aware that Danny and Caroline had come into the room until Cassie suddenly squealed, "Hurry up, Danny! Hurry up!"

"I'm coming." Danny called back. As the boy quickly discarded the bathrobe, Wes smiled to see that a pair of navy-blue underwear was serving as bathing trunks.

"Necessity is the mother of invention," Caroline told Wes with a chuckle.

"Too bad, you weren't just as inventive," he teased. "Maybe we ought to try this again later."

When she didn't follow through with a flirtatious response, he knew she wasn't used to engaging in sexual innuendoes. In some ways, her lack of sophistication was a pleasant change and in other ways it was totally frustrating. How could a man make time with a desirable female who refused—or didn't know how—to play the mating game?

Wes placed the two chairs close enough to the Jacuzzi to be ready for any sudden mishaps. He knew Cassie could be aggressive when she got caught up in any game.

As the two children were bouncing around, splashing each other like porpoises, he could tell Caroline was obviously on guard as she watched their water play.

"Do you like to swim?" Wes asked, fantasizing about those shapely legs and rounded breasts of hers in a bikini.

"I think I would," she answered with a slight frown. "Never had much of a chance to find out. Maybe I'll learn along with Danny."

"He likes the water all right. All boy, isn't he?" Wes said with an unexpected sense of envy.

A short time later, Caroline glanced at her watch. "I've put a load of clothes in the washer and dryer. Do you mind if I leave for a few minutes to tend to them?"

"Not at all. I'll keep everything under control. Don't worry, Danny will be safe," Wes assured her.

"Don't let him get too rough with Cassie."

Wes laughed. "Knowing my daughter, it will probably be the other way around."

She hurried out of the room heading toward the laundry room down the hall. He could tell that she was still reeling from the emotional trauma they'd all been through. Obviously she was apprehensive about letting her son out of her sight. Wes could understand her feelings. He still had reservations about trusting other people with Cassie.

He watched as the two youngsters splashed each other, squealing and laughing. Danny had lifted himself up on the edge of the Jacuzzi and, sitting there, he began furiously kicking the water, drenching Cassie in the spray.

Laughing and shoving back her sopping-wet hair she pointed to his feet. "You have funny toes. You have funny toes," she chanted.

"I do not."

"Do too! They're just like my daddy's."

Wes stared the boy's small toes curled in a funny twist back against the neighboring toe. He couldn't get his breath. Something exploded inside his head. He suddenly felt as if someone just dropped him off a thousand-foot cliff.

Chapter 9

Caroline was in the laundry room longer than she had expected. When she took the clothes out of the dryer, she found a couple of pullovers still a little damp so she decided to give them another ten minutes while she folded the rest of the clothes.

She was just about finished when Stella walked by the door and then stopped when she saw Caroline. "Oh there you are," she said, coming into the laundry room. "Felicia said you were enjoying the Jacuzzi."

"Just the kids," Caroline said quickly. "Wes is watching them while I finish up the laundry."

"I wanted to apologize for this morning. When Wes and I butt heads like that, I need some time to myself to cool down. I really didn't mean to ignore you."

"I understand," Caroline quickly assured her. "I wasn't in a very good mood myself."

"And for good reason! This whole thing is crazy.

Why would anyone think up some dangerous game like that?" she asked and in the next breath she answered her own question. "Someone who knew the kids were into treasure hunts, that's who. I haven't seen the map, but I'm wondering if there's a clue as to who might have drawn it. You know, handwriting or kind of pencil or pen? I don't want Shane to bear the brunt of all this unfounded suspicion. It's not fair!"

Even though Caroline had to question whether Shane merited his mother's faith, she knew she'd feel the same way if it were her son involved. Still, she wanted to remind Stella that Shane was at fault for not stopping Danny and Cassie when he knew about the map.

As Stella continued to blow off steam about Wes's unfair attitude toward her son, Caroline managed to hold her tongue.

"Shane always knocks himself out to please Wes. That's what makes all of this so unfair. I want to see that map. I'll know in a minute if Shane had anything to do with it."

"I'm sure Wes will gladly show it to you. We all want to find out who's responsible."

"I hope this unfortunate incident isn't going to affect moving ahead on our redecorating plans," she said bluntly. "I mean, even losing one day here and there can add up, you know."

Caroline knew then Stella was resentful that she'd accepted Wes's invitation for the kids to enjoy the Jacuzzi.

"Maybe we can put in a full day tomorrow, for a change?" Caroline responded sweetly.

Stella nodded. "I guess neither of us is in the mood to look at paint charts and fabric swatches today."

"I'd like to get your decorating plans finalized as

soon as possible," Caroline told her. More and more, she was feeling the necessity to complete her contract and have the security of some money in the bank. Then, go home.

As they parted in the hall, Stella headed in one direction and Caroline in the other. With her arms filled with folded clothes, Caroline hurried back to the Jacuzzi room.

Danny and Cassie were playing toss in the water with a large ball. She quickly apologized to Wes for being so long.

"Have they been behaving themselves?"

He stared at her for a long moment as if he hadn't even heard her question. Then he seemed to mentally shake himself. "Yes, fine."

"I had to wait for the dryer," she said, deciding not to mention her conversation with Stella.

He just nodded as he picked up the towels and walked over to the steps. His expression displayed impatience as he said, "Time to get out."

Cassie shot her father a quick glance as if she knew from his tone not to argue. As she quickly dropped the ball, Danny grabbed it for one more throw.

Caroline couldn't tell whether Wes was going to reprimand Danny or let it pass, but the way his eyes narrowed on her son made her intervene. "Danny, let's go."

As they made their way back upstairs, Caroline was at a loss to know why Wes was no longer the relaxed, cordial host he'd been. She'd never seen him in this kind of mood.

For some reason he'd erected a wall between them. He seemed ready to explode about something. The hardness of his jaw and the way his hands were clenched frightened her.

When they reached her door, she quickly said, "Thank you. I know Danny enjoyed it."

"Me, too," Cassie said.

If the children hadn't been there, Caroline would have demanded an explanation. Obviously something had happened while she was in the laundry room—but what? He wasn't even like the same man. With a curt nod, he took Cassie's hand and walked away with his back and head as rigid as a board.

Wes was on the phone to headquarters in Houston as soon as Felicia left his suite with Cassie. It was almost closing time but his secretary, Myrna Goodwin, was still in the office. She was a woman in her fifties who had also been his father's secretary.

When Myrna answered he said, "Good! I'm glad I caught you."

"Oh, hi, boss." Her tone was relaxed and friendly. "What's happening?"

"I need a telephone number. That private investigator who did that good job for us last year."

"Detective Delio?"

"That's the one." Wes waited with pen in hand.

After she'd checked she gave him two numbers. "One is his office and the other is his home. I don't suppose his cell phone will do you any good at the lodge."

"Give it to me. I may have to make a trip to Denver."

She knew from experience that he'd fill her in if and when it was necessary. She didn't ask why or try to find out what was on his mind.

He thanked her, hung up and fought an impulse to

call Delio immediately. He knew that getting his emotions under control before making decisions and acting on them had served him well in the business world.

He'd never been faced with such a personal challenge as this one. The unusual curl of little toes had been a family aberration for several generations. Some blood relatives in the same family passed it on and some didn't. Wes had inherited the trait from his father but his brother, Delvin, and his son, Shane, had missed it.

Wes left his desk and began pacing the floor.

Caroline and Danny ate dinner early and she had just put him down for the night when she heard a knock on the sitting room door.

Who could that be?

Her frown changed to an expression of surprise when she saw Wes standing there.

"How about a nightcap? I decided we ought to end the day on a better note. What do you say?" He was smiling and holding two wine goblets and a bottle of chardonnay.

Her spirits lifted. His mood had made a hundred-and-eighty-degree turnaround. "I think I could handle that."

She realized how her feelings for him had moved into dangerous depths when his disarming smile sent a welcoming warmth through her. Somehow, she'd let this man touch her on emotional levels she'd jealousy guarded since Thomas's death. She'd never expected to feel that wonderful, compelling kind of euphoria again, but her heart had quickened just seeing him standing there, smiling at her.

"No ice but the wine is chilled," he assured her as

he placed the glasses and bottle down on the small coffee table.

They sat down on the sofa, he poured the wine and handed her a goblet. Then he lifted his and toasted, "To the future."

"Whatever that may be," she agreed.

"The future is whatever we make it, isn't it?" he asked.

As his eyes met hers over the rim of his glass, she sensed his words had a double meaning, but she just sipped her wine and relaxed against the cushions beside him, grateful for his company.

He kept the conversation light and seemed comfortable talking about the difficulties of raising a child and the challenges that went with parenting. She didn't know how the conversation led into a personal sharing of her past.

"Was your husband good with children?" he asked as he poured her a second glass of wine.

"Thomas was a good father and loved Danny deeply. Unfortunately, he didn't get to spoil him very much because he didn't have the time. His developing medical practice demanded a great deal." She sighed as she swirled the wine in her glass.

"That can happen," he agreed. "I've been there. Sometimes you have to have something shake you up before you realize what's important."

His fingers visibly tightened on his glass and she wondered if he was thinking about the loss of his son. "I don't know what I'd do if something happened to Danny."

"He's lucky to have a mother like you. I expect you wanted more children," he said in a sympathetic tone.

The wine had loosened her tongue. "Yes, I wanted two boys and two girls, but it didn't happen." She felt at ease sharing her feelings with him. "I'll be forever grateful for Danny. I'd almost given up hoping."

"You had trouble getting pregnant?"

Her chest tightened with remembered pain as the past suddenly seemed as fresh as yesterday. Something in his voice brought all the disappointments flooding back. Her hand shook slightly as she set the empty wineglass down on the table without answering.

"I'm sorry," he quickly apologized, putting an arm around her shoulders and leaning his head close to hers. "If you don't you want to talk about it...?"

Strangely enough as she rested in the warm cradle of his arm, she realized how desperately she did want to talk about it. Maybe it was time to try and release all the pain and heartache of the past. She had kept it all bottled up much too long.

Taking a deep breath, she said, "I conceived two times. A boy and a girl."

"And you lost...the girl?"

"I lost them both."

He stiffened. "Both?"

She swallowed hard. "I couldn't carry either one of them to term. Some irreversible physical weakness causes me to miscarry." She finished her wine in two large gulps as hot tears spilled from her eyes and dribbled down her cheeks.

"But Danny?"

As if he heard his name, there was a movement inside the bedroom door and he appeared rubbing his eyes.

"Mommy?"

"What is it, honey?

"I'm thirsty. And you're making too much noise," he whined as if someone had said those same words to him a few times.

"Let me get you a glass of water, Danny." Wes was instantly on his feet. "And I'll tuck you back in bed just the way I do Cassie, okay?" He took the little boy's hand in his and off they went to the bathroom.

Caroline leaned her head back against the sofa. Her head was swimming. How many glasses of wine had she had? Only two but she'd drunk them fast.

The alcohol had loosened her tongue. She couldn't believe she'd been divulging such personal things about herself. And to Wes Wainwright, of all people! She had no idea how the conversation had taken that direction. Her childlessness was not a subject for polite discussion, especially with a man she barely knew.

She could hear Danny's responding giggle as Wes tucked him in bed. His continuing attention to her and Danny surprised her.

When Wes came back into the sitting room and sat down closely beside her, he said, "He's a great boy. I envy you having a son like that."

"He's changed my life," she admitted. "And after Thomas passed away, I was doubly grateful we'd made the decision to take him. I love him as dearly as if he were my own flesh and blood."

"He's adopted?"

She nodded. "My husband knew I was devastated after my medical condition was determined to be irreversible. Thomas pushed for adoption. In fact, he arranged everything."

"Everything?" he echoed.

"Thomas didn't even tell me he'd located a baby boy until most of the legal work had been done."

"I see." Wes swirled the wine in his glass for a long moment and then set it down without taking a sip. "I guess being a doctor, he'd have access to adoptable babies."

"I never met the young unmarried woman who gave the baby up," Caroline admitted. "Nor the lawyer who handled the adoption. I didn't want to know any of that." She firmed her chin. "From the moment Danny was put in my arms, I knew he was mine. All mine."

When Wes didn't respond, she looked up at him and instantly felt contrite. What a fool she'd been! The conversation must have brought back bitter memories of losing his only son under devastating circumstances.

"I'm sorry. I shouldn't have gone on like that. I didn't mean to bore you with all the episodes of my personal soap opera," she apologized quickly.

"No, I'm glad you did. Very glad. And I wasn't bored in the least. I'm grateful you were willing to share with me."

"So am I."

As she lifted her face to his, he gently brushed back a trailing curl on her cheek. His lips brushed her forehead with a light kiss. Then, to her surprise, he drew back and firmly set her away from him.

She was at a loss how to lighten a situation that suddenly had become terribly uncomfortable.

His expression hinted at a guarded control as he rose to his feet. "I'd better let you get some rest. It's been a long day. Maybe I'll see you and Danny at breakfast?"

She nodded, not knowing if it was an invitation or a casual comment.

He paused at the door and looked back at her for a long moment as if he were tempted to come back and kiss her. Then he abruptly said, "Good night," and left.

After the door closed behind him and she heard his fading steps down the hall, she wondered why she felt more totally alone than she had before.

Wes went straight to his desk and located Detective Delio's home telephone number. His hands were sweaty as he dialed the number. He knew it was late to be calling him, but he was filled with an urgency that defied common sense. It was as if six years of tortuous waiting had suddenly been swept aside. Danny was adopted.

He ignored an inner voice warning him that he could be inviting more heart-wrenching disappointment if what Caroline had said about the unmarried birth mother and the adoption was true. Still, she had admitted that her husband took care of everything. Maybe the good doctor had been less than honest. Wes knew he'd never rest until he was certain beyond any doubt that the boy's physical resemblance to his family was just happenstance.

When he had Delio on the line, Wes wasted no time with small talk. He'd worked with the small, energetic Italian before and they understood each other. In the past, Delio had been paid handsomely for getting several investigations done well and quickly. If the private investigator had been around six years ago when his son had been snatched from the nursery, Wes believed Delio might have uncovered some vital leads in the kidnapping.

"I need you to look into a Colorado adoption," Wes advised him in a crisp, businesslike tone.

"All right. I'll need some details."

"I don't know what agency handled it, but Thomas and Caroline Fairchild had a lawyer who was paid to take care of the legal process. I want you to come to Denver and scrutinize every detail of that adoption."

"What am I looking for?"

"Any evidence that the infant boy they adopted might be my son."

Delio gave a low whistle. "If I didn't know you better, Wes, I'd think you were guilty of wishful thinking."

"The boy has a physical trait like one inherent in my family line. What we need is some hard evidence and I'm willing to go to any lengths to get it. I have to follow through on this even though it seems like an impossibility in some ways."

"I understand."

"Good. Get on it right away."

"Sure thing."

"Call me here at the lodge as soon as you've checked out the adoption."

"Will do. And Wes, don't get your hopes up. This sounds like a real long shot."

"Maybe not," Wes countered briskly.

After he'd hung up the phone, he sat there for a long time staring at nothing. He'd had gut intuitions before, but never as strong as this one.

His thoughts raced ahead.

Caroline.

She'd touched him on an emotional level that he hadn't felt for a long time. He admired her independence, her courage and a feminine softness that she tried to hide. He was physically attracted to her. If things had been different... But they weren't!

He told himself that personal considerations had no place in correcting a terrible wrong like this one. He hated using Caroline's feelings in his efforts to find out the truth, but he had no choice. He had the right to claim his son and he couldn't let sentiment stand in the way. He vowed to do whatever was necessary to exert that right.

A peppering mixture of snow and ice hitting the windowpane was the only sound in the echoing rooms as he readied himself for the impending battle with Caroline over the young child who conceivably might be his son.

Chapter 10

Caroline and Danny overslept the next morning. The snow storm had left behind a mantle of glittering white that was almost blinding in the bright sunlight.

"Let's get a move on, Danny," she said as she glanced at her watch. "Trudie will be clearing off the breakfast buffet."

They hurriedly dressed and were just about ready to leave when there was a knock on the bedroom door. They were surprised to see Cassie standing there.

"Felicia says to have breakfast with us. We've got cinnamon rolls with lots of frosting." Grinning at Danny, she rolled her eyes. "Yummy, yummy."

Danny perked up immediately and gave his mother a begging expression. "Can we?"

"Yes, of course. That's very nice of Felicia to invite us," Caroline said quickly, secretly relieved that she had an excuse not to face Wes this morning. She was totally embarrassed at the way she had dumped such an emotional load on him last night. Who could blame him for making a rather abrupt exit? Never had she talked so openly about her disappointing miscarriages—and to Wesley Wainwright of all people! She was mortified just thinking about it. He'd probably make a point of avoiding her from now on.

As that thought crossed her mind, the disappointment she suddenly felt surprised her. What had happened to her usual common sense? According to Dexter's gossip, Wes enjoyed having romantic affairs, but the fact that he'd never remarried made his intentions clear enough. A moment's pleasure was on his agenda.

Well, it's not on mine!

She resolved to put Wes Wainwright out of her mind and have the good judgment to see the situation as it really was. Her next challenge was pressuring Stella into finalizing the details for the redecorating project. The sooner, the better!

Much to Caroline's surprise and consternation, Felicia insisted on talking about Wes at breakfast. She waited until the children had eaten and were parked in the living room playing their car-racing game.

"Wes hides a heavy heart, I'm afraid," she said as she fixed her dark eyes on Caroline.

"Don't we all?" Caroline responded with a slight shrug. She wasn't in the mood to chat about a man who was dominating her thoughts too much already.

"You're very much like him."

Caroline lifted an eyebrow. "In what way?"

"Your heart needs mending, too. That's what the cards tell me."

"Maybe you ought to exchange them for a different deck," Caroline replied with a smile. "I assure you, Felicia, my heart is in a very good state and I intend to keep it that way. Your concern is misplaced."

"Your aura is not good." She seemed to be focusing on something above Caroline's head. "Very disturbed."

"Probably due to a lack of sleep," Caroline quipped.

Felicia sighed as she reached over and patted Caroline's hand. "I only want to prepare you."

"For what?" Caroline had never gone to a fortune teller or consulted a psychic and this kind of talk made her uncomfortable.

"I don't know. Something is not right. Like you, Wes hides his feelings. I'm afraid someone is going to get terribly hurt."

"I appreciate your concern, Felicia, but you and your cards are way off base. As soon as I finish my commitment here, it's not likely there'll be any occasion that I'll see him again."

When Felicia fell silent, Caroline decided it was time to take her leave. "Thanks for breakfast. I'll collect Danny and get to work," she said as she rose from the table.

"You're not leaving him with me?"

"I think it's better if I keep a short rein on him."

"You think I made the treasure map." She fixed her accusing dark eyes on Caroline. "How can you think such a thing?"

"It's not that—" Caroline began.

"Protecting Cassie and her father is my life! Nothing else matters. I'd do anything for them. Anything. Don't you understand?"

"Yes," Caroline replied. Obviously, the poor woman

was riddled with guilt because she'd failed to save Wes's infant son from the kidnappers. A chill went up Caroline's back as she wondered how twisted that devotion might be.

Danny put up a fuss about leaving, but Caroline was firm. Felicia had done nothing to reassure her Danny was in good hands under her care. In fact, her obsessive allegiance to Wes and Cassie sounded a warning. It wasn't Danny's welfare that would come first in any situation. Caroline decided she'd bring her son back to play with Cassie when she could stay with him.

Danny grumbled all the way to the workroom. Caroline knew she'd have to find a way to keep him busy and out of trouble while she moved ahead on the redecorating plans as quickly as possible.

She was surprised and delighted to find Stella in the workroom, waiting for her. The last time she'd seen her was in the laundry room while the children were with Wes in the Jacuzzi. Stella's bright smile was a relief.

"I've gone through these," she said, pointing to several open books. "And I have some ideas to run by you."

"Great," Caroline said. "We'd better line up some workmen to get started before winter really sets in."

"I've made some inquiries and found some reliable services in Telluride," Stella assured her. "We'll have to provide room and board for the workmen as we need them, but that's no problem. There are several rooms off the kitchen that are suitable for temporary occupancy."

A load of frustration rolled off Caroline's shoulders. Once the projected changes were approved, she'd know how quickly her responsibilities would be over and she could make her plans accordingly. She'd have the money from this job to give her time to find the next one.

"Shall we go down to the main room and go over your selections?" Caroline asked, picking up her notebook.

Stella eyed Danny. "Isn't Felicia going to watch him?"

"Not today," Caroline answered smoothly.

"Why not?" Stella asked in her usual forthright manner. "Is something the matter?

"No, not at all."

"I know Felicia can seem a little eccentric at times," Stella persisted.

Caroline decided not to go there. "She's very good at relating to children, I can see that."

"She's spoiled Cassie, that's for sure," Stella said flatly. Caroline avoided commenting as she handed Danny a tablet and a pencil. "You can be my helper. We'll draw pictures, okay?"

"No bears in the room?" he protested, wide-eyed.

"No bears," she reassured him. Thank heavens, the antler chandelier didn't seem to bother him.

"I'm with him," Stella said, obviously hiding a smile. "And we're not going to put up any mangy old trophies on our walls, are we, Danny?"

He solemnly shook his head.

As they looked over the main room, Caroline suggested to Stella that they visualize the space as empty—empty of furniture, shutters, pictures, rug and all hangings.

The morning flew by and Caroline was delighted with the progress they made blocking out conversational areas. Two brocaded wingback chairs and a coffee table were to be placed in front of the windows overlooking the lake. Three large burgundy sofas were chosen to be placed in a U-shape in front of the huge fireplace for a conversational setting. Caroline recommended selecting wooden cornices for the tall windows and removing the shutters which would allow more natural light into the high-ceilinged room.

They discussed other possibilities at lunch and had just returned to the main room when Wes interrupted a conversation about wall hangings.

"What do you think, Wes? See anything you like?" Stella asked in a tone which indicated she knew who would be paying the price tag. She handed him photos of various art treatments recommended for large wall areas.

"I like the picture Danny drew," he said evasively as he picked up Danny's tablet showing a stick figure of a boy and a weird-looking horse complete with saddle and reins. "That would look great on any wall."

"You can have it," Danny said quickly.

Caroline smothered a chuckle. She knew her son would be expecting to find it displayed the next time he visited Wes's suite.

"Thank you very much," Wes said solemnly. "Let's leave it in your tablet for now. You may want to make a whole book of drawings for me to chose from."

Nicely done, Caroline thought, pleased with the way Wes was dealing with her son. Without Cassie around, he was paying a lot more attention to Danny.

"How would you like to go sledding this afternoon, Danny?"

Caroline's smile quickly faded. "Oh, I'm afraid that's not a good idea. Stella and I are really making headway. I'm afraid we're going to be at it for several more hours."

"Oh, I wasn't planning on interrupting your work. I'm sure I can handle both of the kids myself."

"They don't have to go far," Stella quickly assured Caroline. "There's a small slope close to the lodge."

"You can watch from the front windows if you like," Wes told her, obviously a little irritated at her protective manner.

Danny tugged on her arm. "Please…please."

Even as she hesitated, she realized that she really had no basis for refusing. After all, one parent supervising the activity was all that was needed.

"All right."

"Yippee!" He grabbed Wes's hand. "Let's go."

Wes laughed. "First, you change into some warm clothes. I'll go tell Cassie." He smiled at Caroline. "Say twenty minutes. I'll meet Danny back here."

Caroline was thankful Danny's snowsuit had been at the cleaners when the fire had destroyed their house. After putting on knitted cap, gloves and boots, he was ready and they returned to the main room.

Danny waited impatiently and kept looking out a front window as if he was afraid they'd leave without him.

"Through the years, the lodge has collected all kinds of accumulated sleds, ice skates, tubes and rubber rafts," Stella told Caroline. "Believe me, they've been tested by kids of every size and age. Wes will find the right sled for Danny, don't worry."

"He can't use mine," Cassie piped up as she came into the room with Wes. She looked like a snow bunny in a white furry hat and matching white snowsuit and boots.

"He gets the Red Flyer," Wes said quickly. "It's the

best one for a boy." He'd changed to gray ski pants, a matching parka, gloves and snowboots. "Come on, let's go. Tim is bringing the sleds around to the front."

The two children bounded out of the house ahead of him. Caroline and Stella watched them through a front window and saw Wes give each of the children a sled to pull, taking the largest one for himself.

They tromped through the snow to a place where the ground sloped gently down to a meadow bordering the lake. As they made their first run down the hill, Caroline wished she'd dropped everything and gone with them. Danny was laughing as he bounded off his sled and began pulling it back up the slope for another run. She was relieved that Wes was making sure they made their downhill runs one by one so there wouldn't be any collisions.

Stella turned away from the window. "Let's get back to work. We'll make out the orders for the furniture and materials and then call it a day. I want to think about the room accessories. I am still undecided about an area rug."

They'd been working only a few minutes when they heard the sound of a car engine outside.

"That's probably Dexter coming back from Telluride," Stella said. "I wonder why he didn't drive around back to the garage like always?" She looked out the window. "Damn," she swore.

"What is it?"

"Company."

Caroline moved to the window. Dexter was holding the car door open for an attractive, stylish young woman with red hair.

"Who's that?" Caroline asked.

"Nicole Kitridge. Her family owns half the mining interests in these mountains. She and Wes had a thing going last year. Bets were down that Nicole would become the next Mrs. Wesley Wainwright," Stella said with an edge to her voice.

"What happened?"

Stella shrugged. "Who knows? There were plenty of wealthy men lined up for her attention. Personally, I think it was jealousy on Wes's part. He can't stand competition in any form, which stands him in good stead in the business world but it wears thin in a personal relationship."

Nicole must have seen Wes because she immediately headed in that direction. As Nicole reached him and the two embraced, Stella said dryly, "I guess they made up."

"Apparently they have." Caroline remembered Wes saying he and Dexter were late getting back from Telluride the last time because they'd spent time with some friends. She wondered if Nicole was the real reason.

Dexter joined the couple and they watched Danny and Cassie take a couple of runs down the slope.

"They're coming in," Stella said, smoothing back her hair and pulling down her knit sweater.

Caroline watched at the window as the group turned toward the lodge. The woman helped Danny pull his sled, Dexter took Cassie's and Wes pulled his own. When they reached the lodge, Wes was laughing at something Nicole said and Caroline was foolishly annoyed by the obvious harmony between them.

When they came into the room, Stella greeted the visitor with an effusive, "How nice to see you, Nicole."

Caroline deliberately gave all her attention to Danny.

"Did you have fun, honey?" she asked as she helped him take off his snowy jacket. "Your cheeks are rosy."

"I went down the hill—really fast," he bragged.

"Me, too," Cassie piped up. "Didn't I, Daddy?"

"Yes, indeed," Wes assured her. "Both of you are ready for the junior Olympics."

Danny pointed at Nicole. "She won a medal. She told me. A real one...for bobby-sledding." He frowned when they all laughed.

"What fun to be here." Nicole smiled at Wes as she unbuttoned her fur-trimmed, green suede coat. Wispy red curls framed her face and a hint of freckles dotted her perky nose. "When Dexter offered to drive me here for a visit, I just couldn't refuse."

"Always at your service," Dexter replied with mock gallantry as he quickly took her coat and laid it on a nearby chair.

As Nicole's gray-blue eyes traveled to Caroline, Wes quickly introduced her. "Caroline Fairchild. She's our interior decorator. Stella has her busy with all sorts of plans for the lodge."

"Yes, Dexter told me. It's quite a challenging project, I would imagine," she commented as she glanced at the pile of material and books.

"We're just in the exploring stage," Stella said quickly as if she didn't want Nicole putting in her two cents' worth.

Dexter shifted impatiently. "Why don't we all have something to warm us up?"

"Good idea," Wes agreed as if he was uncomfortable with the women's chatter.

"Come on, Stella," Dexter urged. "Let's see what we can wrestle up in the kitchen for a snack."

Wes took Cassie's hand. "We'll get a fire going in the social room."

"It's no fun in the house," she complained. "Why can't we go out and make a snowman?"

"Maybe later," he answered shortly as they disappeared down the hall.

Caroline would rather have excused herself, but she didn't know how to manage it without seeming rude. She was surprised when Nicole fell into step beside her and Danny as they followed Wes and Cassie.

"You have a darling little boy," she told Caroline as she beamed at Danny.

"He's very special," Caroline agreed and squeezed his hand.

"I bet Wes is enjoying having him around. Men are really partial to boys, aren't they?"

"Oh, I don't know. Every child is very special. Wes certainly loves his daughter and they seem to have a very close relationship."

"Perhaps, but there's a sad loneliness in him that all his money and prestige can't seem to fill. He clearly has a deep longing for more family. He ought to get married and have more kids."

"All redheads?" Caroline couldn't believe her own ears and was mortified she'd spoken aloud. Deciding the best defense was offense, she added quickly, "Stella told me you and Wes were an item. I was just guessing there might be a wedding in the future."

Nicole measured Caroline with her steady gray-blue eyes. "Do I detect some personal interest in his future plans?"

"Only that I wish him well," Caroline said evenly. "He seems deserving of happiness."

"One way or another Wes usually gets what he wants," Nicole said thoughtfully. "Once he makes up his mind."

Caroline had the good sense just to smile and keep her mouth shut. She was glad there wasn't opportunity for further exchanges.

Wes and Dexter monopolized Nicole's attention while Stella served hot drinks and freshly baked muffins. Caroline sat on the sofa between the two children. Nicole was a vivacious conversationalist and the adult talk centered on people and events Caroline had never heard about. It was obvious that Dexter was enamored with the attractive redhead and he did his best to be charming.

In contrast, Wes gave his attention to building up the fire and seemed rather preoccupied. He kept looking at his watch and when Tim Henderson poked his head into the room, Wes swung around with a questioning look on his face.

Tim nodded. "That call you've been waiting for is on the line."

"Good." He turned to Nicole. "Excuse me, I have some business matters to take care of. You'll be staying the night, of course?"

"If there's room in the lodge," she replied in a coquettish tone.

"I think we can find one," he said rather briskly.

Caroline was surprised when he shot her a quick look before he hurried out of the room. The sudden hardness in his eyes made him a stranger and she felt an invading chill in the warm room.

Wes shut the door to his office before he sat down and punched the blinking button on his phone. When

Delio identified himself, Wes said curtly, "I've been waiting for your call."

"I flew into Denver on a red-eye last night. I could tell you were impatient for a report so I covered as much ground as I could today." He paused, as if searching for the right words.

"What did you find out?" Wes demanded impatiently.

"I'm not sure."

"What in the hell does that mean?" Wes could summon extreme patience when handling business matters, but something personal was a different story.

"It means I didn't find anything. Nada!"

"Why not?" Wes's tone indicated the fault must lie with the investigator.

"Because there's no official record of any adoption by Thomas and Caroline Fairchild."

Wes's hand was suddenly sweaty on the telephone receiver. "You're sure?"

"If the supposed adoption took place, it wasn't registered with the State of Colorado."

A jolt went through Wes as if someone had landed a punch in the middle of his stomach. No adoption?

"Apparently the husband located the baby and arranged for all the legal work," Wes told him.

"What was the name of the lawyer who handled the legal forms?"

"I don't know."

"Can't you get me a name?" Delio pressured. "I could check that way and might be able to come up with something that makes sense."

"I'll try. I need more information to know what the real story is."

"That's wise," Delio admitted. His tone held a warning. "Innocent or not, Wes, we need to handle this very carefully."

"I understand," Wes answered as a heaviness settled in his chest. He didn't want to hurt anyone. He just wanted his son back. He felt guilty treating Caroline with such deceit, but he had no choice. Until he knew the truth, he couldn't let his feelings get in the way. "I'll try to get more information as quickly as I can."

"In the meantime, Wes, I'll gather as much personal history on both Thomas and Caroline Fairchild as I can, undercover. Since the husband was in the medical field, I should be able to find plenty of people who knew him. Interrogating coworkers might uncover someone who can verify the source of the adopted baby. It could be that everything was on the up and up, despite the lack of Colorado records and I'll get some leads that will answer our questions."

"He graduated from the University of Colorado," Wes offered. "That's where he met his wife. She was raised in eastern Colorado and both parents are dead."

"How did you meet her?"

"My sister-in-law brought her to the lodge. She's an interior decorator." Wes realized then how little he really knew about Caroline even though she had touched him in ways that were deeply personal.

He couldn't allow any feelings to detract him. Not now, when there was a chance that a little boy with curved pink toes might be his own flesh and blood.

Chapter 11

Wes had not returned from his telephone call by the time the children had finished their hot chocolate and Felicia had come for Cassie. Nicole was happily entertaining Dexter and Tim with a flirtatious story that had brought a frown to Stella's face when Caroline made her excuses and left with Danny.

They had made their way upstairs to the second floor and Caroline was just opening their door when Wes came out of his suite at the far end of the corridor.

Danny bolted away from her and ran down the hall to meet him.

"Can we make a snowman now? Can we?" he begged with childish impatience.

Wes laughed and took his hand as they walked toward Caroline. "Let's wait for more snow. Then we can make a really big one."

"How big?" Danny asked with rounded eyes.

"One so tall you'll have to stand on a ladder to put on his ugly nose," he promised.

Danny giggled as if he was already imagining the snowman's funny face.

Wes's smile faded when they reached her, and Caroline wondered why he seemed so guarded. "I'm sorry. Is Danny pestering you again?"

"Not at all," he answered quickly. "In fact, I'd like to spend more time with him."

"I'm sure he'd like that. Danny's always on the go and I'm afraid that sometimes all that bouncing energy gets him into trouble."

"He just needs someone to give him more attention."

She raised an eyebrow. Where did this overinvolved businessman get off telling her what her son needed? She didn't like his dictatorial tone and bristled at his unwarranted criticism.

"I rather think he may be getting too much attention. He doesn't have much competition for my time." She paused for emphasis. "No pressing business and social obligations."

Nicole's vivacious voice suddenly floated down the hall as if to punctuate Caroline's last remarks. "There you are, Wes, darling. I wondered if you were lost to us forever."

When she reached them, she looped her arm through his. "Stella didn't seem to know where to put my overnight things."

Without looking at either of them, Caroline said to Danny, "Let's get you a warm bath."

She wasn't about to stand in the hall while Nicole and Wes discussed their sleeping arrangements. She took his hand and closed the door behind them.

"Why are you mad, Mommy?" Danny asked as she helped him bathe and dress to go downstairs to dinner.

"I'm not mad."

"He's a nice man, Cassie's dad. Isn't he?"

"Yes, of course," she answered quickly.

"Then why don't you like him?"

"I do." *Your mother's jealous.* Somehow, the silent admission made her feel better.

All right, so she was physically attracted to Wes Wainwright. She straightened and firmed her shoulders. That didn't mean she couldn't rein in any serious romantic feelings for him. No telling how many romantic partners of his had crossed the threshold of his mountain retreat. Obviously, he and Nicole knew how to play the game. Her best bet was to give them both wide clearance while she did the job she'd been hired to do.

When she and Danny went downstairs to dinner, her defenses were up but Wes and Nicole didn't show. *Probably having dinner in his suite,* she thought, rather wistfully. Her longing to be with him challenged her pride. She'd been foolish enough to respond to his sexual charm. Just remembering the feel of his mouth on hers sent a rippling of desire through her.

When Stella joined her and Danny at their table, Caroline had trouble keeping her imagination free of thoughts about what was happening upstairs. She had to force herself to focus on what Stella was saying and pretend to be receptive to her instructions.

"We'll spend the morning clearing out the main room and getting rid of all the collected bric-a-brac, newspapers, magazines and such that has collected over the years," she told Caroline in her employer tone. "That way we'll have all clean shelves and tables for new purchases."

As Stella continued with a litany of plans for new lamps, accessories and rugs, Caroline nodded without comment. She knew Stella well enough by now to know she wasn't asking for any two-way discussion about the new purchases.

As soon as they had finished eating, Caroline made her escape, after promising to meet Stella at nine o'clock the next morning.

A growing discontent stayed with her even after she'd tucked Danny in bed. She lay stiffly looking up at the ceiling, trying to forget the strange way Wes had looked at her just before Nicole arrived and slipped her arm through his.

The warm blankets failed to quell a sudden chill as she remembered the way his eyes had narrowed when he looked at her. It was almost as if he were judging her in some way and finding her lacking.

The next morning the feeling of discontent was even stronger. Caroline awoke with a knowing that permeated her total awareness.

It's time to leave.

Logically, the intuitive decision made no sense. Nothing had changed in her finances. The insurance company was still marking time about settling. She had no assurance she would be paid for the time she'd already devoted to the redecorating plans. Still, a nameless urgency flowed through her like the swift current of a river.

As soon as they were dressed, Caroline hurried Danny downstairs to the telephone in the hall alcove.

She dialed Betty McClure's number and was relieved when her friend answered with her familiar, "Hello, Betty speaking."

"I was afraid you might have already left for the store," Caroline said quickly.

"Caroline! How in the world are you? We've been dying to know how the mountain project is going."

"I'm sorry, I didn't call sooner. It's…it's been a challenge."

"Oh, what kind?"

Caroline almost laughed. Such a simple question but such a tangled answer. "I'll try to explain later. At the moment, I'm wondering if there have been any other inquires about my services. I could be back and on another decorating job by the beginning of next week."

"My goodness. You're not going to finish the Wainwright contract? Is it really that bad?" she prodded. "It sounded like such a wonderful opportunity."

"It's complicated," Caroline answered quickly. She couldn't make sense of all of it herself, let alone try to explain to someone else the undefined urgency that had overtaken her.

"Well, I'm really sorry. Gosh, I don't know what to tell you. People aren't in the mood to redecorate this time of year," Betty reminded her. "You know how it is. Come springtime, Caroline, you'll probably have plenty of work. The Wainwright recommendation would be invaluable, you know."

Caroline took a deep breath even as her hand tightened on the phone receiver. She knew her friend was right. Defaulting on this job was irresponsible. And letting her feelings for Wes Wainwright dictate her career choices was juvenile. Financially, she could not afford to just pack up and go back—and to what?

"I guess I'd better give it more thought," she admitted reluctantly. "Thanks for the counseling session."

"Anytime. What are friends for? I know this is a rough time for you. Have you heard from the insurance company?"

"Not much. Only that an arson investigation is holding up settlement. Apparently there's some question about whether I burned down my own house to collect."

Betty muttered a swear word. "Hang in there. They can't dally forever." Her tone brightened. "I've been looking at some homes in our area that would be perfect for you and Danny. With the money you're going to get from the lodge contract, you'll be able to move into something even nicer than you had. Keep the faith."

After Caroline hung up, she realized Betty was right. She shouldn't let nebulous feelings dictate decisions that lacked definite validity. Maybe she should have shared her tangled feelings about Wes? She needed someone to tell her how big a fool she was.

During Caroline's talk with Betty, Danny had been playing with Cassie's pretend telephone. When she heard him ordering a pizza with everything, she smothered a smile.

"Does that mean you're hungry and ready for breakfast?" she teased.

"Is that what we're having? Pizza?" he asked, hopefully.

"Probably not," Caroline admitted. "But something just as good, I bet."

Danny looked skeptical.

Caroline braced herself against the possibility of

finding Wes and Nicole having breakfast together, but there was no sign of either of them in the room. She realized then that they were probably having a private breakfast in his suite.

Dexter was the only one seated at a table. After she and Danny filled their plates and moved away from the buffet, he stood up and held out a chair for her at his table.

She couldn't bring herself to intentionally snub him. As it turned out, she was glad that she hadn't. The conversation was very enlightening.

"I'm taking Nicole back to Telluride this morning," he told her.

"So soon?" she asked in what she hoped was a casual tone.

"Yep. Apparently, her single room last night wasn't to her liking—if you get what I mean." Dexter winked suggestively. "Too bad. I guess Wes wasn't in the mood for company."

Caroline's heartbeat suddenly quickened. Deliberately, she gave her attention to helping Danny cut up his slice of ham. Her outward lack of interest didn't seem to deter Dexter in the least.

"Nothing so dead as an old love, I guess," he continued in his gossipy manner. "They made a nice couple but Nicole certainly doesn't need his money. Not like some of the women who chase after him." His pudgy smile included Caroline. "I think Wes gets a little bored with all the feminine attention." He sighed. "Ah, if I could be so lucky."

"What do you do for a living? Or do you?" Caroline asked pointedly. She was irritated with his insulting innuendoes.

Dexter chuckled as if he was amused by her directness. "You might say my business is entertaining myself. My dear papa left me enough bucks to enjoy life and I intend to do it handsomely." He looked at her over the rim of his coffee cup. "I bet you've never really let yourself go, Caroline. Maybe surrendered to some wild joy just because you felt like it?"

"No, I haven't," she answered honestly.

"Maybe you ought to try it."

"Some of us don't have that luxury," she countered rather impatiently. "My father left me a dry land farm, mortgaged to the hilt. On the other hand, he left me something more important. The strength to make it on my own."

"I admit I've been lucky," Dex admitted, the meaning of her jab missing him entirely. "Really lucky to have friends like Wes. He's been the most important person in my life. To be truthful, I'm glad he and Nicole didn't connect this time." He looked a little sheepish. "I admit I get a little jealous when he gives too much of his attention to someone else. On the other hand, I don't like it when I see him unhappy."

"Is he unhappy?"

"I reckon so. He saddled up Prince early this morning for a solitary ride. Wes does that when he's got a problem to solve. He likes to get away and think it through. Something's bothering him. Do you know what it is?"

"Why don't you ask him?" Caroline countered evenly.

"He's almost as tight-lipped as you are. Well, I guess I'll have to wait and see if what I suspect is going on under my nose." He pushed back his plate and stood up. "I've got to get Nicole's luggage and bring the SUV around. She wants to have breakfast on the way. My guess is the lady's pride is hurt and she wants out of here before Wes gets back."

Caroline nodded without comment.

"Will you tell Wes that I may decide to spend the night in Telluride, consoling the lady and all that?" Without giving her a chance to refuse the role of messenger, he got up and sauntered out of the room.

As Caroline poured herself another cup of coffee from the table carafe, she thoughtfully digested the information Dexter had given her.

Wes had not spent the night making love to Nicole.

The tightness in her heart eased. She had imagined him touching Nicole with his soft trailing fingers and igniting her flesh with heat. Now, she knew his lips had not played upon hers with the inviting promise of a lover's caress and—

"What's the matter, Mommy?" Danny peered up at her with the curiosity of a six-year-old. "You look funny."

Caroline smiled as she brushed down a wayward tuft of his hair. "Are you about through with your breakfast? Finish your cereal and you can have one of those chocolate doughnuts."

As Danny attacked the oatmeal, she leaned back in her chair and gazed out the window.

The view of the snow-covered ground and lake was like a winter postcard with a clearing blue sky and dazzling shafts of morning sunlight splaying through the snow-laden branches. She blinked at the brightness and was about to look away when a dark, fast-moving horse and rider came into view. She quickly set down her coffee cup.

Wes! He was heading for the stable.

Just then Cassie and Felicia came into the room. When the little girl saw Danny, she ran over to the table. "Goody. We're going to eat with you."

"I'm going to have a doughnut," Danny said as if that somehow put him ahead.

"Me, too."

Caroline stood up when Felicia and Cassie were ready to sit down at the table. "Felicia, will you keep an eye on Danny for a few minutes? I have something I need to do."

"Yes, of course. We've been missing Danny, haven't we, Cassie?" She seemed relieved that Caroline had decided to leave him with her. "Take your time."

"I won't be long," Caroline promised as she quickly left the room. Even though she was wearing a heavy sweater, warm slacks and her walking boots, she shivered at the onslaught of crisp air that hit her as she left the lodge.

By the time she got to the stables, Wes had already unsaddled Prince. Without him noticing she lingered in the doorway and watched as he threw a blanket over the stallion and began rubbing down his glistening black hide.

The bond between man and horse was unmistakable as his hands moved gracefully over the horse's shoulders, thighs, lower legs and rump. A deep caring and an outward expression of love was evident in his every stroke.

As Caroline watched him, a warm stirring of sexual desire crept through her. Every movement of his body was a tantalizing promise of his commanding masculinity. As his hands traveled the warm contours of the stallion's body, she felt his gentle strokes on her own skin. She'd never felt that kind of instant desire before. An aching need that rose full-blown and demanding brought beads of perspiration to her brow.

She should leave, walk out the door. Cool the physical desire sluicing hotly through her. It was insanity to want this man so passionately. An exhilarating kind of madness. Not at all like her usual self-contained person.

She must have made a sound that swung him around to face the door. When he saw her, his expression was one of surprise. For a moment she thought he was going to roughly demand what she was doing there. As his gaze traveled over her, his shoulders seemed to relax and his frown eased. "Well, hello. You're too late for a ride this morning."

"That's too bad," she replied in the same even tone. Now that she was face to face with him she couldn't think of anything suitable to say. She fell back on the excuse Dexter had given her.

"I had breakfast with Dex and he wanted me to tell you he was taking Nicole back to Telluride this morning in the SUV." She watched his expression and his eyes narrowed slightly.

Without comment, he turned back to the stallion and finished currying him before he put him in his stall.

They walked back to the house, side by side, and the total content of his conversation was about the weather and early warnings of another snowstorm. Somehow, their former easy companionship had completely vanished.

Once inside the main room of the lodge, Caroline

decided that she needed to make a few things clear to him. "I know Stella is going to be upset, but I'm considering breaking my contract with her."

"You can't leave!" He stared at her as if she'd hit him in the middle of the stomach and he couldn't get his breath.

"I have another job lined up," she lied gibbly. "I would appreciate receiving a fair compensation for the work I've already done."

He just stared at her as if his thoughts were whirling like an off-balance gyroscope. "No."

For a foolish moment, she thought he was going to declare some deep feelings for her. His eyes fastened on her with the force of a grappling hook as he put his hands on her arms.

"I can't let you go."

The words were right but there was no lover's caress in his tone. His angry demeanor made her pull away from him.

He ran an agitated hand through his hair. "We... we have to talk. Please. There's something you have to know."

His manner warned her it wasn't something inconsequential. As her heartbeat quickened, she asked, "What is it? Tell me."

"Not here." He sent a furtive look around the room as if someone might have been watching the emotional scene.

"I need to get back to Danny. I left him with Felicia eating breakfast."

"He'll be fine. Nobody will be in the reading room this time of morning." He grabbed her hand and pulled her down the hall.

Once inside the room, he shut the door and motioned for her to have a seat on the couch. He seemed undecided whether he should sit down beside her or remain standing. He ended up leaning against the library table and looking down at her.

"Do you remember the afternoon we spent watching the kids in the Jacuzzi?"

She nodded.

"You left to go to the laundry room, remember?" He seemed to run out of breath for a moment. "Well, something happened while you were gone."

She stiffened. "Was it something you should have told me about?" At the time she'd been puzzled by the change in him when she returned to the room.

"I probably should have, but I wasn't sure of anything then." His mouth tightened. "You hadn't told me Danny was adopted. At least not until later."

"What does that have to do with anything?" Her voice was suddenly sharper than she intended. Something deep inside registered an unnamed danger when he hesitated to answer her question.

"The boy has the same physical characteristics in his toes as my father, grandfather and other members of the Wainwright family."

She stared at him blankly.

"Don't you see? My infant son was kidnapped when he was only a month old. Already his tiny feet showed the family's trait of curved little toes."

"What are you saying?"

"It's conceivable that you have adopted my baby boy who was taken from our nursery six years ago."

His words stunned her. Not because she found them valid. She couldn't believe that he'd come to such a ludicrous conclusion. She'd judged him to be an intelligent and perceptive man and was appalled that a longing for his own son had twisted his cognitive reasoning in such a bizarre way. Caroline felt a deep sympathy for him.

"It's certainly a coincidence," she admitted gently. "And I can see why any physical similarities to your own family would be startling. But these things do happen. Danny's birth mother or father must have passed along an aberration that resembled yours. It's as simple as that."

"Maybe not as simple as you think," he argued. "What do you know about the birth mother?"

His sharp question took her back for a moment. "Not very much, really. She was a young unmarried woman—"

"Did you meet her?"

"No, Thomas handled everything about the adoption. He and the lawyer took care of all the legal business."

"And this took place in Denver, Colorado." At her nod, he added, "What would you say if I told you there is no record of such an adoption?"

"I would say you're misinformed." A swell of anger brought a hot flush to her face. "Have you been looking into Danny's adoption without my knowledge?"

"Yes, I hired a reputable private detective, Clyde Delio, to look into the adoption." His eyes bit into hers. "Caroline, Delio can't find any adoption registered in your name in the state of Colorado."

"Then I think you should fire him," she flared as she stood up. "I have Danny's official adoption papers in a metal box I saved from the fire. I'll go to my car and get them. That ought to prove how wrong you are." And with that, she practically ran out of the room.

Chapter 12

Wes laid the papers out on his desk and Caroline watched as he examined every word, line, paragraph and signature.

She could not believe this was happening!

He was trying to claim her son!

She felt sick to her stomach realizing how he'd played her for a fool. Plying her with wine and caresses, he'd encouraged her most private confidences until she'd told him what he wanted to know—Danny was adopted. He had hired a private investigator without even a hint of his intentions.

Her eyes stung with threatening tears as a mixture of anger and hurt swept over her. She hated him for deceiving her, for letting her believe that he really cared for her. Now she knew the bitter truth. His attention to her had been a calculated means to achieving his own ends.

Was this what Felicia was trying to warn her about? Caroline had viewed the nanny's behavior as eccentric, but maybe Wes had gone off the deep end like this before. Did any male child who was his lost son's age come under this kind of scrutiny? Maybe Felicia had seen signs that Wes had become fixated on Danny. Caroline had noticed Wes had a genuine liking for her son, but now it appeared that his interest had been something deeper and threatening.

Well, she'd made enough of a fool of herself. Better to have discovered his real intentions now rather than later. She folded her arms and waited impatiently until he finally finished looking at the papers and put them down.

"Satisfied?"

"They seem authentic."

"They *are* authentic!" she snapped.

As she reached for them, he stopped her hand. "May I make some copies?"

A dark, guarded solemnity had settled in his eyes and he seemed like a total stranger. Was this the same man who had held her tenderly in his arms?

"What for?"

"I'd like my investigator to take a look at them."

"A waste of time and money, but I guess you have plenty of that," she jabbed.

"I just have to be sure." His eyes held a haunted look. "Damn sure."

She started to refuse because of the bitterness she felt inside. Even with concrete evidence in front of him, he was refusing to accept the truth. Only the need to settle his obsession as soon as possible made her decide to let him copy the papers.

"Where's your copier?" She wasn't about to let the papers out of her sight.

Because his suite office seemed fully equipped, she wasn't surprised when he pointed to one on a nearby stand.

"All right. Let's settle this once and for all."

She stood closely by his side and watched as he fed the papers into the machine. She was prepared for any trickery and took them away from him as he made a copy of each one. Once the adoption papers were back in her hands, she turned on her heels to leave.

"Caroline!" He stopped her before she reached the door. "Please understand—"

"Oh, I do!" She swung around and faced him. "I understand perfectly. You've exploited my feelings to gain the information you wanted. Now you have it and the charade is over! Once your investigator verifies the adoption papers I'll leave with my son and trust that I'll never see you again." Turning her back on him, she fought back tears as she fled down the hall.

Wes immediately called Delio and alerted him that he was faxing copies of the Fairchild adoption papers to him at his hotel.

"Where'd they come from?"

"The mother had copies."

"I'll be damned."

Wes would have suspected a slipshod job if it had been anybody but Delio. He was too damn good. There had to be a logical explanation why the private dectective had missed the papers.

"George Goodman is the lawyer's name on the papers. As far as I can tell everything looks in order. As soon as you've checked them out, get back to me."

"Will do."

Wes's hand was sweaty as he hung up. Waiting for anything or anybody had never been his strong point. He'd always been a doer, but what kind of action could he take in a situation like this?

Caroline's hurt and outrage weighed heavily with him. All the years of passion and desire that had lain dormant since Pamela's death had exploded into feelings he hadn't known he still had. Somehow, she had touched him in vulnerable areas he'd always kept protected from other women. It hurt deeply to see the scathing look in her eyes, but it couldn't be helped. He had to know the truth! The need to verify Danny's parentage outweighed everything else.

He was glad he'd kept Nicole at a distance during her surprise visit. She'd tried her best to renew their early romantic fling, but playing games with her was the last thing on his mind.

When Caroline checked on Danny in the dining room, she found Felicia had taken him with Cassie to her apartment after breakfast.

The door was ajar and as Caroline went in, she saw that the two children were playing some kind of dice game.

"I'm winning," Danny bragged when he saw his mother. "Can't I stay?"

"Please let him," Cassie begged.

"We've been missing Danny," Felicia said, adding to the chorus as she rose from her nearby chair. "And you, too."

As her penetrating gaze settled on Caroline, she asked, "Is something the matter? I sense turbulence in your spirit."

"I'm not sure *turbulence* is the right word. *Fury* might come closer," Caroline muttered with tight lips.

"Perhaps you'd like to stay for a cup of my tansy tea?" Felicia offered quickly.

Caroline suspected the invitation was for more than sipping tea. Undoubtedly, Felicia would direct the conversation to satisfy her curiosity. Well, two could play that game. Caroline had a few questions of her own. Besides, she was in no mood to face Stella in the workroom.

"Yes, I think I would like a cup of tea, Felicia. Thank you."

Felicia quickly set out cups on the kitchen table and prepared a pot of a fragrant scented tea. She allowed Caroline a few minutes of quiet contemplation before she sat down and remarked pointedly, "Your aura is a worrisome gray this morning."

Caroline managed a weak smile. "Gray? Not a fiery red?"

Felicia handed Caroline a cup. "This will help."

Under other circumstances Caroline might have enjoyed the unique taste of the tea but she had too much on her mind. "Felicia, I need to talk about something that I know must be painful for you. I wouldn't do it if I had any other choice."

"It's all right. I gave up being offended a long time ago," she replied quietly. "It's Wes, isn't it?"

"How did you know?"

"The vibrations between the two of you are hard to miss."

Caroline moistened her lips. "I need to know about the kidnapping. What did Wes do to try and recover the baby boy?"

Felicia didn't seemed the least bit surprised by the question. "Everything humanly possible," she answered readily. "The kidnappers could have named their ransom and Wes would have gladly paid it. He offered an enormous reward, hired a fleet of detectives and followed up every possible lead. Nothing."

"No suspects at all?"

"None. Even the FBI failed to come up with any viable leads."

"Surely they must have had some suspects."

"Wes had plenty of competitors who were jealous of his growing financial empire. The kidnapping could have been in retaliation by some revengeful investor." She paused as she took another sip of tea. "But I don't think so."

"Then who?"

Staring at her cup, Felicia slowly twirled the liquid. "I've asked that question for nearly seven years. Someday we'll know." She leaned over and patted Caroline's hand. "You have to be kind to him."

Caroline jerked her hand away. "He's trying to claim my son."

Felicia didn't say anything for a long moment. "I don't understand. What do you mean by claim? If he wants to help you raise your son—"

"No, that's not it at all. He's trying to claim Danny as his own."

Felicia listened intently as Caroline told her about the family resemblance, the investigator Wes had hired and his report that no record of Danny's adoption existed.

Felicia's eyes rounded. "You mean—"

"The investigator's report is a bunch of crap!" Caroline retorted with an unladylike word. "Danny's adoption was totally legal."

"Are you certain?" A sudden glow brightened her dark eyes. "Maybe—"

"No!" Caroline snapped and then drew in a deep breath to settle her voice. "My son's birth mother was a young unmarried woman and my husband and lawyer handled the adoption. I have copies of the legal adoption and I showed them to Wes. He's going to send copies to his investigator and that will be the end of that!"

Felicia's expression changed and Caroline knew she would have preferred for Wes and his investigator to be right. Undoubtedly everyone at the lodge would line up against her when they learned of Wes's interest in Danny.

Caroline pushed away the teacup. "I have to go."

As she stood, she felt a little unsteady on her feet. Placing her hands on the table, she braced herself as her legs threatened to give way.

"You'd best sit down," Felicia said quietly. "Tansy tea has that effect on some people."

"Then why did you give it to me?" Caroline asked in an accusing tone.

"Because you needed it. Now sit down and collect yourself. You'll not do yourself any good chasing phantoms of your imagination."

"It's not me who's imagining things." She sank back in the chair and put her heavy head in her hands to hold it up. "I can't believe any of this."

"You've fallen in love with him, haven't you? I knew I should have warned you. Poor Wes, he doesn't have a heart to give to a woman. Pamela broke it before she died."

"Didn't she love him?"

"As much as she could, I guess."

"It wasn't a happy marriage?"

"Wes gave and she took," Felicia said sadly. "Even with all the attention and flattery that came Pamela's way as a beauty queen, she never had enough love to share with anyone." She eyed Caroline. "He's very protective of Cassie, as you can understand. If there's a chance that Danny is his…"

"There isn't!"

Caroline rose to her feet again and this time the adrenaline rushing through her body seemed to counteract the effects of the tansy tea.

She left the kitchen. "Come on, Danny, we have to go."

"Can Cassie come, too? We could play games while you work."

"Can I? Can I?" she begged.

Caroline waited for Felicia to tell the little girl no, but she didn't. "If it's all right with Danny's mother," she said smiling in that secretive way of hers.

Caroline silently groaned. She didn't feel up to battling all three of them so she gave in. "If they'll amuse themselves, I guess it will be okay. Stella and I are going to be cleaning out the main room."

Felicia quickly gathered up a few toys and games for them to take along. "I'll come and get Cassie in a couple of hours," she promised.

Stella was already in the main room. She frowned when she saw Caroline had the two children with her. "Is Felicia ill?"

"No."

"Then why are the children with you?"

"They won't be any trouble," Caroline said, avoiding a direct answer. She had too much on her mind to argue about watching the kids for a couple of hours. As quickly as she could she settled them on the rug in the corner of the room. "Play nicely."

Stella had decided to tag all the furniture she wanted removed. "I'll have Tim put everything in the storage room until we decide what to do with it. Maybe we'll find a secondhand dealer in Telluride to haul it away. Right now, we'll have to clean out all the drawers and cabinets. There's a lot of family stuff that Wes will want to save."

Under other circumstances, Caroline might have enjoyed looking through boxes of old photographs and yellowed newspaper clippings. There were even bundles of letters hand-written by members of the Wainwright family.

In Caroline's state of mind, every piece of memorabilia looked threatening because it seemed to contain a warning that this rich, powerful family took what they wanted when they wanted it.

"Daddy!" Cassie leaped to her feet and ran across the room as Wes came in. "Come play with us."

Caroline kept her gaze on the pile of photograph albums and avoided looking in the direction of the doorway.

"Oh, good, Wes, I have a job for you. We want to get this room cleared out. I was just going to get Tim and Shane. You can help them move some of this stuff."

"My lucky day," Wes replied dryly. "I think I'd rather play games with the kids."

"I'm winning," Danny announced proudly.

"I won the first one," Cassie bragged.

Wes laughed. "Well, you two are too good for me. I think I'd better help pack boxes."

Stella made some under-her-breath remark as she left to summon her son and Tim. Caroline stiffened when Wes eased down on the rug beside her.

"What's all this stuff?" he asked, pointing to the boxes she was filling.

"The kinds of things a family collects through the years."

"Oh, I recognize some of the photograph books," he said as he took one out of a box and began turning the pages.

He was sitting so close to her that their shoulders almost brushed as he began turning the pages. The familiar scent of his warm body assaulted her. She knew that any friendly overtures on his part were nothing but a calculated strategy to camouflage his real interest—her son!

"Look at that." Chuckling, he pointed to a photograph of a grinning young boy holding up a large fish. "That's me. The feisty thing almost pulled me into the water before I landed him."

Caroline only gave the photo a fleeting glance. Her interest in anything about him and his family was zero.

"That's Delvin. He was two years younger than me." He held the album so Caroline could see.

She stiffened when his studied gaze went from the colored photo of a little boy petting a dog to Danny who was sitting on the floor nearby,

Was he trying to find a family resemblance?

Both youngsters had light-brown hair, slightly wavy, a full face and slender bone structure—just like a million other little boys. Caroline wasn't about to sit there looking at his family album while he searched for family resemblances to her son. He must have felt her withdrawal because he quickly closed the album and grabbed her hand before she could get to her feet. "Caroline, you have to know I'm pulled in two directions on this. Until I know for sure..."

"Well, that shouldn't take very long." She jerked her hand away and stood up. "If your private snoop is any good at all, he'll verify the adoption papers in quick order. Then we both can put this little charade of yours behind us."

"Charade?" He stood up and faced her. "Is that what you think?"

"Don't insult me by pretending your romantic interest in me has been anything but a calculated effort to gather information about my son."

Heat flared in his eyes. "You seem to forget my so-called romantic interest in you was there before the Jacuzzi discovery."

She answered in the same accusing tone. "You deliberately turned my feelings into an advantage when you needed more information. And I gave it to you. Now you don't have to pretend anymore. And neither do I!"

Before Wes could reply, Stella came back with Tim and Shane. She sent a questioning look at Wes and Caroline as if puzzled by their stiff postures and facial expressions.

Caroline was relieved when Wes ignored Stella's jibes about not staying to help and quickly disappeared.

Delio's call came in about four o'clock that afternoon. Wes's hand tightened on the receiver when the detective identified himself.

"I hope you're ready for this, Wes," Delio said in a warning tone.

"I am. What do you have?"

"The papers are fraudulent. Phonies. They're remarkable copies of the necessary legal adoption documents. Interestingly enough, the lawyer's signature appears to be authentic. I've compared the handwriting with other documents of George Goodman, the lawyer who supposedly handled the adoption. He closed up his office about four years ago and apparently left Colorado. I haven't had time to try and track him down."

"You're saying Goodman falsified the adoption records?"

"That's my guess. Thomas and Caroline Fairchild might have been completely unaware that their lawyer was only going through the pretense of a legal adoption." Delio cleared his throat. "I have no proof, Wes. Not yet. Goodman could have been raking in money on illegal adoptions. You know, providing innocent couples with black-market babies for exorbitant fees."

Wes found it hard to breathe. His mind raced with the implications of what Delio was saying. *Fraudulent papers. Black-market babies.*

"We're still a long way from verifying that the kidnappers of your son were part of this illegal traffic," Delio cautioned. "It's going to take time."

"I want this resolved! Hire all the help you need. Double your own fee."

"That isn't necessary, Wes. Calm down. The little boy is in good hands, isn't he? Just keep on eye on him. Is there a chance the mother would agree to some DNA testing?"

"I doubt it. Her attitude isn't very promising," Wes

admitted. "When I tell her about the fraudulent papers, she may cooperate."

"Give it a try. I'll do my best to get a line on George Goodman and any other adoptive parents who might have gone through his office. Maybe I can locate a secretary or another office worker who worked for him and who would be willing to talk."

"Offer them a bribe if you have to," Wes ordered. "And get back to me as soon as you have something."

"Will do," Delio promised and hung up.

As Wes leaned back in his chair, he mentally reviewed their conversation. Every new discovery seemed to validate his belief that Caroline Fairchild's adopted son could be his. Now, he had no choice but to pressure her to cooperate, even though that meant destroying every remaining thread of tender feelings between them.

Chapter 13

After putting Danny to bed, Caroline stood staring out the window, her thoughts as scattered as a startled flock of pigeons. She hugged herself against a deepening chill as Wes's voice kept ringing in her ears.

Until I know for sure...

What more proof did he need? He'd seen the legal papers. His detective would verify them. Then what? Would Wes put all his power, money and influence to discredit her personally? If he failed to get Danny one way, he might try another and continue forever.

When a demanding knock sounded on the sitting-room door and she saw who it was, she just stood there, blocking the doorway.

"We have to talk."

"What about?" she asked without moving.

Wes scowled. "I don't think we should have this discussion with me standing in the hall."

"I don't think we should be discussing anything at all," she snapped.

"It's very, very important."

She had no choice but to step back and let him into the room. "What, no nightcap this time?" she chided. "Didn't you find out everything you wanted to know the last time?"

He motioned to the couch. "Let's sit down."

She stiffened. Did he really think she going to sit lovingly beside him as she'd done before? The memories of his tender touch and light kiss on her forehead were torture enough. "I prefer to stand."

"Caroline, I think you'd better sit."

"Are you trying to frighten me?"

"I have some important information that you should know about."

"From your detective, no doubt," she replied in a sarcastic tone.

"Yes."

"Well, I guess I'd better hear his excuses for missing the adoption records in the first place." She eased down in a nearby chair.

Sitting on the edge of the couch, he leaned forward and the way he was looking at her brought a sudden tightening to her chest.

"Delio called me and gave me his report."

Her voice was strained. "And—"

"Caroline, there's no easy way to tell you this. He checked Danny's adoption papers. They're fake."

Unexpected laughter was her initial response. What kind of manipulation was this? Did Wes really think she'd believe such a preposterous lie? He must take her for a fool. She wasn't some fluffy-headed woman he could manipulate any way he pleased to get what he wanted.

"How interesting, Wes. And how did your high-paid investigator come to that conclusion?"

"Delio was able to verify that the papers are fraudulent. No legal papers were ever filed. That's the reason Delio couldn't find any official record of Danny's adoption when he searched."

"Really?" she replied in a scathing tone. "And how did you manage to arrange that, Wes? Pay enough people to alter the truth so you could back up this outrageous claim?"

His eyes hardened. "I know this is a shock—"

"The shock is that you would stoop so low. You think your power and money can take away my son because you lost yours!"

His temper flared. "You can't believe that!"

"That's exactly what I believe. And I'll tell you something else. I'll never give Danny up, no matter how you manipulate the truth or how many people you pay to lie!"

"That's enough!" He clenched his jaw and took several deep breaths as if to bring his temper back under control. "There's a way we can settle this quickly, Caroline. Just give your consent for DNA testing."

"And trust you not to manipulate the results?" she replied in a scathing tone. "I was married to a doctor, remember? I know how easily tests can be manipulated and twisted if they fall into the wrong hands. What guarantee do I have that you won't use your money and resources to falsify the results?"

He stared at her. "You can't really believe what

you're saying. I only want to know the truth…for all our sakes."

"I know the truth."

"Do you? You told me your husband and his lawyer handled everything. You admitted you never met the woman they said gave the baby up for adoption. How do you know she really existed?"

"Because I have no reason to doubt it. No, I won't consent to the tests. Absolutely not."

"If I present the situation to a judge, I'm sure I can get a court order." He stood up and moved quickly to her chair. "Please, Caroline, don't destroy everything between us." He grabbed her hands and pulled her to her feet. "You have to know how I feel about you."

"I do now," she said, remaining rigid and stiff in his arms. "You played me very well. I never suspected that romancing me was just a means to an end."

"That's not true. I was falling for you even before the question of Danny's parentage arose." He gently eased back a lock of hair drifting down on her forehead. "And you have deep feelings for me, I know you do."

"Wrong again," she lied. "I never took our touch of romance seriously. When Nicole arrived on the scene I was glad I hadn't."

"You were jealous?" His mouth eased into a faint smile. "For your information I told Nicole how I felt about you. I confessed that at long last I'd found a woman who was everything I wanted. How can we have any kind of a future together until we resolve this? Don't you see, darling, I love you." He brought his mouth closer to hers.

Her senses were suddenly filled with his scent, the warm pull of his body and the caressing sensations of his hands tracing the smallness of her waist and the warm curves of her hips.

"We need to know the truth for both our sakes," he whispered.

The truth!

The word challenged her on every level of her being. She pulled away from him. "I already know the truth. You're willing to lie, cheat and bribe to get what you want."

He looked as if she'd slapped him.

She turned away without saying anything more and as she shut the bedroom door behind her, she leaned back against it and let a flood of hot tears stream down her cheeks.

After a tortuous, sleepless night, Caroline decided that staying at the lodge any longer was out of the question. She had to leave. The decision brought up a myriad of problems that would have to be faced. Somehow, she'd have to cope. No home. No job. No money. At the moment none of the problems were as dire as was remaining under the same roof with a man who had manipulated her feelings and who coveted her son.

She wasn't quite sure how she would explain her sudden departure to Stella, but when she and Danny went down for breakfast she learned Felicia had already told Stella about Wes's interest in Danny.

"I never heard anything so ridiculous," Stella said as she joined Caroline and Danny at their table. "Wes has always brooded about the kidnapping, but I never thought he'd go off the deep end like this."

Caroline shot a meaningful look at Danny. "Let's not talk about this now."

"Oh. Oh, yes," Stella said quickly, getting the silent message. "We'll talk about that later. Anyway, I was wondering what you thought about making some long-distance calls today. We could put in some orders and arrange for workmen to get things started."

Caroline pretended to listen to Stella's monologue, but her stomach muscles were tight and her thoughts heavy with too many unanswered questions. Stella didn't seem to notice.

After breakfast she decided to leave Danny with Felicia for the morning. She didn't want him around when she informed Stella of her decision to leave. Things might get a little heated when she demanded payment for time spent on the project. She didn't kid herself—breaking her contract might mean no money at all.

"Oh, goodie," Cassie said, clapping her hands when she saw Danny. "We'll play racetrack!"

"I want the red car," he quickly declared.

Felicia smiled at Caroline. "Are you feeling more yourself today?"

Caroline wanted to light into her for talking to Stella about Wes and Danny, but with the two children standing there she had to hold her tongue.

"I'll be back to pick him up for lunch," Caroline told Felicia and left.

Stella was already in the workroom and was standing looking out the window when Caroline came in. Heavy clouds hung low and a gray mist was seeping down the mountainside, draining all color from the trees, boulders and remaining patches of snow.

"Looks like another storm brewing," Stella said as she turned around.

Caroline stiffened. She hadn't given any thought to

the weather. Getting snowed in certainly wasn't in her plans. A new sense of urgency sluiced through her.

Stella sat down at the work table and started talking about materials they needed to order before workmen were scheduled to arrive.

Caroline took a deep breath. "I'm sorry to interrupt you, Stella, but we have to talk."

With a questioning frown, Stella put down the catalog she had in her hand.

"I really don't know how to explain all of this," Caroline began and then faltered.

"I'm listening," Stella responded in her businesslike tone, obviously impatient with the delay in carrying out her agenda for the morning.

"I'm glad you know about Wes's fixation on Danny. You'll understand why I can't remain here any longer."

"What are you saying?"

"I'm sorry, Stella, but I've made up my mind. I've decided to leave right away."

Her eyes sparked with disbelief. "No, you can't! We have a contract."

"Yes, I know, but I was hoping you'd understand the situation, Stella, and pay me for time spent." Quickly Caroline began listing the decisions that had been made in the selection of furniture, window dressings and accessories for the main room. She avoided mentioning the remaining areas in the lodge on the redecorating list.

Stella was silent throughout this recitation and Caroline wondered if she had even been listening. She waved a hand in a dismissing gesture when Caroline had finished.

"I don't intend to finish this decorating project alone," she declared.

"You don't understand…" Caroline began.

"Yes, I think I do. Wes has put you in a very uncomfortable position. I certainly don't blame you for wanting to put some distance between the two of you." She paused. "And I think I know how to achieve that."

"How?"

"Wes leaves instead of you." She smiled as if the solution was so simple there was no question about it. "You stay. He goes."

"Are you serious?"

"Wes has overstayed his planned time here, anyway. I'll talk to him. He'll go back to Houston and that will solve everything. You can complete your contract and get paid the generous full amount we agreed upon." She glanced at her watch. "I bet I can catch him in his suite right now."

She was heading for the door before Caroline could tell her about the detective Wes had hired and Delio's false accusations about Danny's adoption.

"Stella, you don't know the whole story," Caroline called after her, but she just gave a wave of her hand and turned down the hall in the direction of Wes's suite.

Caroline rested her head in her hands. She could imagine the conversation between the two of them. After Stella heard the fabricated story about Danny's adoption, she'd fall in line and support Wes. Family ties were stronger than hired help. Trying to collect any money from either of them was a long shot. It made more sense to get back to Denver and try to line up another decorating contract.

She walked out of the work room and went downstairs to the telephone alcove. Taking a deep breath, she called Betty at the store.

"Things have gotten worse here," Caroline told her. "I plan to leave the lodge very early in the morning. Can we be your house guests again?"

"Of course. Love to have you," Betty responded quickly. "What's going on, Caroline?"

"It's complicated. I'll tell you when I get there." Caroline swallowed hard. "I may need a good lawyer."

"Oh, you've decided to shake up the insurance company? I don't blame you. It's about time they paid up."

"No, it's not about the insurance. It's personal."

"Uh-oh. That sounds ominous."

"It is." After promising to tell her everything when she got to Denver, Caroline hung up.

She sat there staring at the telephone for a long moment. When she heard a muffled breathing nearby, she swung her head around. Dexter was loitering a few feet away.

"Do you make a habit of eavesdropping?" she snapped.

He just smiled as he sauntered over to the telephone desk. "Why do you need a lawyer? You aren't thinking about suing the almighty Wainwright family, are ya? Don't tell me you're going to try to put dear old Wes on the rack?" he chided with an amused curl of his pudgy lips. "Collect for breach of promise or the like? Not that he hasn't been there before. I have to warn you, though. It'll be harder than a steel bullet to collect anything from him. He likes to romance them and leave them."

"And you're telling me all this because…?"

"I've been watching what's going on between you two. I knew Wes was just playing you along. Couldn't figure it out—not that you're not attractive and all that. Just didn't seem his type."

"Well, I guess you were right about that," Caroline said as she stood up. "Now, if you'll excuse me…"

"Are you really taking off in the morning?" His tone was plainly hopeful.

"Yes."

"Then maybe Wes and I can get back to carrying out some of our plans."

"I guess that's up to him," Caroline replied just as bluntly. If she hadn't been caught up in her own emotional whirlwind, she would have realized Dexter was jealous of the time and attention Wes had been giving her. She'd come between two old buddies. No wonder Dexter was glad to see her go.

Clearly she'd made an enemy without even realizing it. Had Dexter been the one to put the children in danger with that treacherous treasure-hunt game? Maybe his jealousy over Wes's time extended to them, too.

She felt Dexter's eyes boring into her back as she went down the hall. Instead of going upstairs, she decided to check out the main room for the last time. Maybe she could take care of one last job before she left in the morning.

The large room was stark and nearly empty. As she moved about, her footsteps echoed on the bare floor and gusts of wind whistled in the dark fireplace. The lonely sounds matched the emptiness she felt inside. She closed her eyes and was visualizing the beautiful room that she would never see when she heard footsteps in the hall.

She stiffened when Wes appeared in the doorway a moment later. After last night, she was hoping to avoid him altogether.

"Dex told me he thought you came in here," he said and quickly crossed the room to where she stood. "Stella told me you're leaving. If you do that we'll never be able to settle the conflict between us."

"You'd better believe it's already settled," she countered.

"What if I promised to pull Delio off the investigation? Would you stay then?"

"Why on earth would you do that?"

"I can't let it end like this. I've waited too long to find someone like you." He put his hands gently on her shoulders. "And you love me, I know you do."

She ignored the warmth of his nearness and met his gaze squarely. "I'm leaving and there's nothing you can do to stop me."

Deep lines of defeat etched his face. "All right, you win. I'll do what Stella wants. I'll leave. You stay and finish the job. I promise to halt the investigation until we talk again. You have to believe me, I won't do anything that jeopardizes yours and Danny's happiness."

As if to seal his promise, he bent his head and before she could protest his lips captured hers possessively and his quick tongue sent desire racing through her. She was breathless when he pulled back and searched her face.

"You're a better liar than I am if you claim that didn't mean anything."

As he turned away and walked out of the room, she muffled a cry to call him back.

Chapter 14

Caroline didn't see Wes the rest of the day. Stella seemed to think everything had been settled to her satisfaction and didn't make any reference to their talk. Caroline decided Wes must have convinced her that he'd leave so she wouldn't have to.

"Begin checking on businesses we can hire to make basic renovations," she had ordered with her usual briskness when she found Caroline in the main room. "Try the Denver and Colorado Springs directories first, but I doubt we'll have any luck getting them to come this distance. Probably, Grand Junction is our best bet. We have to get them on the job right away."

Caroline nodded. Her decision to leave in the morning had not changed. She'd make a list and leave it for Stella. Even if Wes left, there was no assurance he wouldn't return before her job was completed. Nothing would have changed. Their conflict would be the same.

As soon as she and Danny returned to their rooms after an early dinner, she began packing.

"Whatcha doing?" Danny asked when he saw her putting everything in their suitcases.

"Packing."

"What for?"

"We're driving back to Denver tomorrow."

"Is Cassie going with us?" he asked with eager innocence.

"No, she has to stay here…with her father."

He scowled. "Why can't we stay, too?"

"This isn't our home."

"But we don't got one. It burned down." A worried look crossed his expressive face.

Caroline sat down on the bed and put an arm around him. "I know, honey. It's going to be all right. We'll stay with Betty and Jim until we get another one."

"I like it better here. Why do we have to go?"

She held him close and rested her chin on top of his head. "It's time."

"Why?"

"Because mommy's job is finished here," she lied. As he snuggled back against her, she whispered. "I love you a whole bunch, my Danny boy. We're going to be just fine. I promise. When we get back to Denver, we can go to the zoo again and see all the new baby animals. You'd like that."

She continued her breezy chatter as she tucked him in bed. "What book would you like me to read tonight?"

"Who Am I?"

For a moment his answer seemed like a question. She stiffened before she realized he was just repeating the title. Would he ask the same question of her someday? The story seemed more poignant than ever.

When he was sound asleep and all the suitcases except one had been packed and closed, she dropped down in a chair and put her face in her hands.

Maybe they wouldn't be safe in Denver!

Fearful thoughts raced through her head. What if Wes convinced the authorities that she was keeping Danny illegally? If his high-priced lawyers successfully proved she was guilty of breaking the law, the authorities could take Danny away from her.

She went over everything that had happened. At first Wes had tried the easy way to get his hands on her son by romancing her. His declarations of love were hollow and had been coldly manipulative under the present circumstances.

Caroline rose to her feet and began restlessly moving around the room. She didn't believe for one minute his promise to halt his investigation. She was positive Delio would stay on the job, searching for some kind of entrapment that would further Wes's determination to claim Danny. She needed to be prepared. But how? Where would she get the money to hire professional help who could verify the truth—an unmarried young woman had given Danny up for adoption. If DNA testing was required, she wanted to have a controlled situation in place where the Wainwright millions couldn't influence the outcome. She knew how easily someone who handled the testing could manipulate blood samples—if the price was right.

All of these thoughts raced through her head with growing intensity. Outside her window, thickening clouds in the dark sky hid the stars and moon from view.

She could hear a high-pitched moaning wind whipping through tall ponderosa pines. No sign of snow yet, thank heavens. If they left the lodge early enough in the morning, they ought to be able to reach the main roads before any potential storm settled in.

She quickly changed into her flannel pajamas and impulsively slipped into bed with Danny. As she nestled close to him, the familiar scent of his soft hair and the warmth of his little body created a rush of emotions that brought tears to her eyes. She clung to a simple truth. *I'm his mother.*

Wes was still awake at midnight when the first icy snowflakes hit the windows. He got out of bed, fixed himself a Scotch and soda and put a couple more logs on the fire. Sleep seemed a long way off.

He kept going over the last scene with Caroline. He'd handled everything wrong. For a fleeting moment, she had responded to his kisses with the same fire and passion but cold rejection had flashed into her eyes as she pulled away.

It was all his fault. A weird set of circumstances had fired a hope that his son was still alive and he'd been so focused on finding out the truth, he'd failed to be concerned whether or not Caroline might be threatened by his actions. He'd moved too fast. Now he had to find a way quickly to repair the damage. Somehow he had to gain back her confidence and love.

After a restless night, he was up early. Without taking time to make his usual pot of coffee, he hurried downstairs.

During the night, the storm had settled in. Already this second snow of the season was piling up drifts as falling flakes whipped across the ground. Wes knew that sometimes October storms in Colorado were as fierce as those in midwinter.

Trudie was busy setting up the buffet when he came in. She was the only one in the room and gave him a look of surprise. "My goodness, look at you. Up and about this early?"

He glanced at his watch. He'd wanted to make sure he didn't miss Caroline at breakfast. "I guess everybody's sleeping in this morning."

"Nope. Just the opposite," she said, shaking her head. "Usually it's another hour before anyone shows up. Not this morning, though. You just missed having company for breakfast."

"Who?"

"Caroline and her little boy were here first. Then Tim came in and joined them. They just left a few minutes ago." Trudie shook her head. "Tim went to bring her car around front. Can you believe it? She's going to start out in this storm with that little boy."

Wes didn't hear anything else. Trudie was still talking when he bolted out of the room. Racing down the hall to the lodge's main entrance, he threw open the front door and looked outside.

No sign of Caroline's small car.

Maybe they'd gone to the garage with Tim.

Snowflakes instantly coated his hair as he dashed around the corner of the building. All five garage doors were closed, but there was a light on in the small office.

Tim was just coming through an inner door when Wes burst into the room. "Are they still here?"

"You just missed them. Not more than five minutes."

"Why in the hell didn't you stop her?"

"I tried. She's one stubborn woman. I knew it was a foolhardy thing to do, but I just take orders around here, remember? What did you want me to do? Hogtie her?"

There was a bitterness in his voice Wes had not heard before. Tim was always so soft-spoken and accommodating, it was easy to overlook his feelings, but Wes didn't have time to worry about that now.

"I've got to stop her before she's driving blind in the snow, down those hairpin curves."

He pushed past Tim and ran to where his Jeep was parked. A glance at the gas gauge told him Dex had not filled the tank after taking Nicole back to Telluride. He swore as he backed out of the garage into a whirl of snow that his windshield wipers failed to completely clear.

Caroline had scarcely made it past the lake and started down the narrow serpentine road when she realized she'd made a terrible mistake. Her hands were rigid on the steering wheel as she hunched over in her seat. Whipping snow assaulted her headlights and blew blinding snowflakes against the windshield. She had only a small area of visibility as the wipers pushed the snow aside.

Forced to drive at a snail's pace, Caroline realized that her plan to make it to the main highway before the storm worsened was going to be impossible. Trees and rocks on the hillsides were already masked by layers of thickening white and snow on the road was building up at an unbelievable rate. She had no choice but to turn around and go back to the lodge.

Turn around where?

The narrow road was cupped on both sides by vaulting rock cliffs or thick stands of evergreens. She could barely make out the edges of the pavement. The wind quickened with every passing minute, sending more snow whipping across the road and obscuring her vision.

"I don't like it," Danny said, sitting in his car seat behind her.

"We'll turn around and go back," she told him with false calmness.

"Right now?"

"As soon as there's a wide spot in the road."

She hoped there would be a pull-out space ahead every time the car navigated a serpentine curve. Even though she couldn't remember any, surely the road had to widen enough for a turn-around before long.

She fought the mesmerizing effect of snowflakes swirling into the feeble radius of her headlights.

And then it happened!

Even at a snail's pace, she lost control without warning. The car hit a slick patch of ice! In a split second, it left the pavement and went over the side of the mountain road.

Careening downward, the small car was caught in a slight trough where a natural runoff of water from above had frozen and created an icy chute down the hillside into a mountain stream below.

Behind the wheel of the Jeep, Wes maintained a speed that drew on his familiarity with the roads. Wes had driven here often enough to have memorized every twist and turn. He hoped with every curve to see Caroline's car just ahead. If she was driving with any caution, she couldn't have gotten very far. He knew the storm was settling in with a vengeance. She had no business trying to drive anywhere in this weather, especially in that car of hers!

He was rehearsing a good bawling out in his mind when he glimpsed her taillights just going around a curve ahead. Good. He'd make her pull over and get herself and Danny into his car. There was an old forestry road for a turnaround about five miles ahead.

He came around the curve and was about to put a hand on his horn to alert her when her taillights suddenly disappeared.

What in the—

Leaning forward he strained to see ahead. He would have passed the place where her car had plunged off the road if fresh tire tracks in the snow had not indicated the spot. In a matter of minutes, the tracks would have been filled with snow and he would have missed them.

He braked and leaped out of the Jeep. As fast as his boots could cover the ground, he rushed to the side of the road. Shielding his eyes from the snow, he searched the snowy terrain below.

There was no sign of the car in the smooth whiteness of rocks and trees. He focused on the tire tracks that plunged downward out of sight and saw they stayed in a kind of ravine made by years of water runoff from above.

The car could have slid all the way down.

Wes knew that if by some miracle a car reached the bottom of the steep mountain slope without being smashed, it would be engulfed in the paralyzing cold water of a mountain stream.

Panic sent him scrambling downward at a dangerous speed as he bounded over snow-covered boulders, through trees heavy with white branches and down steep, slippery banks.

The pain in his chest from the cold, thin air grew with every breath. He knew at this high altitude hypothermia was a real threat.

His worst fear was realized when he broke out of the trees and saw the car half-buried in the stream. It was wedged in between large boulders that had fallen from the slopes above. The front of the car was nose-down in the water not very far from the bank. The back half of the car was in the air with its rear wheels raised and dangling.

As Wes splashed his way into the snowy stream, layers of thin ice broke under his boots. His legs were numb in the few seconds it took to reach the car. Since the front windows were submerged, he scrambled up on a slippery rock to reach a back door which was half raised out of the water.

"Caroline! Danny!"

The cold air made his voice thick and muffled. He jerked with all his might to try and open the door but the rock on which he knelt held it firm.

He couldn't hear anything inside.

If Caroline was unconscious in her seat belt, she'd be underwater.

Only a small portion of a rear window was free of the large boulder and clear enough to see through. Frantically, he rubbed the window with his jacket sleeve to try and clear it. He thought he could see the top of Danny's head but he wasn't sure.

"Danny! Caroline!"

He made a move to go around to the other side of the car. Maybe that door and window weren't blocked by rocks. When he heard a faint noise, he froze. Was it only the sound of moving water fooling him?

"Wes…"

This time there was no mistake.

"Yes, yes," he shouted. "I'm here!"

When she pressed her face against the tiny area of the window he could see, an unbelievable relief washed over him. Her hair was drenched, blood coated a small cut on her forehead and her eyes were glazed.

She was alive! For a few seconds he couldn't think beyond that miracle. She must have scrambled into the back when the front of the car filled with water. His heart leaped in thankfulness a second later when her face disappeared and Danny pressed his against the windowpane.

The little boy's tearful eyes widened when he saw Wes and he put his little hand against the window in a wordless plea.

"Yes, I'll get you out. Just hold on! I'll check the other side."

Quickly, he let himself down into the stream again and waded around the car. The granite boulders wedged against the other door were just as heavy and immoveable. Once again he was unable to shift them enough to allow passage even if they broke the windows as a means of escape.

Only one other window remained free of rocks and water.

Wes climbed around to the back and studied the car's narrow rear window. It was the only possible exit free of rock and water. Standing on built-up slabs of rocks that had tumbled from the hillside above, he would be able to break the glass and help them through the cleared window frame.

Danny would be able to slither through, but a grown woman?

When he brushed away the layer of snow on the narrow window, he could see them huddled together.

"I'm going to break the window," he yelled. "Turn away." His fingers were numb under his gloves as he grasped a wet stone and shattered the window glass. When he'd cleared the frame of jagged shards, he looked through the opening. Half the interior of the car was submerged in water. Caroline had her arm around Danny as they cowered on some piled-up suitcases.

"Okay, let's go!"

Quickly, Caroline helped Danny up to the window. Wes took hold of him from the other side and guided him through. Then he turned and set the boy down on the closest snowy boulder.

"Stay there until I get your mother."

"I'm…cold…" The child looked like an abandoned waif hunched there. Fortunately Caroline had put him in his snowsuit for the trip.

When Wes quickly turned back to the window, he saw that Caroline was already halfway out. Thank heavens for her slim and supple figure, he thought as he helped maneuver her through the narrow opening. She was coming out head-first and he pulled her into his arms as the rest of her body dropped free of the window frame.

They clung together with a fierceness that defied any words. Caroline's tears and blood smeared his face as his numbed hands and soaked gloves held her firmly against him. There was only time for a brief moment of thankfulness. Danger still lay in a growing storm that could claim them before they reached the road.

Shivering, lungs hurting and limbs turning blue, they started the strenuous climb upward. Would they be able to make it up to the warmth of the Jeep before they were all overcome with frozen limbs?

Wesley ended up carrying Danny on his back. Caroline valiantly tried to keep up but fell repeatedly to her knees.

Several times, Wes railed at her when she crumpled and seemed ready to give up. "Move! On your feet. Now!"

He knew what torture she was going through. The temperature of his body had fallen to dangerous levels and he could feel his heart and lungs beginning to protest.

Every time he squinted upward, he thought the rim of the hill was receding farther and farther into the distance. His eyes began playing tricks on him when he saw two headlights shining down on them.

Then he heard a shout. His eyelashes were so heavy with snow, he could barely see a dark figure moving down the slope toward them.

"Hold on. I'm coming!"

Wes recognized Tim's voice even before the big man was close enough to see. Never in his life had Wes felt such total relief. With Tim helping Caroline, Wes's strength seemed to be renewed and the burden of carrying Danny seemed easier.

They were closer to the road than Wes had realized. In a matter of a few minutes they were in the warmth of the SUV.

They used everything they could find in the SUV

to wrap around themselves—hunting jackets, lap robes and seat blankets. All three of them were suffering from hypothermia.

Danny whimpered as Caroline held him close. Shivering in her arms, his little face was drained of color. Her voice was weak and strained as she tried to soothe him.

"I'm getting you all to the Alpine Medical Center," Tim said in a tone that told Wes he was no longer in charge. "Dr. Boyd needs to have a look at you,"

Wes couldn't have argued if he'd wanted to. His body was floating away in numbness which had sapped his muscular strength and was threatening to make him helpless against an invading drowsiness.

Chapter 15

Wes knew Dr. William Boyd personally. He was a handsome man in his early fifties who could have been chosen for the cover of a Colorado outdoor magazine. His rugged build and a complexion weathered by sun and snow betrayed his love of climbing, fishing and skiing.

He'd been a guest at the lodge several times and when Wes was brought into emergency on a gurney, he took a double look as if he couldn't believe his eyes.

"Wes! What in blazes happened to you?"

"I… I went swimming…in a creek," he croaked. "Look after the others. I'm…fine."

"The hell you are. We'll have a look at all of you… now!" He nodded to his staff.

Caroline and Danny disappeared and a couple of nurses took charge of Wes. One stuck a thermometer in his mouth, the other one began stripping off the wet clothes.

After wrapping his chilled body in an electric blanket, they warmed his feet and gave him a mug of tea to drink.

"Your core temperature is only ninety degrees," Dr. Boyd told him when he returned a few minutes later. "You're damn lucky you all got here when you did."

"What about Caroline and Danny?" Wes asked anxiously.

"They're better off than you are. I hear you're some kind of hero. Jumping into a frozen stream, breaking glass to get them out." He winked at Wes. "Of course, you've always been a fool for a pretty lady."

"This one's special."

"Oh, it's like that, is it? Well, glad to hear it. Time you settled down."

"Yes," Wes agreed.

"She was lucky that her car took a nose-dive into the soft bottom of the creek instead of plowing into something solid. Fortunately her airbag protected her enough that she could climb into the back seat for the boy. Neither of them suffered anything more than a few bruises and scratches."

"Thank God." Wes breathed.

"The little boy's a sharp one." The doctor smiled. "The nurse offered him some warm tea and he asked very politely, 'Haven't you got any hot chocolate?'"

"He's quite a boy," Wes agreed, not wanting to think how close they'd come to losing him.

"The good news is the three of you ought to be able to leave emergency later today. I don't see any evidence of lingering frostbite. Once we get the core temperatures stabilized we'll release all of you."

What would Caroline do now? Go back to the lodge or find other transportation to Denver?

"All of you need to stay warm, though," the doctor added. "Because of lingering fatigue I suggest all of you spend the night in Telluride. The weathermen are saying it's going to snow the rest of the day but will move on sometime before tomorrow morning."

Wes nodded. He wasn't about to make the trip back to the lodge. "I'll need to talk with Tim."

"The poor guy has been pacing the floor. I'll tell him you want to see him."

When Tim came in a few minutes later, he looked worried and asked anxiously, "How you doing?"

"Good. Caroline and Danny, too. The doctor's going to release us this afternoon."

"Great." He let out a breath he'd obviously been holding. "You guys had me scared. I called Stella and told her what had happened. Boy, was she surprised! She didn't even know Caroline had left the lodge. She really ripped into me like you did for not stopping them." He shook his head. "I'm sorry, I guess I really dropped the ball on that one."

"This isn't your fault, Tim," Wes assured him. "Thank you for coming after us the way you did. And I shouldn't have yelled at you. Anyway, it's over and done with. Contact the Stonehaven Hotel and make reservations for all of us tonight. Oh, yes, and telephone the lodge and have Dexter and one of the men take the Jeep back to the lodge before the storm gets any worse."

"Stella will want to know if we're coming back tomorrow."

Wes took a deep breath. "I'm not sure." He didn't want to tell Tim that everything depended upon what Caroline decided to do. She might insist on him taking her to Denver as she'd planned. At the moment, he only knew he would make whatever concessions he had to in order to mend the situation between them. He'd pushed her too hard, too fast.

When Dr. Boyd told Caroline he was dismissing the three of them later in the day, she was surprised and relieved. Danny had bounced back without any problem. Once they'd moved him into the same room with her and once she knew her son was all right, her concern had centered on Wes.

"Wes is okay then?" she anxiously asked the doctor. She'd been terribly worried about him. By the time Tim had driven them into Telluride, Wes's face had been void of color, his mouth had an unhealthy blue tinge and his eyes wavered with an unfocused gaze.

"Yes, he's fine, but another couple of hours could have made a serious difference. He's one brave man." He eyed her as if he was about to say something more, but just gave her a smile as he left the room.

Caroline couldn't believe how Wes had totally ignored his own safety to rescue them. It touched her deeply the way he'd plunged down the steep mountainside and waded in icy water and blowing snow to get them out of the car. She'd never forget the way he struggled back up the rugged slope with Danny on his shoulders. Just thinking about his selfless action brought tears to her eyes.

"Why are you crying, Mama?"

She swallowed hard. "Because I'm grateful...for everything."

"I don't like it here."

"I don't either but the doctor says we can go soon."

"Back to Cassie's house?" Danny asked hopefully.

"I... I don't think so."

"Where?"

She was searching for an answer when Wes walked into the room. Obviously he'd overheard Danny's question. "How about a nice hotel with a warm swimming pool?"

"Goody! Can we, Mom?" Danny begged.

With both of them waiting hopefully, and knowing she needed time to sort things out, there was only one answer she could give.

They left the medical center about three o'clock in the afternoon. Tim drove them to the fashionable Stonehaven Hotel. Built of pink stone, an old-world charm was evident in the building's irregular roof line, wooden balconies and large recessed windows. Wes had stayed there many times before and when they registered, he was assured that his usual suite of rooms was available and ready.

Since Tim had friends in the area, he declined Wes's offer of a hotel room. "I'll check with you first thing in the morning," he told him. "You'll probably have made some decisions by then. I promised to call Stella as soon as I know anything. I bet she'd be here in a flash if the weather were decent."

Caroline ignored the questioning look Tim sent her. No doubt, Stella was having a fit about her quitting so abruptly. Handling the present was all she could manage at the moment. They'd lost everything in the half-submerged car. She'd escaped with nothing—not even her purse or the metal box with the records.

The hospital had dried their clothes so they had something to wear immediately. She knew it would take time to get her credit cards reissued and alert her car insurance. All these details seemed rather insignificant when compared to the wonder that they had escaped with their lives.

She had exchanged only a few words with Wes on the way to the hotel and had even less to say to him when they entered the luxurious lobby with its high ceiling, leather carved chairs and sofas. There was a European elegance about the decor which pleased Caroline and she silently complimented the interior decorator who had achieved such a look of wealth and grace.

A mirror-walled elevator sped them upward to a tastefully decorated suite of rooms with its own balcony and stone fireplace. A luxurious sitting room, marble bathroom and exquisite bedrooms resembled pictures Caroline had seen of Old World luxury hotels.

Even at her best, she would have felt terribly out of place. Trying to cope under the circumstances left her drained. Danny, on the other hand, bounced in and out of the elegant rooms with bubbling curiosity.

"Why don't you and Danny take this room." Wes motioned to a spacious bedroom which was definitely feminine in a mauve-and-pale-green decor. "I usually have the one on the other side of the living room."

And this one is reserved for your lady friends?

Ridiculous tears threatened to fill her eyes as she turned away quickly. "I think I'll have a warm bath and rest."

"Good idea."

"I want to go swimming," Danny said as if he had a vote.

"Maybe later. You and I are going shopping while your mother rests," Wes told him. "I bet there's a toy or two in the gift shop you might like."

"What about Cassie? Can I get her one?"

"We'll see," Wes said as his eyes met Caroline's.

She ignored the questioning lift of one of his eyebrows. Emotionally and physically, she wasn't ready to make any firm decisions about what was going to happen next. There were still too many things unresolved between them.

Danny's eyes were dancing with excitement. She suspected Wes was going to have a hard time refusing him anything.

She gave him a hug. "You behave."

He nodded and bounced over to the door.

"You get some rest," Wes told Caroline as he put his arm around her.

She nodded and relaxed in his comforting embrace for a long moment. All of her defenses were down. She needed time to sort out all the emotions that were still reeling like a whirlwind within her.

"Come on!" Danny urged impatiently.

"Okay, buckaroo." He kissed Caroline lightly on the forehead.

She heard her son's excited chatter as they closed the door and made their way down the hall. A delayed reaction from the death-defying experience seemed to hit her all at once. After quickly taking a warm shower, she put on a terry-cloth bathrobe provided as a courtesy of the hotel and slipped into the double, deluxe bed with its heavenly comfort. As the warmth and soft bedding enveloped her like a cocoon, her tight muscles began to relax.

She must have fallen into a deep sleep when the nightmare began. A prodding voice in her subconscious kept telling her to wake up. But she couldn't.

I have to find Danny! Wes never brought him back! The suite was a jumble of doors as she ran through the rooms, searching. As she bounded out into the hall in her bathrobe, a myriad of stairs went everywhere. She kept climbing them, shouting, "He stole my son! He stole my son!"

When she jerked awake, her heart was pounding. Filled with lingering panic, she jumped out of the bed and flung open the door to the living room.

Empty. The only sound was the peppering of icy snow against the windows. A wall clock told her they'd been gone over two hours. She had to find them! She dashed into the bedroom where she'd left her clothes and was just pulling on her boots when she heard a commotion at the hall door.

She dashed out into the living room and as the door opened, an entourage of hotel people came in carrying all kinds of boxes, packages and various pieces of luggage.

As Danny bounded in carrying two sacks, he squealed, "Surprise! Surprise! See what we bought! Lots of stuff. For me and you and Wes!"

Caroline just stood there, unable to find her voice.

"Just pile everything on the chairs and sofas," Wes told the two young women as he set down his own packages on a nearby table. They gave Caroline an envious glance as they put down at least a dozen various-sized bags and boxes labeled Modern Boutique.

An older man smiled at Caroline as he put down the luggage. "I think that's everything."

Wes took some bills out of his wallet for tips and thanked them all. After they left, he walked over to Caroline and took her hand. "You can fill in with other things I missed, but I think this should tide you over."

She blinked as tears tricked down her cheeks and she struggled to get control of her emotions.

"Are you all right? What's the matter? Do you need to go back to the clinic?" He moved quickly to her side. As he put his arm around her, she leaned into the warmth of his embrace. "I shouldn't have left you."

"No, I'm all right," she assured him. "I... I just had a bad dream."

"And no wonder. Any other woman would have been a basket case." He lightly traced her cheek with his fingertip. For a long moment their gaze held in a wordless connection that made his voice husky. "What do you say I fix us both a drink to celebrate?"

She nodded.

While he went to the small bar and fixed a couple of highballs, Caroline looked at Danny's new toys as he played on the floor in front of the sofa.

Wes sat down beside her and put an arm around her shoulder. "I ordered dinner from the Sea and Steak Restaurant downstairs. I didn't think you'd want to go out. Maybe we can come back another time and enjoy Telluride's charm." He searched her face. "Is there going to be another time?"

A brisk knock on the door kept her from giving an uncertain answer to the question.

Danny dominated the conversation while they ate and Caroline was glad when he began to rub his sleepy eyes.

"It's time for bed," she said firmly. "Tell Wes good-night."

"Can we go swimming tomorrow?"

"Maybe. We'll see."

"Okay." Caroline was surprised when Danny gave him a peck on the cheek and said, "Thanks for getting us out of the car."

After tucking Danny into bed and waiting a few minutes until he fell asleep, she returned to the living room. All during the meal, she had been aware of Wes's causal touch and a sexual awareness vibrating between them.

She walked over to where he stood in front of a picture window and for a long moment they stood side by side, looking out at the silvery-white landscape and majestic peaks etched against the night sky.

"Beautiful," she said with a catch in her throat.

"Do you have any idea how close I came to losing you today?" he said in a hoarse voice. "And it would have been my fault."

"No," she protested as she turned toward him.

"Yes, it's the truth. My obsession drove you away. I could have lost you both. Please forgive me." He tipped her chin and looked straight into her eyes. "I'll settle for any part of your life you're willing to share with me. I'll do whatever you say. Be whoever you want me to be. Just don't cut me off from you or Danny."

"I couldn't do that. Not now."

"I love you," he whispered. "Please let me take care of you."

All of her built-up resistance melted away as he kissed her with a hunger that matched her own.

As they lay together, his slow, deep kisses sent a heady supply of desire flowing through her. She delighted in the brush of his chest against her breasts and the caressing touch of his fingers. As his hands molded the curve of her thighs, drawing her beneath him, her surrender seemed brand new. Never had she given herself so completely.

The endearments he whispered as he made love to her mended her shattered emotions. She felt whole, complete.

When he slipped away from her, she lay in the circle of his arms, fulfilled and renewed. With a deep sigh, she closed her eyes, curled against him and fell into a deep sleep.

Chapter 16

A bright sun was streaming through the window when Caroline awoke. For a moment she was disoriented.

Strange room. Strange bed.

Then she remembered!

Quickly she turned on her side. No Wes. Only a tell-tale dent in his pillow remained. A moment later, she heard a murmur of voices and Danny's high-pitched laughter in the living room.

Glancing at her watch, she was startled to see how late it was. Her clothes were still in a heap where she'd dropped them, but an inviting terry-cloth robe lay across a nearby chair.

She smiled as she slipped out of bed and put it on. Wes's thoughtfulness stirred her in a strange way. She wasn't used to being cared for in such a fashion.

She was totally surprised when she opened the bed-room door and saw that Danny was already dressed in one of his new outfits. Apparently, Wes had taken care of him while she slept in.

Room service had brought up a breakfast cart and Wes was wiping a chocolate-milk mustache off Danny's mouth as they sat on the sofa. She felt a little selfconscious as she smiled at them and said, "Good morning."

"You're a sleepyhead!" Danny teased.

"But a beautiful one," Wes added as he quickly stood up and embraced her. "How are you, sweetheart?"

His remembered touch instantly sparked a spiral of unexpected desire in her, and his eyes twinkled as if he knew exactly what his caressing hands were doing to her as they slowly traced the curve of her back.

She felt herself blushing as she drew away. "I think I'm ready for some coffee."

"Wes says we can go swimming this morning," Danny informed her.

"If it's all right with your mother," Wes quickly corrected.

"We'll see," she said in true mother fashion.

After he'd poured her a cup of coffee and offered her several choices from the room-service cart, he commented, "The weather report is good. Everything will start moderating this morning and by afternoon the roads should have been plowed." He searched her face. "We could start back to the lodge right after lunch. If you…"

She knew he was asking if she was going back with him. The question was hardly relevant under the circumstances. She loved him. He knew it.

"Maybe we ought to stop at the clinic before we leave Telluride," she suggested quietly.

An alarmed expression instantly crossed his face. "Is something wrong?"

"I don't know. That's what we need to find out. I think we should consult Dr. Boyd about those blood tests you've been wanting."

His reaction was not at all what she had expected. If anything, he seemed ready to reject her offer. He glanced at Danny and then back at her. "Maybe we should just let things be for the moment."

She knew then he was afraid to know the truth. "I don't think that's a good idea," she said quickly. "The question will always be between us."

She knew their future relationship would be threatened by this fixation of his. When the tests proved a negative match—and she was positive they would—she had to know whether or not he would reject the happiness the three of them had found together.

After a long silence, he nodded. "All right. I'll call Dr. Boyd and set up an appointment for this afternoon. Then we'll head back to the lodge."

"Whoopee!" Danny exclaimed. "Wait 'til I show Cassie all my stuff." His smile faded as he told Wes, "She'll be mad if we don't bring her something."

"Do you think so?" he asked solemnly.

"I bet she'd like one of those Indian dolls we saw."

"All right, we'll buy her one. I think Cassie's found someone to look after her." Wes said as he leaned over and kissed Caroline. "Just the way we're all going to look after each other."

She could tell he was relieved that she'd given in to the DNA testing. Obviously, he was trying to prepare her for the shock that Danny wasn't legally hers, but she was still convinced he was the one heading for an emotional disappointment.

* * *

While Wes spent time with Danny in the swimming pool, Caroline packed everything in the new luggage. They left the hotel right after lunch and drove to the medical center.

Caroline wasn't sure how to explain to Danny what was going to happen. She guessed they would take a vial of blood the way they did for other tests.

"I'll go first," Wes volunteered. "It's a piece of cake."

Danny frowned. "They give you cake?"

"I'm sure we can find some when we're through," Wes assured him.

"I want chocolate."

"Okay, chocolate, it is."

Caroline smothered a chuckle as she took his hand and the three of them walked into the clinic. The whole procedure took less than fifteen minutes and the nurse didn't draw any blood after all.

"We just do a buccal swab for DNA," the nurse explained.

"What is that?" Caroline asked.

"We just swab the inside of the cheek. And that's that."

"We'll express the samples to a reference laboratory in Denver. It usually takes about a week to get the results."

"That long?" Wes protested. "Isn't there any way to hurry them up?"

"'Fraid not. In fact, if the lab is backed up, it might even be a few days longer," he warned Wes.

Caroline slipped her hand into his. "It's okay. We can wait." She could tell he was anxious.

"Yes, I guess we can," he agreed, smiling. "Let's head for the cafeteria and get Danny that big piece of cake."

* * *

As Wes drove the SUV back to the lodge, he could tell that a snowplow had cleared the road that morning. He was glad he had a contact with a firm in Telluride to keep the lodge road plowed when a storm deposited more than four inches of snow. He made arrangements for a tow truck to use a road near the bottom of the creek and pull out Caroline's car.

Caroline sat closely beside him in the passenger seat and Tim was in the back with Danny. When they reached the place in the road where he'd left the Jeep, there was no sign of it. Someone must have returned it to the lodge as he had ordered.

He was aware of Caroline's tension as she sat stiffly beside him, seemingly looking for some clue to where her car had gone over the edge.

"We already passed it," he finally told her gently.

"And if you hadn't been right behind us—"

"But I was," he interrupted quickly. "And you're both here safe and sound. That's all that matters."

She nodded, but her face was still bleached of color and he knew she was reliving that perilous drop down the mountainside and into the water. The horrifying drama would live with both of them forever.

An early-afternoon sun touched the ice-covered lake with a reflected brilliance as they passed it. When they reached the lodge, Wes had barely braked the car when the front door flew open and Stella came rushing out.

Tim chuckled as he admitted, "I called her just before we left the clinic. I'll bet you anything, she's been staring out a front window for God knows how long."

Even before Caroline had her door open, Stella was

at the window, smiling at her. The woman's relief was so obvious, Caroline felt a pang of guilt. She'd always prided herself on going the extra mile to make sure she gave a hundred percent of time and effort to any commitment. She wasn't used to letting people down. And running off like that had not been fair to Stella.

As Caroline stepped out of the car, Stella eyed the new burgundy suede slacks and jacket Wes had bought for her. "Wow, that's some outfit. You've been shopping?"

"Wes bought a bunch of stuff," Danny bragged. "Boxes and boxes. And we got a doll for Cassie, too."

"I'm glad everything turned out okay. When Tim told me what had happened, my blood turned cold. I'm glad Wes came to the rescue." She glanced from Caroline to Wes as if she were trying to figure out exactly what had happened between them.

She had her answer when Wes turned to Tim. "Will you take all the luggage up to my suite? They'll be staying with me."

Tim nodded as if the instructions came as no surprise. He smiled, picked up the two new pieces of luggage and disappeared.

Caroline was surprised to see Trudie wiping her hands on her apron as she hurried to greet them when they entered the main room of the lodge.

"Glory be!" she exclaimed, giving Caroline a hug. "When we heard what had happened, I felt horribly responsible. I should have stopped you from going out that door in such weather. Are you and the boy all right?"

Stella spoke up briskly before Caroline could. "They're fine! Can't you see that, Trudie?" As Stella's knowing smile swept from Wes to Caroline, she added, "In fact, I'd say things are very much all right."

Trudie obviously didn't get the veiled implication. Her mind ran on a different track. "Have you had lunch? I can set out something—"

"No need, Trudie, thank you," Wes responded. "We ate before we left the hotel. Maybe we'll like some refreshment later in the afternoon."

"I want to go see Cassie," Danny declared, holding up the doll box he'd taken from the car.

"First, we'll get settled," Caroline said firmly.

Danny gave her his lower-lip pout as they made their way upstairs.

Tim had unlocked the suite door with his house key and left the luggage inside. Caroline decided he must have taken one of the back stairways down to his office and made a mental note to thank Tim for all his help.

"What room would you like, Danny?" Wes asked. "When Cassie stays with me, she picks the bedroom closest to the kitchenette." He lowered his voice to a confidential whisper. "I think Cassie gets up in the night and raids the cookie jar."

Danny's eyes lit up. "I'll take that room."

"Smart boy." Wes winked at him and left him in the room looking over some of Cassie's collected toys.

Caroline followed Wes into his bedroom. After putting down the luggage, he turned to her and quickly drew her into his arms as if he'd been too long without the feel of her body cupped against his. His kisses matched a hunger of her own. His murmured endearments ignited a flame of desire between them. With obvious reluctance, he sighed as he slowly set her away from him. If they'd been alone, she knew they would have ended up in bed, but there was Danny.

As if to punctuate his presence, the small boy bounded into the room and plopped himself in the middle of Wes's king-sized bed.

"Why do you need such a big bed?" Danny asked with innocent curiosity. The question was obviously one that Wes was not prepared to answer and Caroline smiled as he deftly sidestepped it.

"Would you like to take that doll to Cassie now?" Wes asked. "I want to let her know I'm back. You could even stay and play with her if it's all right with your mother," he added in all innocence.

"It's all right with his mother," Caroline replied with a knowing smile.

Cassie made a big fuss when she saw Wes and he picked her up in his arms and swung her around. "See who I brought back?" he said as he set her down. He knew his daughter well enough to add, "Danny brought you a present."

"Isn't that nice?" Felicia said in a prompting tone as if she was afraid Cassie was going to forget her manners.

"What is it?" the little girl demanded suspiciously.

"Something you want," Danny said, firmly holding on to the box.

"How do you know?"

"'Cause you said so once." Slowly, he held out the box but made Cassie walk over to him to take it.

Wes smiled. *Good, Danny. You're a smart boy.*

Cassie's squeal of delight when she saw the Indian doll brought a big smile to Danny's face as he said, "Told you so!"

Wes ignored Felicia's questions about Caroline and Danny's return to the lodge. "For the moment, everything will go on as before," he told her.

Her dark eyes seemed to narrow as if she was well aware he wasn't speaking the truth. "I sense big changes. Not good! Not good at all."

Ignoring her doomsday predictions, he promised to pick up the kids later for afternoon refreshments and quickly took his leave.

Returning to the suite, he found Caroline lounging on the bed with the soft coverlet barely covering her nakedness. He quickly joined her and drew her to him with the sure touch of a lover. The zenith of passion and desire they had known the night before flared between them as they made love.

Caroline had fallen asleep in the curve of his arm when he heard the insistent ring of his private phone. He debated answering it, but he remembered that Delio had promised a report; Wes wanted to advise him that DNA testing was under way.

Wes gently eased out of bed, pulled on his shorts and hurried to his office.

The private detective's voice was thick with excitement. "I succeeded in contacting the ex-wife of George Goodman, the lawyer who supposedly handled the Fairchild adoption."

"Good work!"

"She told me he'd skipped to Mexico a few years ago after their divorce. When I mentioned I was representing a family involved in a questionable adoption, she really let loose." He paused. "Wes, you're not going to believe this but it's the God's truth. She swears that in the midst of one of their drunken quarrels, her no-good husband admitted he'd placed a black-market baby from a rich family for adoption. He bragged that a woman in the family had paid to have a boy twin kidnapped so that her own son wouldn't lose his position in the male line and lose the entitled inheritance. I thought you should know—"

Wesley slammed down the receiver. "Good God!"

"What is it, Wes?" Caroline stood in the bedroom doorway, putting on her robe.

"Stella! I'll kill her with my bare hands!" He told Caroline what Delio had learned. After quickly dressing, they began searching the lodge with the urgency of a ticking bomb. Stella wasn't in any of her usual places.

"We'll have to tell Felicia to keep a close eye on Danny until we locate her," Caroline said anxiously, and as they hurried to Felicia's apartment, she debated whether or not she should stay close to Danny and let Wes confront Stella.

The decision was taken out of her hands when they found Felicia alone in her apartment. No children were in sight.

"Where are they?" Caroline and Wes demanded almost in unison.

Looking puzzled, Felicia slowly put down her knitting. "Stella came by for them. I thought it would be all right. She took them ice skating on the lake."

"Ice skating!" Wes bellowed in fury. "My God, the lake isn't frozen hard this early in the winter!"

Caroline was close behind him as they raced through the lodge and bounded out the front door.

Their worst fears were realized. Below, on the lake, they could see two small figures moving clumsily a dangerous distance away from the bank. Caroline knew her son could barely maintain his balance on skates. Danny had only been skating a couple of times on a little ice-skating pond that one of the Denver malls maintained for children in the winter.

She shouted his name as they raced down the snowy slope but her voice was driven back into her throat.

Stella was standing on the bank, her hands in her pockets, watching the two clumsy skaters.

Caroline and Wes rushed past her to the edge of the lake.

"Cassie, stop!"

"Danny, come back!"

Caroline kept shouting as Wes moved out gingerly on the thin ice toward them. Both of the children turned around, but it was almost too late. With a warning crack the ice fell away behind them as they slowly started skating toward the bank. Caroline watched with excruciating terror as more and more ice sank into the water.

All three of them might have gone under in the rippling effect of sinking ice if thicker layers of ice spanning out from the edge of the lake hadn't allowed Wes to reach them. Grabbing a small hand in each of his own, he herded them safely back to the bank.

"Get them to the lodge," he yelled at Caroline as he turned toward Stella with wild fury.

"S-sorry," she stammered as she backed up. "I didn't know that the ice was thin."

"Liar!" He grabbed her. "You're going to tell the truth if I have to choke it out of you."

Caroline waited restlessly with the children in the suite for Wes's return. Her emotions were racing at such a pace she couldn't process anything in a calm, rational manner. Everything had happened too fast.

She couldn't see anything from the windows to know what was going on because the view was obscured by tall, snow-laden ponderosa pines that brushed against the side of the lodge.

Fortunately Danny and Cassie seemed unaware of the drama unfolding around them. They didn't realize how close they'd come to losing their lives. As they sat on the floor playing a Sesame Street game, they laughed and quarreled with childish innocence.

Caroline was still struggling to absorb the traumatic upheaval of the last few hours when Wes returned to the suite nearly three hours later. She'd managed to settle Danny and Cassie down for a nap and was pacing the floor as her mind raced with unanswered questions.

As he came in, he held out his arms and she went into them with a grateful sigh.

"It's all right," he said wearily as tension underlined his voice. "An FBI agent from Durango took her into custody."

As they sat down on the sofa together, he told her that Stella had admitted everything. "She arranged the kidnapping because she was afraid Shane would lose his inheritance as the next male heir specified in the Wainwright inheritance entitlement. She hired a lover, one of the ranchhands, to kidnap my infant son. Apparently, Stella thought that he'd killed the baby until a couple of months ago."

"How did she find out he hadn't?"

"Because the bastard found out he was dying of cancer and admitted to her on his deathbed that he'd sold the baby to a Colorado lawyer, George Goodman, who handled the adoption of black-market babies. He also told her that a couple named Fairchild had paid big money for the adoption."

Caroline was stunned. How could something that had seemed so right—have been so wrong?

"Stella came to Denver, deciding to check the story out. When she was convinced that Caroline Fairchild was the adoptive mother and Danny Fairchild was my legal heir, she planned to finish the job herself."

Caroline stiffened.

"She set fire to your house, intending that neither one of you would survive. And when you did, she decided to hire you to redecorate the lodge and wait for an opportunity to arrange a fatal accident."

Caroline's eyes widened. "She drew the treasure map!"

His jaw tightened as he nodded. "Sending the kids up that treacherous mountain path to the cabin might have easily resulted in a fatal fall or given her the chance to arrange an accident at the cabin before we found out where they were. She hadn't planned on them showing the map to Shane."

Caroline whispered in a strained voice, "Then Danny's been in danger every minute we've been here!"

Wes tightened his arm around her shoulder. "Apparently, I was paying the two of you too much attention to give her the opportunity she needed. I thwarted her plans without even knowing it. When we returned today and Tim told her about the DNA testing, she knew she had to move fast."

Caroline closed her eyes against the imagined horror of two innocent children drowning because of one woman's determination to secure an inheritance for her son.

They sat in silence for a long time and as she stayed curled in the loving warmth of Wes's arms, the world's ugliness seemed far, far away.

She smiled when he whispered, "Let's go look at our children." Then he added with a smile. "Cassie's always wanted to have a cookie party in bed. What do you think?"

"I'd like to come," she said as she gave him a soft kiss.

She was surprised to find herself laughing as they carried the cookie jar and a carton of soda pop into the bedroom. The two six-year-olds were curled up and asleep and looked like cherubs.

Wes stood there for a long moment, looking down at his precious twins. His voice was husky as he reached out and touched them.

"Wake up, sleepyheads. It's celebration time!"

Epilogue

The Wainwright family home was a few miles out of Houston and had been built in the tradition of a Southern mansion with white columns and porticos. Wes's grandmother had been a Southern lady before her marriage and she'd brought that refined lifestyle to the Texas broad prairies when she married his grandfather.

"Of course, you'll probably want to make some changes to suit your own taste and style after we're married," Wes had assured her when he showed her through the mansion. "My parents left it pretty much the same while my brother and I were growing up."

"It's lovely," Caroline assured him. "There's a wonderful sense of color and style." She couldn't believe that in a few days she'd be the lady of the house and not a wide-eyed visitor.

"Pamela was never comfortable here and spent most

of her time in our Houston townhouse," he told her. "The ranch is about fifteen miles from here and the house there is roomy but not very fancy. That's where Stella and Shane chose to live." He sobered. "I've bought Shane some nearby acreage where he can develop his own ranch if that's what he decides to do and I'll provide some seasoned help for him. If he decides to go on to college, I'll take care of the finances." His voice broke. "I don't know why Stella didn't trust me to treat him fairly."

"Jealousy can twist everything," Caroline said softly, seeing the pain in his eyes. The past few weeks had been rough on him with the FBI investigation, Stella's indictment and closing up the lodge. The one bright spot was the DNA tests report which proved what they already knew but gave them some much-needed closure.

Caroline wrestled with the knowledge that Thomas had lied to her about Danny being the baby of a young, unmarried woman. Maybe that was the story Goodman gave him and Thomas pretended to know the girl personally in order to set Caroline's mind at ease. She was positive he didn't know the truth. Grateful for the miracle that had brought Danny to her, she knew Thomas would be glad for her newly found happiness.

A few days later Caroline smiled at her reflection in a free-standing floor mirror in a luxurious bedroom. She wore a pink silk dress, cut low at the neck with delicate lace-edged sleeves. A long, slightly flared skirt fell to matching satin, high-heeled shoes. Wes's engagement present of diamond drop earrings swung saucily at her cheeks and a beautifully designed diamond ring sparkled on her finger.

"Don't you look absolutely perfect," Betty McClure exclaimed as she came into the guest bedroom. She and Jim had flown in from Denver the day before so Betty could be Caroline's matron of honor. Her light-blue gown with its straight lines and sheer overskirt was perfect for her.

"And so do you!" Caroline said drawing her over so they stood side by side in front of the mirror.

"I hope there are a dozen photographers snapping pictures," Betty said, grinning.

"Only one," Caroline said, smiling. "But we'll probably make the newspaper. I have no idea how many illustrious guests are coming to my wedding, but you're here and that's all that matters. Thank you for being my family," she said, hugging her.

"Uh-oh," Betty said as the strains of organ music floated up from the formal parlor downstairs. "I hope Cassie and Danny stayed put the way I told them. If they've run off, I'll skin 'em." Then Betty added, "Shane was there waiting for Wes. I think he's a little nervous about all of this."

"I'm so glad Wes asked him to be best man," Caroline said. "He needs some strong family support right now."

"You'll win him over," Betty assured her as she handed Caroline her rosebud bridal bouquet. "Time to go. That handsome man of yours is waiting." She kissed Caroline on the cheek. "Isn't it amazing how wonderfully things turn out sometimes?"

"Yes," Caroline agreed with misty eyes. Last night when she and Wes had walked and talked in the garden, the velvet softness of his deep voice had been like a caress. She knew that the promises they made when they stood in each other's arms were as binding as the ones they would now repeat for others to hear. When Wes and Caroline had told the children that they were twins, Cassie had clapped her hands and Danny had given them a broad grin. They were a family now.

As Caroline descended the curved staircase, her happiness overflowed when she saw Danny, the ring bearer, and Cassie, the flower girl, waiting there.

The Wainwright twins were grinning happily at each other as if they had known from the beginning exactly who they were!

* * * * *

SPECIAL EXCERPT FROM

(H) HARLEQUIN
INTRIGUE

*When she discovers high-level corruption at her job,
accountant Allie Burton finds herself—reluctantly—in
desperate need of a bodyguard. Tall, ruggedly handsome
and terse, Hale Scribner goes all in to save lives, even if it
means staying on the move, going from town to town. But
once they hit the bucolic Conard County, Allie puts her foot
down and demands a traditional Christmas celebration…
which may be how they lure a killer to his prey…*

Keep reading for a sneak peek at
Conard County: Christmas Bodyguard,
part of Conard County: The Next Generation,
from New York Times *bestselling author Rachel Lee.*

"You need a bodyguard."

Allie Burton's jaw dropped as soon as her dad's old friend Detective
Max Roles spoke the words.

It took a few beats for Allie to reply. "Oh, come on, Max. That's over-
the-top. I'm sure Mr. Ellis was talking about all his international businesses,
about protecting his companies. He said he'd put the auditing firm on it."

Max was getting up in years. His jowls made him look like a bloodhound
with a bald head. Allie had known him all her life, thanks to his friendship
with her father, who had died years ago. She trusted him, but this?

"What were his *exact* words, Allie?"

She pulled them up from recent memory. "He said, *exactly*, that I
shouldn't tell anyone anything about what I'd found in the books."

Max shook his head. "And the rest?"

She shrugged. "He said, and I quote, *Bad things can happen*. Well, of
course they could. He's a tycoon with companies all over the world. Any
irregularity in the books could cause big problems."

"Right," Max said. "I want you to think about that. Bad things can
happen."

Allie frowned. "I guess you're one of the people I shouldn't have told
about this. I thought you'd laugh and wouldn't tell anyone."